THE WATER WITCH

BOOKS BY JESSICA THORNE

The Lost Girls of Foxfield Hall
The Bookbinder's Daughter

THE QUEEN'S WING SERIES
The Queen's Wing
The Stone's Heart

THE HOLLOW KING SERIES
Mageborn
Nightborn

THE WATER WITCH

JESSICA THORNE

bookouture

Published by Bookouture in 2022

An imprint of Storyfire Ltd.
Carmelite House
50 Victoria Embankment
London EC4Y 0DZ

www.bookouture.com

ISBN: 978-1-80314-254-8
eBook ISBN: 978-1-80314-253-1

Ar gwir garantez zo un tan ha ne c'hall ket bevañ en e unan
True love is a fire that cannot live alone

Ur gaou livet zo heñvel ouzh ar wirionez
A good lie is like the truth

To my family and all the wonderful times we have spent together in Finistère.

PROLOGUE

Ur wech e oa...
   Il était une fois...
   Once upon a time...

The waves crashed against the walls, their rage beyond control. The skies darkened, black clouds blotting out the sun. Servants lit lanterns and frantically secured the shutters and the doors. They pushed sandbags against the cracks and the entrances. The water still found its way inside, as water will, until damp permeated everything.

In the ballroom, the dancers whirled and laughed, without a care in the world. The musicians played furious reels, drowning out the sound of the storm. The king drank the fine wine from the south, rich and red, in endless supply, ignoring them all, even the priest who whispered urgent warnings, muttered prayers and tried to raise the alarm.

But the king did not listen.

No one listened.

The princess swept through the ballroom, her silks rustling as *she walked, a gait that was more like a dance, so graceful, so beautiful. In her hands she carried her mask, intricately crafted, a work of art. The glazed porcelain shimmered with decorations in gold and lapis lazuli, the image of a human face made inhuman.*

They called it her favour.

And the stranger watched her, drinking her in. The princess smiled and he returned the expression, the lazy, desire-filled darkening of his eyes mirroring her own. All men loved her. They couldn't help themselves, and she was used to that power. She could command and compel anyone who took her fancy.

He was the most handsome creature she had ever seen. From the moment he arrived, every eye was drawn to him, heartbeats sped up at a glimpse of his bewitching looks.

Her decision was made.

She would give him the mask, grace him with it. And with it her body... for the night, at least.

And if he lied, as others had lied, there would be a price... he would never know, until it was too late.

There had been many, so many, vying for her favour, lusting for her and the power she embodied.

But their love was never true. That was her tragedy. It broke her heart. It cost them their lives. The mask had been a gift and she treasured it. It protected her fragile heart.

But this time, for the first time in years, she hoped... she desperately hoped... There was something in his eyes.

'The mask compels the truth and you can see it,' her first lover had told her, when he gave it to her. He was Death's right hand, called Ankou, and she had known the dangers of dancing with him, but the magic he taught her was too addictive. He was too addictive. He'd left her in the end, as he had always warned her he would have to though it broke his heart to do so, and she had sought the same love ever since. In endless faces, the mask showed her only that they lied, that they would never really love her as Ankou had. And if they lied while wearing the

mask, it killed them without mercy. Ankou's gift to her, his protection.

This lordling was different, she was certain of that. And she wanted him.

They danced, they flirted, they teased, they slipped away unseen and made love.

'Put it on,' she whispered. But he smiled against her lips and refused. He set the mask aside.

'I can't wear another's face for you,' he said so sweetly, so compellingly, that she believed him.

She trusted him. He would be true. He could not lie to her, not when he looked at her that way.

While the storm raged outside, the skies turned black and the sea rose, lashing itself against the city walls, they lost themselves in each other.

And afterwards... afterwards, his smile faded like the first flower in the garden.

Around her neck she wore a golden key and while she dozed, sated and happy at last, he took it.

She woke with a start and cried out in alarm.

'Give it back.'

'Alas, that I cannot do,' he replied, mocking her. The kindly, courtly lover was gone. He made for the door without a backwards glance.

'Then die, you faithless traitor.' She spat the words at him, summoning powers that commanded the wind and the wave, magic taught to her by Ankou himself.

'Your magic has no power over me, princess,' said her latest lover disdainfully. 'I am protected.'

The princess threw on her robe and rushed after him. Though she ran and he walked, she couldn't catch him. Invisible weights dragged at her, as if she was running through deep water. Nor could she seem to raise the alarm. Her voice didn't carry. The dancers danced on, her father spoke only with the priest, the servants tried in vain to hold back the storm and the guards stood like statues, oblivious.

Her lover strode onwards and she followed him out to the sea wall, to the great gates, which strained under the press of the wild waves. From across the courtyard, he smiled back at her, triumphant, as he slid the key into the lock on the sea gate and opened it to the raging ocean.

'Are you mad?' she screamed over the roar of the storm. 'You'll kill us all. The city will drown.'

'Oh yes,' he replied. 'The sea will have you. This is my intent.'

'But why?'

'Why? For every death, for every life exploited, for every family destroyed by you and your kind. I am the Mac'htiern of my people, their protector.'

The water was rising now and he stood above it on the wall leading back to the promontory, to safety. The water rushed towards her.

She saw her people begin to panic and flee, saw her father on his magical horse, riding across the waves, and for a moment she thought he would rescue her. But the priest behind him damned her with his words and her father left her to drown.

With her last breath, she cursed the Mac'htiern, her faithless lover, cursed his line, cursed everything and everyone he would touch. Cursed herself for ever trusting him.

'I would have loved you,' she cried as the sea rushed in around her. 'I would have been yours. And one day I will have vengeance, even if it takes forever. I'll wait in the land beneath the waves. The sea will take you too. It will take all your menfolk, and all who stand with you, and leave your women weeping. Until the day you save my city, until you give your all to protect Ys, I curse you and yours to drown.'

The cold hand of death took her, even as she raged, even as she cursed, even as she poured every last ounce of power into her words. She looked into the face of Ankou, the Servant of Death, who had loved her and left her, who would do anything for her. She cried for her lost city, her lost love, her shattered dreams, and he took pity on her, releasing her.

The water took her and made her its bride.

CHAPTER ONE

Ari had never intended to come back here. In fact, she had told
Jason as much the day she refused to return for the funeral.

*Nothing on earth will ever drag me back to that godforsaken
place.*

The ends of the earth, Finistère, Brittany, this promontory
of bare rock and raging waves, wild and angry at the rest of the
world, stubborn to the last.

'Just like you,' her brother told her. He always was a smart-
arse.

The wind tore at her hair and she tasted the salt carried on
it like old tears, all the way across the Atlantic with nothing to
stop it. The cliffs fell away beneath her feet and the sky— She
had forgotten about the sky here. It just seemed so much bigger
than anywhere else, a vast dome of shifting greys and myriad
blues which could change like a transient mood. Sea and sky,
and the rocks between, the white of foam and clouds, all the
colours of the Atlantic. Bright overhead, darkening as it swept
towards the far western horizon, where it deepened to indigo
and blended with the endless sea.

Beautiful, she would have said once. Long ago, she hadn't

conceived of anywhere more beautiful. When she'd been in love with the region, and the peninsula of Cap Sizun in particular. And Simon.

But losing him had stolen everything.

It still felt like he was here, as if he lingered at her shoulder, or failing that, at any moment he would clamber back over the rocky outcrop to the left, scrambling through bracken and wild honeysuckle, and join her once again. He'd grin. That reckless, devil-may-care grin.

And she'd feel it all through her body, the joy. Love.

Had it really been two years? Two years since the letter from him which had changed everything. Since the phone call that had made it all even worse.

She let the wind whisk her tears away from her face and fixed her gaze on the distant place where the sea and the sky melded together, seamless and dark, threatening oblivion. Seagulls wheeled overhead, crying out in those long, drawn-out screams.

To her left, the Pointe du Raz cut like the bow of a ship through the treacherous passage of sea. Beyond it stood the lighthouse, La Vieille, the Old Lady, named for the sea witch, or *groac'h*, who lived beneath the rock on which it stood. After that, the Île de Sein, called Enez-Sun in Breton, hung like a mirage, a flat stretch of isolated land, five miles away. After Sein, barely visible, even on so clear a day, the final lighthouse, the shadowy form of Ar Men, the Rock, clung to last scrap of land. Then there was only the ocean, the vast Atlantic.

Qui voit Sein, voit sa fin.

Who sees Sein, sees their end, or so the saying went, before the sea took them, the rocks tore them apart and the ocean swallowed them up.

Like Simon. She shied away from that thought.

The sea around here was dangerous and the rocks around the island had claimed so many lives. Between the point where she stood now, and the Pointe du Raz, the nearby bay was named for it, la Baie des Trépassés, or the Bay of the Dead, a stretch of idyllic sand with a dark history.

Simon would wax lyrical about the region. He told her tales his grandparents had told him, which their grandparents had told them in turn. His family had once been as entwined with this place as the rocks, the sea and the sky. And she would listen, rapt in the spell of his voice as he spun stories out of places and place names, out of snatches of history and half-remembered folklore – how Sein was once home to nine priest-esses with power over life and death, how the barge of the dead would ply these waters looking for the lost, how during a storm you could still hear the bells of the sunken city of Ys, or how on still days a booming echo rang out across the water signifying its destruction when the sea gates were flung open by the full force of the Atlantic.

Had he heard those sounds of legend? When the sea took him?

It wasn't actually the most westerly point of mainland France, but it truly felt like the end of the world. That was what the Romans had called it. Finistère.

Ari walked on. This late in the season and midweek, the Pointe du Van was almost deserted. It was the gentler sister to Raz, less commercial, a wildlife preserve with carefully curated clifftop walks and the squat little chapel of St They, hugging the edge of the last place on earth.

On either side of the path, gorse, bracken, heather and countless wildflowers stretched out to the cliff edges. Little wires kept wandering feet from disturbing them.

Simon had loved it here, loved to wander and get lost on the pathways, to sit and stare out to sea. He preferred it to the busier Pointe du Raz, with its tourist buses, cafés and shops. From here, he said, he could wander home and never encounter a car. He could pretend he had travelled back in time. He knew the clifftop paths intimately, every lichen-stained rock, every drystone wall, every dip and curve. His family might all be gone from Sainte Sirène, and he might have lived away for years, but he remembered it perfectly. And every story associated with it.

Ari knew she shouldn't have come. She hadn't meant to. But she had reached the turn on the D7 for Sainte Sirène itself, and she'd just kept driving west until there was nowhere else to go.

A sudden tremor shook its way through her and she leaned against the rough wall of piled-up stones, closing her eyes to fight off the inevitable grief, rising like waves in the Raz de Sein behind her, that treacherous and deadly passage of water between the point and the island.

She shouldn't have come back. This was Simon's home. And Simon was gone.

Her phone rang as she reached her car. Jason – his photo flashed up on the screen, a few years old now, fresh-faced, grinning, the grin that always meant trouble.

Reluctantly, Ari answered, expecting the big brother tones she knew too well.

'Where are you?' he asked.

'I'm on my way.' It wasn't exactly a lie.

'You should have been here hours ago, Ari.'

She could argue, lie, say she'd been delayed, tell him she'd get there in her own good time and he didn't get to boss her around anymore. But what was the point? And as for bossing her around? He'd do that anyway. He always had. And she had always ignored him.

'Fifteen minutes,' she told him. 'This had better be good, big brother.'

If he heard the warning in her voice, he didn't let on. He wouldn't care anyway. Jason Walker was afraid of no one, least of all his little sister.

'Oh it is. I promise you.'

Where had she heard that before? Jason's promises. They

were legendary.

She sighed, not even willing to disguise it for him. 'I'm on the way.'

'Where are you anyway? You aren't driving. Are you—?'

He stopped. Perhaps he heard the wind on the line. Perhaps it was something else. But he knew exactly where she was.

'I'm fine. I'm on the way.'

'OK. Drive safe.' She didn't know that tone of voice quite so well. Chastened, worried. That didn't sound like Jason at all. But for once she decided not to argue.

The roads rolled across the landscape, past little white Breton houses with their Atlantic blue shutters, granite lintels and slate roofs. Riots of hydrangea filled the gardens and spilled over the low grey walls, blue and purple, pink and red.

She set out across the flat, mist-shrouded landscape of rambling fields and low hedgerows. Hardly any trees here, not at the coast. She remembered Simon explaining it was to do with the soil and the stones, the salt in the air and the sea, like everything here. Everything came back to the sea. Everything here, everything, reminded her of Simon.

Because when your fiancé drowned in the place he loved most in the world it tended to stick with you. And ruin that place forever.

By the time she reached the junction by the windmills at Trouguer, her stomach was churning and she was half tempted to turn and just keep driving in the other direction. To forget she ever had a brother.

But she couldn't do that.

He had begged her to come and Jason never begged.

The turning looked like no more than a laneway. Only the fact it had road markings – at least at the beginning – betrayed it. There was a sign, but foliage obscured it. The road, such as it was, dipped down and turned, revealing the village in the distance.

She could make out the spire of the chapel, rising through the stunted trees which managed to dig into the earth here, a little further inland. And beyond that Sainte Sirène, nestled by the sea, cliffs jutting up on either side to protect it, while the headland known as Castelmeur stretched out, shielding it all from the wildest the Atlantic had to offer. There was an ancient chapel, a graveyard, a crêperie, a bakery which only opened until midday and a *bar-tabac* which doubled as the local shop and just about everything else. In the summer, there was a little museum, filled with local oddities and knick-knacks. And the manor house, the seat of the du Lac family.

You couldn't see the manor from here. Probably by design. If you were the local lord oh so many years ago, in an area famed for smuggling and dark deeds, a hidden home was probably your greatest asset.

But she wasn't heading for the manor house. She'd only seen it at a distance anyway.

Simon had, long ago, secured a deal to use one of the gîtes on the estate. Or, rather, on the parcels of land that had been the estate. His family had an in, he'd said, with a half-smile, old favours owed and shared secrets, no doubt. Her brother had followed him. What had been supposed to be an archaeological expedition had quickly transformed into a treasure hunt.

Jason Walker always landed on his feet. He could charm the apples off the trees, her mother used to say, handsome, easygoing, but with a passion that surprised and inspired anyone who met him.

Ari was about the only person immune to him. And even then, she couldn't always resist. The fact that she was here was proof enough.

She parked next to a jeep that had seen many better days and a somewhat battered red Renault with a canoe strapped to the roof.

Nico's car hadn't changed. And probably never would. But

it was good to know he was still here too. If anyone could keep Jason in some semblance of check it was Nico. The charm didn't work on him either.

The whole place looked like some kind of hippy encampment, sprawling out of the cottage and across the grass, a scattering of tents in the garden, equipment in various stages of repair and an elaborate flag – the black and white Breton flag in the middle surrounded by smaller flags of all the Celtic nations – hanging over the doorway. She even spotted the Irish flag on it and wondered if Jason had complained it was too small.

Ari shook her head. There weren't as many people as she'd expected. Usually, Jason gathered an entourage for his expeditions. From the patches in the grass, it was clear some people had already upped sticks and left. Well, summer was over, after all.

'There you are!'

Before she knew what was happening, she had been swept up in a pair of strong arms and crushed against her brother's chest.

It shouldn't feel this good. It really shouldn't. He was a pain in the arse and she still hadn't forgiven him for... well, everything. He smelled of the sea and sweat, with a lingering aroma of surfboard oil which told her immediately it wasn't all work around here.

But it never was. Not with him.

Ari disentangled herself, hiding her reluctance to do so. She had to be strong, especially when it came to Jason the feckless wonder.

'So I'm here,' she told him, and Jason grinned down at her, that goofy grin which never changed at all. 'Where's this amazing find of yours?'

He shrugged. 'Oh, that's in Brest already.'

The world seemed to freeze around her, her stomach plummeting and her head reeling.

'It's *what?*' The words came out on a strangled breath and she stepped back from him. She had come all this way for him. He'd begged her to come and see the treasure he claimed to have found, which he had promised was real, was special, was what Simon had always dreamed of, was the very reason they'd followed him out here... and it was already gone?

'It's a sixth-century coin, Ari. They weren't going to let us hang on to it here. Look at the place. It's hardly secure, is it?'

'Jason... I was working. It's the start of term. I had to get someone to cover for me. I took unpaid leave and I—'

She couldn't finish the sentence, couldn't form the words. She pressed her fist to her mouth and fought to make her body inhale again. She was not going to have a panic attack, not here and now, especially not in front of him. She had come all this way, to *this* place...

Jason just carried on like he didn't even hear her.

'I have the photos. And the report. And more. Come on. I'll show you where I found it.' He held out his hand, just as he always had done when they were kids.

He could have emailed all of that. She could be sitting in her flat reading the details. Safe. Quiet. Not here.

'And where did you find it?' she asked coldly, dreading the reply.

'Where Simon said it would be.'

This wasn't just about the coin, she realised. She could see that in the glow that spread through her brother, the pride, the wonder, the triumph. Jason was a believer.

Simon had been adamant. Unswerving in his belief about the lost city. And it had cost him his life.

It had cost her Simon, even before he died. This place. This stupid place.

Ari couldn't take it. 'You're still looking for Ys? *Jesus*, Jason, don't you ever learn?'

CHAPTER TWO

'I'll tell you a story,' Simon said.

They sat side by side on a picnic blanket, on the headland overlooking the Baie des Trépassés. The breeze rippled the heather and it was alive with butterflies. Stretching out her legs, Ari tilted her head back to feel the sun on her face. It was a glorious summer, before she went away, before he'd sent that awful letter which changed everything... before he died.

'Go on then.'

'So, this is the Pointe de Van, right?'

'Got it in one, genius. It's almost as if you know the place.'

He laughed, a deep chuckle which did interesting things inside her. 'And that is the Chapelle de Saint They.' He pointed to the squat church perched on the cliffs a little distance away. 'He kept watch here on the night Ys sank, its golden roofs and red walls swallowed by the sea. When he saw the water rising, he rang the bells to warn his master of the incoming flood and the saint was able to alert the king just in time. The two of them escaped on the king's horse, Morvarc'h.'

'The one that could run on water? Handy,' she teased and tapped the pendant hanging from a leather thong at his throat.

She'd had it made for him, a bone carving of a horse and waves. Then she reached up further to bury her fingers in his hair, caressing him, pulling him closer.

'Who's telling this story, Ariadne Walker?' *he scolded in mock-sternness.*

She had pouted and he'd kissed her before continuing. Ari, who much preferred the kissing to the story, sank into his embrace.

'The king's daughter Dahut cried out to him to save her, and he tried, but he couldn't pull her from the water. In fact, he almost came off the horse, so strong was the pull of the waves on the woman.

'"She's a witch," the saint told him. "She has caused this disaster. Her lusts led your people to their doom. Let the waves have her. Let the curse of Ys take her."

'So the king let his own daughter go and the horse bore them to safety to the sound of the chapel bells. He founded Quimper instead – a new city to rule.'

'What a bastard,' *Ari remarked.* 'Typical king, I suppose. Why is it always the women that have to die in these stories?'

'She was a monster, enchanting the menfolk and murdering them. Pay attention. Anyway, she didn't die. Dahut became a creature of the waves and the storm, a groac'h, or a mari-morgen, a water witch, and she still haunts the Mer d'Iroise, from the Chaussée de Sein up to Lostmarc'h on the other peninsula over there' *– he pointed to the north –* 'right in as far as the port of Douarnenez itself, dragging those who see her in the water to their deaths and singing her seductive songs.'

She grinned, enjoying teasing him when he was so serious. 'Psycho mermaid. Got it.'

Simon kissed her and she lay back beneath him. 'The bells of the chapel still ring out whenever there's a storm on the way, all by themselves.'

Ari gave him a stern look, that was only half in jest. 'You *know as well as I do, old stories are not reliable sources. We don't even know that any of those people existed, Simon, let alone what really happened if they did. Locations change, motivations, even names. Stories change with each telling. You can't base research on them.'*

'I swear to God, Ari' – he placed his hand on his chest, his eyes large and liquid – *'every word is true.'*

She glanced at the chapel. The bell was visible, suspended in the steeple, open to the elements. *'You do realise that any gust of wind would make that bell ring, right?'*

'No, it's magic, you wicked woman. A warning that the water witch is coming and will drown the unwary.'

'Are you unwary?' she'd asked with a low, throaty laugh. She rather liked the idea of being a wicked woman. Especially with him.

'You're the only siren I need in my life,' he had replied, framing her face with his strong hands while she laughed at him. But he was in earnest, his eyes fierce. *'It would take more than Dahut to steal me away from you, Ari. More than the sea itself.'*

But, in the end, the sea had been stronger than his promise.

And even before that, his promise hadn't been worth very much at all.

———

Photos. Jason had dragged her back here just for photos. She should have bloody known.

Ari pinched the bridge of her nose and stared at the report spread out on the kitchen table. Jason had hurriedly cleared away mugs, bowls of half-eaten cereal and various bits of crockery and cutlery to make space. She sat in the wooden chair, trying to focus on the reports he'd printed out. Jason couldn't bear to read things on a computer screen. Oh no, not him.

Her brother stood over her, waiting. He shuffled his feet and cleared his throat and every movement was a barb in her brain.

'Go away, Jason.'

'I just want to know what you think.'

'What I think? I *think* you lied to get me back here.'

'I didn't lie. Nico, did I lie?'

Ari glanced over her shoulder to see the familiar form of the broad-shouldered French diver who was her brother's best friend and right-hand man. It had always been the four of them – Simon, Jason, Nico and Ari, comrades in arms.

Now there were only three.

Nico shook his blond head and grinned. 'You're not sucking me into this, Jase. I know better. Ari, it's good to see you. A bit of sanity around here will be a bonus.'

She smiled, and the next thing she knew, Nico drew her into a hug. He kissed each cheek in greeting.

'I've missed you too,' she told him. 'Is this really legit?'

He tilted his head to one side, pursing his lips while Jason gave an affronted growl which they both ignored. 'The archaeology unit in Brest seemed to think so. They were all over it. There's a woman heading them up, not the most pleasant of people, but she knows her stuff.'

'She called us treasure hunters,' Jason cut in. The tone said it all for him. He was disgusted.

'Well, we *are* treasure hunters,' Nico replied calmly. He was so patient with Jason. Nothing fazed him. She envied him that. 'And you found treasure. *Bravo.*' He returned his attention to Ari. 'Have you eaten, *chérie*? I can make you some lunch. An omelette maybe. The chickens run wild here. We're plagued with eggs.'

The other thing about Nico was his legendary ability with food.

'Please,' she said and, right on cue, her stomach rumbled.

But Jason wasn't going to be put off. 'No food until you've read that and looked at the— Here, this one. Look at it.' He shook a large black and white photo at her, the coin on it blown up, the image sharply defined. A woman in profile, with long hair elaborately dressed with what looked like seashells and pearls. And something else. Possibly eels. Or snakes. Ari couldn't make out the writing, it was too worn.

'It's beautiful.'

'And sixth century. Exactly the right period.'

She didn't want to start the usual lecture about only looking for things that confirmed the story he already wanted to tell. It wasn't worth it.

'So who is she?' Ari asked.

'You know who she is.'

'Probably some governor's wife or—'

'Ari, come on. It's *her*.'

The problem was actually not the image. She'd already seen the dating information on the printouts and it was pretty conclusive that the coin dated from the right time period for the legendary city of Ys. As to the woman's identity, that was just conjecture, but she wasn't going to be able to shake Jason of that conviction. She knew that. The problem was it became too easy to spin the facts into his narrative, rather than follow them to their natural conclusion.

'All this means is that it's from the right period,' she said with a sigh. 'We know there were settlements here from the earliest periods, long before the sixth century. It doesn't prove Ys existed.'

'We were diving here.' He ignored her and poked at the map, not far off the headland north of them, the Pointe de Castelmeur. There was a cave system there, a treacherous and difficult area to dive, even in good weather. The tides here made it all the more perilous and the cliffs were crumbling.

Ari glanced at Nico, wondering what Jason had been

getting him into, but he was busy with his back to her, clattering about at the ancient cooker. On purpose, she suspected.

'You were diving in the caves?'

'No. Not yet. This was outside. I think it got swept out, or maybe when some of the cliff face came down, it was dislodged. And I don't think it's the only thing. But... look, you've kept your diving certs up to date, haven't you?'

She nodded, dubiously. She always kept them updated. Nico had drilled the importance of it into her when they'd first started working together. No one could dive if they didn't have their certs. She'd spent the early part of the summer doing just that. 'Of course.'

'We need another experienced diver,' Nico interrupted, turning back from the cooker, his eyes keen. 'Don't put it off any longer, Jason. Tell her.'

Oh. Of course. This was why he wanted her here. Not technically to rub the find in her face, or bring up all her grief all over again. He needed her to work. After all, she was the one with the qualifications, even if she had run away from archaeology and everything to do with it. Like it or not, she could lend him legitimacy.

Jason pulled that picture-of-innocence face that made her want to jab him in the ribs. There was nothing sharp to hand. He'd made damn sure of that. 'The coin in itself isn't much,' he admitted. 'But it cements what we've been doing here... Look, Ari, I need you.'

'You're an archaeologist, Jason... At least you used to be.'

'I've burned a lot of bridges.'

He certainly had. Even with her.

But he was still her brother. 'Jason... I can't. I mean, this place... you know what happened. You of all people know.'

'Simon would have wanted—'

She pushed herself up to her feet, sending the papers sliding across the table. 'Don't you dare!'

'Ari, please—'

'You may have found something, but you didn't invite me back here to find peace. You just want me to do something for you. Again. Even though I told you I don't want to be here. This place took Simon from me. I see him everywhere. Don't you get it?'

Ari strode out of the house, her hands buried deep in her fleece pockets, her head down. Jason didn't come after her. He knew better. Besides, she didn't have anywhere else to go. Not here. Maybe she could get a hotel room and ignore him until her ferry home in a week. She could turn this into a proper holiday.

But she wouldn't.

She knew it and Jason knew it. Hell, even Nico knew it.

But they let her walk away, for now.

That was probably Nico's idea. Jason would keep nagging her, just like he always did. But Nico knew, as he had always known, that sometimes Ari just needed to walk it off.

Simon had understood that too.

Oh God, Simon...

They didn't know what had happened. They didn't know about the letter or why she hadn't come back after he died. Why she hadn't wanted to come here at all. They thought it was simply her grief.

She lifted her head as she reached the cliff path, the trees far behind her now, the little village and the church out of sight. All that lay ahead were the cliffs and the sea, the water swelling around the rocks turning white as snow. But in the still areas between, the depths leading down to the finest pale sand, the water turned the colour of sea-glass, green-blue and shining. Magical. Under the blue and cloudless sky like today's, it looked tropical, a glimpse of paradise.

This had been their place, the two of them, this corner of the world, this headland especially, reaching out like a causeway to nowhere. This had been his dream, finding something here.

Finding Ys, the lost city.

'Might as well try to find Atlantis,' she'd told him.

'Same thing,' he'd replied. 'Ys. Atlant-Ys.'

God, she *hated* when he did that. It was a spurious correlation, based entirely on a sound from two different languages. But when she told him that, he just laughed.

Simon always laughed.

He was a true believer. He had grown up on the stories, the ones the locals told each other, because he was one of them too. His family had always lived here, until he was the only one left. His family history was entwined with this shoreline and with the tales of Ys.

'We are her children,' he used to say. 'The lost children of lost Ys, the ones who got away.'

Only he didn't get away in the end. He never left. And now he couldn't.

Her eyes filled with tears. She could blame the wind, but there was no one there to see her. Besides, the tears didn't flow anymore. She had cried all her tears.

I should tell you this face to face, he had written in that last letter, *but I do not possess that kind of bravery...*

Ari glanced down to the water again, down to the little cove below her, and what she saw there struck her like a punch to the guts.

A body floated in the water, just drifted there, arms outstretched, face to the sky.

CHAPTER THREE

Coming home was never going to be easy. Rafael might love this place and everything here, but he had been away for a long time, apart from the odd brief visit. Everything seemed smaller somehow, less impressive. There was something worn and ragged about it.

And then there was Mémé to deal with. His great-aunt was nothing if not predictable, causing chaos with her projects and her obsessions. He'd come back to find plaits of seaweed on door handles, and little linen bags of God knew what hidden in the most unexpected places. Charms and amulets, protection, the magic in which she believed so adamantly.

Mémé was not going to listen to anyone else. The money she was drawing from her accounts wasn't huge in the grand scheme of things, but there was no paper trail and he didn't like that. It looked suspicious. She was an elderly woman and he feared that people were taking advantage of her.

She might have listened to his father. With no children of her own, he had been like a son to her rather than a nephew, but Rafael's father was dead. Thirty years dead. Rafael had only been a child when the sea took him. As the sea always took the men of his line. From the lowliest fishermen to the CEO of a successful multinational.

Mémé could tell you all about it. At length. With examples, photos, a family tree and, if she had ever managed to get her head around the wonders of technology, a PowerPoint presentation. Inevitably, they ended up arguing. But Rafael didn't suffer such superstition, even when the inevitable seemed to be clawing its way closer to him with each passing year.

As he always had done when he needed to escape, Rafael made his way down to the sea. The little cove below his home had been his safe space as soon as he could walk. The cliffs rose sheer on either side, the rocks a curious mixture of colours: black, pale grey, white, yellow. The sand there was the finest he'd ever encountered. He would make his way down here to swim whenever he got the opportunity, much to his mother's horror.

'In the sea, Rafael,' she would say, 'like some fisherman's brat. Anything could happen.'

But he never felt in danger here.

The sheltered inlet was once the heart of Sainte Sirène, where the boats had put out and come ashore for generations. Now they used one of the ports in Douarnenez, safer and more practical. Rafael knew every inch of it.

Perhaps understanding that the sea would only take him when he was thirty-five, like the rest of the men in his family, was a safety net. Or at least it had been, until he actually approached that particular birthday.

It was stupid. A superstition. Nothing more. He reminded himself of that constantly.

And yet... and yet...

His father, his grandfather, great-grandfathers aplenty... all the men of his line. Fishermen and farmers, lawyers and soldiers, lords and sailors. All taken by the sea.

He stripped off and left his clothes on the rocks flanking the slipway. No one else came down here, not really. There were barely fifty people living in Sainte Sirène outside of high season. People went to the Baie des Trépassés to surf, or the safe and family-friendly beaches on the southern coast of Cap Sizun to swim. Not here.

Without hesitation, he waded into the whispering ocean braced for the cold. The waves lapped up around him, caressing his skin. Not as chilly as he'd expected – it was the Atlantic Ocean, after all, not the South Pacific or the Caribbean... But this was almost welcoming.

The sand beneath his feet was soft and gentle. He skirted rocks draped in fine green seaweed like mermaid's hair and waded out into the open water, lifted by each gentle wave.

Rafael laid himself back in the sea water, the salt buoying him up, and closed his eyes, letting the rolling motion take him. Sunlight played on his face and suddenly it seemed that the sea was all around him, rocking him, caressing him. It was like a song, something distant and half remembered, only heard under the water. He sank back further, only part of him in the world of air and sunshine and the rest... the rest somewhere else.

He breathed out, relaxing into the sea's embrace, feeling it against his skin, feeling each ripple and current, letting it take him and trusting it completely. Tension ebbed out of him like the tide, and he drifted away.

He should invite Elena and Georges here over the holidays. That could be nice. Something to build their relationship on, perhaps. Something to share. It had been like this when he was a child, when he would come down here, when it was his escape instead of... what?

No, the cove was still his escape. But Sainte Sirène was—

A distant shout made him open his eyes, only half heard through the water. And the splashing, like a horse thundering through the surf towards him. A pair of hands grabbed him and he flailed wildly, going under the surface. Salt water filled his mouth and nose, choking him, drowning him, but then his feet found purchase on the sandy seabed and he launched himself up, ready to hit whoever it was who—

A woman, drenched and clearly terrified, stood over him, chest deep in the water, her upper body heaving with exertion and fear. Her eyes were huge, bright blue and wide in alarm. She hurriedly backed away, her hands held high as if to defend herself from a monster. Her wet grey T-shirt was plastered to her slim athletic body.

Rafael spat out the sea water – half the cove, or so it seemed – coughed violently and staggered towards dry land, cursing with what little breath he could still manage. She followed him, torn between trying to help him and not wanting to touch him again.

'Oh my God, I'm so sorry,' she said in rapid English. 'I didn't mean to... I thought, I just... I'm so sorry...' Then she seemed to catch herself and switched to French. Not bad French, a little too precise, but practised. 'I'm so sorry. I thought you were drowning. I thought—'

He coughed again, bent in two, finally clearing the last of the water from his throat. Long wet strands of his black hair hung over his eyes and he looked up at her pale, frantic face. 'So you decided to drown me a second time just to make sure?'

He said it in English. It was easier. The language was second nature for him. He'd lived there, studied there, and frequently visited London and New York.

The woman flinched, clearly embarrassed by her actions, worried he was right. She opened her mouth to protest and Rafael held up his hand to stop her.

'Don't. I'm fine.'

'I really am sorry,' she whispered. All the colour had drained from her skin, her blue eyes very wide. Such blue eyes. Like the sky overhead, the Breton sky. Copper hair, cut short at the back of her head, long strands framing her high cheekbones and delicate features, stuck there and darkened to bronze by sea water. For a moment, he couldn't look away. A slim leather thong encircled her neck. The small pendant dangling from it looked like ivory or bone, intricately and delicately carved with the figure of a horse or a deer. 'I just...' Her gaze trailed down his chest to his abdomen and then shot back up to his face. A blush spread up her pale neck and blossomed across her cheeks.

Damn it, he was naked. He was standing here naked on the beach, with all the seagulls and the whole Atlantic Ocean laughing at him.

Rafael sighed and raked his hand through his wet hair, pushing it back from his face. It had been a long day, a gruelling journey and his great-aunt had been so difficult when he finally got there. He'd just wanted to relax, to spend some time alone, to unwind. Not this.

'Excuse me,' he said as politely as he could manage. She didn't move at first, but when he took a step towards her, she backed up. He schooled his voice to patience. '*Mademoiselle*, my clothes are behind you.'

Flustered, she turned around and then back to him. She opened her mouth, presumably to apologise again, but didn't. He wondered had she made all her apologies now, or was she just dumbstruck at the sight of him? No, he wasn't so arrogant to think that.

But she was clearly uncomfortable and truly embarrassed.

His phone started to ring, making her turn once more, like a startled cat this time, and Rafael sighed, walking by her to grab it out of the pocket.

'Where are you, Rafael?' His great-aunt sounded irritated rather than concerned.

'I'm on the way back, Mémé. I just went for a swim.'

'You should be more careful, swimming here. It isn't safe. The water is treacherous. Your father would not be so foolish.'

Oh, but he had been, Rafael thought. Didn't she remember

how he died? He couldn't say it out loud. Sometimes he feared that Mémé didn't even remember that his father was dead, and that was more worrying than anything else.

His would-be saviour walked back up the slip and sat down next to the memorial to the local World War Two resistance. She shoved her feet into the pair of hiking boots which she must have abandoned there before taking to the water. Then she bent forward, her head hanging low as she breathed slowly in and out, as if fighting off a panic attack. She didn't look well. He ought to help her, probably.

His great-aunt's voice went on in his ear, chiding him until he interrupted.

'Mémé, I'll be back there shortly. I promise.'

'I'm going out. I'll be back for dinner. I'll see you then.'

She hung up before he could ask where she was going. Unbelievable. How could she just take off like that? Anything could happen to her. Cursing softly to himself, he pulled his clothes on as quickly as he could, chinos, and a T-shirt Jacqueline had bought for him in Paris, which had probably cost more than he cared to think about. She loved her obscenely expensive clothing lines. Rafael, not being one who needed to check such things, had constantly let her get away with it.

His supermodel ex would never be seen dead wearing shorts and a T-shirt like the woman who had launched herself into the ocean to save a stranger. Even if he didn't need saving. Come to that, Jacqueline would never deign to enter a mundane and chilly expanse of sea like the Mer d'Iroise. She had never come here with him and definitely never would now.

A fleece jacket had been flung on the beach, presumably as the woman ran for the water. He picked it up, feeling the weight of keys and a phone. Not something she would want to lose then, for the sake of what was in it at least, even if it did come from a commercial, mass-produced supermarket line.

Oh how his ex-girlfriend would sneer. That wasn't even her least-pleasant habit.

'Is this yours?' he called and she looked up. Her fingers played with the pendant on the leather thong around her throat again and she froze, as if caught doing something she shouldn't have. Her face was wet, not with sea water but with tears. Her skin looked as pale as the piece of carved bone in her hands.

He knew that look. He had seen it on too many faces in this village in his life alone.

Something struck his chest like a blow, the look of grief and loss on her beautiful face making him want to take a step back, while, at the same time, something else, darker and determined, told him to comfort her, to wrap his arms around her and shelter her from the shadows.

It was a ridiculous thought.

She cleared her throat, and stood up, turning away from him for a moment while she wiped her face with her hands.

'Yes,' she said, turning back, and the haunted expression was gone. She wore a mask now. It might look like a calm, collected face, but he knew a mask when he saw one. 'I apologise, for everything.' She made her way to him and retrieved her jacket. She was still soaked, shivering now. She slipped the fleece on and huddled into it. But she didn't make eye contact, eager to get away from him. 'You're clearly OK, so I'll... I'll go. Sorry.'

Rafael frowned as she retreated back towards the path leading up towards the point.

'Wait, are you...' He couldn't say OK. It was a stupid question. She clearly was not OK. 'Are you staying nearby?'

She looked back at him as if to ask what he was doing. Why did he want to know? He'd like an answer to that himself. 'Yes, for a few days anyway.'

A tourist then. She had to be. Late in the season, but people came through all the time, walking the coastal paths mainly.

What did you say to someone who had tried to save your life, even if you hadn't needed them to? He would offer her a lift, but she didn't seem like she'd happily climb into a car with a stranger. Sensible.

'Can I buy you dinner?' The words came out before he knew what he was saying.

Her mouth opened as if to reply and then she shut it again, wrapping her arms tighter around her chest. She looked as perplexed as he felt.

'Dinner?'

He shrugged, that gesture that came so easily to him, part of his nature. 'You came to my rescue. You could say I owe you.'

The smile that flickered over her lips transformed her. She had been beautiful, but that smile... It was something else. An unknown feeling inside him unfurled at the sight of it, a reaction he knew was dangerous. He would be better to ignore it. To push it down inside him and deny it had ever appeared, let alone examine it or recognise it for what it might be.

'Or you could say I accosted a naked man in the water. Why were you naked anyway?'

It was Rafael's turn to flush. 'I just felt like a swim.'

'Naked.'

She kept saying that word. He wished she wouldn't. It sounded like such a stupid thing to do now. He had the feeling she was teasing him and he wasn't sure how he felt about that. People didn't tease him.

Well, two could play at that game.

'There are a lot of things I can do naked,' he told her, casting her what Jacqueline used to call his finest smoulder.

The tourist, the woman, gave another one of those smiles. It said she knew exactly what he was trying to do, and that she wasn't impressed. But rather amused. 'I'm sure there are. But I don't hook up with strange men in the sea – strange men, by the way, who should know better than to swim in this region. The water's treacherous here.'

She sounded like Mémé.

'I'm well aware of that. I know the sea here better than anyone. And I know where the currents are too, where it's safe. It's my home.'

She laughed and the sound was music. Even though he already knew she was about to wind him up even more. There was something thrilling about it he didn't quite understand yet. 'Oh, right. You're a merman? That explains so much. The swimming, the nakedness. Grand so, I'll see you around, Ariel.' She turned away and climbed quickly up the narrow path through the heather and bracken.

Ariel? The little mermaid?

She was calling *him* a *mermaid*?

'I'll hold you to that dinner,' he called after her.

Her laugh floated back down. 'Sure. You find me and we'll have dinner.'

And then she was gone.

Rafael shook his head, bemused. Like the Itron Gwenn, the White Lady his great-aunt liked to spin fairy tales about. A ghostly, magical creature who appeared and disappeared on a whim. Mythical, ethereal.

The old woman lived in a world of myths and stories.

Mémé's moods were becoming increasingly fragile. It was the real reason he was back, after all. To see how bad it had become, to make a decision. To stop her taking on projects that haemorrhaged money to charlatans. To protect her interests because no one else would.

He made his way back towards the car parked at the end of the road leading to the cove, promising he would track down his elusive would-be saviour later on and thank her properly. Maybe he'd even apologise for his rudeness. Sainte Sirène was a tiny village. If you could even use a word as grand as 'village'. And he knew every inch of it.

He stopped for a moment and laid his hand on the memorial, shaped like a menhir, but carved with a ship in full sail. Beneath it was the double cross of Lorraine, the symbol of the Free French forces. And then the names: *Brochard, du Lac, Heussaff, Kerdaniel, Pascal, Poullain, Ruellan...*

He knew them all. They were friends, they were family.

This was his home. It had been home to his family for longer than history itself.

And it had been waiting for him all this time.

CHAPTER FOUR

Ari had almost made it back to the gîte before she'd managed to get her thundering heart under some form of control.

What had she been thinking?

But she had stood there, on the crest of the hill overlooking the cove, she'd seen the body in the water and she'd known, just known. An awareness deep inside her, a terrible sense of dread, a hollow ache...

She sometimes thought she'd known when Simon died, before the phone call, before Jason had told her what happened. Even though she had been in another country, she had felt it. A sense of foreboding, maybe. The letter should have been a clue that something was wrong, but she'd been too caught up in her own pain.

And that poor man had just been trying to have a swim.

A very naked swim. A very handsome man.

Her face burned with the embarrassment of it. She'd made a fool of herself. A total fool.

And then the flirting. Once it had started, she couldn't help herself. He was good at it too. Good at lots of things, she was sure of that.

Had she completely lost her mind?

It was a defence mechanism, that was all. A way of turning people aside so they didn't ask questions, of defusing situations, of making light of what had just happened.

Which was nothing really. She would never see him again. Even his threat of dinner was empty. He didn't even know where she was staying. Once she had sorted all this out with her brother, she'd head back home and hide herself away. She'd go back to being that elusive and tragic teacher the students hoped to get until they actually met her and saw the workload she had for them.

She had a couple of weeks or so before school actually reopened. Technically, she could do her preparation from here. And, of course, Jason knew that. He'd been counting on it.

There was a hotel in Dinan she liked. She'd go there. Short notice meant it would cost her, but she didn't care. Anything to get away from Sainte Sirène and her brother.

And her memories.

But Nico wasn't about to be that easily put off. He never had been. He was waiting for her in the door of the house. Whether Jason had sent him or not, she didn't know. And she didn't care.

No, that was unfair. Nico looked out for her brother no matter what. And her.

'There you are. Did you walk it off?'

She sighed, pushing her hands into her pockets, and didn't answer. Water dripped from her sodden clothes.

'You're soaked,' he said. 'What were you doing?'

'Nothing. I just went for a walk.'

He nodded slowly, still staring at her, taking in the wet clothes and hair. 'Well, you aren't Jesus anyway, so maybe you should stick to dry land for now. Down at Pors Sirène, were you?'

'Are you my dad now?' She wasn't in the mood for this. She

hadn't been in the mood for it from the start. This just made it even worse.

'Sure.' He dropped his voice to a gruff rumble. 'Get yourself indoors, young lady, and change into some dry clothes before you catch your death of cold.'

She couldn't suppress the laugh. Nico could always do that, cheer her up. 'You sound more like Mum,' she told him.

The faux voice didn't change. 'Don't you talk about your mother that way, Ariadne Walker.' He grinned, that gentle, easy-going grin she knew so well. 'Come on,' he continued, his own voice soft music. 'Get changed, come and spend the day with us and try to relax a bit. Let us show you the dive area. You used to love to dive.' She still did. At least she hadn't lost that. 'You can stay for a few days anyway, can't you?'

Could she? The thought of the hotel still tempted her. Maybe she could even change the ferry to a nearer date. She'd get a flight instead if it didn't mean leaving her car behind here. She'd never see it again. Jason would probably sell it for spare change.

'Nico, I don't want—'

'—to be here. It hurts. I know. But you are here. Besides, there's something else.'

A look passed over his face, a flash of guilt maybe, something he didn't want to share but couldn't justify keeping from her.

'What? Is something wrong with Jason?'

'No. I mean... No, nothing like that. We just... we found some of Simon's things upstairs. So we thought... you might want to go through them. Jason thought...'

Jason. Thinking. That would be a first.

'What sort of things?' she asked on a whisper.

'Papers mainly, photos, keepsakes. That sort of thing. Some of his research, from the looks of it. I couldn't make head or tail of it, but you knew him better than anyone, worked with him. I thought… I mean, Jason and I thought… you'd want them. Simon was on to something, we're sure of that. But we couldn't work out what he thought he'd found. Maybe you can figure it out. Maybe he left you a clue.'

Suddenly her throat was tight and her eyes burned again. 'I don't know,' she managed to say. She couldn't imagine Simon leaving her anything, let alone a clue to find Ys. Not that she believed in it to begin with.

But he had sent her the pendant. Guilt, probably.

'Whenever you're ready. There's no rush. I'll leave them out for you.'

She shook her head before she could stop herself. 'Jason should have told me.'

'He was afraid you'd tell him to get stuffed and never talk to him again.'

Tempting, she thought. Very tempting. But this time she didn't answer.

Nico pressed on, gentle and persistent. Relentless, some would say. 'Come on, Ari. Give him a chance. He's been so desperate to find something, for Simon's sake. In his memory. To prove him right. And he needs you.'

Ari swallowed hard on the lump in her throat, rising up to strangle her.

For Simon. He was doing all this, the whole project for Simon. Or at least for Simon's memory.

No one had asked him to.

But Jason was hurting too. She knew that. She just didn't know how to talk to him about it, how to share the pain. Because somehow it felt like, if she shared it with someone, if she let it out into the world, it would just grow and grow, become something even more monstrous and out of control. If she let it go, just for a second, it would swallow her whole.

Nico knew it too. Perhaps Nico was the only one holding things together. Or at least giving a really good impression of it.

Maybe she owed it to him, at least. He was looking after her brother. Just like always.

And they needed her help. Needed her to work out what Simon had been doing, and use her own expertise to find a lost city that probably never existed. Easy.

'My bag's in the car,' she told him. 'Give me a hand?'

There was a shower. It even had hot water. And it was in the en suite of her room. Except it wasn't her room and it wasn't going to be her room for long, even if she did decide to stay. But the bed was wide and soft, and the window looked out across the headland, towards the sea. Nico had left fresh towels and her bags on the chair inside the door.

No sign of the threatened box of Simon's things though. Not yet. They didn't want to scare her off. That was still waiting for her somewhere, lurking.

They'd picked the best room in the house for her, mainly, she suspected, as a bribe.

It was definitely nicer than any hotel she could afford right now. Especially after the cost of getting here at short notice in the first place.

What they didn't know was that this was the room she and Simon had shared when she visited. How could they? They hadn't even been here. They hadn't arrived to work with Simon until after she had gone away.

Simon had smiled at her when she'd told him about the job offer and then he'd looked so sad. They'd been sitting right there, on the edge of that bed, with the sunlight streaming through the window. She could almost hear him even now.

'I'm not going to be the reason you give up an opportunity like that,' he told her. 'Ari, think about it. If one of your mates said they were going to pass up a job like that for a man, what would you say?'

She had to laugh. Even now. The solemn and chiding look on his face. The way he held her hands. She couldn't doubt how much he loved her.

'It isn't for very long,' she said.

'And it's not like I'm going anywhere.'

That was the problem. He wouldn't leave. She couldn't stay. She had to go, if only for a while.

So she'd taken a lecturing job at St John's in Oxford, as close as she could get to the prestigious Oxford Centre for Maritime Archaeology, and she could visit their parents back in Dublin easily enough, much to their delight, since Jason was off gallivanting around the world in search of whatever shiny thing had captured his fancy at that moment.

And she'd loved it. Loved the students, the atmosphere, the work, the city. And she was good at it; so good that a short-term posting had become a longer one. OCMA were talking about a research fellowship. It was a dream, or would have been if Simon was with her.

Simon never complained. Her visits to Sainte Sirène became brief holiday breaks. His visits to her had been a job. She'd got him to be a guest lecturer on a number of occasions, an assistant on any number of digs, and he was such a hit with the undergraduates – smart, sexy, charming, her handsome Frenchman. What a team they had been.

But their holidays always had to come to an end. He came back here, she went back there. And they always promised that next time... next time...

He'd written her letters. Beautiful, romantic letters, page after page of his elegant handwriting, like something from an earlier age. Simon always said letter writing was important, a lost and dying art. One of her colleagues had called it contrived and pompous, but Ari didn't care. Simon's letters weren't like that. They were a glimpse into his soul. She loved them like she loved him.

But the last letter had been something else. She'd never told anyone about it, never shared it with anyone. She had stood there, in shock, holding the pendant which had slipped out with it in her numb fingers, reading the words, unable to believe they came from the same man.

My dearest Ari,

There is no easy way to say this. I should be brave and say it face to face, but I do not possess that kind of bravery...

And then, still reeling from the letter, she got the call from Jason.

'There's been an accident.' He'd said it so simply that she thought he meant a fender bender, or a broken arm. But the weight behind the words, the heaviness in his voice, set every instinct ringing with alarm. She knew her brother, knew him inside and out.

'He was in the water...'

She'd fallen apart.

By the time she picked up enough of the pieces, that dream life, the job at the pinnacle of her field was gone. She'd found another job in a private school, teaching classics, history and any other gaps she could fill in their curriculum. She'd found a crummy flat, which she only used as a place to sleep and store her belongings. She'd turned her back on archaeology, putting it, with Simon, firmly in the grave. She had run away. From her life, from her job, from her brother, from everything.

Now she was back here, the ghosts of Simon Poullain, his search for Ys and that lost life were everywhere.

Ari hadn't meant to sleep. She'd cried again, harder than she had cried in years, and eventually there were no more tears. She woke up suddenly, from a dream which faded as soon as she opened her eyes, flowing out of her mind like a wave retreating down the beach. Her throat was tight and uncomfortable and the sense of the sea all around her – the smell of it, the chill touch, the currents turning her this way and that, manipulating her helpless body – took another moment to fade away.

There was a knock at the door. 'Ari? We have a visitor who's dying to meet you,' said Jason. And then he was gone.

There were voices, hushed tones. Like whispers on the edge of her hearing, calling her.

Ari dragged herself up off the bed, pulled on her clothes and splashed cold water on her face until she made a fairly believable impression of a functioning human being. She dragged her hands through her pixie-cut hair, just to even things out. Then she made her way downstairs to find out what her brother had gotten himself into this time.

An older woman sat in the armchair beside the wood burner in the living room, facing the door. As Ari descended the stairs, she looked up and her piercing eyes examined the new arrival. Her long dark hair was shot with silver, and piled up at the back of her head in a carelessly elaborate bun. Her clothes looked sleek and elegant. It was difficult to tell her age. She could have been sixty or eighty, ageless in that way the super-rich often were. Ari knew the type instantly. Benefactresses – that was what Jason called them, and he could spot them in an instant. He charmed them, collected them, nurtured them. He didn't go beyond flirtation. He didn't have to. And he flirted with everyone anyway. The Irish blood in him, he said. He couldn't help himself. They loved him.

The woman's smile was gentle, her expression knowing.

'Oh good, there you are,' said Jason. She hadn't seen him standing just inside the doorway. Now she did, she was surprised to see how nervous he was. No one else would notice, but she knew those tell-tale signs he worked so hard to hide. 'Madame du Lac, my sister, Dr Ariadne Walker.'

Aha, Ari thought, it was prize pony time. Her title was the giveaway

She schooled her face to politeness and made a mental note to tear Jason a new one as soon as they were alone again.

'Yes,' Madame du Lac interrupted him. She held out her hand to Ari like a queen receiving a supplicant. 'I know who Dr Walker is. Your reputation precedes you. I heard you arrived and came to meet you.'

Who had she heard that from? And what reputation was she talking about?

Ari glanced at her brother, who was desperately trying to communicate something with his eyes, some furtive glances and the twist of his mouth. She didn't know what.

It didn't matter. No doubt Madame du Lac saw this as a great honour for them, for Ari in particular. Ari was used to it from the school, meeting people who could be sources of funding was an occupational hazard and a constant trial. It wasn't just Jason who played this game. He wasn't even the best player she had met.

The du Lacs... she remembered Simon talking about them. They owned everything around here. Even the roof over their heads right now. The family were ridiculously rich, running a multinational foundation, endless businesses and owning a whole portfolio of property all around the world. And Ari saw at once that Madame du Lac was the most formidable of them all.

She could evict Jason from the whole area if the mood took her, refuse them permission to use her buildings, complain to the Ministry of Culture, who oversaw marine archaeology, and the whole expedition, insane as it was, would be over. They were only here because she allowed it. If Madame du Lac decided this was all over, it would be. It would break her brother's heart.

Not to mention her money was funding them. And now Jason needed even more to keep going.

'It's a pleasure to meet you, *madame*.'

'Ah,' the old woman laughed. 'If only you knew who I was.'

Ari couldn't help but smile in return. It wasn't often you met someone so rich with any degree of self-deprecatory humour. 'I have to presume you're funding my brother's explorations here.'

Madame du Lac raised a slender hand, bearing rings that looked both ancient and priceless, and waved it regally. '*Brava*. Although, more properly, our foundation funds him. I am merely the board member who lives closest. In the Manoir. For my sins.'

'What sins could you possibly have, *madame*?' Jason said smoothly.

She laughed that same youthful laugh. The very sound made Ari grin before she could stop herself. 'Far too many to confess to a boy like you, Jason Walker. It would turn your hair white.'

Nico arrived from the kitchen with a glass of something that looked like wine on first glance, but had that syrupy aspect which suggested something altogether more lethal. Lambig, probably, the distilled liquor made locally, sometimes called *eau de vie* – the water of life.

'*Yec'hed mat*,' the old woman said.

Cheers, one of the few phrases of Breton Ari knew because Simon had tried to teach her, and saying cheers was his first step.

Madame du Lac sipped her drink delicately and then set it down on the table beside her. 'A fine *gwinardant*,' she said with some satisfaction when she saw Ari watching her. 'The best. It's made just up the road. Bernez Heussaff makes it himself and has done for fifty years, his father before him, all of them for generations. I have a taste for it, a hereditary thing. It flows easily, warms the blood. Young Nicolas always finds the best producers in the area for all products, don't you? Old Bernez doesn't give up his treasures easily, not even to my household.'

Nico smiled at her with genuine affection. 'I bribe him. Speaking of which, I have some cake fresh out of the oven.'

'Oh now, you will get me into trouble. My family say I do not eat properly. I indulge myself too much. Can you imagine?'

Ari couldn't. The woman looked like a bird.

'Lemon cake,' Nico teased and Madame du Lac shook her head, holding up her hands in defeat.

'You are a demon, Nicolas.'

They were interrupted by the sound of a car engine, tyres tearing up the dirt drive, and Ari caught Jason's frown.

'Ah,' Madame du Lac sighed as if the weight of the world suddenly sat upon her shoulders. '*Pa gomzer eus ar bleiz, Emañ e lost e-kreiz.*' She muttered the phrase and took a larger sup of her *gwinardant*.

'I don't understand,' Ari said.

'An old proverb. Let me see, it translates as "Talk of the wolf, its tail appears". Or in English you might say "Speak of the devil..."'

She finished the glass decisively, and with relish.

'Mémé?' The voice from outside sounded not just angry and frustrated, but worried as well. '*Es-tu lá?*'

More rapid French ensued as Nico shot out to the door, his tone at once both placating and reassuring. But his magic didn't work. Not this time. The man who burst into the house wasn't in the mood to listen to anyone. Jason took a step back and so did Ari. She couldn't help herself.

Not so Madame du Lac. She fixed a withering glare on the newcomer, but that didn't deter him, not for an instant. He spoke far too quickly for Ari to keep up with, but she got the gist.

What were you thinking just taking off like that? I've been worried sick. How did you get here? What are you doing? Who are these people anyway?

The old woman drew in a breath and let it out slowly. 'This one, the one with no manners at all, is my great-nephew, Rafael. Rafi, this is Dr Walker, come all the way from Oxford to help us. I came to say hello and—'

The man turned to Jason, enraged, ignoring Ari completely and immediately making that one fatal mistake people always made. The worst one. The most infuriating thing anyone could do, as far as she was concerned. 'I don't know what you're playing at, or what kind of doctor you pretend—'

'*I'm* Dr Walker,' Ari interrupted pointedly but firmly. It didn't matter if she barely used the title now. It was still hers. She had earned it. She might teach history now rather than unearth it, but still... 'It's archaeology and we are *not* "playing" at it.'

'And I am not quite so old as to need her expertise just yet,' his great-aunt cut in, grinning wickedly, delighted to see him caught out in such a spectacular way.

The man turned around, trapped in his confusion, the bewilderment in his dark eyes making him even more attractive. She couldn't fail to recognise him. Because, of course, it had to be him. At least he wasn't naked this time. He wore an outfit that cost more than Ari's car, possibly when it was new, long before she owned it.

'You?' he gasped. 'What are you—?' He seemed to run out of words, probably aware, as she was, that she was enjoying this particular moment a bit too much.

'Hello again, Ariel,' she said with a satisfied grin.

CHAPTER FIVE

It shouldn't have been quite so amusing to her, and Rafael himself was clearly not in the least bit amused. Shocked perhaps, and embarrassed, but clearly still worried about his elderly, wandering great-aunt and now taken completely off guard. He cleared his throat, and she watched him gather his control in an iron grip. The stillness that came over him was honestly impressive.

'My apologies, Dr Walker,' he said, her name and title clearly articulated this time and bound to be remembered. His accent, she noticed again, was less pronounced, his English perfect. His words carried hints of London and New York, and other places too. He'd travelled. He'd lived abroad, probably studied too. Perhaps he'd spent more time abroad than he had spent here. 'My great-aunt is an elderly lady and prone to—'

Madame du Lac rose to her feet abruptly, cutting him off, and held out her hand for the walking stick. Jason hurriedly supplied it. 'You may take me home now, Rafi. We have had quite enough of your tantrums for one day.' She turned to Ari, and she was surprised to see the old woman's eyes twinkling. '*Doctor* Walker, I came to invite you and your brother to dinner tomorrow night. Nicolas, as well, naturally.' She didn't give them a chance to agree or make excuses. She sounded more French than ever, despite her perfect English. 'Come, Rafi.'

She swept towards the front door, leaving him no chance to contradict her. She also didn't ask if anyone was free, just issued a decree and set off like a flagship leading an armada.

'*Grand-tante*,' Rafael tried to admonish her, but he wasn't getting anywhere. He glared over his shoulder at Ari, clearly flustered, perhaps simply by her use of the obvious childhood nickname when he was trying to order everyone around. That glare, given his sophisticated image, just amused Ari even more, something he didn't fail to notice. 'Very well,' he muttered darkly. 'Dr Walker, it seems that we will have dinner as promised. Try not to go to anyone else's rescue in the meantime.'

As they left, Nico seeing them out, Jason breathed a sigh that sounded suspiciously like relief. He leaned back against the wall, his eyes closed.

'Well, that could have gone better. *Rafael du Lac*, Jesus.' Then he opened one suspicious eye. 'What did he mean about going to someone's rescue, Ari?'

God, he missed nothing. For a moment, she thought she should tell him, but it was just too embarrassing. All of it.

'No idea,' she lied.

'Why did you call him Ariel?' Nico asked when he returned from seeing them off. 'That's the little mermaid, no? Have you met him before?'

'Eh... sort of. It's a long story. I met him at the cove earlier. Who is he?'

Jason barked out a laugh. 'Oh, that is *so* you. You haven't a clue, do you? He's only one of the richest men in France. He's the head of the du Lac Foundation. Well, his mother's the CEO, or maybe the CFO... the money, anyway, but he's... what would you call it? The head of the family. Old blood. It's probably governed by Salic law or something. They used to be royalty, you know? Now they're just richer than royalty.'

Well, the old lady certainly behaved like a queen. Or an empress.

Ari deliberately pushed all thoughts of handsome princes firmly out of her mind. 'Do you see everyone in terms of funding, Jason?'

'Madame du Lac has been very good to us. She's absolutely dedicated to finding Ys and she believed in Simon and his work completely. But her great-nephew is a different kettle of fish. I reckon he's here to rein her in. Or at least make sure we aren't wasting her time. He's the type to want results fast.'

She was sure he was. But archaeology didn't work like that. Treasure hunting, which was more or less what Jason did, even less so. You couldn't just produce things on demand like a magician. Those that did were charlatans and con artists.

Which might be what the du Lacs were worried about. First, Simon had got funding from Madam du Lac, probably based on old family connections, and then Jason turns up out of the blue to take over the baton. They didn't know him from Adam. He might have found the coin, and it might be the right sort of date, but it was flimsy evidence at best when you were looking for a whole lost city.

Nico picked up the plate and the glass to tidy them away. 'Unless he's here to shut us down. You heard him. If he thinks you're ripping off his great-aunt, it could be all over, Jason.'

To be fair, Jason looked more dismayed than angry at that thought. Ripping people off wasn't in his worldview. There was a surprising innocence to her brother, no matter what some people thought of him.

Ari took pity on him. 'Surely he can't just take back the funding you already have...'

He waved her comment away. With a pang of worry, she wondered how much money Jason had already spent here. And how much more he had asked the old lady for. Or maybe he hadn't even asked yet, but something had spooked the family enough that Rafael had come haring down here like the knight in shining armour. 'We need something more concrete. Even once the data on the coin confirms the period... no, that's going to take too long. How do you feel about diving tomorrow morning? I'm sure there's more down there. More coins. Or something better. I saw stuff down there, Ari.' His face took on a wistful look. 'There was something in among the rocks, the type of stuff you'd recognise. If we can tie it directly to the legend of Ys...' Ari glared at him and he gave her the helpless grin of the desperately hopeful. 'The tides are right and everything's set up. Just say the word. We might even have something to show them at this dinner.'

Jason's world, she thought ruefully. Dive for treasure in the morning, dine with royalty that night.

He looked so eager, she didn't have the heart to turn him down. She was here for a few more days. She might as well.

Even if the thought of the water here sent chills through her.

'OK,' she relented. 'You can show me the site. Not promising anything, Jason. But I'll take a look.'

The little harbour nestled into the turn of the bay, the oldest of the many ports of Douarnenez, the Vieux Port du Rosmeur. The green, tree-lined mound of Les Plomarc'h rose above it and the sea was a tropical blue in contrast. All along the Quai du Petit Port, the cafés and bars were still closed but the port itself buzzed with life. Standing so close to the modern Port de Pêche, Rosmeur felt like stepping back into an earlier age.

The dive boat doubled as a fishing boat the rest of the time, but it was big enough to be comfortable for several hours and looked to be well kept. The name had been painted on the wine-red hull in white, *Le Roi Gradlon*.

'Bit on the nose, isn't it?' Ari asked. She was pretty sure her brother had picked it on purpose.

'That our base ship is named for the last king of Ys?' Jason grinned. 'I rather thought it was a good sign.'

Of course he did. That was his sense of humour.

She followed him down the narrow pier. The tide was high. They had driven to Douarnenez earlier this morning than she would have liked and it had not left her in a good mood. The *Gradlon* was tied up waiting for them.

'Great,' she muttered. 'Signs and portents.'

'You love it and you know it. It's what you're all about, sister of mine.' Jason swung himself on board. 'Shut up and say hello to Yana.'

'Yana Kerdaniel, and that's Skipper to you, Jason, *mon cher*,' a slim-hipped woman with dark skin and luxurious black curls called from the helm. She wore a red scarf around her head, which almost made her look like a pirate and she clearly revelled in the aesthetic. 'You must be *la professeure*.'

Ari climbed aboard, ignoring Jason's offered hand. 'Call me Ari,' she replied. 'Everyone does.'

'Welcome aboard. A professional is always welcome.' She cast an arch look at Jason and Ari smiled, liking her already.

'I'm hurt,' he pouted. Still Jason, still flirting. It never ended.

Yana laughed at him. 'I'm sure you'll live. Where is my cousin?'

'He's on the way. With the others. There.' Jason pointed back towards the quay, where Nico and the team were unloading the van.

Her cousin. Ari wondered which one that was.

Several things clicked into place. Jason may have had some money for this, but clearly not enough. Perhaps Nico was right and that was why Rafael had turned up at the house. To stop his

great-aunt handing over more money to her brother. That was a
concern she could understand.

'They're late.'

'No, we're insanely early.' Ari had never been a morning
person. 'I need coffee.'

'The galley's down below,' Yana told her. 'Help yourself.
There's a pot on the stove.'

'You're a lifesaver,' Jason said. 'Really. I think my sister is
ready to kill me. I'd forgotten what you were like, Ari. Go on.
Make yourself human. I'll help load up. Once we've checked
our gear, we're ready to go when you are, Skipper.'

They anchored in the bay off the coast of Sainte Sirène, the
imposing Pointe de Castelmeur sheltering them. Ari sat back in
the staging area, watching them work. Nico didn't mess around,
his orders crisp and clear, his team well drilled.

She'd changed into a wetsuit and waited for him to call her
over. There were four of them going down. Nico and herself,
and Thierry and Madalen, both of them experienced divers.
More so than her really. She knew she was out of practice, but
paired with Nico she'd be OK. Jason would take lead from the
surface and Thierry would operate a camera, letting him see
what they were seeing. The mask and fins felt like second
nature, as soon as she put them on.

When Nico beckoned, she slipped into the buoyancy
control device and clipped it around her waist. It was almost
like a gilet, but would help with descent and ascent, controlled
by the air inflating and deflating it. There was a small knife, a
light and a compass already attached to it. Nico was always
prepared.

The air tank felt heavy on her back. It really had been a
while. And the difference between the Med and the choppy
waters of the Mer d'Iroise felt suddenly stark to her. She fitted

the regulator in place in her mouth and checked the auxiliary line, the octo, the extra air supply needed in case something failed in her equipment, or someone else's.

'Remember to breathe, Ari,' Nico said with a smile as he went over the equipment and then turned so she could check his as well.

The sea welcomed her. It was warmer than she expected and the gently rocking waves cradled her. The buoyancy control device kept them all floating until Nico gave the OK signal to the dive boat and Ari pressed the control on the vest.

Water closed over her, sound fell away and everything became as still as a dream. She wiggled her jaw as they descended, equalising the pressure in her ears, an old trick she'd learned that made it much easier for her. And yes, she had to remember to breathe because, although she knew what she was doing, that was always her first instinct on going underwater, to hold her breath. Nico knew it, joked about it, but still she couldn't shake it.

Peace washed through her. A peace like she never found anywhere else, except with Simon, lying in his arms after making love, or long Sundays lounging around doing nothing. It was as profound as that.

Visibility was surprisingly good. The water here, straight off the Atlantic, had the quality of bottle-glass, bluey-green and crystal clear. Their first safety stop sent a silvery shoal of fish flying around them, too fast for her to identify. They weren't going deep, Jason had promised her. Twenty to twenty-five metres, depending on conditions, to the site where he had found the coin.

And Ari had a clear objective.

Her area of expertise was looking beyond the obvious, finding patterns, whether that was in books, stories or here, on location. Or had been, once upon a time. Jason looked for the shiny things and always had done: the treasures, the high-value items that would make his investors happy. That was what he wanted to find here today – another coin, a treasure trove, something even better. But she looked at the bigger picture, at the wider landscape. She joined the dots together.

From the vantage point of their next safety stop, she surveyed the seabed below. Rocks like ancient monoliths reached up towards her. Others spilled out across the sand, alive with jewel-like anemones and brightly coloured seaweed.

She caught Nico's attention and signed quickly. '*Where?*'

Where had Jason found the coin? She knew the general idea, but Nico knew the specifics. Simon had highlighted these general coordinates, Jason had explained, and a few other locations in the area. What little they had been able to garner from his notes indicated he expected something to be found here and Jason was convinced the coin was just the first treasure they'd find. For her brother, this was a quest, a trail to be followed which he believed would lead to a lost city. Ever the optimist, Jason.

Nico just gestured down and she narrowed her eyes behind the mask. It was hard to be more specific than that underwater though. She followed him as he led them lower and Thierry began to record. There were rocks spread all over this area, buried in soft sand. They looked like they'd come down off the cliffs which rose above them. Pieces of Castelmeur itself.

Gesturing to the sandy bed between two large outcrops, Nico swam down and began fanning his hand at the sand in a small crevice where two of the rocks met. A modest plume of sand and other debris rose from the gap.

Ari swam to join him, examining where he was pointing. It was a dark hole, narrower than she would have liked. Towards the shore, she could see where the seabed rose to join the cliffs. They weren't that far from land. Around them, in a wide fan, she noted the scattering of rocks and stones. It could be debris, she thought. At the very least, there were signs of recent rockfall from the cliffs, which was to be expected, but there was something else here, she was sure of it. She didn't know why.

The stone was heavily encrusted, but if you squinted, it almost looked smooth at the edges, especially when you examined the gap. It could have been worked stone rather than natural. Maybe. It would be impossible to tell without raising it and they didn't have the facilities to do that.

Beckoning Thierry over, she indicated that he should film the area from all angles, and to focus on the stone's edges. Then she swam up a little to get a better look.

Scatter effect. Could be natural. Could be... something else. She glanced up at the cliffs again. The sea surged against them, twisting and rolling high overhead. To her left, there was a small islet rising from the seabed, and she could make out the entrance to caves dotted along the coast.

There was no real evidence here. Not really. Perhaps with sonar, if they had the money for that, or lifting a piece of it, or—

A shiver seemed to pass through the water, all around her, like a boom of thunder far away. Like rock falling or...

She steadied herself and turned towards the cliffs. Above her, the waves were hitting them with renewed force. She could see the surface churning and boiling, the sea pounding against the cliff face and into the caves. A premonition shook its way through her, and in her mind's eye she could see it happening: rocks falling, the cliff sliding away, stones raining down on them. This dive site wasn't as safe as it appeared.

Ari jerked her attention back to the dive, and looked for the others, signalling to Nico for his attention. As he swam towards her and she tried to figure out what gestures would convey the problem, something made her glance towards the others.

Below her, Thierry reeled back from the boulders, almost dropping the camera. Madalen pulled him clear and a dark cloud puffed up in the water from his arm. Blood. Ari darted back towards them, aware that Nico was signalling an alarm.

She caught sight of something sleek and shining, shooting between the rocks and back into the darkness: a conger eel, several feet in length. They must have disturbed it poking around.

She swore to herself and pulled out her torch, shining it into the gap in the hope it would drive the vicious thing off. Something glinted in the darkness. White. Bright and smooth. Not natural. Definitely not natural.

Nico caught her shoulder, jerking his thumb back up, where Madalen and Thierry were already two dark shapes heading laboriously to the surface. He had one hand clamped over his arm and Madalen, now holding the camera as well, was leading him.

Before she knew what she was doing, Ari did the unimaginable. It was pure instinct, an act of desperation. She thrust her hand into the gap and felt it close on something. Not a coin. Too big. Not metal either. It felt smooth to the touch and cool... but not actually cold.

Nico flipped around in front of her, and she couldn't miss his concern. He pointed down and signalled alarm.

The eel was right underneath them, coiling around the rock, coming back.

Fuck. They were vicious bastards and that one looked huge. It had already attacked Thierry. It wouldn't hesitate again.

Archaeological best practice deserted her and she jerked back, her fingers locked around the object in panic. She returned Nico's thumbs up signal to ascend with an OK and kicked off, rising quickly and smoothly away from the seabed, the eel left behind.

She glanced down to see a smooth white thing in her hand, like porcelain. For a horrible moment, she thought it was a bone, part of a skull. But it wasn't. Not quite. This had been worked, carved. Could it be ivory?

No, it was too cold, too smooth. More like a fine ceramic...

Breathe, she told herself again. Breathe.

How had Jason missed this? And what was it even doing there?

She shouldn't have wrenched it out, but she could not have made herself leave it there. Not for anything. It was almost like the eel had been guarding it. A stupid idea. But still, she couldn't shake it.

By the time Ari broke surface a few yards from the boat, the other two divers were already on board and Yana was bending over Thierry while Jason quizzed Madalen.

Nico spat out his regulator, heedless of the sea water. '*Mon dieu*, Ari, you're as bad as *he* is. Get back on the boat.'

'I couldn't leave it there. We need to secure it right away. The site wasn't stable. And besides, that thing could have—'

'It could have taken your hand off. Or worse. Hit an artery. Drowned you. I've seen them take half of a man's face off. Come on. *Now*. No arguing.'

She'd never seen him so annoyed. 'I'm... I'm sorry. I just...'

'You're just...' he muttered as he pulled himself onto the dive platform at the stern and then helped her out of the water. 'Just like your brother. I thought you were better than that. He can't dive, you know that? That's why he wasn't down there with us. He's not allowed to.'

'He what?' Jason had said nothing about that. He'd just said he needed her.

'He messed up his ears, didn't equalise properly. When he found that bloody coin, he came shooting up and got the bends. It could have been so much worse. He was lucky and he knows it. He's off for weeks until the doctor says he's clear. He panicked. Said he saw something down there.'

'Saw something? What kind of something?'

'I don't bloody know. A face. A skull. Something that wasn't there.'

Ari felt the blood draining out of her body, the chill of the

Atlantic rushing in to replace it. Her hand clamped reflexively on her find.

But Nico wasn't finished. 'I told him, I won't dive with him again until he sorts himself out. And I won't take you down either if you're going to do the same stupid things.' He paused, struggling with his irritation, calming his breath, and finally he looked at her again. 'What is it? What did you find? Here.'

He pulled over a low plastic tub and filled it with sea water. Dutifully, she put the thing she'd pulled from the rocks into it as gently as she could. Keeping it in the water would preserve it until they knew what they were dealing with and decided what they had to do next.

Nico grabbed the tub and shoved it up onto the deck. The urge to tell him to be careful died in her throat. He was really annoyed with her, she knew that. But she was pretty sure it was more about his frustrations with Jason rather than her. What had her brother done on his last dive? What had he seen? If it had been hypoxia, he could have hallucinated anything and that was beyond dangerous underwater.

Or had he seen the same thing as her? Seen it and panicked instead of grabbing it.

Meekly, Ari followed Nico, stripping off her equipment as Jason joined them to help.

'Thierry's OK. It tried to bite him, but it's just a graze really. Yana's treating it and— What's that? Did you find something? Ari?' His eyes shone in sudden triumph.

Nico snorted and swore to himself.

A face stared back at them from the shallow water, bone-white beneath dirt and barnacles. No, not a face. A mask.

CHAPTER SIX

Rafael knew it was a dream. It had to be. He knew it of old. All his life, he had dreamed this dream and it was always the same. He was walking along the clifftops at night and the waves crashed against the cliffs, throwing spray so high into the air it was like looking at white towers reaching to the moon. The wind pulled at his hair, plastered it over his face, and when he pushed it back, a man stood ahead of him, broad-shouldered, staring out to sea, unaffected by the storm. A man very much like him, but not him. Not quite.

As Rafael approached him, the man turned and lifted a finger to his lips. His eyes were empty, hollow pools of darkness, and a cloak of storm clouds seemed to wrap itself around him. It wasn't a man, more like the shape of one, a shadow. As Rafael watched, the skin seemed to fade until only a skeleton remained, still holding a single finger bone up in front of his grinning mouth.

Ankou, the Servant of Death, stood before him, bidding him to watch and be silent, the first of the dead, by drowning, murder or suicide, the herald of the lost souls, who shepherded them to safety. When Ankou commanded, no one could disobey. He came for all in the end.

A bell rang out across the water. A lone bell tolling an alarm. It echoed through the air, shivered over his skin and left him chilled to the core. He knew the sound like he knew his own heartbeat. He had heard it all his life.

Bells ringing. Danger coming.

Even as he watched, the figure of Ankou dissolved into shadows on the wind and dissipated, leaving him alone on the headland.

Without meaning to, Rafael walked towards the cliff edge, stood there, right on the precipice while the sea drove against the cliffs and the rocks below it. White foam filled the air and the black sea roared like a monster, a gaping mouth salivating to devour him.

A huge rocky islet jutted from the water at the foot of the point, cleft almost in two by the sea. It looked like two giant boulders, one balanced precariously on the other. Îlot d'Or, the locals of Sainte Sirène called it, the little island of gold. It wasn't even grand enough to warrant a name on a map. In the gaping hole between the two halves, the waves surged forth, flung up into the air like white foam, booming against the inside of the caves riddling the point beneath him.

It was the sound of the gates of Ys. That was what the old people said. The distant echo across time of those doomed gates crashing open as the sea engulfed the city.

A woman stood on the rocky island beneath him, her long hair billowing around her as if she was deep beneath the sea instead of standing on bare rock in the midst of the storm. It was white-blonde, her hair, almost silver, the colour of the sea foam which whipped up around her in a frenzy. She reached out a hand, slim and elegant, beckoning him.

He always obeyed, whatever she asked of him. When she

called him, he couldn't say no. She commanded him, and he was her slave. He always had been. She was waiting for him.

Rafael took a halting step forward, but someone caught his hand from behind him, the touch warm and strong. Holding him back.

He turned, startled, to see her face, her mouth open as if she was saying a name. His name. As if she was calling him back. Her grip tightened on his hand, holding on to him for dear life. His life.

He woke in a tangle of white sheets with her name on his lips.

Ari Walker.

Rafael closed the laptop and swore softly to himself. He'd been awake for hours through the night and had ended up working on the financial records, trying to untie the knot that had been bothering him for months now. Something wasn't right and he couldn't get to the bottom of it. He paced the room, went down and raided the kitchen, and even tried working in the study instead. At least with a house of this size, he could be sure he wouldn't disturb his great-aunt's sleep. Mémé's room was on the other side of the building, a whole wing to herself. It was too big a home for her. He knew that logically. But it would break her heart to leave it.

He'd taken a light breakfast alone and tried to focus on his work. He shouldn't even be here. He should be back in Paris at his desk. There were meetings he needed to attend, and he wanted to talk to the accountants about that strange thing he'd seen in the financial records. He needed to talk to Elena about Georges as well, to touch base with her and make sure everything was OK. He had flights booked to New York for a gala in a week. He would have to cancel that. He didn't want to go anyway. It would have been more Jacqueline's thing, and they weren't going anywhere together now. Besides, he didn't like leaving Laure in charge of the office. His sister wasn't ready, and his mother had too great a hold on the board already. Laure would always cave to Maman's demands. Anything could happen. Meanwhile, his mother was already pushing for the Root Aviation takeover and they'd have to pull reserves from any number of accounts to do it. He'd been unequivocal in the email. He just hoped it was enough. He didn't want to confront his mother. Not yet. It wasn't time.

It had been hard enough to insist that he be the one to take care of this issue with Mémé and her money. Maman had agreed all too willingly, which suggested she wanted him out of the way for some reason. He didn't like it.

'Rafi?' His great-aunt called from the hall outside. 'Rafi? Something's wrong. Can't you hear it?'

She was the only one who still called him that. His father had called him Ael, his Breton name, but after he died, his mother had put a stop to that. He couldn't bear to hear it anyway. Mémé calling him Rafi had been one of his few comforts in that dark time.

'Hear what, Mémé?

Hushed voices came from the other side of the door, someone trying to calm her down.

Rafael got to his feet. He felt weary, worn out to his core. It was this place. No wonder his mother never wanted to come back. If he could have persuaded Mémé to move to Paris, or anywhere else, he would have. The rest of the family had tried, time and again, but she wouldn't budge.

The Manoir had been in the family for generations. And it was beautiful, he knew that, and despite the other members of his clan making plans for it – a hotel, a luxury retreat, even a campsite – he knew he would never be able to give it up. He loved it as much as he loved his great-aunt, as much as she loved it. He might not want to be back here, but that didn't mean he could let it go either.

No more than he could force Mémé to let it go. Even if that had been possible, he didn't have it in him. He didn't want to take that decision out of her hands, but the more he saw, the more he feared he was not going to have a choice. Eventually.

He just hadn't expected it to be so soon, or to be this bad. He had not wanted his mother to be right. But Mémé was not herself.

Opening the door, he saw the housekeeper talking softly to his great-aunt. Nolvene Cariou had worked there for as long as he could remember. She was a friendly and familiar face. She was the one who had phoned him to warn him of the changes in his great-aunt.

Him, he noted. Not his mother. Just as well really.

But then Yvette du Lac was not Mémé's blood, as the old woman was so fond of pointing out. Laure would laugh about it and insist that they were all family, but she always took their mother's side in the end. She was more like their mother than he was. Always had been.

His father had been smitten with Yvette from the moment he saw her, that was what everyone said. Until, some time after Laure's birth, he came back here. There was some kind of affair, Rafael thought, although no one would admit anything. Rumours and hints, innuendo. He didn't know who it was with or what had happened. He didn't even know how his mother had found out, although in Sainte Sirène there were very few secrets.

But Théo du Lac had died before she could confront him. Another thing for which she could never forgive him.

Rafael knew his mother was vain, and shallow, spoilt, and sometimes very cruel. He liked to think it was losing her husband so young that had made her that way, but he wasn't sure. She had inherited a financial empire, but she had always been rich, and expected everything to be laid at her feet.

Perhaps Mémé had realised that from the start and clearly nothing would have been good enough for her Théo. Yvette had never liked Mémé and the feeling had been mutual.

If he left it to her, his mother would see to it that his great-aunt was shut away in a nursing home far from here, far from anywhere, where she couldn't embarrass the du Lac foundation. It would be luxurious, exclusive, beautiful, but it would be as good as a prison to Mémé. And it would be far from her friends, far from her beloved Sainte Sirène.

'What's happened? Nolvene?'

Nolvene was not only Mémé's housekeeper, but also her companion, a middle-aged woman who could always be depended on. But the look she gave him right now was frankly rattled.

'Nothing, Monsieur Rafi. Nothing, she just needs a rest. That's all. Come along, *madame*. Come and have a lie-down.'

Mémé was having none of it. 'I heard it. I know I did. And you did too, Nolvene. Don't lie to him. It does no one any favours. *An neudenn eeun eo ar gwellañ.*'

It was always a bad sign when she was quoting old proverbs in Breton.

He frowned, trying to remember. Once, he knew all her sayings by heart. 'A straight thread?' He looked to Nolvene for help.

'A straight thread is best,' she confirmed.

Don't lie. Be straight with him. Mémé was reverting more and more to Breton, he thought, or at least it appeared that way. Her first language, the one her grandmother taught her. The language of the du Lacs, she would say.

Rafael nodded slowly. 'Well then?'

He waited and Nolvene frowned.

'She heard a sound. Just a sound carrying over the water. Waves in the sea caves or a rock fall on the cliffs. Or something coming over the bay. We hear it all the time. It's just an old story made up to explain it.'

But Mémé was not to be quietened or ignored. 'You know what it is. The gates of Ys are open. My mother heard them when my father died. I heard them when my uncle Fabien died and I was only a child then. A child. And when poor Théo died, even though we thought it was over...'

All the men of his family. His great-grandfather, his father, even Mémé's legendary uncle who'd been executed in the cove by the Germans.

Of course Rafael knew what she meant. That noise haunted him. He'd heard it in his dreams last night.

He shook the thought aside, annoyed with himself. 'Mémé, this is just tall tales and nonsense. These treasure hunters have stirred up your imagination. It's not real. There was no Ys and even if there was, it is long gone. You always said Fabien broke the curse somehow.'

That was a mistake. It tipped her over the top and suddenly she was furious.

'Simon Poullain knew. He believed it. His family knew. They have their stories too. It was his ancestor, Tristan Poullain, who stood by Fabien's side when the Nazis cut them down. They defended the secrets of Ys with their lives and that should have fixed everything. But the curse took Simon as well, that poor boy. With all his future and that beautiful girl waiting for him. We thought the curse was gone until your father died. But I will find a way to stop it. To stop *her*. She will not have you as well. The Walkers will find Ys for me and we will protect it, save it from oblivion. Here, take this. Take it and it will protect you.' She shoved a small linen bag into his hands. Another one. Rafael's heart sank. 'There's a *sou* in there, an old one, so it's good. Not this modern money. And nine stems of nine plants. And nine grains of *fleur du sel*. Keep it with you, Rafi, and it will protect you.'

He wanted to argue, wanted to tell her that this was nonsense, superstition. But he couldn't bring himself to do that. Not now. He tucked the pouch away in his pocket.

'We can't keep doing this, Mémé. You can't keep throwing money at a legend. There's nothing to find, nothing to protect. If it ever existed, Ys was destroyed long ago.'

She stamped her foot at him and turned away. 'It's my family, and my money. I'm not asking for anything from you. I am a du Lac, Rafael. It is my right. It is my duty. I will protect you from her.'

'Who's *her*?' he asked when she quietened. He said it patiently, carefully.

But she shook her head, her lips pursed. She glared at him, but she wouldn't answer, recalcitrant as a child having a temper tantrum.

He knew who and what she was referring to. And he didn't like it.

Mémé thought by finding Ys, proving it was real, she would somehow break a curse on their family that couldn't possibly exist. But she would not be convinced otherwise.

'Come,' said Nolvene at last. 'Let me get you a drink, Séraphine, and settle you down. We're expecting visitors, are we not? You don't want to tire yourself out too early. I'll talk to Monsieur Rafael. You're overwrought, *madame*. Come now.'

Her voice was like a balm and he could see the effect on his great-aunt immediately. Familiarity helped, of course, and the gentleness that seemed to permeate every part of Nolvene's being.

'Very well,' Mémé said, with as much dignity as she could muster. 'We should discuss dinner this evening, prepare a menu. Did I tell you my archaeological team are coming?'

'You did. Of course you did, and we will have a wonderful meal, I promise you. But you should rest so you are at your best for your guests this evening, yes?'

While Nolvene managed to persuade her to her room, Rafael tried to follow and help; he was quickly shooed away. He waited in the hallway like a child, outside her door, feeling powerless. Lost.

It was worse than he had thought. He knew that now.

When Nolvene came out, her face wore a grave expression. 'She'll rest for a while now. She's tired and overwrought, that's all. She must have been dreaming. She wakes in the night often, dreams of danger. Dr Marais has prescribed sleeping pills, but she refuses them. I can ask him to come up and see her again, and to talk to you, Monsieur Rafael.'

He smiled. 'Just Rafael, please, Nolvene. You've known me all my life. I think it's a bit late for formalities.'

'If you say so,' she replied, clearly not convinced. But Nolvene had always relied on tradition and formalities. They were as much part of her as her blood. 'Come and talk to me. You should hear this from me before someone else tries to twist the truth. We look after her here. We always have.'

She strode off towards the stairs and Rafael had no choice but to follow. 'I know you do. But, Nolvene, if she needs more specialist care—'

'That's your mother talking. She would sell this house and cut all ties with Sainte Sirène. That was always her greatest desire. But it cannot be. You belong here. All your line do. And your great-aunt is determined to save you.'

To save him. From a mythical curse. From dreams and nightmares.

'I don't believe in stories. Especially not those stories.'

'Ah, but they believe in you. And that's the problem. I told Séraphine you would not want to believe. I know that. You've been the same since you were a boy. Grounded in the mundane. But now your time approaches. You sense it. And that's why you're back here.'

He had never heard Nolvene talk like this. 'I'm back here for Mémé. Because—'

Nolvene flapped her hands at him. She bustled into the kitchen, Rafael still following helplessly behind her.

'This is not helping her.'

'But she still knows her mind. Your mother would lock her away, you know that. But that will not help either. Quite the opposite.'

He pulled out the linen pouch and turned it over in his hands. 'Who is she trying to protect me from? And why does she think the Walkers, of all people, can help?'

Nolvene set a coffee down in front of him. It was rich and black. She warmed milk in a little metal jug and handed him sugar in an ancient silver caddy, ignoring his questions. Always perfect, Nolvene's coffee. There was not a barista in the world who could rival her. He knew. He'd tried to find them. And failed.

She settled herself down in the seat opposite him. The look she gave him branded him a fool. 'You know full well what she's trying to protect you from, and don't try to pretend differently. Call it what you will, the *groac'h*, the *mari-morgen*, the water witch... If you cannot believe her, at least humour her. She has the sight, and the knowing, your great-aunt. The Walkers can help because they're touched by loss as well. The same kind of loss as your family are, as she is. Simon Poullain, remember him? Gérard Poullain's son.'

'He drowned in a diving accident a few years ago.' Rafael remembered the news stories at the time. Precious little happened in Sainte Sirène, so when something did, he noticed. Besides, he'd been at school with Simon. The same school in Beuzec. They'd been friends once, as children.

'Simon Poullain was the last of the Poullain family. Gérard died in 2001. Eléanor in 2006. It's not often a family so vital to the commune ends. His great-great-uncle was Tristan Poullain, who died alongside Fabien du Lac in the war.'

Mémé's uncle, whose name was on the memorial at the cove, along with Poullain and others.

'Simon was their friend, the Walkers. More than a friend. It ties them to us, to this place, whether they like it or not. Jason Walker buried him, scattering his ashes in the bay as he requested. Imagine, a man so young already having his funeral arrangements laid out.' Nolvene sighed and stared out of the window. 'He was a good boy. They all were, the Poullains. A good family, loyal and true Sirènois. He was determined to find Ys, Rafael. I think he found something, something important and your great-aunt believes... and I believe, he woke something up.'

Woke something up. The words haunted Rafael all day. Even as he tried to work, he couldn't stop thinking about Ari Walker and Simon. And whatever he had found.

Simon Poullain. He should have known. When it came to Ys, and the curse, there was always a Poullain involved, just like Nolvene had said. Not that he could say he knew Simon that well. Only in the same way anyone in a small place knew each other, part of your life, part of your world, when your world extended from school to home to seashore. Rafael had left the school when he was eleven, shipped off to a prestigious boarding school instead. He made new friends. More suitable friends, his mother had said. He couldn't even remember half their names now.

He wanted to go over there and question the Walkers about Simon, about their search, about everything they knew about Ys, but he couldn't. What could he say? Mémé's superstitions were bad enough. Dreams and visions didn't help matters and who would believe him? He'd make a fool of himself and he couldn't have that.

Instead, he googled Simon Poullain and read through the various sparse news reports of his death. It had been his expedition, for want of a better word, his project, and Jason Walker had joined him here in Brittany.

But there was no mention of whatever had been found, if indeed Poullain had found anything at all. Simon was following old stories, stories his grandparents had told him.

Rafael sat back, pondering the stories his own family had told – 1943, for example, during the occupation, when Tristan Poullain died alongside Fabien du Lac, the pair of them fighting in the resistance, helping the Allies land spies in the secret coves and inlets on the north coast, smuggling goods and information, sabotage... Executed on a cold winter's dawn by the edge of the sea with a half-dozen friends and comrades.

One photograph on the screen caught his eye, halfway down the *Ouest-France* article. A group of people standing on a quay, in a pool of sunlight, laughing. Ariadne Walker was there. She stood by Simon Poullain, leaning against him, her head thrown back in a laugh.

Rafael enlarged the photo, intrigued by the expression on her face. Such joy. Her copper hair was longer, ruffled by the breeze. Her blue eyes shone. Simon had one arm around her waist, pulling her closer to him, caught in a moment of intimacy, even with their friends there. It could have been just the two of them. Around his neck, he wore a leather thong with a small carved bone disc on it. It was the one she now wore around her neck. Reaching out, Rafael touched the image of her face, not really sure what he was feeling, not sure why he was so drawn to her. She had lost so much. His heart ached for her.

They'd been lovers, Ari and Simon. She had lost him. 'That beautiful girl,' Mémé had said.

Celebrated local diver drowns in bay, the headline read.

Suddenly Rafael realised why Ari had reacted as she did when she saw him in the water yesterday. If she thought he was drowning, if she thought she was seeing a body where her partner had drowned... Afterwards, she had been so shaken.

Before the walls came up, before the sharp defences came into play.

He felt like such a fool. He'd been so unsympathetic, annoyed with the situation in which he'd found himself. He hadn't thought about her emotions at all. He should have seen, and now he felt terrible. She had recovered her wits so quickly and so convincingly, he hadn't realised that she was genuinely upset. But looking back now, he could see it. Her hands trembling, holding the necklace that had once been Simon's, the way she seemed to find it so hard to draw a proper breath.

Was that why he felt so transfixed by her? It didn't make sense. But he did. She had even appeared in his dream and that was new. Brand new.

In the past, that dream had always ended with him leaping towards the white-haired woman in the sea, with the waves drinking him down, into darkness, pain and death.

Why had she made this one different?

He had to find out more. He needed to know what the Walkers had thought they would find, sure. But, more than that, he needed to find out about Ariadne Walker herself.

Rafael got another two hours of work done before the sound of a car roaring up the gravel drive disturbed him. He frowned, not expecting anyone. But the little Mercedes convertible was instantly recognisable, as was the woman in the driver's seat. Laure.

What was his sister doing here?

He opened the door to her, but she wasn't alone.

A willowy blonde, hair so pale it was almost white in the

sunlight, had joined his sister. She smiled as she saw him, her grey eyes sparkling. She was slender and elegant, a heart-shaped face and a long pale neck. She was as beautiful as she had always been.

Laure spoke first.

'There you are, excellent. I've come for the weekend. You remember Gwen, don't you? I found her in the village. Where's Mémé?'

CHAPTER SEVEN

The last thing Ari wanted to do was go to dinner with Jason and Nico at the Manoir of Sainte Sirène. She wanted to examine the mask, call the university and talk to the experts. But once they had taken photographs and sent them in, and then phoned their contact in Brest to confirm they had received everything, they had little else to do besides look at it. They couldn't clean it. That would need to be the work of a professional conservator.

Oh, but she wanted to look at it. A fine white mask with swirls carved into the cheeks and forehead, traces of some kind of glittering glaze still clinging to it beneath the dirt. Discoloured and worn at the edges, slightly chipped. The whole lower half from the nose down was missing, if it had originally been there at all, but still... it was incredible. She wanted to examine every millimetre of it. She could see colours beneath the patina of ages. It had been painted once, perhaps decorated with gold. She could make out swirls of a turquoise-like colour on the edges as well. A deeper blue than turquoise, she realised. Lapis lazuli? The stone could be ground into powder and used to create the pigment ultramarine. It had been treasured by the Mesopotamians, the Egyptians, and the Mycenaeans. During the Middle Ages, it was more expensive than gold.

So what was she seeing here? A fine porcelain-like ceramic decorated with priceless minerals, wealth from all over the world.

A treasure. An impossible treasure.

And yet, there it was, still in its bath of sea water, and she couldn't take her eyes off it. It was a wonder, but there was something else as well. It sent a chill through her blood. She had a dreadful feeling it was watching her, studying her the way she studied it.

'We're going in half an hour,' said Jason. 'You should at least put on a dress or something.'

She was still in shorts and a T-shirt. She was comfortable like that. She twisted her fingers through the thong at her neck, and then rubbed the pad of her thumb against the horse pendant.

She'd never expected to wear it herself. She still didn't know why Simon sent it back to her. It wasn't until after he died that she felt compelled to put it on. Because it was all she had left then.

'I'm just trying to work out what it is.'

'We will. But not right now. We need to go, Ari. Finding this is the perfect time to press them. It proves we're on the right track. We need to keep the funding. Madame du Lac is generous, but the rest of her family... We need to convince Rafael to support us. Please.'

He held out his hand and, when she reluctantly hooked her fingers with his, he pulled her to her feet.

'I'm not sure what you think I can do.'

'Yeah... I saw the way he was looking at you. Put on a little black number and some heels.'

'Jason!'

'What? It's not like I'm offering you up for a herd of cows or something.'

She glared at him, knowing her brother too well. 'I'm not so bloody sure.'

He looked her up and down and then grinned. His most wicked, teasing grin. 'You're probably worth five. Max.'

He ran before she could punch him, laughing all the way.

The only dress Ari had packed was black and she wished it wasn't, just to spite her brother. But it was easy to pack, appropriate to most situations and relatively wrinkle-free. Good for an emergency. By the time she was ready, Jason and Nico were already standing by the front door. Thierry was back, with a heavily bandaged arm and a ton of pain medication. Madalen and another girl Ari hadn't met before called Lina – a slender blonde with a huge smile – had offered to look after him and he didn't seem to be complaining too much.

Other members of Jason's little tribe wandered in and out, making food, sharing beers and wine, settling in for the night.

'He's meant to be getting some rest and he probably shouldn't drink with the...' Jason's voice tailed off as she appeared down the stairs. Slowly he whistled. 'OK, I said dress up, but I didn't mean give his great-aunt a heart attack.'

'Oh be quiet, Jase,' Nico murmured softly. He took Ari's hand and kissed it elegantly. 'You look beautiful, Ari. He is such a tease.'

They had made an effort too. Best shirts and that sort of thing. It was like seeing Jason in a three-piece suit, even though it was just cotton and chinos. Nico was breathtaking all in black, but then he always was a stunning man. His outfit almost looked as if he had dressed to complement her.

But Ari knew in her heart of hearts that Nico hadn't dressed up for her. She knew she was not his type. And his type, lounging there against the wall like he had nowhere else to be, was entirely oblivious.

'Why don't you just tell him?' she had asked him once.

'And destroy what we do have?' Nico had laughed bitterly. 'I don't think I'm that brave. Let it lie, Ari. It's better this way.'

She still didn't think he was right. But she'd promised and tried to forget it, tried to ignore the glances he cast at her idiot brother and the pain in his eyes every single time Jason flirted with someone else.

And Jason flirted all the time. It was what he did.

The Manoir was one of those beautiful Breton houses which could have been little more than a hundred years old but may equally have been over a thousand. Ari knew she'd find out if she poked around in the right places. Grey stone walls, dark slate roofs, turrets and stone carved in intricate styles, it wasn't large enough to be called a chateau, but there was no doubting the impression the du Lacs of long ago wished to make with it. The building was a stamp on the land. There was something of a fairy tale about it.

Yellow roses sprawled up the wall, hanging over the French doors leading out to the gardens. They were surprisingly formal, beautifully cared for and the setting sun lit them in spectacular fashion. Silver birch trees lined the driveway, their shadows striping the gravel. It was another world from the gîte, or the dismal flat at home Ari was used to.

Rafael himself answered the door, which hadn't expected. She would have thought he had staff for that. For everything. Before she could even say hello, her brother launched into a description of what they'd found, sweeping his hoped-for paymaster into a grand hallway with wood panels and endless portraits. She watched them, wondering if Rafael was listening as intently as he appeared to be, when she saw him glance surreptitiously at her. Their eyes met for a moment, but he looked away quickly. When Jason offered him his phone, he scrolled through the photos, studying them intently.

Jason stood there, attentively, like a puppy waiting for praise. He pointed at something and Rafael nodded before zooming in. A curious expression passed over his face, something cold and distraught. It vanished so quickly, she could have imagined it.

'So, you found something,' Madame du Lac called out from the doorway on the left. 'I knew you would. I told him so. Come into the drawing room. Sit with me. Have an aperitif. Dr Walker, I want to know everything.'

'Go,' Jason mouthed at her and Nico, but he didn't leave Rafael's side.

Just inside the door, Ari was intercepted by two other women and from the moment she entered the room, she felt judged. More than judged – taken apart and examined. She froze, which gave Nico all the time he needed to slip away to Madame du Lac's side. She immediately began plying him with questions.

'Laure du Lac,' said the tall, dark-haired woman, beautiful and elegant, everything about her perfectly tailored. 'I'm Rafael's sister. This is Gwen Morvan, an old friend of the family.'

'Ari Walker,' Ari replied awkwardly, trying to ignore the sleek couture Laure wore and the fact her own dress came from a supermarket. At least Gwen was in something simple, a light summer dress topped with a neat jacket. Ari couldn't guess where she'd bought her clothes and hated herself a little bit for wondering.

'Harry?' Laure laughed as she mangled the name. 'Like Prince Harry, no?'

It was beyond awkward. Ari had long ago given up caring if

people made fun of her name, but all the same. Usually, it was Greek legends and minotaur jokes.

Her great-aunt broke off from her interrogation of Nico, with a note of warning in her voice. 'Ariadne, from the Greek. Dr Walker lectures in Oxford, Laure. We're lucky to have her here.'

Madame du Lac was just an old woman, and possibly a confused one at that. She'd have to explain that she wasn't connected with the university at all in a way that wasn't embarrassing and didn't make either of them look foolish. She was just a teacher now. Had left the academic world behind. Besides, she didn't want to give Laure the satisfaction.

'My PhD was in ethnography and archaeology. I'm just a teacher really. I'm only visiting. My brother's heading the dive team here.' A white lie, since he wasn't actually able to dive. It didn't matter, since Laure hardly acknowledged her but turned back to her great-aunt.

Gwen smiled a dazzling smile as she glanced towards the door. Ari had no idea who she was other than Laure du Lac's friend, but she had that easy comfort which spoke of long familiarity. 'Perhaps you haven't seen Dr Walker's brother yet, Laure. Mémé always had an eye for a good-looking man, didn't you, Mémé?' The teasing tone was gentle and the old lady shook her head and smiled with genuine affection and waved a dismissive hand at her. She was back talking to Nico. The kindness made Ari instantly soften her opinion towards Gwen at least.

Jason had just entered the room with Rafael, the two of them deep in discussion. And Laure's expression changed abruptly as she laid eyes on him.

Great, thought Ari. Just great. Just what she needed.

But then Rafael looked up, his dark eyes locking on to hers, and she knew she was in enough trouble of her own with a du Lac.

Gwen's hand on her arm was cold, startling her. 'You must

tell me about Oxford. I've never been. I believe it is a beautiful city.' Her voice sounded like music, rising and falling gently.

'It is. Do you live locally?'

'I grew up here, much like Laure and Rafael when they were children. Sainte Sirène calls us all back. I love our history, the stories. I look after the *petit musée* in the village, and by extension our heritage and cultural patrimony.'

'Gwen Morvan... it sounds more Welsh.'

'Well, we *are* all Celts, you know? The Bretons came here from Cornwall and Wales to escape the Saxons. But no, my name is as Breton as it can be. You are Irish and not Greek, after all, I believe?'

Ari laughed. 'Our father was just obsessed with Greek myths. Classics professor in Trinity College Dublin.'

'So you have followed in his footsteps. He must be proud.'

Not very far in his footsteps, as it turned out.

Her father, proud... hard to tell anymore. He thought she'd ruined her life, but he wouldn't say it out loud. And it was not a subject she wanted to get into here.

At that moment Jason beckoned her over and Ari made her apologies and escaped.

Rafael watched her approach, his dark eyes perplexed but interested. Whatever could Jason have said to him?

'I've been telling Rafael all about the mask,' Jason explained. 'He wants to hear it from you, Ari.'

'Who is paying for this quest?' asked Madame du Lac imperiously. 'Show me.'

Jason hurried over to her, phone in hand, eager to share, and Ari met Rafael's gaze.

'You look most beautiful,' he told her and the world seemed to tilt a bit off balance.

'I... um... thank you. So do... I mean... you look well.' God, she was babbling. But he did look well. More than well. Handsome. He wore a deep wine-coloured shirt and black trousers and the colours made his skin and eyes glow.

He shrugged, that most Gallic of gestures, as if to say 'This? This is nothing.'

It probably cost more than her monthly pay cheque. She may not be able to afford hand-tailored clothes, but she could still recognise them. He wore the outfit like he'd picked it up off the rack and never thought about it again.

'So, tell me about this find,' he said. 'This mask. It looks amazing.'

'A mask?' Laure exclaimed, moving in on Jason like a shark sensing blood. 'Oh, show me. Look, Gwen. There's a mask in the legend of Ys, Dahut's mask. Do you think this is it?'

Ari was sure Rafael winced. Like he had when Jason had first showed him the photos. He hid it pretty well, but not well enough. He didn't engage with his sister.

'We don't know it's a mask,' said Ari, letting her voice project just a little. Better to put a stop to any speculation as soon as possible. 'And it could be nothing. It has to be properly examined and dated, if that's even possible. We may never know the date.'

Jason glared at her and swallowed whatever his first instinct was to reply. Nico grinned instead, that knowing, teasing look he got when she didn't toe Jason's line.

'But carbon dating or something would work, wouldn't it?' Laure went on regardless.

God bless people with just a little knowledge.

'Not on ceramics. Carbon dating needs something organic. Perhaps rehydroxylation dating might work but...' They all looked at her blankly. 'It's a way to date kiln-fired clay. But given the immersion in water and... well, any number of variables...' She trailed off awkwardly. This wasn't what they wanted to hear. They wanted to hear that it came from Ys, that they had found the lost city. Even if they hadn't. They didn't want fact and science, just fairy tales.

'It's beautiful,' Madame du Lac whispered at last. She sounded overwhelmed and took a moment to compose herself. She reached out and took Nico's hand, squeezing it in her thin fingers. 'And you have it here? Did you bring it with you?'

'Oh no, *madame*,' Jason replied. 'It's secure back at the house. The university team from Brest will want to examine it as soon as possible. We'll take it to them tomorrow, I expect. I'm just waiting to hear back.'

'But the legend,' Gwen said softly, in tones of wonder. 'You *do* know the legend, of course? You've found Dahut's mask. Look at it.' She zoomed in on the screen again and her eyes shone with joy. 'It's magnificent.'

Ari could see what they were all thinking. There it was, straight out of the story Simon had told Ari so long ago, Dahut's magic mask which killed her would-be lovers if they didn't prove to be true. And then she was transformed, cursed to haunt the seas, killing wherever she could, reduced to a monster because of her monstrous female ambition. A thousand feminist interpretations sprang to mind at once.

Could there really be a connection between the mask and the legend? Ari wondered. No, it was a story, that was all. How often had she told Simon that?

Laure peered at it and wrinkled her nose. 'Under the barnacles maybe, and the dirt and the... Oh dear, what's that?' she said, and then gave a sharp laugh. 'It could be Dahut's mask though. If any of that was actually real. Look, Rafael.' She grabbed the phone and lurched at him, her smile widening gleefully. 'She knows you broke up with Jacqueline! She's back to get you after all!'

Rafael shied back, clearly unable to stop himself. The irritation on his face would have sent anyone else scrambling. Not his sister though. Families, thought Ari. They were always the same.

'Oh leave him alone, Laure,' said Gwen. She smiled at him affectionately and something in his face softened. 'He used to have nightmares as a child. Terrible dreams. Does she still tease you about that?'

Rafael rolled his eyes, sharing something in the manner of old friends that instantly made Ari feel like the worst kind of interloper. 'Like anyone could ever stop Laure,' he said and the moment of tension vanished. 'Dinner is ready. Why don't we go in? Mémé?'

'Nicolas,' she held out her arm imperiously, 'will you accompany me?'

Before Ari knew what was happening, Laure had seized Jason's arm and Gwen latched on to Rafael, so she was left to follow them into the next room feeling like some kind of *Downton Abbey* reject.

Jason looked so startled, it was rather funny. Nico was, meanwhile, charming Madame du Lac. Ari bit her lip to hide the smile of amusement, already aware that she was failing at that too.

And, of course, that was when Rafael looked back at her. His dark eyes had the air of something hunted in them and she thought about his riches, his apparent newly single status, his sister turning up with a very beautiful old friend as if by design and suddenly it wasn't quite so funny anymore.

Dinner was delicious, rich and satisfying, each course varied and balanced, and the wine flowed freely. Ari sat beside Rafael, but he was deep in conversation with Gwen, their French rapid and musical. All the same, Ari was curiously aware of his closeness, his cologne intriguing and something else, his underlying scent making her skin warm. Every so often, he glanced at her or asked her something and she felt a peculiar glow inside her.

She tried desperately to focus on other things. The dining room itself gleamed, every surface polished to a shine. Like the house itself, the furniture was ancient but wonderfully cared for. She was beginning to doubt there was anything here from the twenty-first century until Rafael's phone rang.

'Ignore it, Rafael,' Gwen murmured. 'You're entitled to an evening off.'

For a moment, Ari thought he would comply. But when he glanced at the screen, his expression hardened.

'Excuse me,' he said curtly, and left the table as he answered. He was gone for some time and the conversation flowed on. Laure flirted outrageously with Jason and Ari spoke softly to Nico and Madame du Lac, listening to her local stories and general gossip. Gwen made small talk with Ari, but she was clearly distracted, looking for Rafael to return.

That was beyond awkward too. Gwen was carrying a torch for him.

'Ah, the mask, that is incredible,' Madame du Lac sighed, bringing Ari back to the current subject. 'So beautiful. Such a find.'

Ari smiled at her enthusiasm but felt the need to tamp down the rising excitement. 'But we don't really know anything about it. It might not come to anything.'

'Should you really have removed it?' Gwen asked. 'What about the archaeological context?' The specificity of the question surprised Ari. There was a chill behind the words, and Ari knew she was right. Even running her little museum, as she called it, gave her the air of a curator.

'It was in danger of being destroyed,' she replied, amazed at how calm her voice sounded. One thing about public-school politics, it made you think on your feet.

'Was it?' Gwen asked as if she knew differently.

Well, who was she to know anyway? She hadn't been there. Ari's gaze met Nico's, who rolled his eyes to the ceiling. But he stepped into the breach anyway.

'There was a conger eel, an enormous one,' he supplied. 'It attacked one of our divers. Took a huge chunk out of his arm. He'll be all right, but it was hiding in the rocks where we found the mask. I think we were lucky to find it when we did or it could have—'

'Really?' Laure asked, interrupting. 'An eel? But they're like… a fish?'

'So is a shark, *chérie*,' Gwen told her with a flash of teeth that made Laure squeal with laughter. 'So tell me what else you found?'

Jason shrugged. 'It's more about what we *will* find. The coin, the mask, they're all clues, stepping stones. I know there's more down there. Simon always said there was a path leading to Ys and we just had to find it. He was absolutely right. Wasn't he, Ari?'

Her throat closed like a vice. She couldn't get the words out, or air in. Her stomach lurched. Simon. Simon had said many things. Simon was gone.

'Are you quite well, my dear?' asked Madame du Lac. 'You look like you've seen a ghost.'

They were all staring at her. Every last one of them. All those eyes, glittering in the light, expectant, intrigued. She felt so cold, as if all the blood had drained out of her body in that instant.

'Excuse me.' She pushed herself up from the table and tried to stop herself running from the room. Running away again. Just like she always did.

Outside in the dark hallway, she finally stopped, leaning back against the wall, forcing herself to breathe in and out. Tears stung her eyes, but she couldn't burst into tears. She couldn't let herself do that. Not here.

It was a panic attack, that was all. Just a panic attack. She'd dealt with them before. She would again. She had to focus, to lock her feelings and her grief inside and—

'Dr Walker?'

The voice rippled against her senses and she opened her eyes to see Rafael standing in the door to the room opposite her, watching her with that endless dark gaze, a small concerned frown crinkling the skin between his eyebrows.

CHAPTER EIGHT

Light framed Rafael, the golden glow of old blubs reflecting on warm polished wood, as he watched her trying desperately to gather together the shattered pieces of her pride once again. He looked like an angel, standing there. A fallen angel perhaps.

'I'm sorry,' she said. 'I just... I just needed a moment. They were talking about Simon.'

He glanced towards the dining-room door, understanding crossing his features. Then he seemed to reach some sort of conclusion.

'Come in here, sit down. I'll get you a drink.'

She followed him into a study. Behind the desk was a magnificent stained-glass window, containing images of the sea and the cliffs, dark against the night, just outlines, like a colouring-book image waiting for a child to fill it in. Books lined the walls, old and well cared for, leather-bound with gleaming gilt inlays and titles on the spines. In total contrast, there was a laptop open on the desk, the glow of its light pale blue and cold. Some papers were stacked beside it, his phone on top of them. There was also a drinks cabinet from which he took glasses and a bottle of something a rich amber colour. He poured two generous helpings.

'Here,' he said, handing one to her.

'The others will miss—'

'They won't. They're probably on to another subject now anyway. Don't mind them. You need a moment. What happened?'

'It was just...' She sipped the liqueur, sweet and warm, burning its way down her throat. 'That's strong.'

He smiled briefly and drank some of his own. 'It is. Locally made rather than a shop-bought one, so probably illegal if we get down to it. Mémé is a fan, as you probably saw yesterday. What did they say about Simon?'

Ari took another mouthful of the liqueur, probably too much. It made her eyes water. It was definitely that, and not thoughts of her lost fiancé.

'How do you know Simon?' she asked after a moment.

'We were in school together, when we were little. Before my mother sent me away to the academy in Paris. Simon, Gwen, Laure and I...' He sighed and leaned back on the desk, watching her. 'It was a long time ago. A lifetime ago. We were friends, in that way children are when you all come from the same small village. And our families have a long history together. We lost touch ages ago. I didn't realise you and Simon...' He trailed off in that awkward way people did when talking to her about Simon. They couldn't help it. She almost understood.

'We met in college. Another lifetime ago. He was... he was a very special person.'

This was met with silence. Perhaps he didn't know what to say. Grief made people uncomfortable, she knew that better than anyone. She made people uncomfortable, especially those who had known Simon. Their friends had turned out to be his friends and drifted away. She always wondered if they knew what he'd done, but she'd never managed to get up the courage to ask. She withdrew into herself. She had her work and that was enough.

Coming back here was a mistake.

'He loved it here,' she said at last because it seemed like a safe thing to say.

Was it her imagination or did Rafael suppress a shudder? 'Many people do.'

Ari leaned forward, interested. 'But not you.'

He sipped his drink, watching her with those dark eyes, delaying answering.

'My father died here. There is a lot of duty tied to this place for me. Old traditions and family history. That is... difficult. And my great-aunt, of course. Well, you have met her.'

'She's formidable.'

He smiled, a slow lazy smile of genuine affection that made her stomach do something interesting and unexpected. 'She is. And infuriating. But that's family, I suppose.'

Ari thought of Jason and grinned. She raised her glass in toast. 'To family, then.'

Rafael joined her half-heartedly. 'This wasn't what I had in mind when I said I'd buy you dinner, you know?'

'Well, hiding in your study with strong liquor isn't anyone's idea of a sensible dinner, Rafael.'

His name rolled off her tongue, and tasted like the liqueur, sweet and spiced, a little dangerous. More than a little dangerous.

'Let me take you out somewhere nicer.'

Nicer than his manor house on his ancient family estate. Right.

She glanced towards the door. 'Don't you need to be with your sister and your... friend?'

'Gwen? God, no. And Laure is more than capable of getting into trouble by herself. You might want to watch your brother though.'

'Well, speaking of people capable of getting themselves into trouble, she may have met her match. But no, Jason is focused on the treasure hunt. He'll be busy with the university tomorrow and probably for the rest of the week with the mask. So will I, for that matter. And then I'll be gone.'

Surprise flickered through his dark eyes. 'You're leaving?'

Why did he think she would stay? There was nothing for her here. Nothing but pain.

She shrugged the thought away. She couldn't bear it. 'This is only a visit. A holiday really. A favour to Jason. I'm due back in school soon. Students to see, classes to prepare, homework to mark, all of that.'

'I thought you were here to help him for the duration of his excavations – is it still an excavation if it's underwater? – or are you just here to follow stories and folklore?'

'Are you making fun of my discipline of choice?' she teased, feeling more herself suddenly, more at ease with him.

He raised a hand in surrender. 'I wouldn't dare, Dr Walker. But your brother needs your help or he would not have asked, would he? I think you should stay.'

'Oh, you do, do you? I'm sorry, Mr Lord of the Manor, some of us have jobs and bills. I can't live like Jason and Nico, always in search of the next treasure, the next adventure.'

I can't live where Simon died, she thought, but didn't dare say it out loud. Perhaps some shadow of her pain passed across her face because Rafael changed the subject.

'You don't believe there's anything here, do you? Ys or whatever it might have been...'

She frowned. It felt like a betrayal to say it. Simon believed. So did her brother. '"Whatever it might have been..."' she echoed him. 'There's bound to have been settlements here throughout history, especially at the time Ys is meant to have existed. The Bretons arrived, fleeing the Saxons, settling here...'

'Following Conan Meriadoc, founding the House of Rohan,

and Brittany itself. Believe me, I know the stories. My family came with him – I have the lineage here somewhere – fleeing invaders, looking for safety, finding it here at this place at the end of the world. Following the man who's said to be the father of the King of Ys.'

'But not the king of a city full of wonders and terrors, swept away by the sea. Saved by a magical horse. There are historical factors, I'm sure. That's what Simon...' She choked a little and cleared her throat. 'That's what he thought. And Jason believes it too. He might find something, it's true. But it will be old rocks and scattered remains, maybe some carvings. If we're lucky, there will be more things like the coin and maybe – *maybe* – the mask. But those cliffs and caves are coming down. The sea is relentless. It'll destroy anything remaining there before too long. I don't think they're going to find Ys, do you? Not the Ys of red walls and golden roofs and a thousand wonders.'

He shrugged, his toned shoulders moving beneath the expensive shirt in an entirely too distracting way. 'The local stories say differently. They say there's a pathway to Ys and if you're brave enough and true enough, you'll find it.'

She sighed and rose to her feet. 'I'm sure they do. And I'm sure your family has many tales to tell, just like Simon's did. He was full of stories about this place, about people who found traces, who stumbled on secrets, but really, Rafael, that's all they are. Stories.'

'And how do you explain the mask?'

'The mask?'

He put the glass down on the desk and picked up a book. It was richly illustrated, leather-bound and old. He turned a few pages and then offered it to her.

The page was beautiful, elaborately decorated with colours like stained glass in sunlight. A woman with white hair held a white mask decorated with gold and gleaming blue spirals, offering it out to the viewer. Strands of something like ribbons hung from it, like tendrils of hair, or vines, but they curled in an unusual way, as if they had a life of their own.

'Dahut's mask. The one she used to enchant and murder her lovers. It's all there. I knew I recognised it.'

Ari took the book. It was old, a manuscript, she realised, and she couldn't read the language in which it was written. The ink was still dark and the colours bright. This had been treasured for a long time. Cared for.

'Where did you get this?' she asked, smoothing her finger-tips along the side of the page. Vellum, she realised, not paper.

'It's a family heirloom.'

'And the language?'

'Ancient Breton. A local dialect.'

'This must be priceless.'

He shrugged. Maybe to him many things were priceless. Or perhaps they were until he set a price. 'It has been studied. "A collection of local folktales, gathered together in the Middle Ages, referencing earlier works, handsomely illustrated", and so on. The academic authorities don't believe it has merit beyond local interest. Gwen would love to get hold of it for her museum. Your Simon studied it, I believe. He visited Mémé here a few times. There are a number of copies. Most academics believe this too is a copy. It is not.'

'And you just keep it here? In your house?'

He shook his head. 'It is kept secure, don't worry. We have a vault. I wanted to refer to it. That's why I have it here.'

She couldn't seem to let it go. It was beautiful, ancient. 'Why not make a digital copy, Rafael? Why the original?'

'The original is special,' he told her and took it back, sliding it into a leather case with the greatest care. 'And it belongs to us. To me. I can't pretend I'm not unsettled by this discovery, Dr Walker. The mask is legendary and dangerous. And you found it on your first dive...'

She didn't know what he was implying, but she didn't like it.

'Dangerous?'

She thought of the conger eel, the way it had attacked Thierry, the way it wound itself around the rocks, the way it had been coming back. That had been dangerous. The mask was just a mask.

'So the book says. So our legends say. Dahut of Ys used it to kill and control. It is her symbol. Some might say it heralds her return. She was transformed into a water witch, cursed to dwell in the waters of her sunken home, luring people to their deaths with her beauty and her song.'

'A mermaid?'

'Yes. Of a sort. But not like your Ariel.' He arched a knowing eyebrow at her and she pursed her lips, his dig very clear. She wasn't going to rise to that. 'Dahut is dangerous, treacherous, and thoroughly wicked. Vindictive. She is driven solely by revenge against those who betrayed her and caused the destruction of Ys for which she was blamed.'

'And who were they?'

He gave a single, bitter laugh. 'Why, my family, of course. We thought it was broken, the curse, those who believed in it in the first place. But lately my great-aunt changed her mind. Through talking to Simon, I suppose. And because of his death.'

Rafael stepped in closer to her and she didn't move. His voice transfixed her, rising and falling like music, his accent enchanting, his dark eyes drawing her in.

'Why?' she asked.

'The men in my family die young. We are taken by the sea, just as Dahut promised all those years ago. We have our own version of the stories, written in that book. The city of Ys was beautiful, yes, but it was also a blight on the land here. It drained all wealth into it, took our people as slaves, exploited our natural resources, like a voracious monster feeding off this whole region. My ancestor was the one to seduce her, according to the book, to steal the key to the sea gates and open them to welcome the storm. Looked at another way, he rescued all of Cap Sizun from the tyranny of Ys. And she cursed him and all our line to die unless we saved Ys. But how can anyone save something that was lost so long ago?'

'An ancient curse, really?' She turned away, fed up with this. Everyone tried to spin an ancient curse into their history, especially when it came to archaeology. The Curse of Tutankhamun was probably the most famous, but it was by no means the first, or the last. Logic said it was just a way of making people feel important or to explain away horrible coincidences. A kind of dark wish fulfilment.

Rafael caught her hand before she could leave. He didn't use force. His touch was incredibly gentle, but he stopped her all the same. Just that contact, the warmth of his skin on hers, the inadvertent caress, and she couldn't have moved to save her life. The pad of his thumb brushed the sensitive skin of her wrist and shivers ran through her.

'My father drowned when I was a child. He was thirty-five. Only my grandfather seems to have escaped it. But he died in a car crash when he was in his thirties, so who knows? Not one of them was older than thirty-five. It goes back to time out of mind. All the men in my line, and those associated with us. We die young. We die in water.'

Like Simon. Just like Simon.

God, this wasn't happening, couldn't be happening. Was that what Rafael had been doing the other day? Trying to give himself up to the inevitable? Trying to drown?

She asked the question she really didn't want to ask. But she couldn't help herself.

'What age are you, Rafael?'

His grip tightened for just a moment, a squeeze, and then he released her as if she burned him. When he didn't say anything, she reached out, her fingers brushing his jawline and she felt it tighten beneath the intimate touch. He closed his eyes as if he was in pain.

When he opened them again, they were dark and endless, the deep brown she had admired now looked like the black of the deepest ocean, the darkness of places that had never seen the light.

'Rafael?' she prompted cautiously. This was the reason for Madame du Lac's insistence that the excavation take place now, for the excitement over the mask, over any discovery at all. It wasn't just the whim of an elderly lady who felt her own time was running out, or that her mind was slipping. There was method and urgency in this madness. Ari knew it.

Rafael took a moment before he answered, reluctant perhaps to say it out loud, but she knew he'd tell her. He couldn't help it.

'Next month I will be thirty-five.'

CHAPTER NINE

Just saying it out loud left him shaken to the core. Saying it to someone who didn't know the whole sorry history felt beyond strange, and curiously liberating. Like shining a light on a shadow.

Ari's touch on his face trembled, but she didn't retreat. She was so close. He could smell her perfume, feel the warmth of her body, and the urge to reach out and pull her against him, to kiss her, was strong indeed. The image of doing just that raced through his mind and he couldn't move, couldn't breathe, just in case he gave in to impulse and acted on it.

This was insane. He didn't even know her. He'd only just met her and she had already entered his dreams and his waking mind. As if it was part of this enchantment, part of the curse, his only salvation...

He had never allowed himself to get too deeply involved in any relationship. Why would he? Life was too short. And most of the women he met were like Jacqueline. Money mattered above all else. It was his most attractive quality to them. That made trust hard to come by.

But why her? Why Ari Walker? Why did he want to tell

her everything and have her believe everything? His crazy dreams, all his secrets. It seemed so desperately important. Even if he didn't really believe it himself.

'Rafael,' she whispered solemnly, the voice of reason, and her words made his heart stutter inside his chest with regret. He knew what was coming. He was an idiot. 'No one is going to drown you. No evil mermaids exacting an age-old revenge... It's just... just a string of bad coincidences. And old stories. And—'

Disappointment slammed into him like a blow to the stomach. He lurched back from her, tearing himself free. It wasn't condescension, not quite. But it felt that way. Like he was a child again, telling his ghost stories. But never quite believed.

He'd seen the Ankou stalking around the house, waiting for a death. He'd seen the white ladies walking the clifftops, calling out to the lost, he'd seen the *mari-morgen* swimming in the waters beneath. He'd even seen the *groac'h*, like a princess of legends, waiting for him on the rocks in the sea. Dreams, he told himself. Childhood fancies.

His mother had been dismissive in the extreme. Nonsense, she called it. Laure still laughed at him about it.

Mémé didn't though. She'd promised that the house was protected. She'd given him... He breathed in, realising he'd seen the little linen pouches throughout his life, tucked away, never spoken about. And that each low tide, she collected seaweed from the shore and plaited it into fantastical shapes to hang on the doors. All his life.

'I know that. Logically I know that. And yet, this is my life, Ari. It is very hard to deny. I'm a rational person, I assure you. I deal with international finance, and multimillion-euro deals on a daily basis. There is no place for superstition in that world. But my great-aunt does not live in that world. Not anymore. She lives here and she is afraid. There are no other du Lac sons. Not now. Just me.' A white lie perhaps. But he couldn't say more. Not yet. He barely knew her and some secrets were too precious. He'd learned that the hard way. 'Mémé wants to find the source of the curse and put a stop to it. She makes amulets and charms, thinking they will help. She has worked for this all my life, ever since my father died. She's afraid she's running out of time. On both our counts.'

Ari hadn't moved. She stood as if rooted to the spot, staring at him.

'And what do you want me to do? Indulge her? Lie to her?'

'I want you to do exactly what you've already done. To find something, to find Ys. Mémé believes we need to find evidence of the city, whatever it really was.'

'How will that break a curse that doesn't exist?'

He shook his head. He couldn't answer that. But it might put Mémé's mind at ease. So he ignored the question. 'I will fund everything. Whatever you and your brother need, you will have it. Finance is no object. I'll deal with the universities and the officials, with all the red tape. But, in return, I need you to stay here and find the lost city.'

He couldn't tell her why it had to be her. He was sounding deranged enough as it was. What could he say anyway? *I dreamed about you. You saved my life. I know that you are the one person who can do it.*

No. Mémé might believe that. Something in his subconscious must have just picked it up. It wasn't real. None of it could be real.

But why did it feel so important that she stayed and helped find Ys? He was a rational man and he didn't believe in the legends and stories the way his great-aunt did. Logic told him anyone could do it. Anyone with her qualifications and experience. He could employ the very best in the world.

But looking at Ari right now, he knew that wasn't true either. He just knew.

Maybe she was the best. Maybe it just had to be her.

Every instinct told him that she was the only one. She had

come to his rescue right from the start, even if he hadn't needed rescuing. He had dreamed about her and for the first time ever that dream didn't end with him leaping to his death. Somehow he just knew he needed her to stay, to help him solve this mystery.

Ari shook her head. He knew she would and he could hardly blame her. 'I can't stay. I need to get back to my job. I'm sorry. Jason and Nico will find your myth if there's anything to be found. But not with me. I'm sorry, Rafael. It isn't possible.'

Final words. She was just as stubborn as he'd thought. But she had lost someone too. Here. Why couldn't she understand?

'And what if you could find out what happened to Simon? He died here. Drowned. What if the curse took him as well?'

She sucked in a breath and the colour drained from her face. When she found her voice again, it was shaking slightly, still strong, still determined, but masked now in defiance. 'Why? Was he your brother too?'

Rafael shook his head, realising he had gone too far. He just couldn't help himself. 'We were not related, Simon and I, or at least not directly, not to my knowledge. We're a small community, and we share lives, history, and possibly blood. But while my family bears this curse, the sea takes many people on this coast. Those who stand with us. If you look at the war memorial in the cove, there's a Poullain and a du Lac listed side by side. They died there together. Every family will have a story, at least one, usually many more. A child, a son, a father, a brother. They blame the *groac'h*, the water witch, and her *mari-morgens*, or simply the sea itself. And they blame us too. We're meant to protect them.'

'Protect them how?'

He winced. It was another old tradition, that was all. It often made him uncomfortable, to be honest. And yet, he knew that they all thought it. *Noblesse oblige.* The bloodline always came with obligations to the people sworn to it. Whether he liked it or not, he was the Mac'htiern, the head of a clan, the lord, the prince.

'My family held this land, protected it. There are still echoes of that lingering on. More than echoes. It's expected. And the story goes that if the sacrifice isn't made... the sea takes what it wants.'

The sea always took what it wanted. And here in Sainte Sirène, when that happened, people expected a response. He had a duty. And the sea expected a price.

There were only so many du Lacs, and they rarely had many children. One of his ancestors had written that it was hard to have a son knowing what would happen in so short a time. Mémé had never had children of her own. Rafael understood now, the fear, the knowledge of fate hanging not just over you but over your son as well... He'd never believed it, but now... now... it seemed perilously close. It made his heart ache, just the thought of it.

For a moment, Ari just stared at him. He could see her running her thoughts through her mind, unable to articulate them. For a moment, he hoped...

'Simon died in an accident.' Her voice came out clipped and cold, so very firm.

'An experienced diver.'

'It happens,' she growled. Her hands had balled into fists at her sides and he was sure the nails were digging into the skin of her palms. He'd never seen anyone so possessed of a cold fury.

He'd made a terrible mistake goading her about Simon, he realised. But he couldn't stop now. He knew he was right. 'I don't take no for an answer, Dr Walker,' he told her.

'Well, you had better get used to it,' she replied and as if the spell had finally shattered, she stalked from the study, grabbed her coat and headed out into the night without a glance back at him.

Rafael hurried after her, to the open front door. It was dark out there and the wind was rising. He hadn't noticed the weather deteriorating from inside the house. But Breton weather was notoriously changeable. It could be glorious sunshine one moment and torrential rain the next. *Don't like the weather?* – the joke went – *Just wait a minute.*

He couldn't let her go out in that. The roads could be dangerous on foot and the cliff paths even more so. Cursing to himself, cursing himself, he grabbed a jacket and headed after her.

'Rafael? What are you doing?' Laure called from the dining-room door.

'I'll be back later. Tell them... just... Fuck it, Laure. I don't care what you tell them.'

His sister started to argue, but he didn't listen. If he lost Ari now, he'd never find her in the night. She was probably heading back to the gîte. Where else would she go? But still... He'd caused this and he had to fix it. Why on earth had he brought up Simon? Why had he even told her anything about the madness that surrounded his life? No one sane would believe any of it. His family only knew it through bitter experience. They had no proof, just old stories and a string of dead men.

'What did you do?' Laure called after him, but he was already running down the drive, looking for Ari Walker.

The storm came in from the west. Storms in Paris could be dramatic, but they didn't warrant the same name as the wild tempests that lashed the Atlantic coast. He could smell ozone in the air and the rain swirled around him, caught by the wind, falling in every direction, even up. The trees lining the avenue lashed from side to side and he pressed on against the gusts threatening to drive him back. He could just make her out, a small figure in the distance, but when he shouted her name, the gale whipped his voice away.

A gap in the racing clouds uncovered the moon, just for an instant, and he saw a shadow, the height of a man. It flitted along beside her, not her own, but something else. Rafael blinked through the rain, frowning. For a moment, he wasn't sure what he saw was real. It wasn't possible.

At the end of the drive, she stopped, looking either way as if making a decision. The figure that could not possibly be there leaned in and whispered in her ear. Rafael called out her name, but the wind stole his voice again. Ari turned and started up the path. She wasn't heading for the main road, or the village, he realised, but out towards the coast instead. This was madness. True, in daylight, in good weather, it was quicker to take the coastal paths back to the Ty Elen gîte. But not now. The trails and paths that wound their way over the open clifftop were barely visible and beyond them, too close for comfort, the sea was wild, throwing foam up to heaven. There were crevices, some of which led to the rabbit warren of caves beneath their feet. Some led directly to the sea itself. It was dangerous to be out here alone in a storm.

Yet she was not alone. It felt like his nightmare all over again as he ran after her but didn't seem to make any headway. The wind pushed him back, the wet ground underfoot hampering him. Clouds scuttered away from the moon again. Striding alongside Ari's slender form, a tall figure cloaked in rippling shadows flowed across the rough ground. As Rafael finally drew closer, it resolved into a man, taller than either of them, wearing a long black coat and a wide-brimmed black hat which the wind didn't touch. Long white hair lifted in the air as if underwater.

'Ari!' Rafael tried again.

She didn't react. Perhaps she didn't hear him. But the figure glanced back over his shoulder, and Rafael caught a glimpse of a bone-pale face, a rictus, skeletal grin. The figure lifted one hand and pressed it to her back. Just the lightest tap.

Ari screamed and went down, vanishing into the ground. The dark figure dissolved into the shrieking wind.

'Ari!' He scrambled after her. She had to be OK. She had to be.

He couldn't think about who, or what, he had just seen or what it meant. He knew the figure from his nightmares. How could he call himself a Breton and not? Ari Walker had just been touched by Ankou. Death's right hand.

'Down here! Help!'

Her voice. She had to be OK if she could call out. But where was she?

In the darkness, he couldn't see her, but he got his phone out and turned on the torch, swinging the beam of light over the ground where she had been.

'Ari? Keep talking. Where are you? What can you see?'

An answering light shone from beneath an overgrowth of bush and scrub, and he saw the fissure in the ground. She'd had the same idea about using her phone. 'Rocks? And... Oh god, what's that? Ugh.'

She sounded so deeply affronted that under any other circumstances it would be been amusing.

As a kid he had explored the caves, along with Laure and other friends, as far as they dared, which wasn't really very far. They weren't meant to go down there at all and if an adult found out, there would be hell to pay.

He reached out and pushed back the brambles with his arm. Her pale face looked back up at him from a gap in the ground. Even standing, she'd have a hard time climbing out alone. It was a couple of metres down.

'Here.' He lay down on the wet earth and reached out his free hand. 'I'll pull you up.'

For once, she didn't argue. She threw her shoes up and grabbed his arm, clambering over the rocks. When she tried to stand unaided, her legs went from beneath her. He caught her before she could fall.

'You're hurt.' It was a stupid thing to say, he knew that.

'Just give me a minute. I'm just... I'm just winded.'

Oh, she was never going to admit that she was hurt, that much was certain. 'Just let me help you. Come back to the house.'

She shook her head. 'Not like this. Look at me. I'm covered in mud and God knows what. I think there was something alive down there.' She shuddered. 'When did this storm blow in? It took me right off my feet.'

'What did?'

'A gust of wind.'

Right. A rational explanation. She liked them, he got that. So what had he seen? A trick of the light? A hallucination? He closed his eyes in despair.

'Ari...' he began with a tone that could hide his dwindling patience. It wasn't safe out here. Not just the weather and the treacherous ground. Something more. How did he explain that? Preferably without telling her he'd seen a mythical creature from folklore? Because after the conversation they had just had, she was not going to believe that. Not for a second.

It had been a trick of the storm and the limited light. It had to be. He was a rational man. This was ridiculous. He'd already sounded like a madman earlier, talking of curses and ancient legends. He wasn't about to compound that now.

But the way it had turned and looked at him. The way it had grinned. He had *not* imagined that.

'Ari, did you see anyone else out here?' he asked, carefully.

'I didn't see anything but an enormous black hole swallowing me.' She tested her weight on her own feet again. This time, she stood, wobbly as a new-born deer. He held on to her just in case, as she sought out her shoes and tried to put them on her numb feet. Then she looked up. 'Do you mean him? What is he even doing out there?'

She pointed along the path to the point, where a dark figure stood on an outcrop of rocks, surrounded by dense undergrowth, the old ruins of a Roman-era settlement, an oppidum. He'd played there as a boy too. It was nothing more than earthen banks and piles of stones now, horribly overgrown. A narrow path cut through it, leading out to the even more exposed far end of Castelmeur.

The figure moved too quickly, leaping down into the darkness between the lichen-covered stones and bushes, eluding them again.

'Stay here,' Rafael told her as he launched himself forward, pushing his way through the bushes and plunging into the narrow maze-like path. Twigs scratched at him, tugging at his clothes, and he had to raise both hands to force his way through.

He almost fell out the other side, where the path dipped precipitously. On the Pointe de Castelmeur, there was no shelter at all. The sea and the wind roared around him and he staggered as sheets of rain struck him like a series of physical blows. He bent forward, leaning into the storm, making himself continue. Because somehow he had to. It was like his recurring nightmare all over again, but this time he was awake. He had to know. He had to see if it was real.

The man in black stood at the far end of the point, right at the top of the cliff, his arms spread wide.

'Who are you?' Rafael yelled. 'What do you want? Ankou?'

Ankou – because it had to be Ankou – tilted his head to one side, the long white hair of a fée creature whipping around his face so as to obscure his features. He pointed down, down to the sea, down to the wave-lashed rocky island below.

Rafael didn't want to look. He didn't want to see her. He didn't want this to be real.

'Rafael?' Ari gasped, struggling to his side. 'What the hell —?' Her voice fell silent, and her hand gripped his arm, her fingers like iron, but he had no doubt he was forgotten. Her voice, when she yelled at the figure, came out harsh against the wind. 'Who are you? Where did you get that?'

A mask, he realised. The figure was wearing a mask. White like porcelain, like old bone. It shone in the rain and the light bounced off the gold and blue decorations painted on it. The mask she'd found. The mask she had plucked from the sea. But it was clean now, shining in the storm, rain trickling down over the surface.

The figure lifted one finger to his lips, not skeletal now, not death incarnate. Carefully, he removed the mask to reveal a man. Just a man.

The man whose face Rafael had been looking at on his laptop earlier today.

Not a stranger at all.

Ari pushed by him and it was his turn to grab her, to hold her back from the edge, from the phantom in solid form, from Ankou, the Servant of Death.

From the creature wearing the face of her dead fiancé.

'Who are you?' she screamed again, with every last breath of air in her lungs. She almost tore herself free of him and Rafael wrapped his arms around her waist, holding her against him. He had to protect her, to stop her from hurling herself to certain death in her rage. 'Who the fuck are you?'

Ankou spread his arms wide now, the mask dangling from his hand like a discarded plaything. He smiled, a wild, gleeful smile, dangerous and terrible. And then, gracefully, inexorably, he let himself fall backwards off the cliff, into the raging sea.

CHAPTER TEN

Ari staggered back to the gîte, sobbing for breath, her clothes soaked to the skin, her mind whirling. The storm dropped the moment they fled the headland, clawing their way back through the undergrowth and running along the path to the point where the lane turned in a huge loop and headed back towards civilisation.

It had been Simon. She couldn't fail to recognise him. She knew him better than any other man in the world.

But it was also impossible. It was like a waking nightmare.

She silently thanked God Rafael was still with her. To be honest, he was probably the only thing keeping her upright, and certainly the only warm and solid thing in her world right now. She clung to him as she moved on numb legs and he wrapped his arms around her as if he couldn't dream of letting her go.

Exhausted, cold and wet, they finally reached the welcome lights of the gîte and almost fell through the door.

'*Mon dieu,*' said Madalen. She was just coming out of the kitchen, a bottle of red wine in hand. 'What happened to you?'

Ari didn't know where she found her voice from. 'There was a storm.'

Madalen frowned. 'There was? Not here. You must have been really unlucky.' She lifted the bottle towards them. 'Wine?'

'Yes, thank you,' said Rafael. 'And a towel perhaps?'

He stripped off his saturated coat and hung it up. Water pooled on the stone floor tiles beneath it. The waterproof had protected his shirt, but the lower half of his trousers and those beautiful leather shoes were destroyed.

Ari herself had not been so lucky. She knew she looked like a drowned rat and she was shivering so hard now she thought her bones might come loose.

Madalen shrugged and left them standing there in the hall. A moment later she was back without the wine and with a pile of beach towels in various bright colours. The sound of a car outside made them all turn and, with a sense of dread, Ari realised her brother was back.

'What happened to you?' Jason exclaimed as he came in. 'Why did you take off?' He was glaring at Rafael, clearly suspecting him of something terrible.

Ari didn't have time for this. Her brother didn't get to play the overprotective idiot with her. Not now, not ever. Besides, she had other concerns. 'Where did you put the mask, Jason?' she asked.

That threw him off track. He jerked around to stare at her, instantly on edge, alarmed. If anything had happened to their find, they'd have problems. More than problems. He knew that. 'The mask? It's locked up in the store. How did you get so wet?'

'There was a storm,' she said. 'Where's the store? Show me. I need to make sure.'

How could she tell him that she was afraid it had been stolen? How could she tell him she'd seen Simon, or his ghost, or... or whatever she had seen?

'What storm?' Jason asked. 'There was a shower. Why are you both so wet? And you're covered in mud. What happened?'

Nico led the way, ignoring him, sensing perhaps her urgency in a way her brother had completely missed. Jason, it appeared, was too caught up in concern for her. That was a surprise. Irritating, but a surprise nonetheless.

Nico fished out a key from a bowl on the table and led the way to the door she had taken for a cupboard or a utility room at the far end of the hall. It was old, the thick wood painted a brilliant white, which contrasted with the black iron of the hinges. The modern padlock on it was incongruous in comparison. He opened it and flicked on a switch so the lights came on. Shelves were stacked with equipment and supplies, like an Aladdin's cave. The box sat on a shelf, still full of sea water, and the mask lurking inside it.

Nico lifted it out and brought it into the kitchen, where he set it on the wooden table.

'Looks all in order,' he said.

They all craned over it, and Nico opened the top. Carefully, he lifted it and Ari gasped.

The mask was still there, but now it was completely clean. The ceramic was bright. Gold patterns glittered in the artificial light and the blue marking looked like ripples in the sea itself, almost like enamel, clear and shimmering with life.

It looked brand new.

The dirt and debris that had covered it swirled through the water in the tub, turning it milky white and then slowly clearing as it all slid to the bottom. It lay there like a sludge, like mud.

'What the hell?' she whispered, before she could stop herself.

'They're never going to believe we found that in the sea.' Nico's voice was no more than a whisper. The shock was palpable. 'They'll think we compromised it by cleaning it at best, or at worst that it's a fake or... What happened to it?'

Jason, meanwhile, stormed from the kitchen into the sitting room, yelling at the top of his voice. 'Thierry? Who was in the storeroom? Who cleaned the mask? What the hell?' He switched to French, angry and full of accusation.

Thierry himself protested his innocence and Madalen joined in. Suddenly everyone was yelling.

Ari swayed on her feet, exhausted, overwhelmed. She stared at the mask cradled in Nico's shaking hands. Pristine, beautiful.

Just the way she had seen it in Simon's hands earlier.

Without a word, Rafael pulled out a chair for her and she sank on to it gratefully. 'Are you OK?' he asked softly, while her brother carried on yelling at his friends, asking everyone in turn a myriad of questions.

Nico stared in horror at the mask, trying to examine it and work out what on earth happened.

Ari found her voice. It sounded breathy and thin, as if someone had punched her in the stomach and driven all the air from her. 'How is that possible? Any of it? Anything we saw? We... You saw it too, right?' She looked up at Rafael, aware in that moment that he was all the evidence that she had that she wasn't losing her mind.

Rafael fixed her with his dark, solemn eyes and nodded slowly. But he didn't answer. How could he? What answer was there?

'They say no one's been in there,' Jason blustered as he came back into the kitchen. 'And no one else has been here all evening. They're all off at that wretched Irish pub getting hammered for Solena's birthday.' He shuddered, sharing every Irish person's dread of an Irish pub abroad. 'What happened to it, Nico? How is that possible?'

Nico slid the mask back into the water, his hand shaking as he did so. The sediment at the bottom swirled up around it like ghostly hands. 'Perhaps I should get clean water,' he said softly. 'I don't know. I don't want to touch it. Maybe it wasn't as secure as we thought. Maybe tremors or something. I don't think it was near anything that might have... Maybe the washing machine vibrations travelled through the floor or...' He looked as lost as Ari felt. 'We'll have to talk to the university. Maybe they have an explanation.'

Jason groaned. 'We're seeing them tomorrow. They won't believe—'

'We have the video,' Ari suggested. They had filmed the moment she had... except they hadn't. They'd filmed up to the moment the eel attacked Thierry. Not the rest.

'The video, sure. Or at least some of it. And the photos. But that... that looks nothing like it did this morning. They'll say we switched it out. We can't...' He seemed to deflate just standing there. 'Jesus, I don't know.' Then he looked up at her. 'How did you know something had happened to it? What happened to you on the way back anyway? You never answered.'

Ari couldn't answer, couldn't find the words to tell him what she'd seen. He'd say she was mad, or hallucinating. That her grief had finally gotten the better of her.

Rafael came to the rescue again. He lied so smoothly, without even a flicker of hesitation. 'Ari wasn't feeling well after dinner and wanted to come back here. I offered to walk her back, over the cliffs. There was a storm.'

'A storm, just on the cliffs, got you that soaked. One no one else noticed?' Jason's voice went flat with disbelief.

'Well, it was windy, and there was rain as we drove back,' Nico offered gently. 'It would have been worse out on the cliffs. You know how exposed they are.'

Ari could have hugged him. It didn't mean much to Jason though, who was clearly on a mission to prove someone accountable. For what, she wasn't sure even he knew.

'Not that much rain. You're saturated. I don't know what's going on, Ari, but don't lie to me.'

She opened her mouth to argue but couldn't think of

anything to say. How could she tell him what she had seen? He'd never believe her.

Jason snorted when she said nothing. He was barely listening anyway, so caught up in his outrage. 'Yeah, I thought so. I don't have time for this. I need to work out what to say tomorrow. I don't know how I'm going to convince them this isn't a joke. That *we* aren't a joke.' Jason glared at Rafael again and then swept from the kitchen, slamming the door behind him.

Ari balled her icy hands into fists. How dare he? He didn't get to take this out on her. And certainly not on Rafael. He was the one going on about how they needed the du Lac money. Had he forgotten that?

'I should go,' Rafael said softly.

'No,' Ari said, a little too quickly. She hurriedly corrected her tone. 'I... I mean, we need to talk.'

A fleeting smile crossed his lips, but it didn't linger. 'I'd like nothing more, but you should get dry and warm. You're shivering and you're tired. We can talk tomorrow. We must. I'll take you out to lunch.'

Not actually an invitation, she noted. But he was right and she was too shattered to argue. She hugged her arms tighter around her body and felt the cold water chilling her skin through her clothes. She shivered, unable to stop herself.

'You'll catch your death of cold, Ari,' Nico told her in as gentle a voice as ever. She'd almost forgotten he was there, but he was, watching the two of them. Her face flushed with embarrassment. 'He's right. Jason will calm down. You know he will. But let him be now. I'll talk to him later. Monsieur du Lac, I can drive you home if you want. I'm sure your family will be concerned.'

Rafael nodded, although he didn't look as certain about that. 'Thank you. That would be most helpful.'

Nico squeezed Ari's shoulder, his touch an unexpected

comfort. 'And you, step into the shower and then go to bed, Ari. That's an order. I'll let Jason know. God knows, if we just take off now, he'll lose the plot completely. Just give me a moment.'

She couldn't argue with Nico. She didn't have the heart. The wave of tiredness sweeping through her was too much to fight off. Was it shock? she wondered. After all, she had seen… Simon…

She looked up at Rafael helplessly.

Tomorrow would have to do.

As Nico left the room, Rafael leaned over the box again, studying the now pristine mask through the veil of water. The expression on his face was unreadable but it made her chest clench tight around her heart. There was some sort of horrible recognition to it. She thought of the illustration in the book. It was so similar.

'Rafael?' she murmured hesitantly. But she had to know. She had to ask. 'You… you saw him too, didn't you?'

He tried to smile again, but it didn't reach his eyes. 'I saw him.'

'But I—' Her throat closed, choking her words, and her eyes began to burn. 'It's impossible.'

She surged to her feet and instantly regretted it. The room swam around her and dark tendrils of shadows like storm clouds closed around the edges of her vision.

He reached out a hand to steady her. Drawing in a deep breath, he paused, as if he didn't want to say what he was about to say, and yet, couldn't avoid it either. His hand cupped her arm so gently and his warm touch seemed to be the only thing real and solid in the world.

'Mémé has always said that this is a land of signs and symbols, Ari, a place of portents. She believes there is meaning in everything if you know how to read it. Nothing is impossible. The veil between us and the supernatural realm is thin here, so they say, stretched out almost too far at the edge of the world. It's all liminal space, all of the Cap Sizun, perhaps all of Brittany. There are pockets where time moves differently, where old traditions are more real, where things not of the modern world still walk – the forests of Huelgoat and Brocéliande, the many islands in the gulf of Morbihan, the Monts d'Arrée where the bare bones of the world thrust through the earth, and here... most of all here, where stone and sky and sea meet in chaos and rage, where everything falls apart.'

His dark eyes searched hers, his voice rising and falling like a song. He didn't sound like the jaded, cynical businessman anymore. He sounded like a poet or a mystic, one of the ancient druids who once walked here. Like someone as old as time, someone who knew this land more intimately than anyone living had a right to.

Rafael had said his family was ancient and royal.

'The ends of the earth?' she whispered. 'Finistère.'

'Yes. That's why. The ends of the earth. But that's not all it is. Only one way of looking at it. A narrow, finite way. The Bretons call it Penn-ar-Bed. The Head of the World, where everything begins. Not the end at all.' He shook his head, as if trying to clear it. 'Forgive me, old stories, old legends, nothing more. But this is a place of legends. Of mysteries. That is all I mean.'

She drew in a ragged breath and forced the words out.

'I saw Simon. And you did too.'

'I saw something. It might have looked like Simon, but I don't think it was. Not entirely. You have to be careful, Ari. He's seen you now.'

'You called it Ankou. Out on the cliff.'

'Ready?' called Nico from the hall outside, snapping their attention back to the kitchen and the gîte, to the here and now, to reality.

Rafael gave that same sad smile, and lifted her hand to his

mouth, pressing a gentle kiss onto her knuckles. His hand was shaking, his lips were cold. 'I've got to go.'

He couldn't. Not without giving her an answer. 'But what is Ankou?'

For a moment, she thought he wouldn't answer and then she saw something else in his eyes. Sorrow. Such sorrow. Real fear. He believed now.

'A herald of death. My death, I suppose. The death of all the men of my line.'

CHAPTER ELEVEN

The morning light came through the gap in the curtains, playing across Ari's face. She hadn't slept, not well, not really, but her body didn't want to admit that or think about it. Never awake enough to get up and do something productive. Nor asleep enough to really rest. There had been nightmares, but she couldn't say what they were. It was just the lingering sense of horror, crawling back with the shadows, morning mist lifting with the sun.

Simon's face haunted her.

A box sat outside the bedroom door and she knew at once what it was. She'd dreaded seeing it. Because she already recognised some of the things in it. His notebooks, some photos taken in better times, papers, a couple of awards and certificates, and all the ephemera of a life cut short far too soon. Ari sat on the floor, staring in to it, unable to bring herself to touch anything. Not at first.

Finally, she pulled out a folder and opened it to reveal photocopies of articles, with his handwriting all down the side and threaded through the text. She scanned the first one – a travelogue about Sainte Sirène written in the sixties – and put it aside. The next one was a study of Ankou in folklore, and she stared at grainy images of the carvings from countless churches, the *danses macabres* painted on their walls. So he'd been researching Ankou as well. Of course he had.

Tears welled in her eyes as she reached for the notebook. His handwriting, sketches and maps spread out before her, filling the pages and trailing off the bottom and up the sides as it always did, because he always ran out of space when his thoughts ran away with him and he never had time to just turn the page like a normal—

She closed the book and some loose pages slipped out of the back.

Not his writing. Not this time. She didn't even know the language it was written in. It looked like some kind of code. Where had he found this? The paper was yellowish, old but not ancient. It had that high acidity of cheap early twentieth-century pages, and the edge of each one was ragged, as if it had been torn out of a notebook.

'What were you up to, Simon?' She sighed and carefully slid the loose pages into the back of the notebook again. She didn't want to think of last night, of the figure on the clifftops with his face.

Ari didn't look at the various photos of the two of them, smiling, arm in arm. She couldn't. It hurt too much, even now. She put the lid back on the box and left it on the desk.

Later. She would deal with it later. She'd have to. But not now.

Instead she went to the drawer beside the bed where she kept her most personal belongings. The letter was at the bottom, tear-stained and crumpled. She'd crushed it the first time she read it, then tried to flatten it out to read it again. His letter. His last letter.

Just one page. She didn't need to read it, not anymore, because the words were burned into her memory.

I've met someone else, here in Sainte Sirène. I was looking for the pathway to Ys, the chemin de l'eau. *I never meant for this to happen, and I have never wanted to hurt you. I cannot see you anymore. I've let the tide take me and surrendered to her. I am so very sorry.*

He had sent the pendant with it, the little carved bone disc, delicate as filigree, with a horse running on water, Morvarc'h, King Gradlon's horse, a gift from his enchantress wife from a land across the sea. Simon had always teased her that she was Irish too. So why had he sent it back? It was his.

At the bottom of the letter, there were numbers – 48065 4688 – just scrawled there, like an afterthought. She didn't know what they were or what they meant. He'd probably noted them down on the page as they occurred to him, or left them there from an earlier note. They were the least of her concerns.

When she had tried to ring Simon, he didn't answer, which seemed even more cruel, like he was avoiding her, letting her go to voicemail. Her calls went there directly and eventually she assumed he'd blocked her. It was brutal. Not like Simon at all. She couldn't believe it.

Then, a few days later, Jason had phoned with the news. She'd never said anything to him about the letter. There didn't seem any point once Simon was dead. No one else knew. She didn't want to taint anyone else's memory of him.

That was when she finally put the necklace on, her last memory of him, of the way he had been before, when they'd been happy, when he had been hers.

She folded the letter up carefully and put it away. As she had countless times. The same way she folded up her own pain and stored it in the back of her mind, tucked it away in the deepest part of her heart. If Simon could not be trusted, no one could. That had been her lesson. Perhaps she had been right to leave Brittany after all.

But last night, like a dream turned nightmare, he had been there.

She needed to talk to Rafael. She needed to find out what else he knew.

The house was empty. A note on the kitchen table from Nico said they'd be back this afternoon, after they had seen the team from the university at Brest. Ari had thought Jason wanted her present for that, but if she was completely honest, she was relieved they had gone without her.

Ari pulled on her running gear and headed out along the clifftops, letting the fresh breeze and sea air chase the cobwebs of nightmare away. Inexorably, her feet took her out to the cliff edge, to the Pointe de Castelmeur.

There was no sign of anything strange or untoward here this morning. No mysterious dark figures. No creatures of legend. She looked for the fissure into which she had fallen but now it was impossible to tell where that might have been.

She pushed her way through the narrow gap in the bushes, lifting her arms high to protect her face. It was like passing through an enchanted barrier, forcing her way through to the otherworld, travelling to Sleeping Beauty's castle or Rapunzel's tower.

On the other side, the world opened up in front of her. The sky was a vast dome, endless, shades of blue fading to the white of the clouds, layer upon layer of tones. The sea rose and fell like a great sleeping beast, peaceful now, not the wild storm-tossed thing of last night. She could see the distant shore of Crozon to the north, and further up, beyond that lay Le Conquet, and the islands of Molène and Ushant.

Sea birds wheeled and cried out overhead, their mournful song echoing across the water. Ari tried to steady her breath, focused on the horizon. She leaned against the rocky outcrop, grey with splashes of yellow and orange lichen, rising like enormous teeth from the ragged grass.

There was no one here now, no sign of anyone. Had she imagined it? Had the storm made her imagine...

But Rafael had seen it too. Him. They had both seen him. Recognised him.

There was nothing here now. It was peaceful. Heavenly.

She walked back slowly, letting the wind guide her. She didn't know where the path was going to lead her, but she was hardly surprised when she reached the village and in its centre the chapel of Sainte Sirène.

There was a plaque on the low wall surrounding it, stating it was restored in the 1970s but it originally dated back to the thirteenth century. It felt older, the grey stone looked like it had grown out of the ground, like the outcrop on the point. The huge oak tree sprawled over the wall beside the entrance, its roots burrowing through the rocks. To the left, there was a holy well, surrounded by its own low walls, and a little replica of the chapel itself over it. There were flowers everywhere, swaying in the breeze coming off the sea.

The red painted door stood ajar, so Ari pushed it and entered.

The interior was dark, light filtering through the stained-glass windows and sprawling across the grey slabs that made up the floor. The ceiling felt like the hull of a boat turned upside down and raised over her head, painted the pale blue of the sky and decorated here and there with white stars. The beams were carved with designs of fish, serpents and, yes, even eels. Ari suppressed a shudder.

It was a mariner's chapel, she realised, tied to the sea by its location and by the souls who had come here down all the long years. Intricate models of boats hung from the ceiling by almost invisible wires. An ancient tradition, one which asked for blessings on those boats, representing the real boats to which those same sailors entrusted their lives every day. She had seen it elsewhere in Western Brittany and always found it touching.

They were old too. Some of them looked truly ancient. She couldn't really see well in the darkness of the church.

'Hello, Ari Walker.' The soft voice came out of nowhere, her name musical when said in that accent.

She spun around, looking for the source.

It was Gwen, standing in the nave, by the bank of unlit candles laid out before a statue of the Virgin Mary.

'I'm sorry,' Ari said hurriedly, backing towards the door. 'I didn't mean to intrude.'

Gwen shook her head. 'Not at all. Everyone is welcome in here. That's what they say anyway. It's not normally open, of course, which makes it a bit more difficult in practice. Apart from high season. The tourists love it. The council lets me open it as part of the *musée*. And, of course, they get an on-site care-taker for free, so it's to their benefit as well. They're a frugal bunch.' Gwen chatted away brightly, as if they were old friends, even though they had only met the previous night.

She struck one of the long matches as she spoke and began to light candles, this in spite of a sign asking for a donation for each one. Ari frowned, watching her as the glow flickered and danced behind her, illuminating her, and the little church.

'Aren't those meant to be lit for prayers? For people who have... you know... passed.'

Gwen blinked, giving her a long and studied look before replying. 'Who says they aren't? Each and every one of them. I could never light enough candles for all those who have lost their lives to the Mer d'Iroise. I could burn all of Sainte Sirène to the ground and never approach the number. No one could.'

'Then why light the candles?'

'There's a *pardon*... a religious festival. That's why I'm opening the church today. And then the *fest noz* tonight. We all look forward to it. Besides...' she said, 'look up.'

Ari couldn't help but obey, tilting her head back, and what she saw stole the breath from her lungs with wonder.

The lambent light struck the ceiling, the blue transforming to moving water, the shadows thrown by the hanging models becoming ships tossed in the sea, a shadow puppet play.

'Magic, isn't it? Like standing at the bottom of the sea.' Gwen moved on to another bank of candles and began to light them too. Her feet didn't make a sound on the stone-flagged floor and Ari couldn't hear anything except her own breath. 'Do you think Ys looks like this? The sea for the sky? Candlelight for the sun? Do you think its people still walk its streets, look up and wish for the air again?'

Ys? Ari shook her head. She didn't want to think about Ys. 'It's just a story.'

Gwen gave her a long measured look. 'To you maybe. To us, the Sirènois, the people who come from this place, whose blood is in this land and in the sea, Ys is as real as anything on this earth. It always has been.'

'It's an Atlantis legend, a golden city, a place of wonders which was lost.'

Gwen laughed. 'Listen to yourself. Atlant-*Ys*. *Ys*. It all comes back to Ys.'

'But...' Ari drew in a shaky breath. Simon had said that. The same thing. *Atlant-Ys...* It shook her for a moment. She wasn't sure what Gwen was trying to draw her into, but she didn't like it. This was none of her business, and she seemed to know far too much about Ari's business. And she sounded far too much like Simon for comfort. Ari didn't want an argument, but facts were facts. 'Plato wrote about Atlantis in 360 BC. Ys is a medieval legend. It may have grown from the legend of Atlantis, but not the other way around.'

But Gwen was just smiling. 'Aren't you clever, Ariadne Walker. Sixth century AD, at most. Your brother could tell you, I'm sure. But that is just the story. And stories come from somewhere. They have roots in other tales, or real events. Simon could have elaborated, certainly. He knew all the stories, inside and out. He could meld them together in ways that revealed all their secrets. His family was always good at that. They stored away so many secrets. Simon was the last of them and he took his secrets with him.'

A chill passed through Ari as Gwen spoke of Simon. She had known him, then. The way she said his name, the stretching out of the first vowel to sound like *Sea*, the curtailed sound of the rest. Very musical, very French. So familiar, so fond. Intimate. Like she had been his fiancée instead of Ari.

A weird and creeping suspicion wound its way through Ari's body and she stared at Gwen, trying to see something, a hint, anything that might give her away.

'You knew him?'

Gwen smiled again. 'Of course I did. He talked about you all the time, how clever you were, how beautiful. He said he could sit for hours and just listen to you. You challenged him. He loved you so much. It was a tragedy when he passed.'

Passed. So simple a word.

Ari stood there frozen, her heartbeat throbbing in her head.

'I should go,' she whispered, not caring if Gwen heard her or not. She didn't want to be here anymore. The church was dark and cold, a place of the dead and lost souls. She didn't want to be here speaking of Ys or Simon or anything else.

'You should,' Gwen agreed. 'It would be better. Safer. Go back home, Ari Walker. You're waking things here that should be sleeping. Digging up things that should remain lost. You and your brother. You may have loved Simon, but that doesn't mean you should continue his quest. It's dangerous.'

A flame of anger licked up inside Ari's chest. 'What does that mean?' How dare she? How dare she say anything about Simon at all? She didn't know anything about their relationship, or anything about what Simon had meant to her or her to him. She didn't have a clue.

'Ys is not a prize to be won.'

'I don't think Ys is a prize.'

Gwen laughed, a thin dismissive sound. 'Your brother does. And he has that way of getting people to do his work for him, doesn't he? Just like Rafael. It will get more of them hurt. Bring more deaths. Some things are not meant to be disturbed.'

Ari shook her head. 'Jason and Rafael are nothing alike. They couldn't be more different.'

'You think so?' Her voice went strangely cold. 'I know the du Lacs of old. When they want something, they get it. They'll use anything and everything at their disposal to have their way. When you have a moment, come to the *petit musée* and I'll show you. Or, better yet, have a look in the graveyard. Look at the names. If they want to keep you here, they will. Ask any of the Poullains... Except you can't. They are all dead now.'

'No one is keeping me here.'

Gwen had the gall to look concerned. 'I'm trying to help you, you know?'

Ari was about to tell her that she'd leave whenever she wanted and not before, when her phone rang, a loud and jarring sound in the silent church. She jumped in surprise, couldn't help herself.

But Gwen didn't move. She just kept staring at Ari, like a statue herself, her pale skin and her long blonde hair drained of colour in the candlelight. Like the statue of Notre Dame des Naufragés on the Pointe du Raz, the pale statue of Mary gazing down in pity on the pleading shipwrecked sailor, but never offering to help.

Ari shook the idea aside and stepped out into the sunlight of the chapel grounds, answering the call as she did so, trying to ignore Gwen and her strangeness, trying not to think about Simon or the du Lacs. Or Jason for that matter. She didn't like any of this and the creeping feeling of being manipulated from all sides was overwhelming. Once again, she reminded herself that she should never have come back to Sainte Sirène. 'Hello?'

'Dr Walker? Professor Carmichael-Danbury here. Apologies for interrupting you, but we've just heard your incredible news. I wanted to assure you that there is no issue whatsoever at our end.'

What was her boss doing phoning her? What news? He'd always struck her as distant and somewhat pompous. Exactly the type of man you'd expect to be headmaster at a school like Gray's College. A self-important stuffed shirt, she'd called him once, carefully out of his hearing.

'Professor?'

'Call me Roger, my dear girl. Call me Roger.' He'd never sounded quite so friendly, or delighted with her. 'Why, the endowment of course. And such a generous one. You stay there as long as you need to. An expert like you is bound to be in demand. We always understood that.'

Stay as long as she needed to? She didn't *need* to. What on earth was he talking about? He sounded like a child in a toy shop.

'I'm not sure what you mean... sir.' No way she was calling him Roger, even if he invited it.

'The endowment means so much to the school. Several contracts can be made permanent and it opens up all kinds of scholarship opportunities. It will fully fund the new sports hall as well. The Classics department alone—'

'Sir, I'm sorry, I don't know what you're talking about. What endowment? What is going on?'

'The du Lac Foundation. Didn't they tell you? They want your continued input on the site at Sainte Sirène. As such, they've offered to reimburse us for your time and—'

Rafael. She'd told him she had to go back to work, and he'd... what? Bought her from them? How could he?

This wasn't happening. It couldn't be.

. . .

Ari stewed in her anger all morning, imagining marching over to his lordship's manor and telling him exactly what she thought of him. Or facing him down in front of his whole family. Or even showing up at his office in Paris and telling him right there, as all his employees and business associates looked on, what an arrogant, insufferable, control freak he was.

They probably already knew. Of course they did.

She'd seen Simon last night, Simon as Ankou, and Rafael had seen it too. He'd promised to help her work out what it meant, to figure out what had happened, but instead he was trying to run her life, manipulating everything to get his way. Not to help her. To trap her, just like Gwen had said. The du Lacs always got their way.

She ought to ring him. She ought to ring him and tell him where to stick his lunch and his endowment and his whole foundation.

Jason rang first. Over the moon. Beyond excited.

'We've got it. All the funding we need. Every last penny and then some.'

'What?'

'The funding. The du Lac Foundation. They're funding everything. They're dealing with the Ministry of Culture, and the subaquatic research people.'

Ari sank onto the bench outside the house where she had been pacing for the last hour like a deflated balloon.

Of course. This too.

She should have guessed. Rafael had said as much yesterday. Before the clifftops, before the madness...

'What about the university?'

'We don't need the university. Not now. Oh, I mean they'll want in on everything we find and any artefacts will have to be handed over, but we don't *need* them now. Not to do the excavations. Doubly lucky after this morning. Do you know they had the nerve to say the mask was modern? They just dismissed it. Can you believe it? But it doesn't matter now.'

Ari closed her eyes and fought the tears sizzling behind the lids. It felt like needles were being driven into her sinuses.

If they want to keep you here, they will. Ask any of the Poullains.

Jason went on, either not noticing her silence or taking it for assent. 'He wants us to head it up, you and me, kiddo. It's going to be brilliant. I told him about your job, but he said he'd sorted it. Isn't it great?'

'Oh God,' she whispered, fighting the pounding in her head. She felt like throwing up. Her head swam and she couldn't quite catch her breath. She was going to be trapped here, unable to leave until Rafael du bloody Lac said she could.

Just like Gwen had said.

'We're going to celebrate tonight. All the champagne. Or cider. Something bubbly anyway. Nico's ringing around everyone who ever worked with us, getting them back here. This is going to be fantastic, Ari. You just wait and see. We'll make them eat their words.'

She wondered what words had been said to Jason this morning at the university, what belittling, thoughtless, disrespectful words...

And then Rafael has swooped in to the rescue with all his money.

If she refused and left anyway, would he pull the funding after all? It would break Jason's heart. He'd blame her. She knew he would.

If they want to keep you here, they will.

The car barely made a sound as it turned off the road and made its way along the dirt track to the house. Ari looked up. Black, sleek, expensive, there was no one else it could belong to.

Rafael.

'I've got to go,' she told Jason. 'Rafael just arrived.'

He let out a hoot of delight. 'Tell him we're on the way back. If he needs anything, *anything*—'

She didn't want to think about what he was implying there.

She hung up as she rose to her feet, ready to confront him.

Only the fire had drained out of her now. The ebbing rage had just left her nauseated, her stomach roiling and bitter, twisting in on itself.

Rafael got out of the car, as sleek and refined as the vehicle itself even though he was casually dressed. It made no difference. The black jeans hugged his legs and the T-shirt made him look like a film star. How did he do that? With just a T-shirt.

'Did you forget about lunch?' he asked, taking in her running gear.

'Did you forget that you don't own me and I am not for sale?' she snapped back.

For a moment it was almost comical, the look on his face, the surprise in his eyes. His mouth opened, but he didn't seem to know what to say, which had to be a first.

She stood there, hands on her hips, waiting.

'Ah,' he said at last. 'I wanted to talk to you first.'

She waved the phone at him. 'The wonders of technology beat you to it.'

'Please let me explain.' He spread his arms wide as he spoke, his voice entirely calm. Like he was trying to pacify a wild animal. Well, she was more than ready to bite right now.

'I don't think there's anything to explain. I've been losing my mind about what we saw last night, on the cliffs, I have no idea what happened and then today... you just tried to buy me? Twice?'

'It's not like that. I was going to ask, I promise. But I had to act fast. I wanted everything in place first. I need your help, Ari.'

'So you can just dictate my life? Is that how you operate?'

'I would never try to do that,' he replied. 'I promise. But I still need you. Especially after last night.'

'You can't buy people, Rafael.'

A smile twitched across his handsome face, sad, tragic, and all too knowing. 'I love that you still believe that,' he murmured. There was a sorrow beneath the words though, a grim knowledge that gave her pause. 'But we come from very different worlds. Clearly. I'm offering to fund your brother's work and to ensure that the school you work for are more than compensated *if* you chose to stay here. I'm trying to make it all go as smoothly as possible. That's all. I'll do whatever it takes. Just tell me what you need and I will do it.'

A thousand answers flooded her mind, none of them good enough. Some were downright impossible, and more than a few were physiologically unlikely.

He was desperate. She could see that in the depths of his dark eyes. The strain around them made her frown. There was something she was missing. Something that was driving him that she didn't know, something far more important to him than all the riches in the world, something he couldn't afford to lose. He would do anything.

It hit her with such a force, she couldn't deny it. He was scared. Alone. Facing the impossible. But last night they had faced it together.

'Gwen tried to warn me about you, about this. She said I should just leave.'

He gave a snort of laughter. 'That sounds like Gwen.'

There was clearly history between the two of them. Ari didn't know what had gone on between them in the past. Didn't want to know either.

'I thought you didn't believe any of this, your family curse and all that.'

She might well have slapped him, he looked so surprised. 'After last night? How can you ask that?'

It was a fair question. She was still reeling from it all herself. At least, she thought, he wasn't denying it or trying to find some rational explanation for what they had seen. Some part of her, she realised, had been terrified he would say it never happened, that it was imagination and they had not seen Simon or Ankou or whatever the hell it was. At least there was this. And yet...

'You aren't telling me something.'

He leaned back against the car, deflated, broken, his gaze fixed firmly on the ground. His shoulders slumped down and for a moment she thought he'd just slide down into the dirt. 'I *didn't* believe in it. I did as a child, but it's been a long time since then. I thought my great-aunt was going senile. I came back here to move her to a home, if that was what it was going to take. I may not have wanted to, but that was what I expected. I... I didn't want it to be true. Ari?' He looked up, his expression pleading with her. No, not just with her. With life, with destiny, with everything. 'I know what I saw last night. Ankou is the harbinger of death, his servant. He takes the form of someone who dies before their time – by drowning or suicide or murder. Or they become the Ankou. It's old magic, as old as time. There's a local tale that Ankou and Dahut were lovers once, that he taught her magic and gave her the mask. But I know what seeing him means for us. And after that... it changes everything. I will do whatever it takes, even throw my lot in with your brother and his schemes. My great-aunt believes that we can break the curse by finding Ys, by saving it from slipping into half-remembered myths. I cannot take the risk that it is all true, that I will die within a month, like my father and all those who went before me. I cannot let it happen. Because if this curse takes me as well... Ari, I have a son. And if it takes me, he will be next.'

CHAPTER TWELVE

In the end, Ari fell back on centuries of well-known Irish tradition which dictated what to do in a crisis and made a large pot of tea. Rafael paced the kitchen while she worked, but eventually gave up and sat down at the table. The same table they had sat at last night. Where Jason had shown him the mask.

He wondered where it was now. Off to Brest with Ari's brother, he supposed. Being prodded and poked, locked away. Probably for the best. The thought of it on Ankou's face made him shudder. But when he'd removed it to reveal Simon Poullain, that was far worse.

Ari slid a mug in front of him, strong, brown, builder's tea, they called it. He recalled his mother turning her nose up at the idea of it: 'They have no idea how to make thé properly on those islands. They think they do, but really...' He winced as he tasted it, but he drank it all the same. Strangely, it helped.

'So you have a son,' she said at last. 'And now you believe the curse is true, so you need to protect him.'

'Yes.' There didn't seem to be much more to say than that.

She nodded, drank her own tea and picked her question carefully. 'Where is he?'

'With his mother. I phoned her last night to check on him. He was fine. Sleeping. He's only three. She wasn't impressed. But I couldn't tell her why I needed to know.'

That was why he had left so abruptly with Nico last night, unable to find the words to explain it to her there and then. He'd wanted to get home, somewhere private, so he could phone and check on his son. And Elena had thought he was crazy. 'Of course he's OK. He's sleeping. He's worn out, the poor love. He had a busy day. What on earth has gotten into you?'

He became aware that he had clenched his hands into fists again and purposefully uncurled them, stretching out his fingers.

'Finish the tea,' Ari told him calmly, watching his every move. 'You haven't bought her off then.'

That was like a slap to the face. He glared at her sharply. 'I'm not a monster.'

Ari just raised her eyebrows at him, her meaning perfectly clear. She still thought he had tried to buy her cooperation. Damn, he had mishandled that like an amateur. He'd have to explain... somehow...

But 'I saw you save me in my dream' didn't seem like the kind of explanation she would accept. Especially not now. Nor would 'Your late fiancé is death incarnate' work either. No wonder everyone thought his great-aunt was losing her mind. They would say the same thing about him soon enough.

He sighed, turning his thoughts instead to Elena and how she would laugh at the thought of him attempting to buy her off: 'Pocket money, Rafael, chéri.' He raked his hand through his hair, pushing it back against his skull. His mother always told him he'd make himself bald. He knew he did that when he was stressed. Looking at Ari Walker, still watching him with those blue eyes, she knew that too. She was intuitive, clever. She watched people.

'Elena's family has more money than God. She'd laugh in my face if I tried. Besides, we have an understanding, and an excellent custody agreement. We're good friends and Elena is a devoted mother.'

'You didn't marry her? I thought families like yours—'

It was his turn to give her a quizzical look. This should be good. 'Like mine?'

She looked away, uncomfortable to be caught in an assumption. Or in the thought of him marrying. Interesting. 'Aristocracy is all about marriage and money, isn't it? Business empires even more so.'

He grinned. He couldn't help it. The simmer of annoyance in her face only amused him further. 'Well, I imagine Elena's *wife* might have something to say about that.'

'Oh,' she replied. And drank her tea again. But then a smile pulled at the corner of her mouth. Acceptance. Less anger now. She lifted a sardonic eyebrow. 'How very French of you.'

He fixed her with his great-aunt's glare. Or at least his best approximation of it. 'I'll have you know, I'm Breton to the core.'

She laughed this time, enjoying the ridiculous nature of the conversation, and suddenly Rafael felt more comfortable sharing this secret with her. There were precious few others who knew and he wanted to keep it that way.

'So your son lives with Elena and her wife and you see him on holidays?'

'Something like that. They're in Tuscany at the moment, so that does make it a little more difficult. But we're working it out. Elena came up with the proposition and I thought... I don't know. She's a friend. I haven't shared it with my family. Can you imagine?'

She clearly couldn't, but he could. His mother alone would be a nightmare. The corporate lawyers she would drag in, the paternity tests, the legal knots she'd get them into, not to mention the trouble she would cause with Elena and the knock-on effects with her family... He suppressed a shudder.

And yet he could tell Ari Walker as easily as opening his mouth.

'And you believe in your family curse now? Because you have a son.'

'I know how it sounds. Accidents happen, people died, but there was always a logical reason behind them. A boating tragedy, someone swimming in strange waters, even a car crash on a wet road. Nothing to do with an ancient curse. I always thought that. Now though... after last night...'

Now he was afraid, he couldn't deny it. Now he had something to lose, someone to lose. If it was just himself, he might risk it. But not Georges. He could never risk Georges.

Ari nodded slowly, her empathy etched on her features. She understood. He had that much. She might not forgive him for going behind her back, but still, the reason was comprehensible to her. 'You could have asked first. Rather than just throwing money at the problem.'

'It's an occupational hazard,' he admitted. 'I apologise. I meant to speak to you first. The sequencing of things just went badly wrong.'

'Sequencing,' she murmured, clearly finding that less impressive. 'Well, at least you've paid for me to have an extended holiday, I suppose. I might still leave. Take myself off somewhere else...'

'And you could. But I don't think you will.'

'Won't I?' She finished her tea and put the mug down on the table loudly. A challenge.

'You like a mystery.'

She snorted and pushed herself up to stand over him. 'Well, we'll see. I'm going to get changed and then you can take me out to lunch.'

'It's too late for lunch. Most restaurants will be closing until this evening now. You're in rural Brittany. Unless we go to one of the tourist restaurants, we aren't going to find much decent until seven now. Unless you know someone.'

She cast him another arch look. They were becoming familiar. And strangely addictive. Each one gave him a thrill of delight. 'I guess that means you do. All right, Mr Millionaire. Throw some money at that instead.'

The restaurant he chose was in the heart of Tréboul overlooking the pleasure port and Île Tristan across the mouth of the Pouldavid estuary and Port Rhu. Two out of three of the main ports of Douarnenez wasn't bad value when it came to the view, Rafael thought. He didn't count the commercial port. No one wanted to look at that.

Part restaurant, part café, part gallery, he had attended an exhibition here not so long ago and bought several paintings to donate to local galleries. Anonymously, of course. Not that anonymous actually meant much around here. They knew who he was. When he phoned to arrange this, he casually dropped his name and the poor girl almost dropped the phone.

A private lunch was hastily arranged and Rafael smiled to himself as Ari took in the chic surroundings and agreed that it was lovely. He ordered an entrecôte and she chose seabass. As they waited, she tore at one of the pieces of soft, fluffy baguette.

She seemed particularly taken with one of the paintings of the island. Perhaps he should buy it for her. Would that be too much? Probably. He was treading a fine line with her. Money didn't seem to be a lure, which surprised him, a pleasant surprise. She teased him about it certainly, but the ability to spend large amounts of it to get his way did not impress her. Quite the opposite, he feared. She found it vulgar and having seen more than enough of that behaviour all his life, he had to agree.

She was still wary of what he had done, his motivations. He understood that. He had made an unholy mess of this. He was lucky she was still willing to talk to him.

Pity, he suspected.

And lurking between them were all the unanswered questions of what they had both seen last night, the ghost of Simon Poullain, or Ankou, the curse of Dahut and Ys. All those questions they couldn't bring themselves to approach head on. Not yet.

'What's it called? The island?' Ari asked.

'Île Tristan,' he replied. 'It is the resting place of Tristan and Iseult. Somewhere over there, two trees grow entwined over the lovers' grave. And in the fifteen hundreds, the pirate Guy Éder de la Fontenelle had his stronghold there.'

'Another place of legend.'

'It even has connections with Ys. Douarnenez means the land of the island. Some say that's all that remains of the great city.'

'Not Jason,' she replied.

No, not Jason. Not her late fiancé either, but Rafael had more sense than to bring that up right now.

'Was the pirate another one of your ancestors?' she asked, valiantly changing the subject for him.

He laughed. 'No. Although my ancestors were involved in his eventual capture. They say he killed 1,500 people in one day. La Fontenelle, they called him. The Bretons had a less poetic name for him – Ar Bleiz. It means the Wolf.'

'Scary,' she teased. 'Your own big bad wolf.'

Their food arrived. Thanking the waitress, Rafael poured glasses of water for them both. He didn't drink during the day by habit. He preferred to keep a clear head. Now more than ever.

She tasted the fish and he watched her as she did, her eyes closing with pleasure, her lips drawing up to a smile. She gave a little sound of delight and it was all he wanted to hear. She hid nothing, Ari Walker. She was like fresh air in his life. He hadn't realised how much he needed that.

'Good?' he asked.

'So good. How's the steak?'

He hadn't tasted it yet, but now he did. Perfectly *saignant*, rather than merely rare. Just the way he liked it and cooked to perfection. The chef here was just getting better and better. 'Very good,' he told her.

She speared two of the frites in the bowl beside his plate before he knew what she was doing. He loved watching her eat, he realised. She did so with relish. 'So what happened to the Wolf?'

'La Fontenelle? He was executed in Paris. He was implicated in a plot with Spain.'

'Convenient.'

She had a point. The people of Cap Sizun had wanted rid of him, high and lowborn alike. 'He was broken on the wheel, the punishment for highwaymen and robbers, rather than traitors, so who knows?'

Ari grimaced at the thought of all that such an execution entailed. 'We have such charming dinner conversations,' she told him solemnly. 'The final resting place of doomed lovers and gruesome executions of murdering pirates. Whatever will we do for coffee?'

He wanted to say that she'd steered the conversation that way with her questions, but self-preservation held his tongue. 'What would you like to talk about then?'

That was the question. She paused, thinking it over.

'Last night, I suppose.'

Ah yes, there it was. The thing they had been skirting around all day.

She put her fork down with a clatter that jarred them both and echoed around the silent restaurant. 'Was it really Simon?'

'Why don't we finish our meal first?' he suggested. Not to put her off. Not really. The food was just too good and it seemed a shame to put the restaurant staff to all this trouble only to leave the meal half finished.

They ate in silence after that and he half wished he had never said anything. Skipping dessert, they each had a *petit café crème* while the bill was calculated. A paltry sum, really, for all the trouble he had put them to. He paid without hesitation, adding a generous tip.

They walked down the hill, past the quays and the marina, to the path which led, through gentle woodland, to the blue-painted pedestrian bridge, the Passerelle Jean Marin. The centre was open to allow a yacht entrance to Port Rhu, and they had to wait, the soft breeze worrying her copper-coloured hair, the sunlight painting it with gold. He tried not to watch her too closely, but it was impossible. She drew his attention like a flame. She leaned against the rail, staring at the island with its dense woodland, the stately white buildings of the former cannery, now the headquarters of the Parc Naturel Marin d'Iroise. The people who worked there guarded the sea in this region, the precious marine environment, the very place where Ys could still be hidden. He still had some red tape to sort out there, but no doubt another donation would solve it. He'd worry about that later. He'd worked with them on a number of environmental projects before and there was a lot of goodwill both ways.

'It's an oasis,' she murmured.

'You can walk there at low tide.' He glanced down at the high water beneath them. 'But not today, I fear. I can arrange a boat, if you would like.'

She looked tempted for a moment, then shook her head. Which left them with nothing else to say.

Apart from all the things they needed to say. They had put it off as long as they could.

'Last night,' he began and the bridge began to lower again, releasing them to the other side of the estuary. It was almost like one of those awful conversations when you'd had too much to drink and fallen into bed together. Except that would have been easy in comparison. 'I'm not superstitious.'

'I know that. Neither am I. I'm not mad either.' Well, someone had to say it. Of course she would be the brave one. 'He had Simon's face. But it wasn't Simon, was it?'

'I don't know,' he replied. That was the problem, wasn't it? 'We could ask Mémé, but I...'

'You don't want to upset her,' she finished for him, understanding immediately. He was grateful for that. Her empathy was a godsend.

They had reached the point where the road curved around, where the slip led to the island. At low tide, there was a path which he had walked many times as a child, but it was deep underwater now. Lost, drowned. Like so much else in his life. The steps and handrail vanished into the water.

On the side of the slip, the mosaic of an eye glared back at him, one of those stylised creations you saw more commonly in the Med. He wondered who had put it there and when. And why? An art project probably.

Perhaps more people needed protection from the sea than just him.

'So Tristan and Iseult are buried over there?'

'That's what the stories say. But as legends go, it's a relatively modern one. Perhaps there's a seed of truth at the heart of it. Who knows?'

'Archaeology has found many things based on stories, myths, legends handed down through generations,' said Ari. 'Troy for one. And Nineveh. Biblical archaeology is basically dependent on the idea. The Viking settlements in Vinland were thought to be legendary for years, but look at the discoveries in Newfoundland. And they found Richard III under a car park by tracing the friary where he was said to have been buried. Why not Ys? That's Jason's theory.'

Rafael knew this was her area of study, the subject of her doctorate. He'd looked it up, even started reading it online, although, if he was honest, it was probably beyond him. But she was an expert and right now he needed all the help he could get. He could see the moment she decided to change the subject, to veer away from mentioning Simon and reliving the pain all over again. But she couldn't escape it entirely. Not now.

'So, Ankou. That's who we apparently saw, right? Tell me about him.'

Ankou, not Simon. It was much easier if it was Ankou. Better the Servant of Death, than her dead love. Understandable. The thought tripped him up, and almost drew a bitter laugh he didn't dare release. She'd never forgive him.

'He collects the souls of the dead, takes them in his boat to the underworld.'

'Why did he look like Simon?' Her voice broke as she said his name and Rafael felt a sudden fierce urge well up inside him to protect her, to comfort her.

But it wasn't his place.

And the man whose place it was…

No… answer the question. That was what she was waiting for. Not sympathy which would unmask her pain. Answers.

'Mémé says that Ankou often takes the face of a lost soul, the first death of the season or the last of the previous—'

'But he didn't die this season, or last. It's been two years.'

He didn't respond to the snap of her voice. It was purely defensive. 'He could simply be one of those lost at sea, unburied… I don't know how it works, Ari. Ankou is a lost soul, who helps lost souls. That's all I know. I'm sorry.'

She shook her head, clearly annoyed with herself. But he saw something else there, a glimmer of understanding perhaps.

'His ashes were scattered in the bay. That was what he wanted. Go on.'

It wouldn't do to press her on it just now, he could tell. He was certainly not going to go into the idea that he was a suicide or a murder victim. Her grief was still there, just beneath the surface, and he didn't want to bring it back up. 'He sails the *Bag Noz*, the boat of the night, or sometimes drives a wagon. When they brought the train here, the locals were afraid of the noise, and said it was Ankou coming for them. Some say each parish has its own Ankou. Perhaps he's ours. Sainte Sirène's, I mean. But all the stories agree that while he protects the dead, he's an ill omen for the living.'

'So we're extra lucky to see him then.'

He snorted out a laugh at her sarcasm. 'Yeah. Something like that.'

'And how does he tie into Ys?'

'He doesn't. Unless he was walking the streets there that night. He's an old legend, older than Ys, as old as mankind, a tale to be told around the fire and frighten the children. Or at least that's what I thought he was. But... but there is another story, not commonly known. The book I showed you implies that once he was Dahut's lover. That he gave her the mask and taught her magic.'

Ari didn't reply at first. He watched as she tightened her hand into a fist and then uncurled it again. She opened her mouth to say something, then thought better of it and decided on another question instead. 'Is there a way to find him?'

'To find Ankou? Are you mad? Didn't you see him?'

She stared at the island, her eyes dangerous, and her voice was suddenly cold. 'Yes. I saw him. And I think... Rafael, he had the mask. Last night. He was wearing it and then he took it off to reveal Simon's face. And he didn't want me there, did he? Because I'd recognise him. That's why he pushed me aside beforehand. He wanted you, wanted you to see him and see the mask. And the mask is now as good as new. I think... the two have to be connected. Don't you think?'

'Maybe?' He didn't know what to think. But she was slotting everything into place so quickly that he wasn't sure he really wanted her to get to the end of that particular path. He didn't like the dark and dangerous places it was leading. But he knew they would have to go there if they were to solve this.

'There's something about the Pointe de Castelmeur. What does the name mean? It doesn't sound French.'

'It isn't. It's Breton. Castel is castle, or fortress and...' His words dried up as he said it. He'd never thought about it before. Not like this.

'And *meur?*'

He grimaced. 'Great, or big. The Great Castle.'

'There's no castle there though.'

'There's the oppidum. That might have been... well, not a castle, but a stronghold. It had walls of sorts.'

It was a pile of rocks, some earthen banks. It was hardly a castle.

She hummed to herself. He could see it now, the way her mind worked. Like her brother, but so much better. A new Schliemann, tracking down the legendary city. Only instead of a copy of *The Iliad*, she had no more than a smattering of local legends.

'He was right at the end of the point, above the little rocky island, the one that looks like it was broken in two. Like he was showing it to us. What do you call that?'

He didn't remember mentioning it, to be honest. 'It doesn't have a name on the maps. It's too small, insignificant really. Like Sainte Sirène. But the locals call it Îlot d'Or. The little island of gold.'

She savoured that idea, rolled it around in that brilliant mind of hers.

'*D'or*? If it was French, that's gold, sure. But the locals speak Breton, or used to...'

The other place names were Breton, or based on Breton words. Why not this one? Because he didn't want it to be. Not now. He swallowed on his suddenly parched throat. 'It means an entrance.'

'Or gates? Like the gates of Ys?'

'That's a leap,' he murmured dubiously.

She wasn't listening. 'We need to go back. I need to see a map. And those scans of the seabed. And the photos we took.'

'Ari, I think you might be making some assumptions here that—'

She grabbed his hand, pulling him after her as she headed back towards the bridge. 'You wanted me to look into all of this, to work for you, didn't you? Well, try to keep up, Rafael, because this is exactly what we're doing. I mean to make sure you get your money's worth. Like it or not.'

CHAPTER THIRTEEN

'Good God, Ari, it looks like a bomb went off in here.'

Jason was one to talk. She'd seen his workspaces and the debris he left in his wake. He made a mess wherever he went. The outrage in his voice broke the spell of concentration surrounding her. She'd been completely immersed, the print-outs spread across the floor in the living room. Alix and Lina, who had been relaxing there, had taken their tea and fled. She'd zoomed in on the sonar images on the laptop and didn't remember the last time she had even blinked. Rafael had dropped her back, but she hadn't invited him in. It might be his money, but he was distracting, and right now she didn't need to be distracted. If he wanted answers, he'd have to let her do this her way. Work was good. Work let her ignore the madness. It stopped her thinking about Rafael. And Ankou. And Simon.

Lunch with Rafael had been a revelation. She'd seen another side of him. When he talked about Tristan and Iseult, about the legends of this coast, and his family history... there was a passion in him she had not expected. He'd inspired her.

The only person who had ever understood her so well, who had made her feel that way, was Simon. At least, he had once.

Before she left him here and he found someone else. When Simon had been the one to tell her stories.

She couldn't invite Rafael into that space. It was Simon's still. Rafael could tell her all the tales he wanted about Ankou and Death incarnate, but she knew who she had seen. He had been real. If only for a moment.

Simon loved to watch her work. He'd let her get on with it. Or worked alongside her, silent and just as enthralled as she was.

Jason, not so much. She was aware of him now, pacing, watching, looking for her attention.

'Where have you been?' she asked, blinking at him. She had no idea what time it was or how long she'd been at this. Her body ached from sitting in the same position.

'Driving back from Brest. We stopped for lunch. We were celebrating. Are you here on your own? Where's everyone else?'

The house was deserted. So was the garden. The washing machine hummed away somewhere in the utility room. She hadn't realised everyone had gone.

'Out, I think. Surfing or something... Jason, what happened? You said they didn't believe you.'

'Well,' he replied with a laugh which always heralded the start of a story with him. Nico came in behind him, his face altogether more solemn. 'They thought we were trying to pull a fast one, of course. They wouldn't even look at the evidence. Just the mask itself. They said it's clearly modern, wouldn't deign to examine it properly. The prof told us the coin is a fluke and we ought to stop messing around like amateurs. *Amateurs!*' To her surprise, he shrugged. 'But then I got the phone call about Rafael's cash. It was glorious.'

Carefully, Ari circled a point on the sonar and deliberately avoided making eye contact. 'Rafael's money came to the rescue in the nick of time then?'

'It certainly makes things much easier, doesn't it? And think about it, Ari. We don't need to have them breathing down our necks anymore. He's promised to take care of everything. He can stand there and let them insult him, if they dare. University or not, they have blinkers on. They don't care, and they won't care until we find something they cannot refute. Damn, I'm hungry. Do we have anything for dinner?'

'I thought you'd eaten.' But she knew the answer to that. Her brother was always hungry. He could go out for a six-course meal and still stop for chips on the way home.

'That was ages ago. I'll lock this up first.'

He stalked off with the box containing the mask.

She glanced at the clock. It was almost eight. When had it got so late?

Ari looked over at Nico, met his concerned gaze. 'Was it that bad at the university?'

'It was awful,' he groaned. 'I actually thought he was going to punch someone. Their head of department told him, to his face, mind, that he's a charlatan. And then, right in front of her, he got the call from du Lac's people. All he could wish for. Then their legal team phoned her and the shit really hit the fan. We had a front-row seat. It was horrible.'

Ari gave him a solemn look. 'But gratifying?'

He held his thumb and forefinger up with a tiny gap between them. 'Just a bit. I think we all could have done without your brother's gloating though. After all his claims of professionalism, it was not a good look. The celebratory lunch was lovely though. You know what he's like when he thinks he's finally won.' He sighed then, looking at the sprawl of papers and the glow of the laptop illuminating her face. 'You've been busy.'

She pinched the bridge of her nose, trying to dispel the headache that had lodged there and was suddenly blossoming. Nothing to do with Jason's return. Or at least she hoped not.

'I had a brainwave. Well, I was talking to Rafael and... I

thought I might as well do what Rafael is paying for as quickly as possible so I can get back to my life.'

'Did he tell you what he was planning to do? The financing?'

'Oh no,' she said brightly, because that was the only way she could handle it right now. 'I had the pleasure of my school ringing me to say how delighted they were he was buying my services. And then he finally told me. When he turned up. Anyway, it doesn't matter now.'

But Nico wasn't put off by that. 'What did you say to him?'

'Nothing,' she lied.

Nico did not look convinced. 'He just decided to fund everything? Just like that? You know what Jason thinks, don't you?'

She gave him a flat look. She did not like the implication. 'Jason would be wrong.'

And if he said it to her directly, she would go through him for a shortcut. He knew better than to do that. He'd just drop sly hints and say it to everyone else. There wasn't much she could do to contradict him except plead her innocence.

She wasn't about to tell them what really happened last night, their encounter with Ankou, Rafael's curse, or his son. None of this was Jason's business and he would only make things so much worse if he knew any of it.

'OK then,' Nico replied carefully. He knew the two of them too well. He knew what the looks meant. 'Are you sure you're OK? You look a bit...'

'What, Nico?'

'Manic?'

She shook her head, defeated, and the rising anger dissipated a little. 'I need a break. Do we have wine?'

He laughed. 'Where do you think we are? Of course we have wine.'

'Better yet,' said Jason, arriving back in, 'there's a *fest noz* on in the village. We should go. Lina texted. They've all headed down there. Tried to tell Ari here, but she was too engrossed in what she was doing.'

She vaguely remembered someone coming in and wittering on about a party, but she'd been busy. Gwen had mentioned a *fest noz* that night, a local festival, with live music and traditional dancing, like a céilí. It was usually accompanied by food and a fairly large quantity of wine, beer and spirits. Simon had loved them. It made him feel like he was touching his roots, he'd told her once.

'Come on,' her brother said. 'We're going out. You look like you need some air. You've got crazy eyes.'

Charming.

'I really don't want to.'

'Can you actually focus properly right now?' he asked, his voice gentler all of a sudden. And this was the Jason she knew and loved. Not the adventurer, not the chancer. Her brother. And he knew her too well. 'You need a break, little sister. You're meant to be on holiday.'

Was she? She wasn't aware that he knew what a holiday was. And hadn't he invited her here to work? 'But I think I'm close to something here,' she protested.

For a moment, she thought he might lean in and join her, that he'd be sucked into this madness as thoroughly as she was. It was his madness after all. But something had changed. Jason looked relaxed for the first time in months, like he wasn't pulling all the weight of this great endeavour by himself anymore. He reminded her of the way he'd been with Simon by his side.

Ari almost fancied she saw a trace of Simon in him, like a ghost drifting around the edges.

The thought of ghosts, and Simon, made her shiver. Of course, her brother saw it.

'Take a break, squirt,' Jason said softly, and his concern showed on his face. 'That's an order.'

Music filled the little square outside the chapel, bright and melodic, call-and-response songs, merry reels and sea shanties. The musicians played a long oboe-like instrument, a set of small bagpipes, and drums, all lit by firelight. It was the kind of music that dug its way into Ari's chest and beat there alongside her heart. There was a harpist as well, a woman with long, delicate fingers which seemed to dance over the strings. No concert harp this. It was a Celtic harp, based on ancient designs, and it sounded like water rippling through the air.

Whirling groups of dancers filled the space in front of them, forming up in lines, breaking apart, laughing, singing, living every moment. Somewhere, someone was roasting a whole pig over a fire, with potatoes cooking in the embers, and the wine was flowing.

Ari clutched her paper cup and moved around the edge of the crowd. Thierry was there, right in the heart of the dancers. He spun towards her, his hand outstretched, trying to get her to join in, but she just laughed and stepped back. Jason was already in the thick of it. He knew everyone here by their first name anyway, fitting himself in to the community with an ease she couldn't help but envy. He always had done.

Madalen, Lina and several other girls were singing the refrain, gathered around the tables outside the bar, their voices high and clear in the night's air. It was heady and exhilarating. They beckoned her over to join them, but she really didn't belong here.

Ari retreated, looking for a way to fade back into the shadows. Parties were not her thing. Jason should know that. Once upon a time, they might have been bearable, but without Simon, without his easy charm and love of life, she just felt lost.

So lost.

The cold weight of grief closed itself around her again.

As she wandered down the narrow cobbled street, she found her vision blurring, her eyes stinging yet again. This had been his home once. Before he lost his parents, before he moved away. But he had never stopped dreaming about it. He'd never stopped loving it. Even when they'd been in college together, all those years he lived abroad, he always talked about it. You could hear the love in his voice. When he had eventually moved back here, it was like he finally relaxed.

A true Sirènois.

She paused, a thought niggling at her. This place couldn't have been called Sainte Sirène originally. That was a French name too, wasn't it? And, come to that, she strongly doubted the du Lac family had borne that name all those years ago. Why had they changed it? And what had the original been?

Rafael might know. Or Madame du Lac...

Folklore often lingered in names. In Irish, it was *dindshenchas*, the lore of the place, and many of their legends began with the details of why a place bore a certain name and the stories that had named it.

High walls loomed out of the darkness. The cemetery. She'd walked out beyond the edge of the village and it was dark here. If she'd wanted to get lost and avoid other people, she was doing a bloody good job of it. She leaned against the high metal gates, her forehead pressed against the cold black curls and twists. She expected it to be locked, but to her surprise, the gate opened.

On the other side, in the darkness, a host of little lights twinkled, like Christmas lights. She stepped inside, following them. They hovered over gravestones and vanished as she approached. There was just enough light to read the names on those graves as she passed. Kerdaniel, Heussaff, Pascal, Poullain...

Ari sucked in a breath and the air was cold as it filled her lungs. It formed mist in front of her face as she breathed out. And through that mist, she saw a figure.

He stood by a crypt in the centre of the graveyard, a huge ornate thing, grey and cold, a tiny fortress with the name du Lac carved over the sealed door. Almost as if he was waiting for her. As if he had called her and she had come, unable to resist.

He wore the same black coat and hat as last night, his long white-blond hair whipping around his face, even though there was no storm now, no wind or rain. And he had never had hair like that. Not while he was alive.

But this time there was no mask. It was Simon.

Unmistakably, irrefutably, Simon.

It shouldn't be. He hadn't been buried here. He shouldn't be here at all. They had done exactly as he requested. He'd been cremated and his ashes scattered at sea, in the bay. Jason and Nico had seen to everything. He didn't have any living family. He had been alone in the world, he had said, before he found her.

But his family could be here, she realised. Here in these neat and regimented rows, surrounded by the high walls, in the heart of Sainte Sirène.

'Simon?' she whispered.

He didn't move. His face didn't alter, but she sensed the hardening in him, the disquiet that rippled through the air around him. She knew it wasn't Simon. Not really. Not anymore.

And yet it was.

'Simon,' she said again, more insistently. She would name him. If whatever she was looking at would insist on wearing his face, it could stand to hear his name and wear that too. The simmering rage inside her demanded it.

He opened his mouth in a snarl, an expression Simon had never worn, all those teeth on display, and Ari took an inadvertent step back, but stopped herself running. Behind her, the gate slammed closed with a clang of metal and she bumped into it. Nowhere else to go.

Deep silence swept over them both. She couldn't hear the music anymore, or the sounds of merriment from the crowd at the *fest noz*. Not even distantly. All she could hear was the sea.

The Ankou swept forward, the long black coat flying out like a cloak behind him, until he stood right in front of her. The cold air around him enveloped her and he looked down into her face. 'You shouldn't be here, Ariadne Walker.' His voice was very soft, little more than a whisper.

'What are you?'

'You know the answer to that.'

'Why, Simon?'

He smiled, a knowing languid expression. It wasn't kind. 'Why not?'

Because she had loved him. Because he would never behave in this way. Because...

Because he had betrayed her. She caught the pendant with her cold fingers and squeezed, feeling the carved surface dig into her skin.

'Simon...'

'Simon is dead. Gone. You know that. Lost. You should let go. Ari...' And something flickered in his eyes, something she finally did recognise, a trace of him still there. 'It's not safe here. You need to go.'

She reached out one shaking hand and it closed on the material of his coat. She half expected it to pass right through him, but he was as solid and real as she was. The fabric was a rich, heavy wool, but instead of the warm softness she expected, it felt like it was dusted with frost. So cold. Beneath the clothes, she could feel the strong lines of Simon's body.

'Simon...' she whispered and looked up into his face.

It was him. The pain in his eyes told her that. And yet it was not.

'I cannot help you. I cannot save you. Ys is not a prize to be won. I should never have tried... Please, Ari. Please, just leave.'

'But you... you're here. How are you here?' She leaned forward, still shaking, and pressed her face to his chest, just as she had done a million times. His arms came up around her, instinctually, so familiar a gesture, intimate and comforting. Even with the touch of ice...

For a moment, all she could do was breathe, the cold entering her body, seeping through her skin, swallowing her up.

'Ari,' he whispered and his voice sounded heavy with heartbreak. 'I'm not here. It's just a dream.'

But it wasn't. She was awake. She was standing here, shivering in his cold arms. This was not a dream, not this time. She had dreamed too often of having Simon back that she knew the difference.

'You're here,' she insisted. 'Why are you still here?'

'I'm not, Ari. I'm just a memory. An echo.'

'But why? Why did you come back?'

And for one brief moment she thought he'd say, for her. That he'd come back for her. That he'd heard all her prayers, and all her tears, and he'd come back for her. That he was sorry. That he had made a terrible mistake. That he had never meant to leave her... For just a moment, before he spoke.

'It was the mask. It transformed me. When I found it... when I found her...'

Dahut's mask. He had found it then, before she did. How did it find its way back to the sea, lodged in a rocky crevice, guarded by an eel? It couldn't have got there by itself.

'You hid the mask, didn't you? Why, Simon? If it proved that you were right...'

'Because it's too dangerous. It is a dark and ancient magic, created by Ankou, wielded by Dahut, cursed by all whose lives it took. She will use it. How could she resist? I had to hide it, protect it. And with it, Ys. When I died...' The words seemed to fade away and he looked confused. 'When I died...' Simon frowned, memories and confusion playing through his haunted eyes.

But Ari had another question, one no one else could answer. It burned inside her, terrible, sickening. And it had nothing to do with Dahut or the du Lacs. 'Who was she, Simon? The woman in your letter?'

He laughed, just once, a brief broken noise, but didn't reply, taking on that cold, aloofness again.

She had to know. '*Who was she, Simon?*'

His eyes grew distant, his gaze shifting over her shoulder, down towards the cove, out to the ocean. 'I couldn't help myself, Ari. She was... she was like the sea itself. Before I realised what was happening...' He held her tighter, just for a moment. Frost ate in through her clothes, speared her heart. 'I'm sorry. Go home, *mon coeur*. Be safe. Live your life. Forget about this place. The sea has taken most of the people here. It always will. You were not meant to come here. The letter was meant to keep you safe, to keep you away. Forget Rafael du Lac. Forget me.'

And suddenly he was gone. Like a plume of smoke, he twisted in the air and he was gone. Ari was standing alone in a deserted graveyard, leaning back against the ice-cold metalwork of the gate, her arms wrapped around her chest, with tears like flakes of snow on her face.

CHAPTER FOURTEEN

Simon's words haunted Ari all night, waking her from nightmares where he held her tightly and the sea rose around them. He'd warned her to leave, implied he was trying to protect her by breaking up with her. And yet he admitted he'd loved someone else. Far more than he had ever loved her, she suspected. By the time her alarm sounded, she had been tossing and turning for hours. Simon had hidden the mask and somehow she had found it. As if it was meant to be. But why had he hidden it? He had talked about protecting it. Protecting Ys. From what?

They were meant to dive that morning, but even as Ari dragged herself downstairs, she could tell something else was off. Jason was in a foul mood, stomping around the house like a petulant teenager.

'What's up?' she asked Nico as he fussed over the coffee on the stove. A plate of crêpes from the local supermarket sat open on the table.

'Thierry isn't back yet.'

'Thierry? Where is he?'

Nico shrugged. 'He stayed on at the *fest noz* last night with friends after we came back. You left really early. Were you OK?'

'Yes,' she lied as firmly as she could and helped herself to a crêpe. What could she say? *I saw Simon's ghost and I think something has transformed him into an ancient Breton death spirit. He found the mask and then hid it again. Oh, and he dumped me but wouldn't tell me why.* They'd lock her up. 'Surely Thierry wouldn't be diving today anyway?'

'No, but Jason wanted him on board for support. Alix was taking his place. He's off trying to get hold of one of the others who doesn't have a hangover. It's not looking good.'

'Well, if he will schedule a dive after a party...' Normally he'd never do such a thing. He had more sense than that.

'He has all that cash to spend,' Nico told her with a knowing smile. 'I think he's afraid it's fairy money and will vanish before he gets a chance.'

She thought of last night and shuddered. What had she seen? What had she spoken to?

'Or du Lac might change his mind,' Jason added as he came in and flopped down in the chair beside her. 'No luck. They're all out for the count. The tides are perfect, damn it.'

'You need to give people more notice,' she told him as Nico handed him a commiserative coffee.

'We're meant to be working here. We're meant to be professionals.'

In case Rafael du Lac saw them, she supposed. And given the interaction with the archaeological unit in Brest, he was trying hard today to make up for his unprofessional behaviour, no doubt.

She cast him a sidelong look. 'Jason, you have been running this whole thing like it's some kind of college spring break. If you want it to be professional, you've got to lead by example. You've got to step up. Rather than...'

'Rather than what?'

He sat there, legs splayed wide, in long swimming shorts decorated with Hawaiian flowers and a T-shirt which read No. 1 Sexpot. He was a living, breathing point waiting to be made. She looked him up and down.

'Rather than be you.'

He narrowed his eyes to a glare. 'Thank you very much.' But he didn't actually sound as outraged as she thought he would be. 'Yeah well, starting tomorrow, I suppose. Hardly going to wear a suit out on Yana's boat, am I? Have you found anything in your trawl of the charts and the sonar readings?'

She shrugged. 'Some interesting features to look at, mainly around the cliffs. And then there are some of the place names. Castelmeur, Îlot d'Or, Kermeur... It's like drawing a line with the place names in the area. What great city or castle do you see around here? What island of gold or gates?'

He gazed at her for a long moment, then drank his coffee without saying a word. He avoided eye contact for a moment.

'What?' she asked.

'Nothing. You just... you sound like him. Like Simon. That's all.'

Her voice shook. She couldn't help it. She'd seen him last night, spoken to him, heard him, touched him... things she had dreamed about. Now they had become a nightmare. She tried to push those thoughts aside. She had to, if she was to keep going. 'I thought that was what you wanted?'

Jason gave her a funny look, like he sensed something was wrong. 'It's OK. Go on.'

She opened her laptop and brought up the map of the seabed around the cliffs and the sonar readings, pointing out the area where they had found the mask. 'I think this is where we need to keep looking. The mask and the coin would indicate it anyway, but there's something else.' She pulled up another document, a map. She'd found it on the online archives. It wasn't to scale by modern terms. Even printed out, it looked more like a sketch. 'This is a sixteenth-century copy. I found it looking for information about Guy Éder de la Fontenelle and Île Tristan.'

'The Wolf? The pirate from Douarnenez? What were you looking for info on him for?'

Of course, he knew who la Fontenelle was. Jason had endless details filed away in that labyrinthine brain of his.

'Oh just... I was there yesterday. With Rafael. Well, not on the island, but we looked at it and...' He arched an eyebrow. 'It doesn't matter. Look at the map: that's not Île Tristan, no matter what it says in the description. The notes say it was his plan for the island, his stronghold. But I don't think it is. Look at the shape, it's all wrong. I mean, I know that's always a problem with early maps, but really, look at it. It's walled, with streets and sea gates. Look at the sea gates, they're on the wrong side. See this causeway? And below it there's a path, like at Tristan, sure, but permanently under the water...'

It was marked *chemin de l'eau*. The water path.

He frowned. Zoomed in on the modern map on the screen. Frowned even more intently at the printout. 'You think it's Ys?'

'The stories said he used the coves up and down the coast to hide his treasure. He may have stumbled on to something else, don't you think? Made this map and said it was a plan, but it can't be. I need to check with Rafael. See if he has anything similar.'

'Why would he have—?'

'Because the du Lacs have all sorts of stuff. They have their own archive, Jason. A vault full of records, books, maps. He showed me this book, a manuscript...' Maybe she shouldn't be telling Jason that. But Rafael had not implied it was a secret.

Jason frowned. 'Simon used to go up there all the time to talk to Madame du Lac. Did he know about this?'

She shrugged, not wanting to talk about Simon. Or what Simon knew. Not now.

He'd found the mask. He'd hidden it again. He was Ankou now.

No. She couldn't say that out loud.

'Look at this.' She pulled up the modern map and enlarged the area around the Pointe de Castelmeur. The shape was unmistakable. 'Îlot d'Or was Enez Dor in Breton which means the island of the door. Or the gates. It's this tiny island here, not much more than a couple of rocks really. So imagine this isn't a headland' – she tapped the Pointe de Castelmeur – 'but a causeway, and turn it this way.' She twisted the printout of the ancient sketched map around, so it matched the modern map on the laptop, until they lined up, more or less. Where the paper showed a walled island city, the screen was the empty expanse of water. The same expanse where they had found the rocks with the coin and the mask, where the cliffs were crumbling into the sea.

'How can we prove this is the same place?'

She shrugged her shoulders. 'I'm not sure we can. Not really. Not unless Rafael has more information than we do right now. Or we find something major. There's nothing much down there, you know that as well as I do. But it's a theory.'

'Well, we need to ask him, don't we? This is his party after all. If he still wants to play.'

He would. She knew that. Now more than ever. Simon... or Ankou... or whatever he was, had confirmed it for her, but Rafael was a believer. He was terrified that the curse was real, and that it would take not just him but his son as well. Rafael would do anything to solve this mystery and break the curse.

Finding Dahut's mask had somehow called forth Ankou, in the form of her dead fiancé. By hiding it, the mask had transformed Simon himself and Ankou had claimed him.

The phone started ringing and Nico grabbed it, but he didn't even make it through the normal greetings. 'What do you mean? Where?' And his face paled. 'We'll be right there. Phone the police. Immediately, do you understand?'

Ari and Jason stared at him as he hung up and leaned on the counter, his arms shaking.

'That was Alix. She and Milo went down to the cove. They've found a... a body.'

Ari's breath caught in her throat, her heart pounding beneath it, trying to force its way out.

The sea has taken most of the people here. It always will.

That was what Simon had said last night. Dahut, the princess of Ys, who became the Siren of Sainte Sirène, drowned anyone she wanted without mercy.

Is *that* who he meant? Is that who he had written about in his letter? Had he met Dahut?

The one person Dahut wanted more than anyone else was Rafael.

But it couldn't be. It couldn't!

Ari had first seen Rafael du Lac down there in the cove, floating in the water, like he was offering himself up. He thought a watery death was inevitable. Or had done. Since yesterday, he had hope again. She was certain of it. He'd as good as told her as much. That she was his hope.

He couldn't give up. He wanted to save his son. But what if Dahut's curse took him before he could do anything, before either of them could stop it? Because she was faffing about with the records here, and meeting the ghost of her lost lover in the graveyard... She hadn't even seen Rafael today. Hadn't talked to him. She'd just... abandoned him.

'A what?' Jason pushed himself up from the chair. Ari couldn't move, couldn't speak. 'What do you mean, a body?'

Nico's face was horribly grim.

'It's Thierry. They found him in the water.'

. . .

Ari barely remembered the rush down to the cove, tearing along the narrow paths at the clifftop because it was faster to go by foot than to take the long looping route by road. Bronze-coloured bracken and long trailing brambles tore at them as they passed, trying to hold them back. The yellow dust of the path was like a beacon dragging them forwards. They clambered over the tumbledown drystone walls, and down the steepest section to the cove itself.

There were police cars and a small group of people speaking in hushed tones, all local by the look of them, no sign of Alix or Milo.

Jason's phone rang again, but he cut it off. Word had already gone around.

A young gendarme at the top of the slip stopped them as they approached. They could see two other uniformed figures further down the beach with Alix and Milo, who stood hunched over, arms around their bodies, heads bowed. Broken by shock and grief.

'We're with them,' Nico said in surprisingly brusque tones. 'We know him... knew...'

For a moment, the young man paused and then spoke into his radio. 'Wait over there,' he said, pointing to the low wall above the beach, not far from the war memorial. 'The inspector isn't here yet. They'll want to talk to you.'

'But he's our friend—' Jason began, before Nico grabbed his arm and pulled him away. You didn't argue with the cops, not even if they looked about fifteen. Ari knew he'd had to explain that one to Jason on more than one occasion.

She followed, not knowing what else to do. A shadow fell over her, a cloud passing over the sun, and she looked out to the sea, the surface of which glittered where the sun struck it. It shouldn't be such a beautiful place. It shouldn't be so perfect. Thierry was dead. And what had he done to earn that?

'Ari?' Rafael called from the edge of the road. He'd just got out of his car and hurried towards them, ignoring everyone else. 'What happened? I got a call from the Mairie.' He took in the fact that Jason and Nico were with her and nodded to them in greeting.

'It's Thierry Jacquet, our diver. We don't know anything. We just...' She held up her hands helplessly. There was nothing more to say. They simply didn't know anything else. 'We just got here. Alix phoned. She and Milo found him.'

Rafael nodded and frowned. 'Come with me.' He started striding back towards the gendarme, who eyed him warily as he approached.

'But we can't just—' she began to protest but he cut her off.

'I can,' he growled. 'Louis Martin, what is going on here?'

The young policeman blanched, but all the same, he didn't budge. It said a lot about him and his training, she decided, because Rafael had gone full-on CEO crossed with a prince and a bastard. 'Monsieur du Lac, you need to stay up there. I have orders.'

'Yes, and I gave them,' barked a voice from behind them.

Rafael turned sharply, but something like relief rippled over his handsome features. He didn't retreat though. 'Alain, it's about time you got here.'

The man coming towards them wore plain clothes, smart but not flashy. Functional. There was a touch of grey in his dark hair and a penetrating gaze behind a pair of wire-framed glasses. And he didn't look like he would take any nonsense from anyone. Especially not Rafael du Lac. 'That's Inspector Vannier to you. Now, let me do my job.'

Rafael ignored the rebuff. 'Alain, I need to know what happened.'

The older man shrugged. 'So do I, my friend. But you aren't the CEO in this case. Step back. Madame...?' He gazed for a long moment at Ari, waiting for more information.

'Walker,' she whispered. She felt like he was gazing deep inside her, searching her thoughts. She didn't like the idea.

'*Doctor* Walker,' Rafael cut in when she didn't supply anything more. 'It's her friend. The victim. Alain, we need to know—'

'No, you don't. This has nothing to do with you, Rafael. It's a police matter.' Then he sighed, relenting. 'I'll tell you what I can *when* I can.'

Reluctantly, Rafael nodded. What else could he do? But he didn't step back. He stayed exactly where he was, watching everything, scanning the shoreline with the eyes of a hawk.

'What happened?' he asked Ari when the inspector had gone.

'We don't know. Not really. He was at the festival last night, and I don't know if anyone saw him this morning. I didn't. Alix wanted to go for a swim. That's her there, with Milo, her boyfriend. They're just students. They're camping around the back of the house and they—'

His hand came up to cup her elbow gently in that way he did, the warmth of his touch a shock. She hadn't realised that she was so cold. Or that she was shaking. She leaned against him, welcoming the human contact. 'Come and sit in the car,' he said. 'I think you may be in shock.'

Shock? Was she?

Well, it made sense. Everything that had happened since she got here felt like a fever dream. Not to mention everything that had happened last night.

Jason jogged over to them, a ball of nervous energy and concern. 'Did you tell him what you found out?'

What she found out? What was he...? Oh, the map and the various alignments in place names. He was talking about Rafael, not the detective.

'No, not yet. It wasn't... It isn't the time, Jason.'

But that light was already in Rafael's eyes. She was beginning to dread it. First Simon, then her brother, now Rafael... the mysteries surrounding Sainte Sirène just seemed to swallow the men in her life whole. It was like some kind of infection. Or madness.

She started at the thought. Rafael du Lac was not in her life. He was just a man, nothing to do with her. The constant attraction she felt to him was a mistake. She knew that. Even with her own grief and the magic of this place interfering with her emotions, what could she possibly be thinking?

'Tell me,' he said. 'Please.'

She winced and glanced back towards the shore. They couldn't leave. But they couldn't do anything helpful here either, could they?

As if he had read her mind, Rafael went on. 'They'd probably rather we weren't here. I'll get them to come to the manor as soon as they're done. They can bring your friends there if you want. Or...'

'I'll wait here,' said Nico. 'For Milo and Alix. You go on ahead.'

Thank God for Nico, she thought.

The Manoir still had the warm and welcoming atmosphere which Ari remembered from the other night. Even though she had run away from it. Best not to think about that. It led to thoughts of the storm and the clifftops, of Ankou standing there, holding the mask, of Simon. And of last night.

Her stomach twisted. While she had been standing in a graveyard talking to a dead man, was Thierry drowning?

No. It couldn't have been that early, could it? She had seen him dancing, laughing, singing along...

God, he'd been alive and now—

'Ari?' Jason said, dragging her attention back to the present. 'Are you OK?'

She brushed away his concern. 'Yeah. Fine.'

'You don't look it.'

She swallowed hard. Well, she had been lying, hadn't she?

'Ah, visitors,' said Madame du Lac when she saw them. She sat at a card table by the window, a colourful deck of Tarot cards spread out in front of her. She turned them over, one at a time, studying the images, distracted.

'Where's Laure?' Rafael asked sharply. 'Are you on your own?'

'Why wouldn't I be on my own? Laure went out. Nolvene is around somewhere.' The vagueness in her didn't sound good and Ari could see his concern mounting. 'Gwen was here earlier. She was looking for you. Something about the museum?'

Ari tried not to shudder. Gwen had warned her all about Rafael, and yet here she was. In his house. Doing what he wanted.

And Simon had warned her too, told her to go before it was too late. And now Thierry was dead.

Rafael frowned and didn't exactly look thrilled at the thought of Gwen either. Before he could say anything more, Madame du Lac looked up, fixing Ari with a suddenly piercing look.

'Dr Walker, come, pick a card.'

'This isn't the time for party tricks, Mémé—' Rafael began, but Ari shook her head.

'It's fine,' she told him. If it amused an old woman, why not? It wasn't as if she believed in such things.

Nor had she believed in Ankou, or ancient curses, or...

She couldn't think about that now.

The back of the cards looked like stained glass, the colours vibrant and bright. It was an old pack though, the edges of the cards worn from use.

'Any card?' she asked.

The old woman nodded and spread her hands wide over the pack. 'Just turn it over.'

Ari reached out for one in the middle of the table, but at the last minute her hand wavered and she flicked over one at the edge instead.

The Moon, a beautiful traditional depiction of it, with the moon appearing between two towers, while two wolves howled at it, all at the edge of the sea. A shiver ran down Ari's back. If you looked at the landscape, it almost reminded her of Pointe de Castelmeur and the landscape around Sainte Sirène.

She looked up at Madame du Lac, but the old woman just stared at the card, a curious expression on her face.

'Something ancient stirs,' she said in that strange, calm voice. 'Beneath the surface. Pick another.'

Ari did as instructed, unable to stop herself.

'The Hanged Man,' said Madame du Lac. 'The sacrifice. He who gives all for knowledge. Another.'

'Mémé,' Rafael said with a tone of warning in his voice.

She still ignored him, staring at the cards, her eyes intense.

Ari had already selected another card. The Star, a naked woman with long white hair flowing around her, one foot in the water and the other on land, pouring water from two jugs. A feeling of relief swept through her until the old woman took it from her and laid it upside down on the Hanged Man.

'A drowning,' she murmured darkly. 'Another one.'

Ari didn't want to play this game anymore. Her hand shook over the cards.

'Enough,' said Rafael, and this time he really did sound distressed.

And yet, she knew she had to do it. It was inevitable. Ari flicked over the final card and knew, even before she saw it, what it would be.

A man in black sat on a barge, a wide black hat on his head, a scythe in his hand. And his face was a skull.

Death. It had to be.

'Ankou,' said Madame du Lac. Her hands trembled and she knotted them together, as if in prayer. 'Oh, children, what have you stirred up?'

'Mémé, please, stop it,' her great-nephew told her firmly. 'Someone has drowned. This isn't funny.'

A shiver of transformation seemed to pass over her, as if something magical drained out of her, all the power and strength in her leaving.

'Drowned?' In that moment, she looked so confused, so very old and frail. 'Who? Rafael? Who was it?' she urged.

'A friend of ours,' said Jason gently, masking the trembling in his voice. 'Thierry Jacquet. He was one of the divers who found the mask. We don't know what happened.'

'He was at the *fest noz* last night,' Ari added. She reached out and grabbed her brother's hand and for once he didn't pull away.

'We were all there together,' he continued. 'But I didn't see him when I left. I thought he'd already gone back. God, I should have checked, shouldn't I? I should have done something.'

'It wasn't your fault, Jason.'

'I'm meant to be in charge of this. That's what you said. That I should act like it? That's what you meant. Safety is one of the main priorities in any dive and I failed—'

'You weren't on a dive. It's not your fault.' She pulled him into a hug and he stiffened in surprise and then abruptly relaxed. She felt him shake against her, his breath cut by grief. She'd never seen him like this.

'I wasn't with Simon either. I was away, in Paris. If I'd been here...'

'It's OK, Jason,' she whispered. And she meant it. It surprised her as much as anything. Jason hadn't caused the deaths, not Thierry's and not Simon's either, and she had blamed him for far too long.

'If I'd been here...'

Who knew if he could have done anything? If Dahut had taken her fiancé, enchanted him, made him love her and then killed him...

She shook the thought away. The spear of pain inside her didn't need awakening now.

'It's OK. It wasn't your fault. Not then. Not now.'

They were good words. Other people had said them to her often enough after Simon's death that she almost believed them. Except for all the ways she didn't. But she had no idea Jason had felt the same way.

A noise reminded her that they were not alone. They weren't even somewhere private. They were in someone else's home. Madame du Lac was rummaging in a sewing basket in the corner and Rafael stood beside her, looking quietly mortified. The old woman pulled out two little pouches and then brought them over, pressing one into Ari's hand and one into Jason's, wrapping her hand over theirs and muttering a prayer as she did so. Ari couldn't make out the words.

Her eyes glistened with tears. 'Keep them safe,' Madame du Lac said at last. 'And they will keep you safe. Rafi, I would like to lie down. I am exhausted. Help me.'

Rafael didn't argue but cast Ari a helpless glance, an apology perhaps. He closed the door behind them, but not quickly enough.

'*Salut*,' a voice said quite loudly, while the main door slammed. Laure, she realised, home from whatever errand had called her away, obviously. The greeting was followed by a hushed exchange between her, Rafael and Madame du Lac which Ari probably couldn't have followed even if she had been able to hear it properly. It didn't matter. She didn't really care. They were probably just telling her what had happened and she didn't want to hear it rehashed again, no matter what language it was in.

Jason turned the pouch over in his hand and then stared at her, broken and devastated by loss yet again. She'd blamed him, she knew, but that wasn't the whole of it. She had blamed herself so much more. But she had needed somewhere to direct the pain and the guilt. She had been in an entirely different country when it had happened. Her brother had been the obvious target, whether it was warranted or not.

And Jason had willingly taken all that blame and added it to his own.

'What is it?' he asked.

Ari smiled. 'A charm of protection. It's an old tradition. Put it somewhere safe.' And she hugged him as hard as she could.

CHAPTER FIFTEEN

Laure was carrying about a dozen carrier bags, all from high-end stores from Quimper. She must have left at the crack of dawn to get there, buy all this and come back.

'The roads were crazy,' she said in her usual bright tones. 'You should have seen it on the—'

'Laure,' Rafael stopped her. 'There's been a drowning.'

She went white. The blood just drained out of her face and her hands went limp, the bags falling from her hands.

'Wh-what?'

But her eyes fixed on Rafael. Because she knew as well as he did that it should have been him. That he could be the next.

'This morning. Or last night. At the *fest noz*.'

She looked thoroughly bewildered. 'But... but *I* was at the *fest noz!*'

As if that made a difference. She knew these stories as well as he did. She'd grown up with Mémé too. And the women of his family were the ones to survive. They were the ones who carried those legends, who held the lore.

But for his sister, everything in the world centred around

her own self. It always had done. She was Yvette du Lac's daughter to the core.

'You were?' Mémé asked. 'I thought you went out with the Morvan girl.'

'I did,' she replied. 'We did. But it was just the *fest noz*. Mémé, remember? I told you. What happened?'

Their great-aunt dropped her gaze and didn't answer.

'Who was it?' Laure pressed on.

Rafael swallowed hard. She wasn't going to stop and the louder her questions, the more likely it was Ari and Jason would hear her. He didn't want them any more upset than they were. Mémé had done enough in that respect. 'One of the divers staying at Ty Elen.'

She drew in a single breath and her face went white.

'Who?' The tremble in her voice was unmistakable.

Rafael frowned and Mémé's hand tightened on his arm. Was that a warning? But a warning of what? Maybe just not to start a fight with his sister right now. As simple as that.

In theory anyway.

'His name was Thierry,' he replied. 'Thierry Jacquet. From Les Sables-d'Olonne originally.'

'Oh,' Laure said at last. 'I... I'm sorry. What happened?'

He fixed her with his sternest glare. What did she think happened? 'We don't know any details. I'm waiting for word from Alain Vannier. He's in charge of the investigation. The body was found this morning, in Pors Sirène, by two of his friends.'

She made a small 'o' with her mouth, her eyes very wide. 'But... oh, that's awful. Was he drinking? Of course he was; everyone drinks at a *fest noz*. Did he go in the water? What do they think—'

A sound from the other room made Rafael look around and he frowned. He really didn't want Ari and Jason to hear Laure speculating.

But it was Mémé who interrupted this time. 'Enough, Laure, help me to my room. I am tired and need to rest. This has all been most exhausting.'

She disentangled herself from Rafael's arm and Laure had no choice but to help her up the stairs, leaving Rafael standing there with her many bags scattered around him.

With a resigned sigh, he picked them up and gathered them into one spot, at the foot of the stairs where she could take them later. He had no idea how long she intended to stay. You could never tell with Laure. At least she took care of Mémé when she was here.

Sort of.

Mémé doted on her, though, and if it made the old woman happy, he was content. There was little else to cheer him at the moment. He didn't know how Thierry had died and it could just have been a horrible coincidence. But he'd been one of the Walkers' divers. He'd been there when they found that wretched mask and had been attacked by the eel. Marked by it.

The sense of danger closing in on him made his head ache.

Alain called by on his way back to headquarters. He was grim-faced and had that strained look in his eyes that boded nothing good.

'They're still here? The Walkers?' he asked without preamble.

Rafael frowned. He didn't like the tone, but he just nodded. He'd left them talking in the drawing room, finally sharing things they should have shared long ago, he suspected. Even Laure seemed happy to leave them to it once she had 'popped in to say hello'. The atmosphere had been tense and he knew they needed this time. 'What did you find?'

Alain grimaced briefly. 'Inside. I shouldn't be here at all.

But the sooner I interview them, the better. How's their French? Do I need a translator?'

'I can help. I'll make coffee,' he said, and for once Alain looked relieved.

By the time he'd brought the coffee up from the kitchen, running the gauntlet of Nolvene, who was busy baking and had no time for interlopers in her domain, Alain had introduced himself and was already taking some notes and contact details.

'He was our friend,' Jason was saying as Rafael came in and looked up at the interruption. As his eyes met Rafael's, he couldn't miss the glistening of tears in Jason's eyes and he looked like a child sitting there on the edge of the armchair. A world away from the happy-go-lucky adventurer he usually projected. Ari was staring fixedly out of the window. Everything about her was a taut wire. She didn't look around at him.

He didn't blame her. This had to be dredging up all her grief regarding Simon. That was unavoidable. And in between their vision of Ankou the other night and another death by drowning in the same place... well... it had to hurt.

He couldn't tell her how many people had died in that cove, or whose bodies had been washed ashore there. It wouldn't help. Simon wasn't even the first Poullain.

He wondered if she recalled the names on the memorial there. Probably not. People didn't tend to read them without a reason. They had been a small group of no great importance, caught by the Gestapo, executed where they knelt in the surf. One after the other, so the story went, but none of them had talked. Fabien du Lac had been the last.

Many similar things had happened up and down the coast.

The urge to comfort her was unexpectedly strong. And wholly inappropriate. He knew that. But that didn't make it lessen.

He set down the coffees on the table. Ari ignored them.

'Was Monsieur Jacquet involved in a fight recently?' Alain was asking.

'Thierry? No. He was the most laid-back man you'd meet. Fighting wasn't in his nature.' Jason took the coffee Rafael offered and held it close, warming his hands on it rather than drinking.

Alain nodded slowly and made more notes. 'And the injury to his arm?'

'An eel attacked him while we were diving the other day.'

Alain frowned and looked up at Rafael for confirmation of the word. 'An eel?'

'A conger eel, I believe. Vicious things.' He didn't mention the mask. It didn't seem relevant and he wasn't sure if anyone wanted it involved in a police investigation. Jason had made no mention of it. 'The Walkers are working for my great-aunt and the Foundation. Marine archaeology. They locate sites which may harbour historic artefacts and dive for evidence of them. Before the university and the state are involved, of course.'

More notes followed, the whisper of his pen on the page, his brow furrowing in thought... Alain gave nothing away and Rafael wondered what he was thinking. All the same, it was fascinating to watch his process.

Eventually, Alain leaned back in the chair and closed his notebook. 'There are some injuries we need to investigate further and the coroner will have a full report for me soon. It would appear to be an accidental drowning.' He glanced at Jason. 'My condolences.'

Jason pursed his lips and looked away.

Alain drank the rest of his coffee quickly, the way someone did when he didn't want to linger somewhere but needed the caffeine nonetheless.

'But he was a strong swimmer,' Ari cut in. 'He knew the area. He—' Her voice choked a little and she went quiet.

'I understand that, *mademoiselle*. The sea here is treacherous and the cliffs perilous. Rip tides appear as if from nowhere like the *mari-morgen* of legend. We will do everything we can to find out what happened. But sometimes accidents just happen. Even to the most experienced. A late night, some alcohol, even just a little, and a fall while walking home along the cliffs, or an ill-advised visit to the shore... we've seen it many times.'

Especially at Sainte Sirène, Rafael thought, but he didn't say it out loud.

Alain rose and said his farewells, leaving them to their coffees and their thoughts. Rafael followed him outside.

'What other injuries?' he asked softly.

Alain gave him a look, half warning, half resignation. He probably felt he shouldn't have mentioned it, but he also knew Rafael would not let it go. 'Some bruising around the neck.'

'Bruising?' Rafael asked.

Alain gave a slight shrug. 'That's for the coroner to say, but there is no sign of foul play. I suspect he may have done it to himself, as he...' He brought his hands up to his own neck. 'Well, I've seen it quite often with drowning victims. Simon Poullain was the last one.'

'Simon?' Ari's voice was unusually sharp and made them both turn. She'd followed them to the entrance hall. Rafael didn't know why, but God, he wished she had not.

'Yes, Simon Poullain,' Alain said and Rafael noticed the notebook was already in his hand again. 'You knew him?'

Alain didn't know. Why would he? Simon Poullain was history here, a death in the past, just one more accident, the records quietly shelved and almost forgotten.

Ari's voice turned glacial. 'I was engaged to be married to him.'

Alain didn't reply at first. He made another note, the pen scratching at the paper too loudly. Then he said something neither of them expected. 'My sincerest condolences, Dr Walker. He was a good man.'

'He... he was,' she replied, more softly now, and wrapped her arms around her chest again, her face pale as parchment. 'Is that not... isn't it weird? Both of them? With the same...' Words failed her and she looked desperately at Rafael for help.

He drew in a steadying breath. 'Perhaps the coroner can tell us why they would both have these marks?' he asked Alain.

'I'm sure he will try. I really have to get on.'

'Keep in touch,' Rafael told him and Alain didn't say another word, just got into his car and drove off.

Ari was still there when he turned around, staring at him.

'Is he really saying Thierry and Simon died in the same way?'

Evasiveness came as second nature to him. He really didn't want to visit this. 'In that they both drowned?'

She narrowed her eyes. She saw everything, didn't she? She saw straight through him. 'You know what I mean.'

The curse. The *mari-morgen*. The *groac'h*. Ys. Dahut. All of those things swarmed to the forefront of his mind. He didn't have an answer. Not one he was able to articulate anyway. It was all his fault. That was his fear.

'I don't think ancient curses figure in Alain's worldview.' He closed the door and walked back to join her. Carefully, he reached out to rest a comforting hand on her shoulder. She didn't pull away. If anything, she seemed to lean in towards him, unbending just a little, welcoming his touch. The warmth of her skin beneath the light cotton shirt was unexpected. 'I can drive you back to the house, if you want.'

'No.' She shook her head as she said it and looked up into his face, her coral-reef eyes so bright, glittering. 'I wanted to ask you for access to your archive since I'm here. I found something, I think. I'd like to see if I can corroborate it here. You have maps, don't you? Old ones?'

'Of course. Whatever we can help with.'

There was a book missing from the shelf. Rafael hadn't noticed it before, but the gap was like a broken tooth, drawing his eye instantly. He didn't say anything, not at first, but he saw it, nonetheless.

Ari, meanwhile, took in the library like it was a sacred space, her head tilted back, her blue eyes wide in wonder, as she turned slowly around. 'I had no idea you had this tucked away. You should have led with this. You aren't Ariel after all, are you? You're the Beast.'

Which made her Belle. He let his lips quirk into a smile but said nothing. If she wanted to think him the Beast, that fitted. Curse and all.

'It's not mine. Not really. My family collected it. Mémé looks after it now.'

It was strange to see it through her eyes – a place of beauty and wonder, polished mahogany shelves which had stood in the same place for lifetimes, the mullioned windows letting the sunlight stream across the oak floor. Bound volumes and boxed materials crowded the shelves, some piled on the desk, a world away from the stark lines of his office back in Paris, or even the neat regimented shelves of the study next door.

His, but not his. Not really. This belonged to his family line, and some of them had made it their life's work to preserve it. All that information on Sainte Sirène and its history, on its folklore and legends, on the people who had lived here, no matter how humble.

He ran his hand along the shelf with the missing book. Someone else had been in here. Mémé? She didn't tend to remove things though. She liked to read in here sometimes, mainly in the afternoons. The library was her pride and joy. She had nurtured it all these years. She'd know, wouldn't she? Surely she would.

'Is something wrong?' Ari asked.

'Someone's borrowed a book.'

'I know that tone,' Jason said. He'd followed them in when Ari had summoned him, not apparently willingly, but now he was just as enchanted as his sister. A library like this, full of rare and ephemeral records of history, was like catnip to them. Adventurers, treasure hunters, seekers after the lost and mystical worlds of long ago... Places like this were where they found the threads they followed.

Like Ariadne of legend, weaving her path through the labyrinth. Like Jason in search of the Golden Fleece.

'I'm sure it's fine,' he replied, aware of the vague tone in his voice. He wasn't sure. Not at all. He ought to go and ask her, but still, he hesitated. It was not a good idea to leave anyone in here unsupervised. Mémé had impressed that on them since they could first talk.

This is the real treasure of Sainte Sirène, crammed into this small space.

She guarded it fiercely.

Which was why a missing book was so unnerving.

Ari picked up on his discomfort. 'What book is it?'

He picked up the neighbouring volume and flicked it open, turning the brittle yellow pages with care. It was a diary, hand-written, in a spidery writing he recognised as belonging to Mémé's uncle, Fabien, one of many he had written in his short life.

Because, of course, he had led a short life. Eventful, adventurous, but short.

'A diary covering the war years, by the looks of it. My great-great-uncle Fabien was in the resistance here. It was a brutal war for Cap Sizun.'

There were memorials dotted all over the peninsula, in

every town, marking the places where his people had fought, had made their stands. The coves and inlets here had been vital to the resistance, stealing people and equipment in and out, like the smugglers and wreckers of old. And the retaliation from the Third Reich had been brutal. There wasn't a family that hadn't been scarred.

Fabien had written in code half the time because he hadn't been an idiot to write down all the secrets which the occupying forces could use against him and his comrades. But there were things Fabien had felt were not so secret. It was clear from the diaries that he'd written quickly sometimes, scrawling down ideas, or brief impressions in a rush.

He'd been in love. Opinion was divided on whom with. Sometimes there were poems. Sometimes there were sketches and maps with no names.

Rafael glanced at the page before him.

I didn't think she would be there again, but when I came out, she was walking along the shore, collecting shells, her bare feet sinking in the wet sand. Tris told me I was imagining things, but there she was. And I had never seen such a creature. Like something from the legends of this place, the ones that tell us we will die and the sea will have us. She looked at me and smiled, her long white-blonde hair catching the sun like candlelight. I asked if she was a White Lady. She laughed and told me her name was Blanche.

Rafael closed the book and replaced it carefully on the shelf. The woman reminded him too closely of the one in his nightmare, the one waiting for him at the foot of the Pointe de Castelmeur. He pushed the thought away as firmly as possible.

'What do you need to know?' he asked. 'How can I help?'

'I need to know more about the early history of the area.

Where the place names came from, for example, and why they changed. Sainte Sirène?'

'Yes. It's a French name. The Breton is Sant Sieren.'

'I saw the signs,' she replied flatly. 'But surely that's just a modern translation back. Who was Sieren? Why change it to the word for mermaid? Do you see what I mean? There must be something else, some other name, something older. Or a story of some kind to explain it.'

Rafael cast a confused glance at Jason, who just shrugged. 'Hey, this is what she does. And she's very good at it. She follows the breadcrumbs left in place names and stories. I just dive and dig stuff up.'

Ari shushed her brother, embarrassed by his praise. 'What I mean is... do you have a map?'

Rafael almost laughed and his mood shifted. She could do that to him easily, like the sun coming out from behind a cloud. 'A map? There are dozens here. More. A modern one? A fifteenth-century one? What do you want?'

Ari grinned. 'Show-off.'

They spent an hour lost in the past. Rafael suspected that, for Ari and Jason, it was easier than dwelling in the present where a friend had just died. He placed item after item in front of her. Books, maps, documents, printed and handwritten, all those priceless things he could lay hands on. It was only when Laure came in looking for them that Ari took a break.

'Have you even eaten?' his sister asked with the pout she always wore when she was being ignored.

'No, we've been working,' he replied. 'It's a thing people do in between shopping and sleeping.'

She pointedly ignored him, shook back her glossy hair and fixed Jason Walker with that perfect Laure du Lac smile. 'Come and help me, Jason. I was going to arrange dinner. You're all welcome to stay. Gwen is coming over. She's fascinated to know what you've found in here.'

'When were you talking to Gwen?' Rafael asked.

'Oh, she phoned. And when I said you were tucked away in here, she wanted to know all the details. She's on her way over now. She'll be after everything you find for her museum, you know? Everything.'

As Jason unfolded his legs and stood up, he checked his phone and frowned. 'I've a ton of missed calls from Nico. I never even heard the phone.'

'The signal can be patchy here,' Laure offered, but Jason was already dialling.

Ari paused in her work and checked her own mobile. 'Me too. Jason?'

But Jason was just listening intently to the messages and looked even more confused. That expression melted to horror as the blood drained from his skin.

'He's in the hospital in Douarnenez. There was a car accident. We've got to... Ari? We've got to go there now.'

CHAPTER SIXTEEN

The drive to Douarnenez seemed to take forever. Rafael manoeuvred the car with ease at the breakneck speed that Ari was convinced all Bretons employed on their narrow roads, but she didn't care right now.

As he pulled up outside the emergency entrance to the Centre Hospitalier, Jason spilled out of the car before she could move and was gone.

'They'll only let one person in to him,' Rafael told her, a note of apology in his voice. 'We'll park and wait until we hear from your brother. OK?'

She nodded reluctantly. 'Yes. Thank you.'

He pulled off again, found the car park and a space effortlessly. They sat there in awkward silence, Ari fidgeting with her phone, Rafael staring at the buildings beyond the rows of cars like he was meditating. There was no pretty sea view here, no fishing boats or island of doomed lovers to gaze at. Just cars and low utilitarian buildings in white and terracotta, interspersed with manicured lawns and shrubs.

'Do you want me to ring and find out more?' he asked.

She had no doubt he was ready and willing to pull rank and

possibly fund a new hospital wing to get answers and the thought made her smile briefly. Before the realisation of what those answers might be stole all humour from her again.

She shook her head and without thinking reached out for his hand. His grip was strong and reassuring and she threaded her fingers with his, relishing the contact. His other hand smoothed over the back of her hand.

'Nico is a good driver. He'd never be in an accident. I just don't understand—' Her phone rang before she could continue and she answered it, her fingertips skidding over the surface.

'He's OK,' Jason babbled. 'He's OK. Just cuts and bruises. They brought him here because the car was a write-off and he might have a concussion or something. But he's OK.'

Ari finally found that she could breathe again. Her eyes burned with sudden tears. Nico had been part of her life for so long, he was like another brother. 'Are you sure? What happened?'

'Here, talk to him.'

There was a brief sound of discussion at the other end of the line and Nico, resigned and fed up from the tone of his voice, spoke. 'Ari, I'm fine. I promise you. They're completely overreacting. I'm happy to go home now.'

'Well, you aren't going anywhere. Not until they discharge you,' she heard Jason say quite clearly. When he did leave, her brother would be watching him like a hawk.

'What happened?' she asked.

'I don't know. The car came out of nowhere and sideswiped me. I went off the road and down into the river. I'm just lucky I got out before—'

'Nico, you could have drowned.'

She said the word before she thought about it and something terrible and cold gripped her chest.

'But I didn't. It wasn't even that deep. I'm fine, *chérie*. Absolutely fine. I blacked out, that's all—'

'Twice!' Jason protested.

'Yes, fine, twice. I fainted when the ambulance came. I just got up too fast. I'm better now. Really.'

He was not winning in his campaign to be released from the hospital any time soon. And now Jason was on his case as well, in no mood to allow Nico to pretend nothing was wrong.

Rafael squeezed her hand in reassurance. She leaned in against him, grateful for the support.

'I'll stay here with him for now, Ari,' Jason told her. 'You and Rafael can head off. I'll ring if the *doctors*' – he emphasised the word clearly – 'think he's ready to go home. Talk later.'

'I'll come and pick you up. Any time,' she told them and Jason hung up. Slowly, carefully, she let out her breath and looked up at Rafael. 'Thank you.'

He smiled gently. 'For what? Driving you here? What sort of host would I have been otherwise?'

She didn't know if it was the sheer overwhelming sense of relief or that growing madness that had been overcoming her for days now. Ever since she had tried to save him and almost drowned him in the process. His gaze met hers and she saw his pupils widen, making the already dark eyes even darker with unmistakable desire. And suddenly she wasn't breathing again and her heart was thundering away at the base of her throat, as if eager to tear itself free of her body. She looked from his eyes to his mouth and back, and leaned in closer at the same moment he did.

Their lips met and parted. She felt herself melt beneath him, his free hand coming up to caress the side of her face, his fingertips so gentle she could hardly bear it. She wriggled closer, aware of the confines of the car, of the seat belt biting into her and everything conspiring to keep them apart.

Rafael breathed her name against her mouth, and there was no doubting his need for her. But all the same he pulled back, gazing solemnly into her eyes.

'Ari,' he murmured gently. 'I want this... I want you very much, but we are not teenagers. Perhaps a car park is not the most appropriate place?'

She had to laugh. She couldn't help herself. It was a perfect storm of emotions, and it swept her away. She didn't care anymore. 'Perhaps not. Maybe you should take me home instead then.' And at the same time, she couldn't believe those words had just come out of her mouth. Why had he stopped kissing her? She wasn't saying stupid things when he was kissing her.

He tried to start the car engine with a bit more speed than was strictly necessary and promptly stalled it. Which really did make her laugh out loud.

They tore their way back to Sainte Sirène, and Ari wasn't sure whose bed they were heading for. Or whether they actually were heading to a bed at all. Because rushing into this, into anything, was not a good idea. The further they drove, the more she realised it.

She had made mistakes like this before. Simon's last letter had torn out her heart. His death had incinerated the remaining pieces. How could she believe anything anyone said again? Especially when her emotions were involved.

It wasn't guilt, she told herself. It wasn't thoughts of Simon. She wasn't running away.

Not exactly.

So much had happened, terrible things. Nico could have died. Thierry *had* died. And here she was acting like a lovesick fool. She couldn't. She just *couldn't*.

As they passed the sign for Sainte Sirène, with the neat Breton translation underneath which made no logical sense, she swore softly under her breath. She still needed answers. And she had so many questions. About Ys. About Ankou. About everything.

'Ari?' Rafael said as they turned toward Sainte Sirène, his tone tentative, as if he was about to broach a momentous subject. As if he sensed her whirling mind, spiralling out of control. Or her change of heart. 'Are you OK?'

The hesitancy in his voice made her heart thud against her ribs. 'Rafael, I need to talk to Gwen.'

He couldn't have sounded more confused if he tried. 'Gwen? Why?'

'Who, apart from your aunt, knows more about Sainte Sirène?'

There was a long pause. 'No one,' he admitted with obvious reluctance. His mouth lifted to a bleak smile, but he didn't argue. He didn't try to persuade her otherwise either. She couldn't tell him how much she appreciated that. She didn't know many men who would take this change of plans so gracefully.

He stopped in Sainte Sirène itself, outside the tiny crêperie, just across the road from the church. He cleared his throat awkwardly.

'Gwen's museum is just over there. It should be open.' Rafael pursed his lips.

Oh God, what had she done? He was already regretting kissing her and now he thought she had been leading him on.

And maybe she had been. She'd wanted to kiss him though, and she had wanted to do so much more, but now... she was afraid of how much she wanted him.

But she needed her questions answered too, the last surviving shred of logic she possessed insisted. Now more than ever. The curse seemed to be closing in on those she loved. If it couldn't have Rafael, it seemed intent on taking everyone else who'd been in contact with the mask. Simon had been the first, if he had been telling the truth, which left herself, Nico and Jason as well.

Much as she wanted to explore the kiss with Rafael, to go further, she was afraid as well. More afraid than she wanted to admit.

But facing Gwen just like that... Gwen who had tried to warn her off Rafael and Sainte Sirène... Gwen who had known Simon... Gwen who seemed to know far too much...

The museum, or *Petit Musée du Sainte Sirène*, as the sign by the door proudly proclaimed, was housed in one of the cottages across from the church. They pushed open the door and stepped inside, Rafael having to duck to do so. Inside was a tiny drawing room, restored to how it might have looked a hundred years ago. There were pictures on the wall, people in traditional costume, those towering lace headdresses and elaborately embroidered waistcoats. In contrast, Ari's eyes were immediately drawn to a large picture of a group of men standing in Pors Sirène, fishermen from their clothes. The photo had been enlarged so it was grainy and their faces hard to make out. There was something about them, though... She peered closer at the label – *Les Maquisards de Sainte Sirène, mort pour la France et pour la mémoire d'Ys.*

'Rafael, who's that?'

There was a familiarity to the figures, even if she couldn't see them clearly. Or to two of them anyway. Two men, grinning at the camera, side by side on the beach, standing so close they could be brothers, or lovers.

He gave a little huff. 'That's them – Fabien du Lac and Tristan Poullain. They were the resistance here, that group, and a few more. The others in the photo are...' He paused as if searching for names.

Another, softer voice came from nowhere. 'Yves Brochard and Pierre Kerdaniel are off to the left and that's Ewen Heussaff in the background. The others aren't in that one, although one of them must have taken it. A lovely picture, isn't it? They look so hopeful, such brave, brave men. It was a tragedy.' Gwen appeared out of the back room. 'Rafael, Ari, how lovely to see you. I'm just about to close up, I'm afraid.'

Rafael reached blindly for Ari's hand. She squeezed his fingers and felt him respond.

The smile Gwen offered Ari wasn't unkind, but it was fascinated. She'd clearly seen the intimate contact. Suddenly, Ari was something to be studied, inspected and examined. Ari didn't like it. She remembered the feeling of Gwen's scrutiny in the chapel the morning of the festival. It was uncomfortable.

Instead, Ari turned her attention back to the two men in the picture. Even with the terrible resolution, she could see the resemblance to Rafael and Simon. It was a strange, unsettling feeling of a different kind. 'What happened to them?'

Gwen shrugged. 'Not a pretty story, I'm afraid. They were using the sea caves, smuggling in arms and spies, helping others escape to England. At the time, the Germans had cleared everything up to three miles from the coast to build their sea wall...' She said it with disgust. 'Well, you've seen the concrete monstrosities they left behind. But Fabien and these boys knew the secrets in and out of the caves, and the things hidden there. And then Hitler's own archaeologists turned up. They were obsessed with Ys, did you know that? For their own dark purposes, to prove their twisted theories by manipulating our past. The resistance members were captured, eventually, tortured almost certainly, but they never betrayed the secrets of Sainte Sirène. They died to protect us all, to keep the secrets of Ys. They are our heroes. There's a memorial in the cove.'

Fabien du Lac died in Pors Sirène, not because of the curse, but with a Nazi bullet in his head. He'd cheated the family fate, at least. In a way.

Ari nodded. 'Yes, I saw it.' This morning, she thought, while the police swarmed over the place and revulsion washed over

her in a cold Atlantic wave. How many people had died there?
It seemed endless.

Rafael cleared his throat uncomfortably. 'Did you hear
about Thierry Jacquet?'

For a moment, Gwen looked appalled, obviously realising
what she'd just been talking about and what had just happened
in the same place. 'I did, of course.' And her features grew
solemn. She didn't move her attention from Ari. 'I'm so sorry.
He was a lovely man.'

'I didn't know you knew him.'

'I know everyone in Sainte Sirène. I make sure of it. I have a
lifelong interest in this little place. It is my home, after all. I
study its history and gather its stories, everything about it.' She
spread her arms wide, indicating the little room, littered with
artefacts and photos, and smiled that glorious smile. 'This is my
domain.'

'I have some questions,' Ari said. 'Quite a lot of questions.'

Gwen smiled, a bemused smile which was quite disarming.
She suddenly looked a little off step and it was a strange sense of
victory to see that. If only for a moment. 'Just like your Simon,'
she replied. The sound of his name on her lips made a chill
ripple up the back of Ari's neck, the way she said it, familiar,
intimate. She remembered Gwen in the church, talking about
Simon in the same soft tones, and something cold and suspicious crept up her spine. 'I suppose that makes sense. I think
you're more than half a Poullain by association. We could sit
down together tomorrow morning perhaps?'

Tomorrow? But anything could happen between now and
tomorrow. Ari didn't want to be pushy, but she really wanted to
talk to Gwen and ask her questions now.

Rafael swept in to the rescue. 'Why not now? We were
about to get a bite to eat. Come and join us. I was about to intro-
duce Ari to real Breton galettes, and perhaps a *bolée de cidre*.'

Ari laughed at the statement. 'I've had galettes before,

Rafael.' She didn't admit that she was more than a little relieved that they weren't rushing off to have sex somewhere anymore. And disappointed. How could she be both? And yet she was.

But rushing never ended up well, did it? If something was really going to happen, it would wait. And doubts still niggled at her. She'd trusted Simon implicitly and look where that had got her. She wanted to trust Rafael, but the very thought terrified her.

'Oh, but you have not had galettes like these,' Gwen told her. 'Buckwheat flour milled just down the road, all local ingredients, the cheese, the cream, and the ham, seafood fresh from the sea, and the cider comes from the heart of the Goyen Valley. Wait until you taste it. It's like autumn on your lips.'

They whisked her off to the tiny rustic crêperie, where they sat at the plain wooden table, on carved wooden chairs which shouldn't have been as comfortable as they were. Pots and pans, the copper polished to a blinding shine, hung on the white painted walls, while black beams crisscrossed the space overhead.

Gwen took her place opposite the two of them, like a teacher facing her class. She and Rafael took charge, promising Ari that she would love what they selected, conspiring like the old friends they were, and Ari had no choice but to go along with it. If Gwen had answers to her questions, she would put up with anything. At least Rafael seemed more at ease now and though Ari knew she would have to address the kiss and all that it implied, this let her put that off for a while longer.

There weren't a lot of men who would kiss a woman like that, with all the promise it entailed and then be overly pleased if she changed her mind. Not that she was changing her mind. Not exactly.

What had she been thinking? She'd been overwrought, her emotions all over the place because of Nico, and everything else that had happened. She'd made a terrible mistake and surely

Rafael thought so too. But that was something for later. Right now, she could avoid facing it and get the answers she needed. Killing two birds with one stone.

But when she looked at Rafael, ordering for them in his lyrical French, she wasn't sure if she was actually doing the right thing.

Her stomach rumbled loudly, reminding her that she still hadn't eaten since the morning. And even that had been a single cold crêpe, like old brown paper in comparison to what she was promised here. The aromas had already set her stomach growling.

The cider came in a pale earthenware jug, accompanied by three bowls. Rafael poured for each of them, although she saw he gave himself substantially less. Was he trying to get her drunk now? Because that really was not necessary as her hormones had already proved once today. Then she remembered the car. Of course, he was driving. God, she was an idiot. And no one was getting drunk on the cider unless they drank a whole barrel. It was good though. Gwen hadn't lied about that.

'So what do you need to know about Sainte Sirène, Ariadne Walker? I thought you were here looking for Ys. I don't think it's on the land anymore. And if it was here, no one has seen it for more than a thousand years.' Gwen laughed, amused at her own words.

'No. I know that.' A stupid thing to say. Of course she knew that. Gwen was joking. She swallowed hard and plunged onwards. 'It's just a legend. There's no city of gold under the waters of the bay, however much my brother would love that. But those tales came from somewhere. So, by tracing the stories back, looking for the origins, we can get clues as to what was really there. And where to look for it.'

'Fascinating,' Gwen replied, sipping delicately at her cider.

'Don't tease, Gwen,' Rafael warned gently. There was real affection between them, Ari realised. A lifelong friendship.

They had been childhood sweethearts, or at least that was what Laure had implied. She seemed to think Gwen was just waiting for Rafael to come back to her. That was the impression Ari had got at dinner the other night.

Gwen batted her long pale lashes at him. 'I'm not teasing. I'm interested. Please go on.'

She looked genuine. But maybe she was a really good actress.

Ari glanced at Rafael, but he just nodded, encouraging her to continue.

'What was the name of Sainte Sirène before it was Sainte Sirène? The Breton name, I mean.'

'The Breton name? Sant Sieren?'

'But that's just a direct translation from the French, isn't it?' Rafael said. 'There was an older name. I thought it would be in our library, but I couldn't find it.'

'You didn't think to ask Mémé? Dear me, Rafael, you're slipping.'

'She was sleeping and I didn't... Look, it doesn't matter. Not now. You're here. You've got to know, Gwen.'

'Let me see.'

She paused as their food arrived and Ari found herself presented with a savoury buckwheat pancake stuffed with scallops, leek and cream. She tucked in, relishing every bite, waiting for Gwen to answer.

'There was a name, but I don't think it's been used in hundreds of years. Ker-Gwagenn. The home of the wave. Sometimes they called it Ker-ar-Groac'h, after the water witch who lived in the caves. Many of our names come from legend. The French changed them. It was a way of stamping out the language and the culture, but it never really worked. And, of course, our mermaid legends lent into the new name. There was no real saint called Sirène. She never existed. The stained glass in the chapel and the sculptures depict someone else.'

'Dahut of Ys?'

Gwen gave a brief, dismissive laugh. 'Perhaps. If such a person ever existed either. More likely, it's just another Madonna. Poor Dahut. She is so very maligned in all our legends, but really she was just looking for true love. Everyone else let her down. She could have been a wonderful ruler for all we know, but the Christians blamed her for everything. Like Eve.'

'She didn't open the gates and destroy the city?'

'Her last lover did. He betrayed her.'

'He had good reason,' said Rafael, putting down his cutlery with an uncharacteristic clatter. 'Her city was feeding like a parasite off the surrounding population. She was a despot, a monster. And her father, the supposed king, did nothing to control her. Besides, she had a habit of murdering the men she slept with.'

'The men who lied to her,' Gwen corrected him gently. 'Perhaps they forfeited their lives by doing that. They craved only her power. And she was powerful.'

'Power corrupts,' said Rafael.

Gwen reached out to tuck a stray lock of his dark hair behind his ear, so simple and intimate a gesture. 'The du Lac version of events. We've all heard them before, Mac'htiern.'

Ari felt like an interloper, a voyeur. They had that easy familiarity of old lovers and for a moment Rafael wore a dazed expression. He'd been looking at her the same way not so very long ago. Well, maybe not the same, not quite. The fire she'd seen in him wasn't there, the pain and passion that had rattled her so much and left her insisting they come here instead. To Gwen.

She'd known Simon, spoke about him with affection. Had he reacted to her in the same way? Ari's heart almost stopped. But Gwen went on speaking.

'Scandalous rumours, put about by the man who betrayed

her. Her mother was an enchantress, a fey woman. Their ways are not the same as mankind's. She inherited Morvan's power, and ruling was her right. Her father had no say in the matter. Even Ankou bowed before her, the Servant of Death himself. Men always think they know best, but seldom do. Every Breton woman knows that.'

'Not just every *Breton* woman,' Ari muttered and caught Rafael's eye again.

A shiver ran through him and he seemed more himself again. He grinned at her.

Such a dangerous grin. It made her think of that kiss again, of the way she'd lost herself in him. She had to force herself to look away and instantly regretted it.

Gwen laughed. 'Oh, you'll fit right in, Ari. Hardly foreign at all.'

'Not French, you mean?'

Rafael interrupted. 'Not *Breton*, is what she means. Even the French are foreign here. Don't mind her.'

Gwen finished her cider and poured some more. 'You're a fellow Celt, Dr Walker, that's enough. I can tell these things. So, you study the stories people tell and the names they give their homes to find the pathway to the past. Like a bard. We'll make you a member of the Goursez Vreizh yet.'

'What's that?'

'The Breton Druids. A modern association, but they try their best.' She sat back, sipping on her cider, watching Ari with an air of speculation. 'What a fascinating area you chose to study, reconnecting us to history, to the places and people we came from, to the land, the stones and the sea. But why here? Why Sainte Sirène?'

Ari dropped her gaze to the wood of the table, old and worn smooth. 'Simon Poullain wanted to find Ys more than anything. He said he was looking for the pathway. I thought he meant figuratively, but I'm not so sure anymore.'

Le chemin de l'eau, she thought, the water path. The pathway to Ys.

'Ah, I see. Simon. A matter of honour then.' No trace of mockery remained in her voice. If anything, she looked briefly stricken. 'Simon was a good man, Ari. A good friend to Sainte Sirène.'

For a moment, the question hovered on the tip of Ari's tongue. How well had Gwen known Simon? Was she the woman he had written about? But she couldn't force the words out of her mouth.

Gwen hummed softly to herself, watching Ari, waiting. Abruptly, she looked up, smiled brightly at the waitress who had arrived with menus for dessert.

'*Trois crêpes caramel au beurre salé maison, s'il vous plaît.* Trust me on this one. There is nothing better. Jeanne makes it herself, the sauce. To die for.'

Ari's phone rang and she glanced at it to see Jason's name flash up. She shoved all thoughts of Gwen and Simon to the back of her mind. 'I have to take this. Sorry.' She fled outside as she answered. 'Jason? Is everything—'

'Fine. It's all fine. They're discharging him. He's got the all-clear, but he has to rest for a week or so. Total rest. Whether he likes it or not.'

Two of them down then. That wasn't good news. Jason wasn't saying it, but he had to be thinking it. How were they going to proceed with his expedition now?

'That's good. That's great. Do you want me to drive back and pick you up?'

'No, we'll get a taxi. Don't drag Rafael all the way back here. Where are you anyway? I couldn't get through. Are you home?'

'No. We stopped for a meal.'

The silence lingered on the line and then Jason laughed, a slow meaningful laugh. 'Oh right. A meal... You and him?'

'Just a meal. Crêpes. Jesus, Jason. Knock it off.'

'Yeah, yeah, crêpes. That's what the cool kids are calling it now. Wait until I tell Nico. He owes me fifty euros.'

For a moment, she didn't know what to say. They'd been *betting* on her? No, probably not. Not really. Not Nico anyway. But her face flamed red all the same. Because Jason was almost right. If Rafael had lived any closer to the hospital, she was pretty sure she would have been in bed with him by now.

'You're ridiculous,' she choked out the words. 'Go and take care of Nico. I'll see you back at the gîte. Ring me when you're on the way.'

She hung up and turned around to see Rafael standing in the door of the cottage housing the crêperie. 'Is everything OK?' he asked.

'Yeah, yes.' God, he hadn't heard, had he? What had she said? Nothing bad. And he couldn't have heard Jason and his insinuation, could he? 'They're discharging Nico. Jason's going to get a taxi.'

'That's good news. Do you want coffee?'

She shook her head. 'I should get back to the gîte. I'd like to be there when they arrive. Rafael, I'm sorry.' The awkwardness of it swept over her. True, no promises had been made, but still. If not made, they'd been implied. 'I really am. I just—'

He raised his hands in a placating gesture. 'I understand. Really. It isn't a problem. I'll just pay the bill and then I'll—'

She cut in before he could finish. 'It's fine. I can walk from here. It would be rude to run out on Gwen like that. Please apologise for me. And thank her as well.'

A flicker of disappointment crossed his beautiful features and she hated herself a little bit. The ghost of his lips against hers wouldn't leave her and she longed to kiss him again. But it was neither the time nor the place. She couldn't just throw herself at him again. Out here on the street, in full view of everyone. She needed to think, to get her emotions in order.

'I could call over later. If you'd like. If it's not an imposition.' His tone was tentative, a question. It was also a plea. Did he think she didn't want him?

How could it be an imposition after what they had shared earlier? 'No, not at all. I'd like that. Please.' God, she sounded like an idiot. And here she was, running away yet again. Well, not running away, not entirely. But putting some distance between them for now. A safe distance. Because she had to. He made her lose all reason. She wasn't ready for the emotions he churned up inside her. No one had made her feel so much since Simon.

Her thoughts drifted back to Gwen, and the way she spoke about Simon, and what Ari suspected... Ari veered her mind away from that as quickly as possible. Back to Rafael. It was dizzying.

He was gazing solemnly at her, studying her, and she wasn't sure she wanted to know what he saw.

'And you will have thoroughly researched Ker-Gwagenn and all the implications by then, I presume?'

She grinned at him, forcing all the bravado she didn't feel into the expression. 'It's like you know me already, Rafael.'

He smiled back, and a softness entered his dark eyes.

'What is it? What's wrong?' she asked.

'Nothing. Just... I've finally graduated from being a cartoon character.'

CHAPTER SEVENTEEN

When Ari got back to the gîte, she was surprised to find it deserted again. There was none of the usual gang who wandered in and out at a whim. Even the tents in the garden flapped wanly in the breeze with no sign of life. Perhaps the loss of Thierry had been too much for them.

The door was unlocked. They had all rushed out so early this morning that they must have forgotten to lock up after themselves.

It was dark and cold, without a single light on inside.

Something didn't feel right.

It was even eerier in the house itself. She was used to there being someone in every room, music playing or the TV on, and at least one argument breaking out at any given moment. But there was nothing.

A cool breeze brushed over the back of her neck, setting the hairs there standing up. Someone had been in here.

She knew it as surely as she knew her own name.

A floorboard creaked overhead.

Was someone still here?

A thousand fears rushed through her, for herself, for their belongings, and then she realised the most precious thing of all.

Running to the store cupboard, she found the lock broken, a mangled mess of metal. It hung there, like a one-armed man clinging to a clifftop.

Ari jerked the door open and searched desperately.

It couldn't be gone. Who knew it was even here? The mask was the one thing they still had that proved they weren't all deranged or deluded. The archaeologists might not have believed it was real, but she knew what she had seen, the condition in which she had found it. Jason was determined to get it dated somehow and Rafael would surely pay for that. If it proved to be as old as they thought...

It was still there. She found herself gasping in relief. The mask lurked in its watery enclosure, the liquid milky and opaque around it, worse than the last time she had seen it, hiding it from easy observation. Almost as if something was bleeding from the mask into the water, polluting it. All the same, she caught a glimpse of the artefact itself, gleaming in the light coming from the open door. It looked even brighter, the gold even more pronounced, glittering through the murk. She pulled the box out and brought it over to the kitchen table to get a better look.

The lid stuck as she opened it, as if it didn't want to let her in, and she had to tug it free. Water slopped over her hands, but she didn't care. She cursed under her breath as she dropped the lid beside it and peered inside.

The mask didn't look old now. Not at all. It shone like something freshly made, a work of art. It was subtly altered and she couldn't quite work out what it was. The mask looked even more lifelike somehow, delicate curves and hollows in the surface that she was certain were not there before. It had been smooth and sleek. But this was something else. Like a human face, weirdly familiar...

The gold lines swirling on the porcelain were thicker and brighter, and there were more pronounced blue lines as well, a bright lapis lazuli. Ari ran her fingers over the surface, and could feel the changes. It felt warm to the touch, almost like skin.

And the face... she knew that face...

'*Put it on.*'

The voice came from the air around her, drifting through the unnatural stillness of the house. She shook her head, trying to focus, but the world shifted sideways into a misty, watery world. Light rippled around her, blue-green, undulating. Her breath caught in her throat and she couldn't breathe, couldn't swallow, couldn't stop herself.

'*Put it on, Ariadne. It will show you everything. It will show you the truth, even the truths you hide from yourself. It will answer all your questions. And you have so many questions...*'

Her hands shook and the mask trembled in them. Tears stung the corners of her eyes. It wasn't possible. She was hearing things, imagining things. But it felt so real.

Shadows rushed in towards her, long and sinuous, like the eel which had wound its way around the rocks when she had found this thing. This cursed thing.

'*Ari, don't.*'

Another voice, Simon's voice. She would know it anywhere. It sounded far-off and distant, like an echo, or a whisper. But the urgency in it was like a coiled spring.

She wanted to listen to him, wanted to obey. But she couldn't.

Something else was at play here, something that was so much stronger than him. Than her. Than anything.

A long low laugh sounded, much closer to her, part of the shadow that wound its way around her, encircling her, crushing her.

'*He tried to tell you, your love, before he lost his way on the*

*path to Ys. He tried to leave you clues and to protect you. But you
did not see. You did not listen. And now it is too late. Put on the
mask. It will show you. It is the only way.'*

Slowly, as if she no longer had control of her body, she lifted
the mask towards her face. And she knew, deep inside her heart,
that she didn't want to do this. Every instinct screamed at her to
put the wretched thing down, to let it go. But she couldn't.

Darkness swept up, wrapping itself around her and pulling
her down into the depths. Drowning her in shadows.

'Ari?'

A spear of light lanced through her with the sound of her
name, grabbing her by the throat and dragging her back to the
surface. She drew in a breath of shock and pain. Not Simon's
voice. Not this time.

She turned so fast she almost dropped the mask. Instead,
her grip on it tightened so much she feared she'd break it
herself. And part of her wanted to.

To shatter it. Crush it. Grind it to dust...

Rafael stood in the door, holding her jacket. She must have
left it behind. Standing there with her mouth hanging open, she
didn't know what to say.

The spell broke and she inhaled the sweet air. Before she
could second-guess herself, she dropped the mask back into the
box and stepped back as quickly as she dared. Her head spin-
ning, she fought for breath and the whispering voice faded
away.

'Ari? Are you OK?'

Suddenly he was beside her, his arms around her, the
warmth of him driving the chill of the darkest depths of the sea
from her bones. He held her close, cradling her against him. She
wasn't proud of it. She clung to him.

'What is it? What happened?' he went on when she didn't
answer. 'You're shaking like a leaf.'

His fingers brushed her hair, stroked the side of her face and she leaned into his touch. The comfort it gave her was unexpected.

She dragged her face away from his shoulder as if it was the last thing she wanted to do. Which it was. Looking up, she met his dark eyes and read the undisguised concern there.

It gave her the strength to tell him the truth. Even if it made her sound like a madwoman. Given what they had seen together already, it was not a leap.

'There was someone here,' she whispered. 'The lock's broken on the storage and... Rafael, there was a voice. Not a human voice. Something else. It wanted me to wear the mask.'

He frowned and shifted his gaze to the mask lurking in the water again. 'It looks...' His voice trailed off, confused.

'Different. I know. It's changed. I don't know how or why, but it was old and worn when we found it, covered in dirt and barnacles and God knows what. And now... look at it.'

The expression that crossed his face married repulsion and fascination.

'It's beautiful,' he whispered and his voice was a rumble against her. 'Ari... I had no idea.'

For a moment, he held her tighter and then released her just as abruptly. He leaned in closer, staring at it.

'It looks familiar,' he said. 'The face, I mean. Like... like someone I knew long ago... something...'

He reached out, his hand hovering over the water. The liquid rippled beneath his skin, moving like a living thing, moving out of his way. An optical illusion, it had to be, but she stood there transfixed as something magic started to unfold before her. She was frozen as he moved closer, the same spell which had swept over her creeping through him. She could see it at work; a blank expression, a desperate need burning in his dark eyes.

All sound fell away, every breath stilled, her heartbeat, everything.

'*Don't let him touch it, Ari,*' Simon's voice whispered suddenly in her ear. '*Whatever you do, don't let him—*'

The enchantment shattered.

Before she knew what she was doing, she grabbed the lid and slammed it back on the box. Rafael recoiled in shock.

'What's wrong?' he gasped. 'What was that?' He staggered back from her, still clutching her coat like it was a totem of protection.

'Nothing,' she said. 'Are you OK?'

She peered at him and he squeezed his eyes tightly shut and then pinched the bridge of his nose as if fending off a headache.

'Yes. I... I think so. Just... a bit dizzy. Sorry. That... that thing is...' He didn't say what he thought of it, but she knew exactly what he meant.

'I know,' she agreed. Picking up the box, she returned it to the storeroom and closed the door. The lock still hung there, forlornly broken. There had to be another one around here somewhere. She needed to lock the mask away, and not just in case of theft. The effect it had on both of them was unnerving. Dangerous.

'Someone broke in?' Rafael asked.

'Looks like it. I don't know who though. There was no one here when I got back.'

'But you said there was.'

The creaking floorboard, the sounds upstairs...

Ari ran up the stairs, her heart pounding in her chest. Her room was empty. The box with Simon's things was tipped over, the papers spilling across the floor. She gathered them up quickly, shoving the notebook and the pages back into it.

His things. All she had left of him. Precious, sacred to her. If someone had taken them, or destroyed them...

But there was no one here. Had they gone while she'd been preoccupied with the mask? Climbed out a window and made their escape?

Or had there really been anyone else here at all?

'Ari,' Rafael said as he appeared behind her again. 'Don't just run off!' He checked the rooms himself. 'What if there had been someone here? A burglar or worse. With what we've seen... Think.'

It was like a slap and she turned on him, angry now. Angry with the situation, with whoever had been here, real or imagined, with the mask, with all the madness, and with him. 'I think altogether too much, Rafael. And I don't need your protection.'

To his credit, he backed up, hands held up in submission, but she caught the smile lingering in the corner of his mouth.

Slowly, he shook his head. 'Even a malevolent spirit would think twice about taking you on. Ari, talk to me. Please.'

'We need to lock that bloody mask away where no one can get at it. I don't care if something supernatural or physical is trying to get to it, or if it's trying to get to us, it needs to be put out of reach. Now.'

'I agree. The vault in the Manoir, it will be safe there.'

She hesitated, the suspicion she felt curdling in her stomach. 'You can't take it alone. It isn't safe, Rafael. Believe me.'

He reached out his hand. 'I do.'

'I know what I felt. What I saw in your face. It wants us. It's manipulating people. I know it sounds crazy, but—'

It had affected her effortlessly. She'd seen the way its magic had reached out to ensnare Rafael just as quickly. What would it do to Jason or to Nico if it was this strong already? What would it want from her brother or her friend? No. She couldn't allow that. She wouldn't. She'd have to get rid of it. Destroy it. Throw it back into the sea.

Is this what it had done to Simon? Had he seen the danger, tried to act – but the mask had taken him all the same? It hadn't even mattered, because the first time she'd gone into the water, she'd brought it back out again. As if it had been intended. Ordained.

To get rid of it would mean destroying their only serious find, the only link they had to Ys. And to Simon…

Rafael's hand closed over hers again, threading their fingers together, and the spiral of panic faded away. Just with his touch. 'Ari, I believe you. We'll take it together. We'll both go, and we'll keep each other safe. OK?'

Somehow she found the ability to breathe again. Slowly, she nodded. 'OK,' she said. 'But it has to stay locked away, Rafael. It's dangerous. Promise me.'

'I promise,' he assured her. And, like an idiot, she believed him.

CHAPTER EIGHTEEN

Rafael led Ari into the Manoir and down a narrow staircase behind the main flight of stairs. The place was quiet, peaceful, and the familiar scents of sea and wood polish swept up around him, calming him. His heart beat hard against his ribs, and the sound of his footsteps echoed that rhythm.

He knew this path like he knew the way through his room at night, like he knew how to breathe.

Ari followed him, her nervousness betrayed with every step, but she clung to the box she had wrapped in an oversized shopping bag. An ignominious state for such a find, but what choice did they have? At least down here, it would be safe.

He didn't know which of his ancestors had built the vault. It was buried in the heart of the cellars, more fundamental a part of the building than any roof or floor. It was, perhaps, the whole reason for the rest of the Manoir. When he was a child, on the rare occasions they had visited here, he had schemed and plotted, tried to figure out ways to sneak inside, convinced that it had to contain treasure and mysteries. He imagined a hoard of gold and gleaming jewels, and possibly a dragon to guard it. Rather than Mémé.

On the day his great-aunt had finally put the ornate key in his hands, he'd hardly dared to open the heavy metal door. The key was old as well, a huge heavy thing which they hid in plain sight as a decoration in the drawing room. No one else knew what it opened.

The door opened with a long, sinister creak. Fitting, he supposed. He often wondered if it was intentional, just to put him on edge when he went in there.

He glanced back at Ari and smiled in an attempt to reassure her. She looked terrified. He didn't blame her.

Rafael had felt the urge to pick up that mask, to put it on and give himself up to it. Some strange energy had possessed him, shaken him, overpowered him without any effort at all. It had almost taken Ari as well. That was what he'd walked in on. And he thanked all that was holy that he had arrived in time.

He flicked on the light. The bulbs flickered and then filled the space with a steady glow. He heard Ari inhale, a sharp intake of breath he couldn't ignore. He didn't see wonder here anymore, but she did.

'What do you have down here?' she blurted out.

He glanced around, wishing he could see the wonder she did. Her eyes shone with it. All he saw were dusty boxes and crates, a few paintings and even more books.

'Are those diamonds?' she asked. 'Rafael? Are those—?'

There was a box of jewellery on the nearest shelf. Mémé must have been storing things down here. Or someone else, long ago. He didn't remember seeing it before, but he didn't know if he would have noticed. It looked antique. And probably uninsurable. No wonder she hadn't mentioned that. A bank vault would probably be more responsible. But the same could be true of many things down here. Sometimes a bank vault was not enough.

Ari set the box containing the mask down on a shelf and

pushed it back, as if keen to get it out of her hands. She turned around, staring at the room. There were no windows, and only one way in, the huge metal door through which they had just entered. The alarms were separate to those protecting the house. He'd had them installed himself. Other than that, just that door, this key and several feet of granite everywhere else kept this place secure. Impregnable. Only his immediate family knew of its existence. And now Ari. It was the most secure place he knew and he had visited more than his fair share of bank vaults in his time.

'Cosy, isn't it?' he joked.

A smile flickered over her mouth. 'Very homely.'

'So, safe enough for your magic mask?'

He had to make light of it, for both their sakes.

She looked relieved. 'Yes.'

'Good, let's get away from it.'

He couldn't disguise how eager he was to do that and neither could she.

But as he turned to go, something else caught his eye. Not jewels, or treasures. It was a small leather-bound book, lying on its side on the shelf just inside the door. Not old, not compared to other things in here. But not modern either. He picked it up, turned it over in his hand, recognising it. It didn't belong here.

'What's that?' Ari asked.

'Fabien's diary, the volume missing from the library upstairs. I wonder what it's doing down here.'

He opened it, his eyes scanning the page. The writing was so familiar. The diaries were relatively well known. People came begging to use them for research from time to time. As a child, Rafael had read all of his diaries, the ones he could lay hands on. All the early ones were easy. It was only when war broke out that Fabien had started using code.

A phrase caught his eye.

Blanche said there was a path leading to Ys, or what is left of Ys. She called it le chemin de l'eau *and I never realised why until we found it, Poullain and I. And there she was, eyes of stone, heart of stone, waiting for us.*

Rafael frowned, glaring at the words, refusing to believe what he was seeing.

Ari leaned over, reading. 'Does that say Poullain?'

'Tristan Poullain. Fabien's... friend. His comrade in arms.'

He knew from the rest of the diaries what Tristan had been to Fabien, even in a time when that was not only illegal but also dangerous. They had died together, after all. He didn't know if Tristan had returned Fabien's feelings. Perhaps Fabien had never told him.

But who on earth was Blanche?

'We saw them in the picture, in the museum,' Ari said. 'And Simon talked about Tristan. His grandfather used to tell him about Tristan and how he found the path to Ys.'

He flicked on ahead. There were pages missing, torn out. That couldn't be good.

He closed the book. 'Upstairs,' he said. 'We need to talk to Mémé and find out why she hid it down here.'

'She hid it?'

'It's his last diary. There's a gap on the shelf upstairs. I don't know when she did it, but I don't think anyone else could have hidden it down here. So what's in it? And what did she want to keep secret?'

Ari was on the phone to Jason when he came back from Mémé's room. His great-aunt was asleep and she looked so frail, he didn't like to wake her. Nolvene said she hadn't been well all day. Lack of sleep last night, bad dreams...

'No, it's fine. It's here. I promise. We thought it was better to lock it up somewhere secure... Yes, it's secure. I checked. It's fine... I don't know who did it. There was no one there when I— Look, I've got to go. Let me know when you're home, OK?'

She hung up and gave him a pained smile.

'How are they?' he asked.

'Still at the hospital waiting for discharge. I just didn't want them to get back and think—'

What she had thought, he guessed. That the house had been burgled and the mask stolen.

'Mémé is sleeping, but I've asked Nolvene to tell us when she wakes up. I didn't want to disturb her.'

'May I see the diary?'

He handed it over with a certain reluctance. It felt like prying and he didn't like it. It wasn't that Fabien's life, and his love for Tristan Poullain, was a deep dark secret. At least, not after so many years. It was tragic, that was all. Just as Gwen had said. In more ways than one.

Ari flicked through it, studying the elegant script, clearly having no real trouble with the language.

'What cave is he talking about?'

'Probably one of the sea caves near Pors Sirène. But it could be anywhere up and down the coast. The resistance used them to bring in operatives and to store supplies, like the smugglers did for years.'

'Like La Fontenelle.' The Wolf of Île Tristan, the pirate who had marauded these shores and used the caves to hide his treasure. The caves were always places of secrets, and those who knew them could benefit from that.

'Exactly. Many of the local men left with de Gaulle and joined the Free French forces. They knew these shores like no one else. Every young man on Île de Sein left, you know? The Germans occupied the island but found only the women, the children and the old men had stayed. It was the same along the coast. But not as obvious. Men came and went and the women covered for them. Then the Germans cleared the coast, relocating everyone.'

Ari frowned at something on the page. 'It says here he was brought in for questioning. He can't have been in hiding then.'

'Not at that point, no.' He scanned the paragraph and then translated. 'They were living in one of the farmhouses, with his sisters. "I was brought in for questioning this morning. The commander, Sternberg, is a thin-faced, miserable man, from the Ahnenerbe..." What's that?'

She frowned. 'Nazi archaeologists. Obsessed with proving the purity and supremacy of the Aryan race. Gwen mentioned them. Obsessed with Atlantis. And Ys, I guess. Go on.'

He obeyed. '"The questions were not what I expected and not at all welcome. He wanted to know about Ys, everything I might know and how it might tie in to the legend of Atlantis. He would not accept my answer that there is no connection and never has been. He has already made up his mind. When I had nothing useful for him, he released me. But they will keep looking. For now, the tides hide the water path. They will be watching me. If I am lucky, that will be all. However, in most things I have never been lucky."'

They sat in uncomfortable silence. Rafael's ancestor had been walking a dangerous line and ultimately he had paid the price. He had died a patriot and a hero of France. If he was also defending the last remnants of Ys from the Nazis, he'd died a hero of Brittany as well. The Mac'htiern, the leader of his people, their protector.

'"The tides hide the water path",' Ari murmured. '*Le chemin de l'eau...* like on the map, the old map. He found it, Rafael. Some part of it is still here. The pathway to Ys. Simon was right.'

She flicked on ahead to where the pages had been torn out.

No way of knowing when or by whom. Along the edge, he could make out a few letters and nothing more. No clues as to what might have been written there.

'And Simon was trying to find it based on the stories he heard as a child. It must have been Tristan's stories, passed on through his family. Who was this Blanche he speaks about?'

Rafael shrugged. 'I don't know.'

'You have records of the people who lived here at the time, don't you? I thought I saw them in the library.'

'Some local records, but not much. There wasn't a census in 1941, for obvious reasons. Most of it is in the departmental archives. We have rent books, perhaps. We can look. I've never heard of a woman called Blanche in relation to Fabien other than here in his writings. Maybe Mémé remembers. She would have been very young when he died, but she adored him.'

Ari was reading again. 'Look at this. "Tris tells me I am a fool and sometimes I believe him. He suspects Blanche of a darker purpose and fears she will lead me to my death. But it is like a spell comes over me when she is near. She is my every dream and she knows the way. She is a keeper of secrets and would share them with us. The secrets of Ys itself. If only we surrender to her and let the tide take us. And then stand beneath her eyes of stone."'

Her voice flowed so sweetly, her translation perfect. Her French was good, for a foreigner, but he supposed that having spent so long with Simon, having stayed here, it was only to be expected. Still, it warmed some part of him he didn't expect her to reach.

But that was Ari Walker, a constant revelation.

'Simon said something like that,' she murmured, more to herself than to him. '"I've let the tide take me and surrendered to her."' And she fell silent again, a deep, heartbroken silence. Thinking of Simon, he supposed. He was a constant shadow between them.

Rafael didn't know how to talk to her about the kiss, about that flare of desire they had shared, but at the same time he wasn't sure that he should either. He hadn't doubted for a moment that Ari desired him, but as soon as she had time to think about it, she had started to doubt herself. Or to doubt him perhaps.

Well, anyone was entitled to change their mind. He shouldn't have rushed her. She was as flighty as a deer, Ariadne Walker, and with good reason. Simon's death had left deep scars.

Simon Poullain. Why did it always come back to a Poullain?

Tris. Fabien had called Tristan Poullain *Tris.* A nickname, informal and intimate. Whereas Blanche was referred to more formally, as if he was talking about a priestess. Or a goddess.

Blanche...

Who on earth was Blanche?

And after almost eighty years, how would they find out what she had known? If she had shared it with Fabien, and if he had written it down, the final pages of this diary were gone now. Probably destroyed years ago.

Ari flicked through the pages and then got to her feet, pacing back and forth as she read. He watched her, framed by the evening light coming through the high windows and slanting across the floor. She looked like a classical statue, beautiful and untouchable, a dream he didn't even know he had until he met her. Not a model, or socialite, not a head of industry or anything like any of the women he had briefly dated. She was a whirlwind, intelligence and brilliance entwined with a quick wit and a fearless spirit.

It wasn't love. It couldn't be. He barely knew her. But it was something he didn't want to lose. He didn't even want to risk that.

He had never told a woman he loved her. It had never been true.

Suddenly, Ari's shoulder's tensed. 'The pages...'

He rose from the table, her alarm infecting him.

She looked over at him, met his gaze and frowned, her eyes wide with shock. 'I think I know where the missing pages are. Simon had them. They're back in the gîte. In my room.'

CHAPTER NINETEEN

Ari tipped the box out on her bed as if unveiling a guilty secret. She only half believed it herself. The idea of Simon stealing something like that, of him tearing out pages from a historical document, a unique archive of his beloved home...

It was so out of character.

And yet, there they were.

Gibberish, that was what she'd thought when she first glanced at the pages.

Rafael took them solemnly. They moved as his hands trembled, as if a breeze shook them. 'But why would he do such a thing?' Even he sounded horrified.

Ari didn't have an answer to that. She was wondering the same thing herself, but she didn't want to tell him. It was not like the Simon she had known. He had such respect for the past. Madame du Lac must have given him the diary, trusted him, and this was how he repaid her?

'What's that?' Rafael asked.

Another photograph, she realised, in the back of the notebook. She pulled it out. It was Simon and, to her surprise, Gwen. She handed it to Rafael, trying to ignore the way the two figures sat close together, their legs kind of tangled with each other.

'What the hell?' he muttered.

Ari's throat had tightened. It was like seeing a whole different side to Simon, someone she didn't know at all. And she didn't like it. It brought the words he'd written in his last letter back to her a bit too vividly. It must have been Gwen. It had to be.

And she had wondered, hadn't she? The way Gwen talked about him, the way all men seemed to be drawn to her... would Simon have stood a chance if Gwen had returned the interest?

'Maybe...' Rafael began and then stopped. He cleared his throat. 'Maybe this was taken before he met you?'

It didn't look that way. But then Simon had always been youthful, handsome, and Gwen was as beautiful as ever.

Why did Simon have a photo of himself with Gwen Morvan tucked away like that?

'I don't know.' She whispered the words and went back to rooting through the box. 'Can you read the pages from Fabien's diary?'

'No.' Her bed creaked as he sat on it. 'It must have been important though. It's not like the rest of the diary back at the house. He's encoded everything. There's a map here too but... well, it might be a map. I don't know... It's just lines really. It's so vague you'd have to know the general location to begin with.'

Fabien had been no fool.

But Simon on the other hand... Perhaps more than she knew.

The caves under Castelmeur. Fabien had been protecting them because the resistance were using them to move supplies and smuggle people in and out. Or that was what everyone assumed. Maybe it was more. He'd mentioned the water path in his diary...

The locations were just a series of numbers, some random lines and squiggles.

She opened Simon's notebook now, and scanned the pages. One after the other, he had laid out his own cryptic notes. But she could follow them. They had always worked together, so this was not a code to her. Just a mess.

How do you save a lost city?

He'd underlined that several times. It was a good question.

Rafael believed that was how they could break the curse on his family, the curse that killed all the men of his line: by saving Ys. But Ys was gone. Centuries gone.

Water path... Eyes of stone... Dahut's mask.

Her gaze skimmed over phrases, questions, so many squiggles and Simon's terrible handwriting.

The numbers caught her eye. *48065 4688*. She knew those numbers. They were etched into her mind.

Beneath them, she found a date, followed by a transcription. Simon had written the whole thing out. He'd broken the code and copied it from Fabien's own diary from years ago.

4 June, 1943.

Low tide 14.05, Wind south-west, 10 knots. Conditions calm.

Tris and I took the boat out and moored off the point at 48.065, -4.688. Water cold but still and visibility good in between the gates. We swam down to the pathway and followed it, surrendering to her, just as Blanche said. We let the tide take us. Beyond that lay wonders, and a heart of stone. While this area can be used for storage, we will have to find somewhere else for Goldfinch. This cannot be shared. The risk is too great. Sternberg and his thugs must not find it.

'Ari?' Rafael's voice called her back to the present.

'Who's Sternberg?' she asked.

'The officer from the Ahnenerbe, I think.'

The Nazi archaeologists looking for Ys. That made sense. It all made sense. Which meant...

'I need to look at... There, that.' She pulled a large chart out of the pile of ephemera Simon had gathered and spread it out on the carpet. He'd made marks there too, tracing locations. One was not far from where they had found the mask, at the foot of the cliffs. They had been so close.

'There?' Rafael asked, leaning over her.

She nodded. 'It has to be. Simon found the mask but hid it again. I just don't know why. The mask would have proved he was right.'

'Would it? The university didn't believe it was real. And the influence it seems to have on us...' He shuddered and Ari had to agree with that. She hated the thing. It felt wrong. Dangerous.

'But why didn't he tell Jason? Why didn't he show anyone this?'

Rafael was still holding the photo of Simon and Gwen. He tapped it on his hand. 'Maybe he did.'

'Simon would have told me if...'

But he wouldn't. He'd sent her a letter telling her he never wanted to see her again. He had sent back the necklace. He had met someone else and he loved her, not Ari. Gwen. It had to be Gwen.

'You were in another country. And maybe it wasn't anything serious. Just a photo.' He didn't sound any more convinced about it than she was. Rafael was trying to be kind, but Ari knew better. There was something about the picture, the way Simon looked at Gwen.

I've let the tide take me and surrendered to her.

Ari shuddered. She didn't like this. More of that part of Simon she didn't know. What had he been trying to tell her in the letter? What had he been trying to say? That he had no choice?

'Ari!' Jason's voice rang out downstairs.

'Shit!' she exclaimed, looking at Rafael as if they were a pair of teenagers caught sneaking around upstairs. She hurriedly started shoving everything back into the box. He still had the pages from Fabien's diary and the photo. 'I don't want them to see that. Especially the photo.' She didn't want them to know what she had discovered about Simon. Even now, she felt the urge to protect his memory.

Rafael nodded and tucked it all into the inside pocket of his jacket. 'We'll have to tell them something. You've found the site, Fabien's path to Ys.'

'Simon found it. Not me,' she muttered. 'I've done nothing.'

Nothing but find out that the man she had adored and idolised had stolen and lied, and cheated on...

No, she couldn't think about that. Not now. She had known that anyway. He'd already told her in the letter. She simply hadn't wanted it to be true.

Rafael reached out his hand to her, but she turned away. If he touched her now, showed her any sympathy or kindness at all, she'd crumble.

'I'll show them the map and we'll arrange a dive tomorrow. Or as soon as possible anyway. We have to confirm this, find the pathway to Ys. Just... just let me...' Her throat closed and she choked on a sob she hadn't expected. Rafael's arms around her were the comfort she needed, but this was not the time. It was going to be bad enough that he was here with her, up in her bedroom. Yes, she was an adult woman, but that was not going to stop her brother.

They made their way downstairs to the living room, where Nico was sitting on the sofa and Jason was busily flitting in and out of the kitchen with tea and cake, and whatever else he could find that might constitute some form of comfort.

He stopped dead when he saw Rafael though. 'Oh. Hello. What are you—' And his eyes swung inexorably towards Ari.

She blurted out the words before he could explode. 'We've found something in Simon's things. A dive site. We think the location...' She swallowed back a comment about finding altogether too many things. 'Can I dive tomorrow?'

Jason frowned, still looking from her to Rafael and back. 'Tomorrow? No one's diving without a partner, you know that. Not here. It's too dangerous.'

'It's not that dangerous. I know what I'm doing.'

Nico cleared his throat pointedly and she cast a glare at him. Just out of hospital, concussion or not, he was not above throwing her last mistake in her face. 'I'm not able to dive for at least a week, and Jason's out for longer. Alix is distraught, as is Madalen. They're the only two with enough experience to lead a dive.'

'I have the experience,' she countered. True, it wasn't recent and it wasn't local, but it wasn't completely unreasonable.

'You are not going alone,' said Jason firmly. Like he wouldn't go in a heartbeat if their situation was reversed.

'What if she wasn't alone?' Rafael asked.

'You can dive, can you?' Jason snapped.

Ari flinched back. She'd never heard her brother talk to anyone quite like that, especially not a donor. The dynamics had shifted and she didn't like it.

'Off in the Caymans for a week, were you? Or at some five-star resort in Indonesia?'

But Rafael didn't back down or show the slightest bit of shame. He was what he was, Ari thought, and never thought less of himself for that. 'Yes. And I'm Sirènois. I know these waters as well as anyone.'

· · ·

The boat rocked gently on the water. It was early afternoon before everything could be pulled together. Yana wasn't particularly happy about it, but the extra pay Rafael offered was duly accepted and nothing more was said out loud. At least not in his hearing. There were still ways she could make her displeasure known.

'Du Lacs have always made the Kerdaniels do what they wanted,' she muttered darkly when Ari tried to talk to her about it. 'Do you know about the Pors Sirène deaths? My family were there too. Boatmen for another du Lac. He won't listen any more than his ancestors did. Just issues his orders and expects them to be obeyed.'

'This isn't his idea. It's mine,' Ari protested.

'More fool you then. What do you even expect to find down there?'

Ari frowned. 'I don't know.'

It wasn't a lie. Not exactly. But she was certain she would find something. Simon had written the coordinates on the letter, whether deliberately or not. The very last letter he had written to her, the one where he broke up with her. And that was where she'd found the mask. He'd found the path, whatever the path might be, wherever it might lead, and she knew he wanted her to find it too.

Yana glanced at her and then turned her attention back to the horizon. 'Hadn't you better get ready? We'll be there soon.'

And, like that, she was dismissed.

Rafael in the wetsuit was another distraction she didn't want to be thinking about. As she checked his equipment, she stepped in against him.

'You weren't lying, were you? You do know what you're doing?' she whispered. She would put nothing past him and, like Yana said, he liked to get his way, no matter what.

'I promise,' he assured her, with a soft smile. He knew exactly what she was thinking. Luckily, he seemed to find it amusing. 'I know what I'm doing. I expect it to be a damn sight colder though.'

She laughed softly. Jason hadn't been too far of the mark with his tropical destination holidays accusations then. She looked up to see her brother and Nico, sitting at the stern, glaring at the two of them.

'What do you think we'll find, Rafael?' she asked.

He didn't hesitate. 'The path to Ys, of course.'

'Yes, but... then what?'

'I'm hoping we'll find a way to break the curse, but as to what that might be...' He shrugged and gave her a rueful smile. 'Proof that Ys was real perhaps? Something to save it from being dismissed as merely a tall tale? They don't call it a mystery for no reason, Ari.'

What would Jason and Nico say if they heard the two of them now?

She had shown them Simon's map and some of the notes in his diary. Rafael had taken the pages from Fabien's diary back to the manor, presumably to return them to the book they came from. Or find a conservator to do so. She hadn't asked. She was too mortified by the thought that Simon would have torn them out and stolen them to begin with.

Jason was still not entirely on board with this, and Nico even less so. And they were right, it could have waited. But then they would be waiting a week or more. They could have waited a month. She had brought up the sea forecast and the window of good weather they'd been enjoying was closing rapidly. There was a storm front coming across the Atlantic and when that hit, they'd be on shore until it passed. The long-range forecast wasn't looking much better. The tides were suitable today. That was it.

Not to mention she knew that waiting any longer to see if Simon had been right would eat them all up inside. When she'd told Jason the coordinates – 48.065, -4.688 – his eyes had widened. 'But that's where the mask was. Are you saying Simon—?'

'Found it first? Put it there? Maybe. I don't know. But I need to find out.'

He hadn't argued much after that.

And as for Rafael, well, he firmly believed that finding whatever remnants of Ys remained would help him to break the curse and save his son. Saving Ys meant preserving its memory, and some physical evidence of it, saving it from becoming just a half-remembered story. That seemed to be what Simon had believed too.

Some of the notes still bothered her though. What was the water path? And when he mentioned 'she', who was he referring to? She'd wondered if it was Gwen. But how? He seemed both enchanted and afraid of her.

'Are you ready?' she asked and Rafael nodded. 'Run through the signals with me again, OK?'

He dutifully repeated each and every one.

'We have mics,' he reminded her. 'I got them specially this morning. It's just a push button and it uses the water to let us talk to each other and the ship.'

Yes, there were advantages to his bottomless wallet. She had to admit that.

'I know. But just in case, we need old-school signals. I have a diving tablet too.' She showed him the little plastic pad with the pen attached on a spiral wire.

'Ari doesn't trust technology,' Nico said, finally approaching. 'Neither do I. Too much can go wrong. Just keep in mind that we were doing this long before wireless mics were invented.'

The system required a different face mask, but it was comfortable enough. Getting into gear without the mouthpiece felt strange. She had no idea how he had managed to get them so quickly, but she was not about to ask too many questions now. Rafael seemed to be familiar with it.

All the same, both Jason and Nico insisted on checking everything again. Every new item was treble-checked. Perhaps they were trying to make her run out of light so she couldn't go down. Her brother ignored her protests, but eventually cleared her to go.

'Ari,' he called as she lowered herself into the water. He leaned over the stern, his concerned expression looming above her. 'Be careful. Don't do anything stupid.'

'When have I ever done anything stupid?' she asked, her voice sounding strange in the confines of the face mask. 'That's your job.'

Jason shook his head. 'There's a first time for everything, kiddo. Let's not make this it, OK?'

She gave him the trademark Walker reckless grin and adjusted the dive weight to take her under the surface of the Mer d'Iroise and into the world of lost Ys.

CHAPTER TWENTY

Ari took the descent as slowly as possible to keep an eye on Rafael and ensure he wasn't in any distress, but he just patiently followed her lead. She didn't know what she had expected really. Some sort of bravado, or for him to attempt to take charge. But he didn't. He swam where she directed, waited when she told him to, and let her check equipment, air and coms until she was content.

'OK to continue?' she asked.

He held up his hand in the universal 'OK' symbol and grinned at her. Well, she had insisted he know the hand signals too.

'Very funny,' she told him.

'I thought so. Shall we?'

'When you're finished flirting?' Jason's voice cut in. They'd lowered a transponder from the boat to pick up Ari and Rafael's voice signals and complete the underwater communication network.

Ari winced. Jason needed to shut the hell up, but Rafael just gave that now familiar shrug as if to say it was up to her.

What was? Up to her if they had finished flirting? No, she was leading this expedition, so she had better get on with it.

Down they went again, into the sea-glass water. She could feel the current shifting around her, the way it seemed to be pulling them in to shore. The mass of Îlot d'Or rose to their right, a great crack running down the middle at an angle. And now... now when she looked at the formation, it really did look like a pair of great stone gates fallen on top of each other.

And in the space between the islet and the cliffs, the fine sand spread out between a scattering of fallen boulders and outcrops. Beyond it, the great sea cave opened up, like the mouth of a leviathan.

'Is that it?' Rafael asked, his voice like a whisper in her ear.

'I think so.'

It shouldn't be there, this impossible opening. It looked so fragile in one sense and in another, it looked ready to swallow them whole.

Time to update Jason. She turned on the mic. 'We're heading down to the bed first. Rafael has the camera. I'm going to try to clear some of the sand and see what's there.'

If Simon was right...

The local stories, the oldest stories, the ones passed down through families by word of mouth said there was a pathway to Ys, *le chemin de l'eau*, like the causeway leading to Île Tristan. Simon had found it. Fabien had found it.

We swam down to the pathway and followed it, surrendering to her, just as Blanche said. We let the tide take us.

The sand was fine and light. It didn't take much work to fan it away. For a moment, Ari could see nothing, but then she caught a glimpse of a strangely shaped stone, unnaturally round, like an egg. Or a cobble. It was the wrong colour too, pale and gleaming like marble. She hurriedly shifted more sand aside to reveal more stones, different colours, laid out in a pattern. It couldn't be random.

'Are you getting this?' she gasped.

'Yes,' Rafael replied. 'Yes, definitely. This is it, Ari.'

'What do you see?' Jason cut in, his voice desperate. It was killing him, she realised, that he wasn't able to see this.

'It looks like a cobbled path, Jason. Some kind of plaza maybe? We're documenting as much as we can, but it will have to be fully excavated by professionals. But it's evidence. Real evidence.'

There was a long pause, longer than she would have expected. When his voice came through again, it sounded like he was in tears. For a moment, she could picture him and Nico, dancing around on the deck of Yana's boat while she looked on in disgust.

'I knew it. I bloody knew it. And we were just on the wrong side of the little island. Bloody hell.'

Something glinted in the sand and she pulled it out. Another coin, much like the last. She bagged it and moved on.

'We're going to approach the cave mouth now,' she told him. 'The path leads in there.'

Instantly, her brother's voice sobered. 'Be careful. You're not geared up for caves right now.'

'Just the entrance, I promise. And I have a torch.'

'Great. A torch.'

There was a noise as Nico grabbed the mic from him. 'Ari, we talked about this. Don't do anything stupid. Especially not with—'

Rafael cut in effortlessly. 'I'm perfectly safe, Nico. We are just approaching the entrance, nothing more. And we are mindful of the currents.'

Ari flashed him a grin as he said that. The danger of being swept inside was not great, but it was still there. The area between the point and the island was narrow and treacherous. Above them, the waves against the cliffs were undulating, stronger than she had thought when they left the surface. She glanced up. Was it darker here? A trick of the light?

'Stay with me,' she said.

The sand tailed off to a scattering of rock debris and stones, things that had been swept in over the years, and that had fallen down as the rock face slowly gave way to the relentless sea. It wouldn't last forever. Nothing did with the ocean involved. It wore away rock and stone, ate the land away from the outside, and from within. The caves beneath the point were its weakness. Every year, they undermined it a little bit more. The geological survey had said as much.

Ten minutes passed, fifteen, as they approached the gaping mouth and she studied it for further clues.

'What's that?' Rafael asked, pointing down between a couple of rocks.

Ari shone the torch down and it glinted. More coins?

No. Something else. More modern. A watch? She waited while he photographed the area with the find in situ. Then she pulled it out and bagged it, trying to work out why it seemed so familiar. A diving watch. She'd seen them a thousand times. Jason and Nico both wore something similar. Metal strap, heavy face with blue highlights and...

And suddenly she remembered where she'd seen it. Thierry's wrist.

She swore and almost dropped the bag.

'What is it? What's wrong?' Nico barked.

She couldn't tell them. Not now. She couldn't even explain it. What was his watch doing here? Had he lost it when the eel attacked him? But that was some distance from here. Had he lost it the night he died?

Rafael swam closer, his hand resting on her shoulder, his head tilted in a question.

She shook her head. She couldn't say anything. She didn't

know what to say. 'It's fine. Nothing. I thought I'd found something else. Trick of the light. Let's get on.'

There was a long silence from the boat while she and Rafael photographed the area carefully, looking for anything else.

It could just be a coincidence. Someone else's watch. Someone else's loss.

They'd find out back on the surface. The boys would recognise it, wouldn't they? Or Madalen?

Ari shuddered at the thought, a chill rushing through her body. Another shadow passed overhead and she glanced up again. The light from the surface had dimmed further and the waves looked like storm clouds gathering. The weather was changing. She could feel it.

'Jason, give me an update on conditions up there?'

His voice broke up as he answered and she tried again.

'Repeat that?'

'—deteriorating. Can you hear—? Return to—'

'Something's wrong,' Rafael said. 'Interference? That shouldn't be possible.' He looked more affronted that his expensive technology was failing them.

'Yeah, we should head back. We've got the place. We've got some evidence.'

'Yes, but... Ari, it's hardly enough.'

'What are you looking for?'

He glanced at the cave, and she could see the longing in his eyes, even through the equipment. He wanted to find Ys. How many times did she have to tell people that there was no lost city? Not the way the legend described it. But they had found evidence, actual evidence. It might not look like much, but real finds weren't piles of treasure where X marked the spot. So what else did he want?

'It doesn't matter,' he said at last and the disappointment was palpable. 'We've run out of time, haven't we?'

She ached inside for the loss, for the despair, she heard in his voice, but he was right.

Jason's voice came through the coms again. 'Ari! Come back. Now. We need to get out of here. Squall incoming. Respond immediately.'

She pushed the button. 'We're coming. On the way now.'

They couldn't rush. Shoot up too quickly and they were going to get the bends. True, they weren't that deep, but they couldn't risk it. The ascent had to be staged. And time was against them.

She jerked her thumb upwards and Rafael nodded, turning to swim back towards the boat as agreed.

Something hard and unseen slammed into her side, sending her flying back towards the cliffs. She twisted around, trying to right herself, and it hit her again, something in the water, part of the water. As if a current had taken on a mind of its own and bore her a particularly vicious grudge. Ari struggled violently, trying to tear herself free. A rip tide? It had come out of nowhere.

She heard Rafael shout her name, his panic igniting hers as the sea cave loomed over her, a gaping mouth, a maw of darkness, swallowing her up.

For the next few seconds, minutes – she had no idea how long – her body tumbled through the water, struck rock face and was dragged along the ground. Silt from the floor turned everything dark, her torch unable to penetrate it, though she managed to hold on to it. She tried to protect herself, to make sure the equipment wasn't damaged, but there wasn't time and, to be honest, there was nothing she could do but let the water take her where it wanted. And pray.

The face mask cracked, the sound deafening, and the water rushed over her face, freezing, overwhelming. Her air supply bubbled up in front of her. She couldn't fight the sea. Nothing could. She knew this better than anyone.

Panic drained away. She couldn't take anymore. It was too late.

Surrender.

The thought came from the back of her brain, from that dark place of loss and despair, that at least this way she'd be with Simon again, going the same way he went.

A curious calm spread over her mind and body.

I've let the tide take me and surrendered to her.

From the darkness, a hand grabbed her wrist and hauled her upwards.

They burst out of the water into a vast domed cavern. The waves surged around them, but Rafael pushed her up onto the ledge where his torch was already lying beside the camera. He pushed her shattered face mask back.

'Breathe,' he told her. 'Just take a moment, go slow and breathe. In and out. Ari, listen to me. Breathe.'

CHAPTER TWENTY-ONE

It all happened so fast, Rafael couldn't stop it. One minute she was there and the next the sea swept her into the cave as if it had reached out an invisible hand to seize her. Without a second thought, he plunged in after her, letting the current take him as well. It was madness, he knew that, but it was just what Fabien had written, the rip tide taking them in along an underwater path. It was a leap of faith. Idiocy, but he couldn't let her go alone. Not like this.

He saw her hit the wall at the back of the cave, with horrible clarity, saw the impact shudder through her body. The silt came up like a curtain, but he pushed on to reach her. For a moment, he thought he'd lost her again and he knew – *knew!* – he couldn't allow that to happen.

He needed her.

The beam of his torch hit the water overhead and he realised that they were near the surface and beyond it was a larger open space. He surfaced briefly, took in the cavern above them and plunged down to find her, grabbing her flailing arm and pulling her to the surface.

The diving mask was cracked and her pale face looked

devoid of life, like the thing they had locked away. Her wet
eyelashes made little points on her lower lids and he thought he
was too late. Then she opened her mouth to gasp for air,
coughing as he hauled her onto the ledge and out of the water.

He removed the face mask, staring at her frantically.

'Breathe,' he told her, smoothing his hand over the perfect
lines of her face. 'Just take a moment, go slow and breathe. In
and out. Ari, listen to me. Breathe.'

'I'm... I'm OK.' She choked out the words. 'I think so
anyway. What happened? Where are we?'

'I think we're underneath Castelmeur. In the sea caves.'

A dim light filtered through the water from outside the cave,
and from the churning surface, the storm was still going on out
there.

'Jason and Nico... they'll be going mad,' she said. 'They'll
think we're— Oh God, how are we going to get out of here?'

He smoothed his hand down her back, trying to comfort
her. 'We'll find a way. Maybe when the storm passes, we can
swim back out.'

She stared at the broken face mask lying beside her. 'I don't
think so. Not me, anyway.'

'It's going to be OK, Ari. *Courage, ma brave*. We'll find a
way out. There are caves and tunnels throughout the point. We
used to come down here as kids. Well, not down *here* exactly.'
He searched the shadowy recesses of the cavern. 'But into the
caves, looking for treasure. Me and Laure. All the kids. It was a
thing. There's going to be a way out. And if not... if not, I'll
swim out and come back for you with help. *D'accord*?'

'You can't. They won't be there. You'll be out at sea.
Besides, we don't know if you've got enough oxygen or if the
tide will let you, or—'

He lifted his finger to her lips, just lightly. It wasn't enough
to actually silence her, but she stopped talking all the same. The
panic in her eyes didn't fade though. 'I promise you. I'll find a

way. We will. Together. Now, *mon coeur*, can you stand? Were you hurt?'

For a moment, she just stared at him, as if dazed. Perhaps she'd hit her head harder than he thought. But then she pulled herself together in front of his eyes, just as he knew she would. She was valiant of heart, Ariadne Walker, like the mythical woman she was named for. And though they might be lost, he knew they would find their way out. Knew it with all his heart. Because she was here too.

'No, I'm fine. A bit bruised, I'm sure. And cold. But nothing's broken. You're right. We'll find a way out of here.'

They had to have been swept some distance into the cave system, he realised. If they were near the end of the point, the sea would fill this space. The light that made it through only lit up the immediate surroundings and he feared the torches they carried would do little more. And once they ran out of power...

No, they needed to move now.

Ari shook off her shock and set to work ordering him around. Normally, it would have amused him, but she was the dive leader and she knew what she was doing. Besides, he was worried that she needed this right now so that shock wouldn't set in. Or despair.

They took off the oxygen tanks and stowed them safely away from the water, up on a higher ledge. If the sea rose further, they didn't want to lose equipment and Ari was adamant that they might still need them. If he had to swim out of here, if he could find the way, and if there was a chance that the boat came back...

For all his insistence that there was a way out of here through the cave system – and logic said there had to be – he didn't know for sure. He had never found a cavern like this in all the years he'd explored here. But Fabien had.

How he had done it without modern equipment and scuba gear, Rafael dreaded to think. The diary said he and Tristan had dived down, so maybe there had been some equipment available. Had Simon found it too? Had he followed the clues in the pages of Fabien's diary or some tale Tristan had told his brothers, passed down by the Poullains? Or a combination of both?

It didn't matter now. Not finding Ys. Not even the hope of ending the curse to protect Georges. He could feel it slipping from his fingers even as he stood there, the terrible twisting in his guts, the failure. That dream was gone. Or at least postponed to another day. What mattered now was finding a way out again, preferably one that didn't involve trying to swim through submerged caves. He had heard too many horror stories about people doing that.

They climbed up to the next ledge and Ari gave a gasp of surprise, her torch sweeping across the rocky incline.

'They're steps. Look. Someone carved steps into the rock.' They were unmistakable, smooth and regular, the perfect height, leading upwards. 'Come on.'

She skipped up those stairs before he could stop her and he had no choice but to follow. 'Ari, wait. We have to stay together.'

She stopped at the top of the steps, but even then, he wasn't entirely sure she was waiting. She was standing there, head lifted, staring in wonder.

And as he joined her, he couldn't help but do the same.

The torchlight illuminated carvings, arches and pillars, worked by long-ago hands into the rocks of the caves themselves. Tunnels led off in various directions, but the main chamber here was the size of a small church, like the chapel in the village. Fish trailed along one wall, eels curling around them in intricate knotwork which reminded him of Celtic art. There were ships carved into the ceiling, reminiscent of Viking long boats and Roman galleys. Every time their pools of light shifted around the chamber, something else was revealed, more beautiful than the last.

Beneath their feet, he felt the rough surface give way to

something still uneven but manmade, cobbles, like the little round stones you sometimes found washed up on the beaches and in the coves. Like the plaza outside. He brought his own beam down and saw the patterned floor in a riot of colours spreading out beneath him, a picture, an image of a building, a street, a city.

'My God,' Ari murmured. 'It's incredible, Rafael. It's...'

'It's Ys,' he replied, hardly able to heave those words out with the enormity of what he was seeing. It was like the old map she had found which may have been La Fontenelle's. Had he stood here too, the Wolf of Douarnenez? Had he seen these wonders and died protecting the secret as well?

Or died because he would have spoken of it? Was there another side to the curse?

The thought shuddered through him, the realisation... they had found it. They had found evidence of Ys.

'This is what Fabien and Tristan discovered, isn't it? This is what they had to protect.'

To save it. They had found this and kept silent so the occupying forces of the Third Reich couldn't plunder it. It had to be. But they died before they could share it with anyone else either. How old was it? Who had done all this?

'Rafael, look!'

She had moved off again, up towards the far end of the chamber, where a raised plinth rose out of the ground, like the sanctum of the chapel. In the centre stood a carved stone, shaped like a throne. On the wall, framed in carvings of every kind of sea creature, her torch illuminated the face of a woman. Long hair spilled out from her head, like she was underwater, waving and coiling like seaweed. Her face held all the impassivity of stone, her eyes staring at him without kindness, without empathy, without any kind of emotion at all. *Eyes of stone, heart of stone.* And she was beautiful, beyond beautiful. She was a goddess to be worshipped, an idol to be adored. Like a Madonna, unapproachable, unfeeling, glorious.

This was what he had to save, this place, this wonder and the power that surged through the stone carvings. He could save Ys. Just like Fabien had.

His mind tripped over the thought. There was something wrong there. How was there still a curse, a curse on all his family, if Fabien had already saved Ys?

'Dahut,' he whispered and the cavern around him took up the echo, her name repeating and repeating, murmuring around him until he could hear only its music. Calling her to him. Strength left his legs and he fell to his knees on the cold stone, right at the edge of the plinth, as darkness swept over him, swallowed him whole.

Cold lips pressed to his, icy hands framed his face. He tilted his head back, succumbing completely to the spell, to *her*. Dahut, the water witch.

There was nothing else to do. She had won. She would always win. She was too powerful for any man to stand against. She was ancient and terrible, a sorceress, an enchantress, the water witch, with a heart of stone, and she had destroyed his line, leaving only him and his own innocent little boy remaining. Soon Rafael himself would be gone too. Followed by his son. How had he dreamed he would be able to break such a curse? He'd been a fool and the air humming with the magic of this place told him that over and over again.

'Rafael? Rafael, please! Talk to me.'

The voice was just an echo, not even real, a dream. He'd had a dream and now it was over. He'd wait here until she came to claim him. He'd wait here in the darkness until she pressed her cold lips to his and made him her own. That was what she wanted.

Just kneel and wait. Just give in. Like a man without air,

beneath the waves, lost. All he had to do was accept it, embrace it.

Surrender to her.

He had done it in the sea, giving himself up to the current, letting it take him where it had taken Ari. It was instinctive, bred into his line, a hereditary memory. He understood that now.

Maybe, just maybe, if he begged enough, she would spare Georges.

'Damn it, Rafael! Wake up! Please...'

Warm hands touched his face, warm with life, trembling from the cold. And then another pair of lips pressed to his. Not the icy kiss he expected, the kiss of the deepest ocean, the lightless depths of the sea. These lips tasted of salt, but also sweetness. They were warm and alive. They were lips he had already kissed and longed to kiss again, to feel again her lithe body against his.

He opened his heavy eyes to see her desperate face, to feel the warmth she generated, the passion he remembered, the only source of heat in this lifeless place.

'Ari?' It came out as a groan, a sound of need and hunger, and that same heat rushed back through him.

'Yes, yes, it's me. What happened to you? Are you OK?'

'You kissed me.'

For a moment, she looked positively guilty. 'I... I know, I'm sorry. I just didn't know... It was that or hit you. Rafael, you spaced out completely. You were saying things, I don't know what. I didn't understand. Another language. I had to snap you out of it.'

So she had kissed him. Woke him with her kiss like one of her fairy-tale heroes.

Instead of arguing, he kissed Ari back, bringing his heavy arms up to hold her against him. For a long moment, he could think of nothing else. She was the air he needed, the warmth he craved, she was everything. He was lost, but not in the darkness. She was a flame, lighting him from within.

'We have to get out of here,' she told him breathlessly, when she could tear her mouth from his. 'There isn't time. There's something weird about it and it's affecting you. Like the mask. Something to do with the curse on your family. And this place. I think... Do you understand?' She said it slowly and clearly, as if talking to an idiot. Which, he reflected, he was. He was a complete idiot.

He nodded. Yes, he could feel it too and she was right. The delirious need to make love to her here and now in the darkness, on the cold stone, was just another symptom of whatever this place was doing to him. It had to be. Because he did not lose control like this. Never.

Later, he promised himself, later, he would beg her to let him explore this further. Somewhere safe and warm. But not here and now.

'I do. We must find another way out of here. Quickly.' He took her hands, and let her help him back to his feet.

'One torch at a time,' she said. 'Conserve batteries.'

'We need something to mark our way, so we don't double back on ourselves.'

She lifted her wrist where she wore a slender white sheath around her wrist. 'The pen from the dive pad. That should do it.'

He was never so grateful for her. Was there even a way he could tell her that? Not now. There wasn't enough time. 'Let's go then.'

They retreated from the chapel-like area, the eyes of the carving of Dahut following them.

Hours passed, hours in the darkness, feeling their way along the walls and squeezing through gaps, trying to head upwards.

They were forced back several times, too many times to keep count of, but Ari's marks on the walls kept them on track. Each time they retreated, she would put a slash through the symbol, curse softly to herself and set off again.

But, eventually, even she grew tired. It was cold down here, and miserable. The situation was hopeless and he knew it. Ari stopped, leaned back against the wall of the cave and slowly slid down to sit on the sandy path.

'Are you all right?' he asked.

She waved a hand at him. 'I just need a minute or two. I'm parched. It's a shame we don't have any water.'

It was. He'd been thinking that himself.

That was when the first torch picked its moment. It flickered and then died.

'Get the other one,' Ari said and he reached for it, ready to turn it on.

She frowned and furiously rubbed at her eyes, wiping away tears she didn't want him to see. She looked so tired, drained. He could see the lines of her face and—

Wait, he could see her?

He could see her face, her eyes, the way her hair, dry now, shifted softly in the breeze.

The breeze!

'Ari!' He surged to his feet, looking around desperately, trying to see where it was coming from. He could smell it, fresh air, air from outside the caves. The ambient light came from their left, filtering down from a steep slope.

They scrambled up as far as they could and found the ground turning wet underneath them. Water splashed onto his face, fresh water. That was rain. He tasted it, like it was a miracle. It was a way out.

The light flashed, bright and blinding after the darkness. Lightning. Outside, the storm still raged.

The gap at the top was narrow, but not too narrow. Ari was

slim enough to get through it, even if he wasn't. She could get help.

'Come on, this way,' he told her. 'Up there.'

'I see it. Can you get me up there?'

He lifted her and she scrambled up the sharp incline, sending a scattering of gravel and dirt down on his face.

'It's a way out,' she called down, then wriggled through and disappeared from view. 'Rafael? I'm out on the cliffs leading to the point, not far from the manor.' Her arm appeared, hanging down, reaching for him.

'Go and get help,' he yelled up.

'No. Not without you. It's wide enough. Take my hand.'

A rumble of thunder shook through the earth around him.

'Ari, don't be silly.'

'I'm not leaving you in there. Come on. And hurry up. It's raining, Rafael, and it's cold. Blowing a gale. Let's go.'

He grabbed her hand and braced himself against the rocks, scrambling up as best he could. She was surprisingly strong, or maybe it was just her determination, but she hauled him out into the storm and fell back, laughing as the rain pelted down on them both, and the wind tore at the low scrubby bracken on the Pointe de Castelmeur. Lightning flashed overhead and the sky lit up, the clouds boiling like the sea.

But they were out in the open.

Safe.

CHAPTER TWENTY-TWO

It was dark by the time they made it back to the manor. There wasn't a light on inside. Barefoot and cold, the two of them made their way to a back door, where Rafael fished a key out from behind a plant pot.

'Highly secure,' Ari said.

'Don't complain. It means we get inside. Besides, they've only started locking doors around here in the last twenty years. We're in the middle of nowhere, remember?'

'Ends of the earth,' she agreed. 'Hurry up. I'm freezing. And I need to ring Jason, let him know we're OK.'

It only took a moment before they were in and the warmth of the kitchen engulfed them both. Rafael grabbed a couple of blankets from the laundry room, wrapping one around her first. He pulled out a chair at the kitchen table and made her sit down before putting the phone in front of her, an old landline, with large buttons.

She dialled, her hand trembling, and waited while the phone rang. But it went straight to voicemail. She left a message – *we're safe, we're back, where are you?* – and tried Nico. The problem was the same there. No answer, just voicemail.

Lost and unsure of what to do, she looked to Rafael. He placed a cup of coffee in her hand and took over.

He made a series of calls and she heard him speaking in rapid French. Finally, he hung up.

'I've let the coastguard know we're safe, the gendarmerie, and the harbourmaster in Douarnenez. Yana's boat is in the harbour, so they made it back. They're probably out of battery or something like that. Or the mobile signal is bad. We get that here with storms. You're shaking.'

'I'm cold.' And she was. She felt frozen to the core and she suspected that shock was also playing a hand in this. She felt like a rag that had been drenched in icy water and then wrung out.

He wrapped his hands around hers. His skin felt cold to the touch as well, but she still welcomed the contact.

'Come with me,' he told her and she followed him up the stairs.

The room to which he led her looked over the front of the house and the sea beyond. The storm raged on, wild and out of control. Clouds raced across the sky and the trees around the property thrashed with the gale.

Rafael turned on the light and pulled the curtains while she stood there, shivering.

It was a beautiful room, decorated with taste and style, modern but with nods to the age of the building. The sleigh bed looked antique.

He made his way to another door, which opened to a vast en suite with a roll-top bath and a walk-in shower tiled in grey, dotted with what looked like hand-painted feature tiles for decoration. Rafael gave it all barely a glance, used to it. He reached in and turned on the shower.

'I'll get towels for you,' he told her, and left.

She stood there, frozen, wrapped in the blanket. This was his room, wasn't it? She could tell. A laptop sat open on the dresser. There were three books piled up on the bedside table. A lambswool sweater lay casually over the back of the armchair in the corner and she thought she remembered him wearing that yesterday. Was it only yesterday?

Warm steam reached her from the en suite. Right, the shower. She was meant to have a shower. Here. In his—

She reached behind her to try to unzip the wetsuit, but she couldn't grab the pull with her numb and clumsy fingers. She half turned, got tangled in the blanket and staggered over.

He caught her before she could fall. She hadn't even heard him come back in, but he caught her all the same.

'I've got you. Here, let me help.'

She wasn't the only one trembling, she realised, as he pulled the zip down at the back of her wetsuit.

'Turn around,' she told him and he glanced at her, doubt passing over his features. 'Or do you think you'll manage alone? I can leave you be. That shower is very tempting.'

But it wasn't the only tempting thing.

A slow, knowing smile spread over his face. He turned around, his eyes fixed on the mirror, and she unzipped him as well, revealing his bare back with the ripple of muscles she had admired the first time she saw him. She pressed her hand to his shoulder. As she reached up, however, a sharp pain lanced down her side.

'What is it?' he asked, turning in alarm. 'What's wrong?'

She'd been swept through a cave system and bashed against a rock wall, that was what was wrong. She turned towards the mirror and pulled down the wetsuit, leaving herself just in the swimsuit she'd worn underneath. Bruises were beginning to blossom all along her shoulder and her thigh, probably all down her side as well.

She looked at his reflection and saw the concern mirrored there. 'Well, at least we're alive. And I wouldn't be if you hadn't come after me.'

'Ari,' he murmured. 'I—'

She pressed a kiss to his skin, tasting salt there. 'I've wanted to do this since I first saw you.' The admission sent a thrill of pleasure through her, but it was nothing compared to the feeling when his muscles tightened.

With a groan of desire, his arms enfolded her and his kiss took her breath away.

For a moment, he was all she could think of, all she knew. He was dizzying, addictive. And he knew exactly what he did to her.

So why did he seem as lost in her as she was in him? They both felt it, she knew that. They were both out of control, and she didn't regret it at all. She needed him. The brief kisses they had shared, the stolen moments between them, they were all leading to this and she would not back away again.

Skin on skin now, stepping out of the remaining layers to stand before each other, she revelled in the taste of him, the warmth of his skin over his toned muscles. Madness. She knew it was madness. She didn't care.

'But you're still shivering,' he told her. 'Into the shower before you die of cold.'

'It's not the cold,' she replied.

He lifted her off the ground, scooping her up in his arms. 'Let's test that theory. What else makes you shiver, Dr Walker?'

The hot water of the shower flowed over their skin. She melted under his mouth, his hands caressing her, drawing her against him. She buried her fingers in his hair and cried out as he entered her, lost in a pleasure she had forgotten how to feel.

Ari slept more deeply than she had in years. The bed cradled her, his arms cradled her. And the storm raged outside. Far away from either of them.

'Ari...'

The whisper woke her, a stir of breath on her cheek or perhaps a gentle caress. She opened her eyes as sunlight crept through the gap in the curtains. Rafael slept on beside her, warm and tempting, one arm flung up above his head, his breathing deep and even. It hadn't been his voice she had heard.

She stared at him. What had she done?

Not that she regretted it. Not really. But still... what had she done?

She needed to get back to the gîte, to Jason and Nico. She had to let them know she was OK and tell them about what they'd found.

That was her excuse and she was sticking to it.

Slipping out of the bed, she backed up towards the antique wardrobe. The wetsuits were still in the en suite, cold and damp. She wasn't about to try to put hers back on. There had to be something she could wear here.

'Ari...'

There it was again, not Rafael's voice. Simon's. She was sure of it.

Ari sucked in a breath and tried to open the drawer silently, not so easy to do with old furniture. It squeaked and groaned open.

'Are you looking for something?' Rafael asked in a sleepy, but amused tone.

Ari spun around guiltily. 'I just... I needed... something to wear.'

'Were you leaving?'

'I have to.'

A frown flickered over his brow. 'Are you sure? Come back to bed, Ari. It's still early.'

She spotted the dressing gown hanging on the back of the door, a rich navy wrap. It was long and soft, silk and expensive. Of course it was. She wrapped it around herself hurriedly and turned back to face him. He was sitting up now, looking suspicious.

Damn, she thought. What could she say?

I'm sorry, but this was a mistake... We were both very emotional last night and... I shouldn't have...

She was such a coward.

'I need to talk to my brother. We've not even spoken about what we saw down there, the carvings, the cave. I have to... I'm sorry. I just—'

'You don't have to be sorry.' The patience was stretched thin, she could hear it in his voice.

'I'm not. I mean... Rafael, this... this was probably not a good idea. We didn't know what we were doing.'

'I knew exactly what I was doing,' he countered. 'I thought you did too. Ari? What is this about? Talk to me.' He rose to his feet, approaching her like he might a frightened animal.

She took a few steps back and he stopped, wary perhaps, or trying to keep his temper now.

'I shouldn't have. Simon—' She choked on his name. She couldn't help it.

For a few hours last night, it was as if she'd forgotten all about him. But now, thinking of Ys and the lost city he'd sacrificed himself to find, her time with Rafael felt like the most terrible betrayal.

Rafael let out a soft rumble of a sigh. 'Simon is gone,' he told her in that calm, patient voice.

'I know that.'

'You can't spend your whole life looking back.'

She shook her head and felt her eyes sting. Panic surged inside her, her heart hammering away. 'I have to go. I can't stay here.'

'Don't run away, Ari. Please. Don't run away from me like you ran away from him.'

Her whole body straightened as if her outrage was steel snapping into place along her spine. 'I beg your pardon?'

'You don't have to beg, *mon coeur*.' He said it with a laugh and she wanted to lash out in a fury.

Perhaps it was a language thing. Perhaps he was just a smart-arse.

'I'm not.' She bit out each word and his humour seemed to fade. 'I'm not begging and I am not your heart. I have to go.'

Disappointment filled his voice. 'So this is it, is it? This is where you run away again. Like yesterday.'

'I am not running away.'

'Yes you are. You don't want to get close to anyone. Perhaps you never did. You ran from Simon as well, didn't you?'

The world seemed to contract around her, her skin tightening over her bones, the air compressing inside her lungs. There was a high-pitched whine in the back of her head, reverberating through her skull.

'*What* did you say?' She ground out the words, her eyes so fixed, she thought they might bore holes through his head.

'You keep running away, sabotaging your own life.'

'I left for a job. A good job.'

'A good excuse.' He calmly crossed to the wardrobe and pulled out another dressing gown. It was something of a relief when he covered himself up, but at the same time, she couldn't shake the horrible feeling that it signalled the definitive end of something. 'Ari, this is not a – how do they say it? – a quick roll in the hay for me. I don't do that.'

'Don't you? With all your supermodel girlfriends?' It was a low blow but she couldn't help herself.

'One supermodel,' he corrected smoothly as he turned back to her.

'Oh, I'm sorry. Just the one then.'

He raised one eyebrow as he studied her. 'You're overwrought. Maybe we should—'

'Stop telling me what I am and what I should do, Rafael. You don't control my life. I can come and go as I please, and I always have done. I left Simon here because that job was every-thing I'd worked for.'

I left Simon. The words hammered away in her skull. *I left Simon.* Was that what had happened? She hadn't meant to but, in fact, she had left. Had their relationship been over long before he sent that letter?

'And did you ask him to go with you?'

She paused. Had she? She must have. But right now she couldn't remember. Simon had told her to go, that she'd regret it if she didn't. But had she ever asked him to go with her? And if he had asked her to stay, to live here in Sainte Sirène with him, would she have?

'That's not...' She couldn't even finish it. 'I need to leave now.'

'Ari,' he tried again, in that cool, calm voice that she knew meant he was at his most logical, that he was looking inside her and pulling her apart. 'Please don't run away this time.'

'I didn't. I don't.'

But he was right. And she hated that he was right. All she did was run away. The moment a relationship got too real, espe-cially now. Getting over Simon had taken everything she had left. She had broken apart, collapsed entirely, and it had taken more than a year to pull herself back together. Now, running away was a survival technique. From her old life, her career, her brother, her memories...

And now from Rafael, if she had to.

And she *had* to. What had she been thinking? Just falling into bed with him like that. Well, she hadn't been thinking, had she? She'd been on fire, desperate, so overwhelmed with need for him that she hadn't thought at all. All she had done was feel.

And that always led to disaster.

His phone rang. Rafael groaned and turned back towards it,

glowing on the bedside table. He must have left it there before going diving, or else it was some kind of backup. That would be like him, wouldn't it?

'You're going to answer that?' she snapped. 'Now?'

'I have to,' he replied, as if repeating her own words back at her, and before she could say another word, he did so. '*Oui?* Louis, yes, I'm here. Tell me.' Concern flickered through his eyes and he frowned again. Without another word to her, without even a glance, he headed for the door.

Ari stared, her mouth hanging open as he vanished. What the hell?

'*Ari...*'

The voice was no more than a sigh. If the room wasn't so quiet, she wouldn't have heard it. It was probably just the wind outside. Only the wind had died down now. And it still sounded like Simon.

Wrapping her arms around her chest, trying to will herself to be brave, she glanced out of the window to her left. Dawn was staining the horizon, a bleak and grey morning, cold and bitter. So still after the night before. The gardens stretched out towards the sea.

A figure stood there, watching her, his shoulders slumped, his black coat and white hair whipping in an unnatural wind, even though the foliage around him didn't move at all. Ankou. Simon.

Ari sucked in a breath, her heart slamming up to the base of her throat. He knew. He was there. He knew what she had done.

Of course he did. He was Ankou now, Dahut's consort, the spirit of this place, the Servant of Death, the lost soul doomed to haunt it...

Slowly, he turned and walked towards the back of the house, out of sight.

'Shit,' she whispered. What was she doing here? What had

she done? She'd just jumped into bed with Rafael du Lac. The man who was funding everything, the man used to buying whatever he wanted... Did he think that included her?

And was he wrong?

He'd paid off the school so she'd stay, and she had. He'd funded the expedition, joined her on the dive, found the cavern and then...

He accused her of running away. How dare he? Who wouldn't run from a man so determined to control her life?

She sank down on the bed, trembling. It still smelled of him, of the two of them together, reminding her of every touch, every caress, every gasp of ecstasy...

'There you are,' said Laure brightly.

Ari surged to her feet and dizziness swamped her.

Laure stood in the doorway, a pile of clothes balanced on one hand. 'Rafael asked me to find you something to wear.'

'He... what? When?'

She smiled. 'Just now, on the stairs...' She ran her gaze down Ari's body and back up to her face. 'Well, so long as everyone got what they wanted.'

'What does that mean?'

But she knew what it meant. How could she fail to understand?

'Don't be naïve, Ari. He's a Frenchman. He has wanted you in his bed from the first moment he saw you.'

She had more or less said the same thing last night, as they undressed each other. But he had been thinking it all along. And now... now he had what he wanted...

Laure wasn't finished. 'You wanted funding, which you got. He wanted to be a hero. You thanked him for rescuing you and your project so very thoroughly. *Brava.*' She said it all so matter-of-factly and gave an unpleasant smile.

'It wasn't like that,' Ari protested.

'Everything is a transaction with my brother, with my

family, as I believe you were warned. Gwen said she'd tried to tell you, and she would know. Oh, not in so many words. She's not a gossip. You should understand it now. Everything is complete, all sides of the balance sheet match. He can move on from Jacqueline. He's had his bit of rebound fun.' She crossed the room and shoved the clothes at Ari, who took them in stunned, unfeeling arms, gathering them against her chest. 'I'll ring Jason for you. I'm sure he'll come and pick you up.'

What was it Gwen had said to her? *When they want something, they get it. They'll use anything and everything at their disposal to have their way.*

From somewhere in the depths of her spiralling despair, Ari summoned up the last remnants of her backbone. 'Don't bother. I know the way.'

Laure shrugged, as if to say 'whatever', and pulled the door to behind her.

Ari dragged on the clothes as quickly as she could. She didn't look at the bed, with its tossed sheets, or the bathroom or... or... anything.

Running away. Well, she wasn't running away. A strategic retreat, perhaps. Entirely different. And if she wanted to run away that was her decision anyway. Not his.

'Don't worry about returning the clothes,' Laure called after her merrily, as she left the room and headed for the stairs. 'They were going to charity anyway.'

God, she was enjoying this, wasn't she? Every second of it. The bitch was loving it.

Halfway down the stairs, Ari heard Rafael's voice again. The light was on in the study and his voice carried, angry but not rage-filled. That same quiet cold that was so much worse. The same tone he had just used upstairs. But even colder somehow, the businessman, the CEO...

'Very well. Cancel the funding. That will take care of it.'

Ari froze on the staircase, caught between dread and

concern. Was she mistranslating that? What funding was he talking about? *Their* funding?

He couldn't.

'No. She won't understand, but I will deal with it. It means nothing. This has to be done and done quickly. A clean break.'

Ari's heartbeat thundered away in the back of her head, deafening her, and she clung to the banister to stop herself from falling. What was he talking about?

It means nothing.

Did he even really care about finding Ys, about ending the curse? He'd been so convincing and she had been taken right in. Everyone had warned her about him, that he would manipulate her, that he was used to getting his own way, that he always got what he wanted...

What had Ari been thinking? That they'd live happily ever after, following one night together? She'd never been that stupid. They were from completely different worlds.

She hadn't even been able to make it work with Simon. She should have stayed with him, or persuaded him to come with her and—

Simon. She'd betrayed Simon. She had run away from him. It was like a punch to the stomach, as if all the air had been driven out of her.

And Rafael was right. She was running away again. But she couldn't still be there when he deigned to come back, waiting to be turfed out like yesterday's garbage.

Ari made for the back door in a breathless rush.

Nolvene was in the kitchen as she entered and gave her a confused smile. 'Oh, you are so early. I almost have *petit dejeuner* ready, *mademoiselle*, but not quite. A *café* perhaps while you wait?'

Ari forced a smile, glanced down at the ill-fitting clothes Laure had provided her with. The shoes were simple slip-on trainers with a garish pink logo on the side. She was going to hurl them into the sea at the first opportunity. 'I'd better just go. But thank you.' She could barely get the words out. She needed to get outside. To find Simon. To explain.

'Are you running? At this hour? It's not even light out yet.' Nolvene gave an exasperated sigh, unaware of the way the word struck Ari. 'Oh, you young people, always running somewhere. I will feed you. You need it.'

And with that, Ari slipped out of the back door and ran as fast as she could through the growing dawn, towards the cliffs and the path towards the gîte.

Away from Rafael du Lac.

CHAPTER TWENTY-THREE

The moment Ari set foot back into the gîte, Jason seized her, pulling her into his embrace and burying her face in his shoulder. She staggered against him, helpless.

'My God, where were you? What happened?' He grabbed her arms and pushed her away, but still holding her so she couldn't escape. He stared at her, at the horrible clothes and at her pale face, examining her everywhere. 'Are you OK? Talk to me.'

'Let me get a word in edgeways,' she told him, her voice shaking far too much for her liking.

'Ari!' Nico yelled from the kitchen and then he was there too, holding her, hugging her, bombarding her with questions.

Jason cut in the moment Nico paused for breath. 'We thought we'd lost you. We thought the absolute worst. I was going to go in after you, but—'

'But he couldn't. Neither of us could, and Yana had to get the boat to safety. We radioed the coastguard and—'

'I'm fine,' she told them. 'Really. I'm fine. We were both...' She choked on the words and struggled not to burst into tears.

They both saw it and the shock on their faces would have

been hilarious under any other circumstances. Because she wasn't fine.

Pushing thoughts of Rafael aside, she decided to tell them of the discovery and pray that distracted them enough that they'd forget her emotional state. She'd rehearsed this the whole way back. 'We got swept into the sea caves, under Castelmeur. There's a chamber with carvings, rock carvings, and mosaics. We found the path, an actual path, and the maps and her – we found her. A rock carving. It's incredible. Simply...'

It was like all hell broke loose at once. 'Did you get photos? Did you bring anything out? Where is it? Can you find it again?'

'I can. I'm sure I can. I marked the way. We didn't bring anything out though. And...'

The watch. She'd forgotten about Thierry's watch and what it might mean. Had he been down there too? How did she explain that to them? She'd left it with the diving equipment, along with the coin and the camera. Shit, she'd had the camera down there. She could have filmed it all. She could have brought evidence back with her. But all they had thought of was finding a way out.

'Damn,' she whispered. 'I left the camera down there. I didn't think—'

'No,' Nico interrupted her in stern tones. 'Don't think like that. If you can find the way back, then we'll go back. Don't you dare regret placing your safety first.'

She glanced at Jason nervously, not so sure he would agree, but her brother just nodded. The concern hadn't left his face. 'You look dreadful. Did something else happen?'

Oh God, he knew. He could see it etched on her features.

'I just want to get changed and—'

'Yeah, where did that outfit come from?'

'Laure,' she said and her control shook once again. Her throat closed over and her eyes stung. 'I think... I think they're going to pull the funding. Rafael and the Foundation... I think I messed up everything, Jason.'

'What? Why would he do that now? What happened? If the two of you found evidence, if he saw it with his own eyes—' And then he stopped, staring at her, and she crumpled in front of him, ashamed and so tired of everything. 'Ari?' he said, his voice unexpectedly gentle. 'What happened? You stayed there last night, at the manor. With him?'

It was excruciating. She nodded and closed her eyes so she didn't have to see the anger on his face.

'What the fuck happened?'

'Jesus, Jason,' Nico hissed at him and steered her towards the stairs.

She ran. Just ran, tore her way up the stairs and slammed the bedroom door behind her. She heard them shouting at each other downstairs, arguing about confronting Rafael, or going to the manor, or heaven knows what, and it was all her fault. Everything.

She tore off every scrap of Laure's clothing and hurled them into a corner before taking herself into the narrow shower – a world away from the luxury of last night – and scrubbed herself from head to toe.

It didn't help. None of it helped.

She pulled on her own clothes, her jeans and a T-shirt, and her eyes fell on the box of Simon's things.

Without a moment's thought, she kicked it as hard as she could, sending it flying across the room to slam against the door. Its contents spilt across the floor.

Ari sprawled on the bed and sobbed.

A careful knock disturbed her from her misery. Aware she was acting like a heartbroken teen, she dragged her hand over her face and sat up.

'What?' she said.

The door opened slightly and Jason poked his head in. 'I've brought tea,' he said, like he was approaching with a white flag.

'Tea's good,' she sighed, because she was a grown woman and she couldn't just keep relapsing into tears and tantrums. 'Thank you.'

Ari cradled the mug in her hands while Jason sat beside her. He handed over her phone and her bag, all the things she'd left with him on the boat. She checked the phone, saw a few missed calls and notifications, but didn't want to look more closely than that. She wasn't sure which would be worse: if Rafael had tried to ring her or if he had not. She shoved it deep into her pocket.

Jason watched, waiting. 'Want to tell me what happened?'

It was excruciating. She gripped the tea even harder. 'Not really. I was stupid. And naïve.' Even saying the word made her stomach twist in on itself. She heard Laure's accent, and her disdain, clinging to the syllables. 'I don't know what I was thinking. Just happy to be alive, I guess. And then... well, when you're in the middle of a fight and he just leaves to take a work call, and then his sister hands you her cast-off clothes and offers to call a lift home, it doesn't say hang around, does it? Especially when I overheard him pulling our funding too. I thought he really cared about Ys but...'

She couldn't tell him about seeing Simon as well. He'd think she was insane. Rather than just stupid.

Jason stared at the floor, and she knew he was controlling his temper. It was a superhuman effort from him. Any second now, he'd yell and call her a fool, and blame her for messing up everything he'd worked for.

But he didn't.

'I've been a shit brother, haven't I?' he said at last.

'What? No.'

He laughed, a brief, dismissive sound. 'Yes I have. Throwing you at him, being a dick about it, threatening to trade you for cows... I'm sorry, Ari.'

The mix of regret and his trademark sense of humour made her smile. Not to mention her own relief. It startled her to hear him say it, though, and she didn't know how to reply. Instead she nudged him with her hip and he shoved his back at her, because they'd always sorted things out that way in the past.

'It wasn't your fault, Jason,' she said at last. 'I should have been more careful.'

'Yeah, but... I don't know. I just thought... it's been two years, and he's cute... I was stupid.'

She shook her head, drank the tea and tried not to cry again. Jason was right. Rafael was more than cute. And it had felt like it was time to move on. He was stunning, challenging, the man of her dreams...

And now all those nascent dreams were shattered into pieces.

Stupid dreams.

'What's that?' Jason asked. The photograph of Simon and Gwen lay on the floor in the sprawl of items from the box.

'Oh it's just...' But he'd picked it up before she could stop him.

'What the hell? Is that Simon and Gwen?'

She nodded, started to make excuses and then... gave up. Instead, she opened the drawer and took out the letter. 'You should read this. I got it the week before he died. I should have told you but... well, when he died...'

Jason took it, frowning, and read in silence.

She noticed when his hand began to shake because the paper did too.

It didn't take long. It wasn't a long letter. When he finished, he looked aghast.

'This was with it.' She flicked the necklace.

'I wondered how you got it back,' he murmured. 'Why did you keep it? If he did this, then why...?'

Ari shrugged. She wasn't sure she had an answer to that.

Not really. 'It was all I had of him.'

'But this doesn't make any sense. None of it. He adored you. I know he adored you. You were all he could talk about. The day I left... Ari, the day I left, he was planning a trip to see you for your birthday.'

She shook her head. 'Well... he didn't.' She didn't know what else to say.

'Have you asked Gwen?'

The very idea horrified her. To confront Gwen, to see if she shared the same grief as Ari. 'No. How could I? What would I say? But, Jason...' Why stop now? she thought. 'Jason, I saw him. Or something that looks like him. Simon's ghost or... Ankou, that's what Rafael called it...'

He looked dubious, but kind. 'When?'

'The night of the dinner at the manor on the cliffs. And at the *fest noz*. There's more. There's so much more. I can't even begin to tell you all of it. But there are things happening here, dark and ancient, dangerous things. I know I sound crazy, but... Rafael saw him too.'

'Oh, Rafael did, did he? And that's why he was back here when we got home, was it? To comfort you? He didn't waste a moment the second time he had the chance.'

'Don't...' she whispered. Because even though it hurt, she didn't want Jason to say that. Maybe she was stupid, but she didn't like the implications.

He put the picture and the letter aside. 'And all this?' He gestured to the rest of the papers.

'You didn't look at it when you packed it away?'

He shrugged. 'I didn't pack it away. I don't know who did. It was just there.' He sifted through some of the photocopies and then picked up the notebook, flicking through it. 'Jesus... he had it all in here. That's how you knew. What's this? *Le chemin de l'eau?*'

'At the mouth of the sea cave. There's evidence of a road or a plaza. And there was a rip tide. Inside, the carvings... If I'd remembered the camera, I could show you. I'm sorry, Jason.'

He turned back to the letter. 'These are the coordinates, on the bottom, the place where we found the mask, where you found the cave. Ari? This doesn't make sense. Why would Simon give you the coordinates and send you the pendant if he never wanted to see you again?'

She didn't know. She didn't know anything. Nothing seemed to make sense anymore. She just couldn't find the words. He'd written those numbers of the edge of the page. Had he even known he was doing that or had something made him do it? The mask, perhaps, reaching out to be found again. Or had it just been a mistake? An idle doodle. He used to do that, she recalled.

Tears welled in her eyes again, burning.

'Here.' Jason hugged her, ruffled her hair like he had always done. 'It's OK, squirt. We'll work it out. You have a rest and then we'll go exploring, OK? Always loved a cave. Endless wonder. All those secrets. Buried treasure is almost as good as sunken treasure. The sooner, the better. I'll get the gear we need and we'll head off.'

The gear. Just like that.

But gear for exploring caves was completely different. And if Rafael really had cancelled the funding...

'But what if we don't have the money anymore?'

'Nico will know where to get it. I'll ask him. Come on.'

But Nico wasn't there when they went downstairs. Jason's car was gone.

Jason fished out his phone and rang, but there was no answer. 'Where've you gone, mate? Call me back.'

As they headed to the kitchen, they heard a car engine outside and Jason turned, relieved, but his expression darkened as he saw not his aged truck, but a familiar sleek black Mercedes.

Rafael.

'Shit,' Ari said, but Jason was already out the door, striding across the dirt yard, a man on a mission, a man outraged, with his sister's honour at stake.

Damn it. She ran after him, knowing exactly how this would go down.

'Jason, no!'

This wasn't going to help. It wasn't going to solve anything. And if she thought it would, she would bloody well do it herself.

Rafael got out of the car, spotted her and in his achingly handsome face she saw... relief? 'Ari, why did you—?'

That was when Jason reached him, drew back his fist and aimed a punch right at his nose.

Ari grabbed her brother's arm and, at the same moment, Rafael sidestepped, avoiding them both.

'Stop it!' she growled at Jason. 'Stop it now. It won't help.'

'I'll feel better.'

'Well, it isn't about you,' she snapped. How dare he? 'Leave him alone.'

'He slept with you and then tossed you out on your arse, Ari!'

Rafael recoiled from them in obvious horror. 'I did no such thing.'

'Oh right, you got your sister to do it.'

'I did not. I don't know what's going on here. I went back upstairs and you were gone.' Thank God he addressed her directly, rather than talking to Jason, who was all but foaming at the mouth anyway. 'Nolvene said you'd gone out running, and Laure didn't know where you were. What is going on? Ari, please, talk to me. With everything that has happened, all that we found in the caves—'

'She doesn't want to talk to you,' Jason snarled and Ari lost it. Only her brother could make her even more angry than Rafael already had. But there he was, as usual, digging deeper.

'Don't speak for me, Jason. Go back inside. I'll handle this.'

For a moment, she thought he'd refuse. She'd never seen him look quite so rebellious.

'Fine. But, dear God, Ari, the men in your life...'

Ice flooded her. She turned on him, daring him to go further. She'd finally trusted him with the truth about Simon and here he was blurting it all over the place. Throwing it in her face. 'Don't! Don't you *dare*!'

Jason threw his hands out in disgust or despair and turned on his heel, heading back to the house. He slammed the door behind him and a strange, pregnant silence fell over the garden.

'I'm going to stop driving over here,' Rafael said, with a half-smile, as if inviting her to laugh with him.

It was the wrong thing to do.

'He isn't wrong.' Ari brought her hands to her hips, and glared at him.

Rafael looked completely bewildered. 'We had an argument. We need to talk. We can work this out.'

'I *heard* you.'

'*Heard me* what?'

'You were on the phone cancelling our funding. Laure said—'

Understanding dawned on his face. 'Oh, *Laure said*? I bet she did. What did she say?'

And suddenly Ari began to suspect she had been taken for a fool, that Rafael's sister had manipulated her, for reasons of her own.

Not to mention she'd allowed her own guilt to control her. She'd slept with Rafael. But he wasn't Simon.

Even Simon had betrayed her in the end. But that didn't mean Rafael would, did it?

And Simon had been outside. She was sure she'd seen him there. Or maybe it was a trick of the light and her grief, her guilt. She hadn't been able to find him.

But she'd been certain it was him.

And Rafael had accused her of running away. Not just from him, but from Simon as well. And he was right. That was the worst part.

Rafael was still waiting for an answer, but she couldn't say that. She couldn't say any of it. The very idea made her throat close over.

'That you... that I...' The words dried up in her mouth. She couldn't say them either. 'I ran away.' Her voice sounded so small.

The confession hung between them and he stared into her eyes as if to say he knew what that confession meant. To her endless relief he didn't crow, or rub it in. He didn't mention it at all. When he spoke, his voice was soft and patient.

'The phone call you overheard was *not* about your funding. My mother has been running the company like her own personal fiefdom and I need to put a stop to it. She's in Dubai and I asked someone I trusted to look into the accounts. That's the funding I meant. Laure cannot resist interfering in my love life. I don't know what she's up to, some kind of power play probably, but it doesn't matter. None of it matters. Ari...' his voice softened, 'I thought... I don't know what I thought. You were just gone. After last night, after our fight, after everything... you were gone.'

He looked devastated and the sudden stab of a new kind of guilt was unexpected. It made her instantly defensive. 'You thought I'd what? Just slept with you and taken off?'

She saw it then, written all over his face. The truth. That was exactly what he'd thought and he didn't like it. Who would?

'Well, yes. It wouldn't be the first time.'

'That's not fair,' she told him. But she wasn't entirely certain about that herself.

'I didn't mean you. I meant it wouldn't be the first time it happened to me. I'm sorry I said you always ran away. That was not fair either.'

The last thing she expected was an apology. Nor to hear the vulnerability he buried deep inside. She hadn't thought about his past relationships. It had all seemed so glamorous when she looked him up online. She drew in a ragged breath. 'I thought... after Simon... after he died...'

Something flickered in his eyes, something dark and bitter, not angry exactly. 'Oh. Simon.' The words were flat and Ari winced.

She met his gaze firmly. There was no point in denying it. 'Yes. Simon.'

It always came back to Simon. She couldn't help that. Even now, she couldn't escape him. He'd come back as Ankou and he didn't seem any better at letting go than she was, despite his letter.

Rafael shook his head slowly, as if clearing a headache. When he spoke, she could tell he was trying to be kind. But all the same, the words he said... 'Simon left you, Ari. Simon was an idiot. Just because he died doesn't change that.'

'Don't you dare—' she began, anger simmering.

'Of course I dare,' he replied. 'You keep pushing me away, falling back to Simon, to a man who let you go to another country, who let you run away, who wouldn't give up anything for you, and in the end gave you up. He was a fool. And so are you if you can't see it.'

She wanted to scream at him, to tell him he was wrong, to defend Simon's memory but... but she couldn't. Because he wasn't wrong. None of what he said was wrong.

Just like this morning. Simon had been there, just long enough to make her leave Rafael, and then he was gone.

A rush of air came from her lungs, like she was a deflating balloon.

Chastened, Ari took a step towards him. 'Then why come after me?'

He smiled, such a sad broken smile, one of long and bitter experience. 'I didn't want to let you go. Can't you see that? Not for anything.'

CHAPTER TWENTY-FOUR

The seconds crawled by, tormenting Rafael as Ari just stared at him, open-mouthed. As he had made his way back to the room that morning, expecting to find her still there, still angry but hopefully less angry and ready to make up, he'd felt a glow of something he had never really experienced before, a satisfaction, a sense of all being right in his life for the first time ever. He felt different. Everything felt different.

And she hadn't been there.

He knew why instantly. Guilt. It had to be guilt. She had run away again. This time from him.

Laure, of course, denied all knowledge. 'You asked me to find her some clothes,' she'd snapped. 'So I did. What was I meant to do? Sit on her?'

His sister had been stirring, but he'd find out what that was all about eventually. She probably just didn't approve. She hadn't approved of Jacqueline either. But this time she was wrong. So very wrong.

While they made love, he knew Ari had been his and his alone, perhaps for the first time ever. Simon's ghost had been banished, if only for a short while. And now it was back. Not

Ankou, not that dark spirit. But the man who had hurt her so badly.

Ari chewed her bottom lip, folded her arms in front of her, and for another dreadful moment, he thought she was just going to tell him to leave anyway. To say his sister had been right. That she wasn't interested. To tell him not to mention Simon and to go to hell.

'You'd better come in. I'll talk to Jason first. Give me a second.'

Well, it wasn't the warmest greeting, but it wasn't an outright dismissal. He'd take what he could get. He allowed himself to breathe again.

He locked his car, waited, and he could still hear their voices inside, bickering as only siblings could. But at least they sounded like they cared about each other underneath it all. He was never sure with Laure. She was their mother's daughter.

And he was going to have to confront her about this. Enough meddling in his life. Enough acting the bitch. Jacqueline had told him as much, but he'd never listened. Even Elena had implied it and she rarely had a bad word to say about anyone. Now, for the first time, he truly wondered. Had he been so caught up in the business and everything else that he'd failed to see that his sister delighted in sabotaging his life? So did his mother, for that matter. They were... well, they had always been difficult. Mémé had tried to warn him too.

He had always told himself it didn't matter. He didn't trust easily. His whole life had been a lesson in not trusting.

Ari had her own trust issues.

But she hadn't always. He knew that instinctively. She'd been engaged to Simon Poullain, clearly had adored him. She still wore his necklace around her neck and in the photos he had seen of them together... no, there was no doubt in his mind.

It was something more than his death. Grief alone didn't explain it. She had run away from the relationship even if it had taken her this long to admit that. She had run away from settling down with Simon and sought out a new life on her own terms. And then she had run away from that when she lost him.

She was the puzzle he longed to unravel. To understand. Even if it took forever to do that. If only he could keep up with her.

The thought shocked him, stopped him in his tracks.

Before he had a chance to examine the feelings any further, the door opened again and Ari waved him inside.

Jason paced back and forth in the living room. He still didn't look happy, but at least there didn't seem to be an imminent risk of assault.

'Jason,' Ari said, her tone all warning.

He stopped, glared at Rafael. 'I'm sorry.' He spat out the words and Rafael realised that that was all he was likely to get from either of the Walkers for the time being.

'Jason,' she said again, more gently.

Rafael fought to hold back a smile, which really wouldn't help right now. The teacher in her was coming out.

'I said I'm sorry. What else do you want?'

'Apology accepted,' Rafael said before the situation could get any more awkward.

'We need to talk about the cave,' Ari cut in before he could say anything else. 'We need to go back there. Gather evidence.'

'Where's the mask?' Jason asked. 'If it's so dangerous, if it has the effect on the two of you that you say it does...'

'Locked away, safe. I can show you if you want.'

'Now.'

'Of course.'

'Jason, it's there, I put it there,' Ari said. 'And it's safe, I promise.'

She had trusted him with that, Rafael thought. That was something, wasn't it? It had to be.

Jason, however, was unconvinced. 'I still want to see it.'

She clenched her teeth and made eye contact with Rafael. She clearly didn't want her brother near the mask and if the effect it had on him was anything to go by, he knew why.

'We need to explain, Ari,' Rafael said cautiously. She wouldn't want to. 'Everything.'

She shook her head, but Jason was not going to back down. Not without an explanation, so slowly, reluctantly, Rafael started to explain. Everything. From the fall of Ys, to the deaths, to the curse on his own family. He told Jason the version of the tale he knew, how Ankou and Dahut were lovers forced apart by death, how Ankou blessed her to be desired and gave her the mask as a protection, how she used it to kill the unworthy and how his ancestor the Mac'htiern freed Cap Sizun from her tyranny, destroying Ys.

And he told him about the curse, how all the men of his line were doomed to be taken by the water: and how it might be broken by protecting the last remnants of Ys. He didn't mention his son and, to his relief, neither did Ari.

Jason, who had sunk into one of the armchairs at some point in the saga, leaned forward and all traces of agitation had gone. 'That's... quite a story.'

'It's true, Jason,' Ari assured him. 'The cave confirms it. Fabien and Tristan found it in 1943. They died to keep it secret. And I think Simon did as well, or at least he was on the right track. He found the mask. He hid it. And it killed him.'

'This ghost you saw... Ankou... are you sure, Ari?' When she nodded solemnly, he closed his eyes. 'Did you ask him?'

Rafael wasn't sure what she was meant to have asked him, but she gave her brother a look of such pain that he didn't want to ask.

'I think Dahut murdered him. That's what Ankou is, isn't it? The unquiet dead, the first drowning, murder or suicide of a season. I think she's hunting all of us, to stop Rafael breaking the curse. I think she killed Thierry too. I think she tried to get Nico when—'

'Where is Nico?' Rafael asked.

Jason's face went a peculiar shade of grey. 'I... I don't know. He took off when Ari got back.'

'Try ringing him again,' Ari said. 'If the car crash is part of this... if she's after him as well...'

Rafael's phone rang and he fished it out of his pocket. Nolvene's name flashed up on the screen and a terrible feeling of foreboding settled on his shoulders like a shroud.

She knew everything that happened at the manor, more so, he suspected, than anyone who lived there.

'It's Séraphine. I brought her breakfast up to her, but... Rafael, I've called Dr Marais. He's on his way now.'

'We'll... I'll be right there. Where is Laure? Could you find her for me?' His sister could have phoned him. She was so thoughtless.

'Of course.' He heard Nolvene walking across the stone flags of the kitchen and from there into the hall and onto the carpets. But when she reached the dining room, she let out a gasp of surprise. 'Oh now, where are they? The cars are still here.'

A sense of something dreadful swept over him. He saw it reflected in Ari's face, and Jason rose to his feet again.

'What cars?'

'Laure's and that nice young man from the gîte, Nicolas. They were having breakfast. He came looking for you, but you had already left. In a state he was, but your sister calmed him down. Where did they get to?'

'Nolvene, just get Dr Marais in to see Mémé. I'll be there in a few minutes. If you see either of them, get them to ring me.' He hung up and met the concerned looks both Ari and Jason were directing at him. 'We need to go to the manor, now. My great-aunt is ill. Nico was there with Laure, but now they've vanished. The mask is there. I have a bad feeling about this.'

He drove faster than he should have along the narrow road up to the manor, with Ari beside him and Jason in the back seat. No one said a word on the short trip, each one of them lost in their own fears.

Sure enough, Laure's sleek little sports car was there, as was a truck which had seen better days. The doctor's car, a new Citroën, was parked on the far side of the entrance.

Nolvene met him at the door, fussing as he came in. 'I'm sure it's nothing, Rafael, but it's not like her.'

'I know. Let me just go to see her.'

'The doctor is in with her now.'

He took the stairs two at a time and ran to Mémé's room. She looked very small and frail in her bed.

She blinked at him. 'Rafi?'

The doctor was packing up his bag and gave him a curt nod. 'Nothing too much to worry about, Monsieur du Lac,' he said. 'She slept poorly and is perhaps sickening with a cold. I've suggested she rest and keep warm, lots of liquids, and, of course, if she worsens ring me immediately. I'm just down the road, is that not so, *madame*?'

He smiled at her with genuine affection and Mémé waved him away. 'Let me talk to my nephew. He's drugged me, Rafael. Drugged me!'

'A very mild sedative, as per your prescription, *madame*, nothing more.'

Rafael shook Dr Marais's hand as he left and closed the door behind him.

Trying to make himself calm and reassuring, he sat on her bedside. 'I'm here. Are you well?'

'Yoú heard him.' She squinted at him. 'He's a child. His

father, now *there* was a doctor. He'd have you up and out walking in no time. But, yes, I am tired. I dreamed of them, of Fabien and his friend, poor Tristan. Of your father and my father, my brothers. Of Dahut… and I… All night, the Ankou stalked around this house. It took all that is in me to keep him out. Do you understand, *chéri?*'

'Keep him out? What do you mean?'

Ankou. Simon. Here. A chill ran through him at the thought. Did Ari know? Had she sensed him or seen him? Was that why she'd left?

'He cannot enter here.' She sank back onto the pillow, her eyes closing, and he sat there, caught between rising and looking for help and an inability to leave her. 'I will not allow it. You have the charm I gave you, do you not?' Her protective charms and amulets… Given all he had seen, he was not about to mock them again. How did he know she hadn't kept them safe? But at what price?

'Yes, Mémé,' he told her solemnly.

'Show me.'

Luckily, there was one in his pocket. He shifted on the bed so he could take it out and show it to her. It seemed to satisfy her.

She pressed it back into his hand and closed his fingers over it. 'Put it away. It will keep you safe from her enchantments. From all evil. Keep it with you.'

He nodded and slid it back into the safety of his pocket again.

He waited until she drifted off to sleep at last and went back downstairs to find Ari and Jason standing awkwardly in the main hall.

'Is she OK?' Ari asked.

Rafael held his hands out palm up, a gesture of helplessness. Her guess was as good as his, but the doctor had done what he could and was ready to come back at once if necessary. Nolvene would look after her. She'd been straight back into the room to sit with her the moment he appeared at the door.

'Did you find Nico?'

'No,' said Jason. 'The car's still locked, but there's no sign of him or your sister. We looked outside as well. Where could they have gone?'

And that was the other thing dragging nails across the back of his consciousness.

He walked into the drawing room and felt over the mantel-piece. The key was missing.

'Damn,' he said. 'The vault.'

He didn't pause to see if they followed, but he knew they would. They both understood the implications of this. What had he been thinking, storing it here? He'd been arrogant enough to believe that the walls of his family's vault would keep its malignant influence from reaching out to others. Like his sister. Like a man Dahut had already set her mark upon. He'd just wanted it away from Ari. To keep her safe.

The door stood open. In the middle of the shelf where he had left it, the plastic box full of water was still there, but the lid was off. The mask was gone.

Jason let out a torrent of curses. 'Who was it? Your sister? Nico? What the hell is going on?'

'Where have they gone?' Ari asked.

He led them back upstairs and as he reached the hallway again, his phone rang. Sick to death of this, he answered without looking and barked out a single word. 'What?'

'Rafael?' It was Laure, and she sounded terrified. Her voice echoed strangely, the sound twisted and faint. The signal cut in and out, making her voice flicker. 'You have to come, you have to come *now*. Please. He put on the mask and he... he *changed...*'

'Where are you? What's happened?'

'The caves,' she whispered and the line cut off completely. She was gone.

CHAPTER TWENTY-FIVE

It was nothing more than a little tower of rocks, marking the place where they had crawled out of the darkness and into the storm last night. Ari remembered it. She'd made it herself, realising that they'd never find the gap between the boulders again without a marker. It wasn't far from the place where Ankou had shoved her to the ground, she realised now. Perhaps he had been aiming for here after all. Trying to show her the way.

Wishful thinking, she told herself. Whatever the Ankou was, he wasn't really Simon and she couldn't trust him. Even if she wanted to.

Simon had proved she couldn't even trust him, she reminded herself. Better to trust no one at all. And as for Rafael... well... he'd been right about why she'd left. Which didn't make her feel any better. She'd panicked and, to be honest, she was still panicking. She couldn't think about the two of them right now. Not with Nico in danger.

Rafael had found a couple of torches and some rope in the manor's storeroom. That was all they had. So much for the gear Jason had said they'd need. But this wasn't an expedition into the cave system in search of treasure and a lost city. It was a rescue. Rafael's sister was in trouble, Nico too, and although Ari knew damn well who she cared about more, she wasn't going to let anything happen to either of them.

'Nico wouldn't hurt her,' Jason protested again. 'He just... he wouldn't.'

'I don't know that. No one knows that.' Rafael uncoiled the rope and looked for the biggest rock he could fine. He moved like he'd done this before, wrapping it around the boulder several times and then tying an elaborate knot.

'Will it hold?' Ari asked.

'If it holds me, it will hold either of you. That's why I'm going in first. Do you think you'll be able to find your marks again?'

She nodded, hoping they were still there, that nothing had happened to them. Because if they were gone, they wouldn't have a hope of getting in or out.

'We should have called the police,' she told him.

Both Rafael and Jason turned on her in the same instant. 'No!'

'We don't know what's happened,' Jason went on. 'I don't want cops swarming all over here and anything going wrong. Someone could get hurt. I refuse to believe Nico kidnapped her or whatever *you* think was happening.' He glared at Rafael, who ignored him coolly.

'The police will never understand,' said Rafael in calmer tones. 'I'm not sure Nico knows what he's doing. If he put on that mask...' He trailed off, no doubt recalling the sensation himself.

Ari remembered the feeling of helplessness, the way the mask, or whatever possessed it, had crawled into her mind in a bid to control her. Nico might not have any choice in what he was doing.

And Laure was a du Lac. There was a curse on her family.

She locked eyes with Rafael and nodded, understanding. Like it or not, it was up to the three of them.

Rafael went first, Jason lowering him carefully. Once down, he released the rope and Ari tied it around her waist.

'Just be careful,' said Jason quietly. 'And if anything happens, get the hell out and get help, OK?'

'I could say the same to you,' she told him, and slid down through the gap between the stones into the darkness.

Rafael caught her and helped her down. He didn't extend the same courtesy to her brother, she noticed, but then again, Jason probably would have clocked him one if he tried.

There was more light filtering through the caves than the last time they'd been here, almost enough to see some metres ahead, until the tunnel turned.

Rafael's torch was more powerful than the ones they had carried last night, more like a lantern, and they followed the beam of light through the twists and turns, picking out Ari's marks at each junction.

They emerged into the cavern. The pool at the far end glowed with light from outside, throwing up a rippling, moving pattern on the roof, illuminating the carvings. There were more than Ari had seen at first. It was like standing under the ocean, looking up at schools of fish, boats, and a city with seven towers and a grand harbour. There were candles at the far end, so many candles, ranging over every surface, filling the chamber with a golden flickering glow. They hadn't been there before. Who had done this?

Jason let out a sound like a low groan, somewhere between wonder and shock.

The floor beneath them was patterned too, coloured stones like cobbles, those curious little egg-shaped stones often found buried in the sand on the shore here, in green, red, black, white... every shade. The map of Ys as it had been, stretched out at his feet.

And facing them, in the chapel-like space at the far end of the cavern, her face watched them.

'Dahut,' Jason murmured. 'This... this isn't possible...'

'Jason, wait!' Ari called. 'Look.'

A dark shape sprawled on the ground between them and the dais, a man wearing a white mask.

'Nico!' Jason cried out in alarm, his whole demeanour transforming.

Nico jerked back, trying to lift himself up on his trembling arms. He half turned towards them and gave a hoarse growl of pain. The mask rippled against his skin, white lines snaking down to coil around his throat like the arms of an octopus, digging into his flesh. The surface caught the light, gleaming and real, like a living thing, a man's face with high sculpted cheekbones, the fine tracery of lines giving the impression of veins. The gold gleamed and the blue was vibrant as the sky, all the treasures of the world...

Jason reached him first, trying to grab him, to hold him, to gather him into his arms. Nico's body contorted with pain and the mask tightened its grip, slowly choking the life out of him.

'What happened to him?' Jason croaked. 'What's wrong?'

Ari wanted to answer him, but she couldn't find the words. Someone else did.

'Oh, he's pure instinct now, but he won't last much longer. I think because he fights it so hard. It pulls the life out of him even faster. It's fascinating.'

They spun around to see Laure, half in shadows, sitting on one of the broken pieces of carved stone in front of the podium. The throne, Ari realised. Sitting on an ancient throne like she belonged there. The carving of Dahut spread out behind her, illuminated by the rows of candles. But it cast her in shadow, a silhouette, perfectly poised, a spectator.

'Laure? What have you done?' Rafael's voice sounded like thunder.

'What, this?' She lifted her hands to gesture the cavern. 'Reclaiming my birthright, brother. Taking what is rightfully mine. After all, I'm descended from the same line as you, from the Mac'htiern. I've wanted to do this for years. *Years.* I planned everything. But the time wasn't right. Plus, I didn't have the mask. That idiot Simon found it for me and then refused to hand it over. He hid it and wouldn't tell me where. But I can be very persuasive.'

'I don't— Laure?' His voice shook and he reached out blindly to Ari, his hand seeking hers. His fingers shook as she took them in hers, trying to reassure him, when in fact she was as bewildered as he was. It was like his whole world had turned on its axis. 'You aren't in danger? I thought...' He glanced down at Nico.

Her cold laugh brought his attention snapping back up to her. 'You thought what I wanted you to think. You always have, when you can be bothered to pay attention to anything. Now, come here, and kneel before her. We're going to bring her here to finish this and I can claim my rightful inheritance.'

'Her?'

'Dahut, of course. The Queen of Ys, the water witch. She owes us, Rafael. We've kept her secret for years. I mean to call in the debt.'

With Rafael keeping her talking, Ari crept carefully forward, towards Nico's prone body. The mask was icy cold to the touch, but it wouldn't come away from his face. She pulled harder.

'Oh, I wouldn't do that if I were you,' Laure warned in a sing-song voice.

The tentacles around his neck tightened abruptly and Nico's mouth opened around the gag as he started to choke again. Behind the mask, his eyes opened wide in panic. They fixed on Ari, just for a moment, and she knew him. Nico was still in there, somewhere. He gasped for air, his hands clawing against the stones. The mask dug in tighter, his skin turning white beneath the appendages.

'Ari, no!' Jason pulled her away. 'You'll kill him. It'll kill him.'

She fell back, looking for Rafael, but his attention was fixed on his sister in disbelief. She could hardly blame him. Laure du Lac sat like a queen beneath the carving of Dahut, and it was hard to see a difference between the two of them. But she wasn't watching them now, or Nico. She had what she wanted. Rafael.

Together, Ari and Jason hauled Nico back into the tunnel, out of the way, out of sight. The voices of the du Lac siblings echoed around them, their argument the distraction Ari needed. Nico was what mattered now. They needed to get the mask off him. But how?

Ari helped lower him down and that was when Nico moved, and his hands closed on her arms in a bruising grip. His eyes gleamed beneath the mask, so full of pain and fear she hardly recognised the gentle man she knew and loved like a brother.

'What has she done to him?' said Jason. 'How do we stop it?' He sounded so desperate, his words sharp with grief.

At the sound of his voice, Nico's hands relaxed a fraction and he looked back at him, like a flower seeking sunlight.

'Keep talking to him, Jason,' she said, struggling free. Jason's voice was what Nico needed. Jason was what he needed.

'Nico,' Jason whispered, his voice hoarse. He swallowed painfully and took her place, bringing his hands up to take Nico's. Slowly, he pulled him up into his arms, wrapped him in an embrace. 'Nico, please talk to me. Just talk to me. Please.'

Nico gasped something, tried to speak, and the mask twisted into a smile, the porcelain around the eyes crinkling, the cheeks drawing up into a grin, the brow, alive with glee, a monster.

It wasn't Nico's smile. It was nothing like him. This wasn't going to work.

'Nico, please,' Ari said. 'You have to fight it. You can fight it. I know you can.'

His fingers tightened on her brother's, the knuckles white, and his mouth opened in a silent grimace of pain. The gasps were sharper, more desperate. He was running out of time.

'What do we do? We can't leave him like this,' Jason gasped.

She wracked her brains, every one of the notes and stories and things that Simon had written down in his notebook, anything. The books, the maps, the sketches, the diary entries. Fabien and Tristan, who had somehow overcome all of this with...

The one thing Dahut wanted was true love. It was the only thing she wanted. It was her mask. Ankou had given it to her. It showed her true love.

'Tell him the truth, Nico,' she whispered urgently. 'You have to tell him the truth.'

Jason didn't get it. He never did. 'What truth... Ari, I—'

Oh, but he knew. Of course he knew. She could see it written all over his face.

Nico shook his head, despair and pain making the movement wild and uncontrolled.

'Nico, you have to tell him the truth. And let him tell you. Now. Jason, tell him how you feel.'

Her brother frowned. 'He knows how I feel...' His voice was gruff and shuttered and he looked away from her. Right at Nico. 'You know how I feel. Talk to me.'

'How?' Nico spat the word out, barely recognisable as a word. He had almost no breath left to him. But as he spoke, the tentacles gagging him withdrew, curling back against the body of the mask. Some little part of the pressure loosened. His voice was broken, hopeless. 'How would I know? I've loved you for years. Always you. But I... How did you know?'

Jason's face crumpled in dismay. 'In a thousand things, little things. But I didn't want to wreck everything, our friendship... Nico, you have to know.'

'You flirt... you string me alone... like everyone else... you...' And the mask's grip tightened again, his voice dying, his eyes welling up with burning tears.

Jason glanced at her and then she was forgotten. He grabbed Nico's face and kissed him.

A sound like a crack of thunder filled the chamber. It echoed back and forth, reverberating through stone and air. The rocks shook, the water of the pool boiled and a rain of dust fell down on them.

The mask fell from Nico's face, clattering on the stone floor, and he drew in a deep, shuddering breath. Livid red lines marked his throat and face. He gasped for air, great racking sobs, but Jason held him close, murmured words she couldn't hear. Nor should she. They weren't for her.

As fast as she could, Ari grabbed the cursed mask and hurled it away from them. She heard the noise of it clattering on the stones and prayed it would smash into a million pieces.

'Jason... have to go,' Nico murmured, as if still caught in a dream. 'The voices said. The voices in the mask. She's coming and she's angry. So angry. You can't be here. Death comes with her. Surrender to her.' His eyelashes fluttered against his cheeks as he went limp.

Ari grabbed her brother and shook him hard. 'Get him out of here,' she told him. 'Get him back to safety. There are marks on the rocks. Follow them.'

The ground shook again. They could hear the rocks shifting and in the distance a sound like a sonic boom coming through the water. The gates of Ys opening, the coming of Dahut.

'Ari, this place, this find—'

'Is worth nothing if we're dead. Get Nico out.'

He didn't argue again, didn't dare perhaps. He manhandled Nico to his feet and half carried, half dragged him back down the tunnel.

But when Ari looked for Rafael, both he and the mask were gone.

CHAPTER TWENTY-SIX

Rafael stepped out into the cavern. He knew he needed to buy the others time, to let Ari and Jason find a way to help Nico. And escape. God, he prayed they would escape.

'Laure, what have you done?'

'Me?' She laughed, that light little trill of satisfaction he found so irritating, so artificial. He didn't know when she'd learned it, but he hated it. 'God, you're such a fool, aren't you? Pretty but dumb. Maman always said you were just like Papa.'

'What are you talking about?'

She surged to her feet and real anger filled her beautiful face. 'Don't talk down to me, Rafael. You aren't in charge here. You aren't in charge of anything anymore.'

He heard a noise behind him and something hit his feet. Glancing down, he saw the mask lying there, waiting.

Laure's smile grew even wider. 'Pick it up,' she whispered in delight, her voice echoing around the chamber.

He bent before he thought better of it. Suddenly, the cool weight of it was in his hands.

'Put it on. You know you want to. It's been calling you, hasn't it? And then we'll find the truth of you. That's what it does, did you know that? It makes you tell the truth, no matter how harsh. And if you lie...' She ran her perfectly manicured fingernail over her throat and grinned like a hyena. 'It takes you.'

The rocks shook again and the water in the pool surged, slopping over the edge as if something huge had stirred underneath it.

Rafael's mouth had gone dry as he swallowed and fought every instinct in his body telling him to obey her. Put on the mask and he was lost, he knew that.

So did his sister.

But why? Why was she doing this?

Truth was not his forte. Not him. Not anyone in his family.

Everything was quiet. All he could hear was his own breath and the water of the pool, as if he breathed in unison with its movement. The mask was just a cold weight in his hands. He felt nothing of the obsessive need to put it on he'd felt the last time. There were no voices, no whispers. Almost no magic at all.

'Laure,' he tried again, schooling his face and his voice to patience. 'I don't know what's happened to you or why you think—'

'Don't you dare try to talk me around. You've always dismissed me. Stupid, vapid little Laure, who can't be trusted to do the simplest thing. You stormed in on every project I tried to run, took credit for every idea I had that worked. You've done this all my life, the bloody golden boy of the du Lac Foundation. Mémé's favourite, Papa's favourite, always destined to lead. If only they knew your real destiny, brother. The destiny of all the du Lac men, to kneel here and give themselves up to her.'

The sheer force of resentment took him aback. Had he really done all those things? He knew he'd been forced to step in and rescue any number of her bright ideas which had gone spiralling out of control over the years. As for taking credit, no, he'd always made sure she was acknowledged. He was sure he had.

'Laure,' he tried again. 'Let's just talk about this...'

'I don't want to talk about it.' She pulled a gun from somewhere and pointed it at him. That explained how she got Nico down here, he guessed. Or had she just promised to show him wonders? Anything was possible, or so it now seemed. He didn't really know his sister at all. 'Put the mask on. I want you on your knees and ready when she gets here. Then she can deal with you and we can all move on. Maman and I will make sure Mémé's taken care of, if that's worrying you. You always cared more about her than us.'

He stared at the barrel of the gun, unable to believe what he was seeing. Or what she was saying. They were both in on this? His mother and his sister?

'*Maman?* She knows about this?'

'Maman has known for years. Our father showed her the cave when they were first married. He was a lovesick fool, desperate to impress her with the family secret. The "real treasure", he called it, not that she was impressed. Dahut had forgiven us, forgiven our family, because Fabien sacrificed himself to protect this place. He and Tristan Poullain died to protect the secret, haven't we been told that for years? But we didn't realise what that meant. It was all over then, no curse any more, not since '43, he said... but the story lingered on. And then...' She gave a sigh. 'Papa had to go and have an affair. He was going to leave Maman, take you and me away from her. No way would anyone give her custody of the du Lac children. So she did what she has always done, she *dealt* with it. The women of our family have always had to *deal with it*, haven't they? She killed him, dumped the body in the pool here and let the legend take its course. Genius really. But even she didn't realise what she'd woken up.'

His mind reeled around inside his head. It wasn't possible.

She didn't know what she was saying. He had his differences with Maman, but...

And yet, here was his own sister holding a gun on him.

'Maman... she killed Papa?'

'Better than losing everything.'

'She would have got a settlement.' It didn't make sense. None of it made sense. But somehow, horribly, it did.

'He betrayed her, Rafael. An affair. He was going to dump her. You may have thought he was a saint, but he wasn't. You barely knew him. He was the same bastard du Lac lord of the manor they all were. Now put on the fucking mask.'

He jerked back at the violence in her voice, the way her face contorted, and most of all at the way the gun shook wildly. If it went off, she might not hit him. Or she might take his head off. It was impossible to tell. His sister was deranged.

The chamber trembled, a rain of fine dust falling from the ceiling, the waves in the pool slapping against the stone around it.

Rafael kept his voice as calm as he could, stretching out his open hands towards her in a gesture of peace, or at least that was what he hoped. The last thing he wanted to do was put on that mask. He remembered the sensation of the voices crawling under the surface of his skin, controlling him, manipulating him. But this time... not a murmur... why? 'If you shoot me, you aren't going to get anyone to believe I was the victim of a curse.'

Her right eye twitched in irritation. 'It doesn't matter. I can just leave you down here. No one will find you.'

'The others know I'm here.'

'And I can take care of that too.'

'Three more murders? What about Simon? Thierry? What did you do, Laure?'

She pouted, twisting her mouth to one side as she did so, like a petulant child. 'Simon was working for Mémé and he found the mask. I told him to give it me and he refused. He was obsessed with Gwen by that stage and I tried to reason with him, told him I'd tell his beloved Ariadne, ruin his life, but he wouldn't listen. Next thing I knew, he'd hidden it and he wouldn't say where.' Her grip on the gun tightened, her knuckles white. 'He wouldn't say when I trapped him down here, or when I strangled him.'

'You... you strangled him...' He echoed the words like a hollow log, hardly able to believe they were real.

Laure nodded with a frightening enthusiasm, her eyes shining. 'A garotte. It was La Fontenelle's favourite method of torture, did you know that? You think you know everything, don't you?'

Rafael shook his head and she laughed at him. 'What about Thierry?'

'The diver? Well, when it was found again, I had to test the mask, silly. Make sure it was the real thing.' A slow smile trickled over her features. 'And it is.' The sneer she threw his way wasn't pretty. 'Do you even realise how much the Foundation is worth, Rafael? Accidents happen all the time, especially to divers, to men who drink too much and to people who wander into caves they don't know. Sometimes they're never found. Besides, I don't need to shoot *you*, brother of mine. Do I, Dr Ariadne Walker?'

The muzzle of the gun swung to his left and, to his horror, he saw Ari stop by his side. She reached out to grab his arm, her cold hand on his skin. She was shaking. He didn't blame her. But what on earth was she doing here? She could be far away with her brother and Nico by now, safe, or at the very least raising the alarm. But she was here. With him. She'd come back. For him...

'You do know she's just a teacher, don't you?' Laure went on dismissively. 'They're conmen, her and her brother. People believe whatever they want to believe.'

Ari didn't answer, but her grip on him tightened. He could

see she was angry. More than angry. But he couldn't afford to let her tackle Laure. She'd shoot Ari in an instant, the way her mind was right now.

'And yet they found this place. Just as they promised.' He wrapped his free hand around Ari's and pressed her gently against him, trying to keep her calm, trying to let her know that he would handle it. Somehow.

'Of course. You had her thoroughly researched, didn't you? All the little company spies scurried off to report back to you as soon as you laid eyes on her. Did you know that he does that, Ari? Did you know he investigated every aspect of your life as soon as he heard your name?'

Laure wasn't lying. He had done that. Of course he had. And he wasn't entirely sure how Ari would react to that truth. It had been the last thing on his mind until this moment. She was still angry with him, he suspected, angry that he had accused her of running away. And yet, here she was by his side.

Not running away at all when it really counted.

She cleared her throat, glanced at him briefly, and then fixed her gaze on the gun. She was no fool. 'He does have a habit of throwing money at things.' Her voice was extraordinarily calm.

'Well, it works,' he said. Then, aware of their situation, he felt he ought to elaborate. 'Sometimes.'

'Depends what you throw it at, I guess,' she murmured.

He had always thought Laure had enough money of her own. Clearly not. She wanted it all. And she wanted him out of the way.

'Shut up,' Laure spat. 'Both of you. If you'd just stayed away like you were told, Dr Walker, this would have been so much simpler.'

Like she was told? When had she been told to stay away?

'But then you wouldn't have the mask,' Ari said quietly. 'What happened with Simon, Laure? What did you do?'

'I gave him everything he needed, all Fabien's clues. Gwen even helped, although she didn't realise what I was doing. But you found it again, so maybe you're right. Maybe you're meant to be here after all. A witness. And I know how to take care of witnesses.'

'Laure, we can talk about this, negotiate something,' Rafael tried again, because he had to try. But she wasn't even listening, he knew that. Her gaze had drifted over to the pool, where the water churned and frothed. It had grown wilder, as it had the night of the storm, but the light still shone through it. It glowed. 'Ari? Is that... is that normal?'

But Ari wasn't looking. Before he knew what she was doing, she took the mask from his unresisting grip. She ran her delicate fingers over the smooth surface and then her eyes met his.

'Get out of here,' she told him as she gritted her teeth. And then she put it on.

For a moment, nothing happened. Her hands released the mask, but froze, framing her face. The mask didn't fall. It seemed to stick to her, and, as he watched in horror, tendrils worked their way out of it, wriggling against her skin and through her hair.

'No, what have you done?' he hissed, but Ari didn't answer. He grabbed her shoulders and spun her around to face him, heedless now of Laure and her gun. She was still a danger, but nothing compared to this, to the unnatural madness of this.

Ari drew in a shaking breath. 'I can hear it. Hear... voices. Jesus... Rafael, so many voices. They say Dahut is coming. Surrender to her. Give up. She wants the truth. She wants... she wants revenge.'

Her body trembled and then jerked as if something had stabbed her. The white tendrils of the mask thickened, tightened, crawled across her skin, wound around her neck.

Panic seized her. She clawed at the mask in a futile effort to pull it off. 'No. No, please.'

Laure swore loudly, her rage drawing his attention back to her. 'Did you think you'd save him with this futile action? You're so stupid.'

'Shut up, Laure,' he roared. 'You've brought us here. You've done this. You and your endless greed.'

The gunshot was deafening in the caves, the sound echoing and reverberating around them. The rocks above them shifted, screaming against each other, and the earth shook. Rafael ducked instinctively, trying to shield Ari even as she scrabbled at her own face, trying to tear the thing off again. Her body arched in pain against him.

Laure had missed. Maybe on purpose, maybe not. Still cursing, she came closer, the gun shaking in her hand. She wouldn't miss again, not at this range, no matter how out of control she was.

'Ari,' he whispered. 'Close your eyes. Just close your eyes.' He turned his back on Laure, offering her more of a target but covering Ari's trembling form. If he could just protect her...

And that's when he saw it, rising from the pool, a swirling pillar of water.

Laure must have seen him freeze, must have followed his attention. She gave a shout of alarm and fired again, straight at the apparition, shot after shot, emptying the gun in panic. All around them, the chamber shook as if to tear itself apart, the whole cave system grinding down on it, ready to fall.

And suddenly everything went still.

A figure formed from the water, clear and pale green-blue, like sea glass. It shimmered with reflected light, a million colours swirling in the depths, resolving themselves to something tangible, a woman's figure. It took another step, walking onto the cave floor, leaving a trail of wetness behind it, then footprints. Pearls threaded their way through her sea-foam white hair, and a string of brightly coloured shells glittered around her neck.

Her face was the last thing to take shape, but he knew it. He knew it the moment he could make it out. He had known it all his life.

'Gwen?' he whispered in disbelief.

Gwen smiled, that bewitching half-smile she always used when he had finally figured something out, but she didn't acknowledge him.

Her bare feet left wet footprints behind her as she crossed the cave floor, walking towards the carving of Dahut as if it was a ritual procession. Behind her, the pool went as still as a mirror. As she passed Laure, however, she stopped and stretched out her hand. She trailed her fingers up the length of the gun and the metal changed, discolouring, corroding and then crumbling to the ground. Laure cried out and released it before Gwen could touch her hands, staggering back. Only then did she catch herself and draw her body up to her full height.

'Gwen— My lady, my queen,' she corrected herself. 'I've brought him for you. You can have your revenge. You can take him. It's Rafael. You always wanted him. Please, just take him.'

'Oh, Laure,' Gwen sighed and her voice was as soft as the lapping of waves on the cove. 'You really have no idea what you've done, do you?'

'I've done what you wanted. I brought your mask. And my brother.'

Gwen shook her head so slowly, like the rise and fall of a wave. 'You killed Simon. My Simon.'

Her hand, still glistening with sea water, pressed to Laure's cheek, like a caress, and Laure's eyes went wide at first with wonder, and then with panic.

She dropped like a stone to the cave floor.

Rafael yelled her name and started forward, but as he moved, Ari fell to her knees, her hands balling to fists as she gasped out in agony. Torn between them both, he froze, helpless, for a moment. But when Ari cried out again, the spell broke and he dropped down beside her, trying to cradle her, to comfort her, to do something to help.

Gwen continued towards the carving, looked up at it briefly, and then turned around, seating herself on the throne like a queen. Her watery robe spread out around her and she looked regal, lit by candlelight. Part of him wanted to fall at her feet.

But the rest of him... the rest of him only knew that Ari was in pain, that she was suffering because of him.

'Help her, Gwen, please.'

Gwen studied the two of them, her expression remote and alien, so different from the woman he thought he knew, the girl he had known growing up. Or thought he did.

'There's nothing I can do, Rafael,' she said. 'She put on my mask. She made the choice.'

'Only to stop me. So Laure wouldn't make me do it. Ari did it for me.'

Gwen smiled, a cold hard smile. 'Have you thought to ask her why?'

'Because she... because...' He had no idea. Not really. They'd slept together. He wanted so much more from her than she was ready to give yet. But she might be. One day. For the first time in his life, he had dared to dream he could have a relationship that might go somewhere. If they broke the curse, that was. And part of him dared to hope she wanted the same from him.

She wanted to save him? She loved him? Is that what this was? Love? How could she love him enough to sacrifice herself this way? They'd barely known each other a week.

But he had dreamed of her saving him.

Not like this. Dear God, not like this.

'You made it,' he tried again. 'You have to be able to control it.'

'No. It is a far older magic than mine. Ankou's parting gift to me. He said it would keep me safe, let me test my lovers to be sure they were true. And if they were not... well... you know the rest.'

'You killed them?' Rafael asked, bitterness souring his voice. 'All of them?'

Gwen laughed, as if he was a fool or a child. 'No. The mask did.'

But he wasn't finished. The surge of anger inside him broke out, all the resentment, all the betrayal. 'You killed my father?'

'I haven't killed a du Lac in over a hundred years.' She smiled, an expression tinged with mockery. 'Really? Is that what you think of me? And here I thought we were friends.'

Friends... He'd thought they were friends, him and Gwen. And all this time...

'I think... I think you're ageless, if you really are Dahut. That's the curse, your curse. It trapped you as well, made you a *groac'h*, a water witch. I knew you when I was a child...'

'Sainte Sirène is my home and it has been forever. I told you. It was called Ker-Gwagenn, the home of the wave. Or Ker-ar-Groac'h, which is less flattering. I appear as I must, that's part of the magic.'

'The curse.'

She shrugged, dismissing that. 'The curse is broken. It has been for almost eighty years. Fabien du Lac and Tristan Poullain protected this place, saved it. They proved themselves to me, proved their love. For me, for Ys, for each other. The mask couldn't take them. Their love was true.'

Rafael took this news with dismay. 'Then how—?'

'I didn't kill your father, Rafael. Nor did I murder Simon, or Thierry. You must look closer to home for that.'

Laure. She had to mean Laure. Rafael's face fell and his gaze slid towards the prone form of his sister. Well, she had already admitted it, hadn't she? He could try to deny it all he wanted, but he'd heard the truth of it from her own lips. Laure and his mother...

'I loved Simon,' Gwen continued. 'Isn't that strange? I know men are drawn to me. That's my curse, the one Ankou left me with and gave me the mask to guard against. Drawn to my power, my beauty, my magic. They cannot help it. I thought he was the same, but he wasn't. He was torn between Ari and me. And I tried to tell him there was no future for us, that he'd only ruin his life, but he wouldn't listen. When did he ever listen? Ari had left him and he could feel her drifting away. He couldn't leave our home... wouldn't...' She shook her head and closed her eyes as if driving back tears. 'Perhaps he already guessed his fate. I thought maybe he took his own life. I thought the worst.'

Rafael held Ari tighter. She gasped for air, every tendon a wire of pain. 'Gwen... help her. Please.'

'Ariadne Walker wears the mask of Dahut,' she intoned as if she was passing judgement. Maybe she was. 'Now she has to face the truth, no matter how painful. If she lies, it will kill her. Try to take it off, and it will kill her. That's what it does. It was part of an ancient magic. It is without pity. As I was, once upon a time. It took so many years for that to change. But I am a living thing. It is not. It is a thing of death itself. And Death must have a witness. Death must provide a judge.'

Rafael didn't know what she meant. It sounded like she was performing a ritual. Gwen, or Dahut, or whatever she was, couldn't help. And if the sorceress princess of Ys couldn't help them, who could?

He stared down at Ari, cupped her face with his hands. 'Ari, can you hear me?'

Ari looked up, whispered something through her gritted teeth and a cold breeze flooded the chamber. Rafael shuddered and held her tighter. But it was useless. He knew that now.

'*I'm here, my love,*' said the figure of the Ankou, still wearing Simon Poullain's face. He materialised out of the shadows, dressed as ever in black, his long white hair stark in contrast, and the brim of his black hat pulled down to shade the dark eyes that scoured with obvious distaste across Rafael before resting on Ari.

She gave a sob, the sound wrenched out of her by grief alone. As he watched, she reached out her hands towards her lost fiancé, the pain in her face not just physical now. She was in torment.

And Rafael felt the heart he didn't even realise he had lost to her begin to shatter.

An unseen force tore her from his arms and lifted her into the air. She hung there, like an angel, her head tilted back as icy wind whirled around her. The light from the candles bounced off the water and up onto the roof, rippling waves of light like the sky of the underwater world of Ys.

CHAPTER TWENTY-SEVEN

'Put on the mask,' the voices had whispered. *'You can save him. No one else can. She is coming. Surrender to her. If he puts it on, he will die. You're already dead inside.'*

And she was, she knew that now. Something had died in her with Simon. Something had died the day she got that letter...

The mask felt strangely cool against her face, as if it was sucking the life from her, feeding on the heat in her body. And when the warmth in her faded, pinpricks of pain took its place. It was everywhere, all at once. She could feel tendrils crawling on her skin, digging into her flesh, tightening around her throat.

The moment Gwen appeared, she finally understood. Ari watched her approach through a veil of tears, watched her disarm Laure and take her throne and knew her for all that she was. A spirit of the sea, endless, immortal, terrible, glorious...

The voices still whispered, a sibilant chorus, tormenting her. Rafael couldn't hear them, she realised. They were just for her.

'Give up. You don't have to fight anymore. It's over. Just accept it. You're too broken to fix. Submit to her.'

Voices of the dead, voices that had been absorbed into the mask, all those people it had swallowed up, all those lives it had devoured. So many of them...

Rafael was talking, trying to reach her, to help, but she couldn't hear his voice. He was drowned out. Rafael who held her so gently, who clearly would do anything to stop this, but couldn't.

If she hadn't grabbed it, he would have put it on. Once she held it, she knew what she had to do. She'd seen what it did to Nico. She couldn't let Rafael put himself through that. He didn't deserve it.

She, on the other hand... she was used to pain.

Or at least, she thought she was.

But not pain like this. It flowed like lightning along her veins, it boiled in her lungs, and all the while, the tentacles tightened, cutting off her breath, making spots dance before her eyes.

The world went cold and dark. The fire of the pain she felt became ice, and it was even worse. And then she heard him.

Just as she knew she would.

'*I'm here, my love,*' Ankou's arctic voice whispered, in harmony with the voices of the mask.

She forced her eyes open and saw him, peering at her, the look on his face one of fascination rather than concern.

All the same, she reached out for him. She couldn't help herself. All she wanted was Simon back, and yet...

The mask clamped itself around her throat, winding tight and harsh against her skin, crushing her windpipe. Tendrils slithered under the leather thong and crushed the little bone pendant, scattering the fragments. She tried to cry out as something pulled her away from Rafael.

His voice reached her, as if through a hurricane.

'Ari, please, you have to fight it. You have to—'

'Fighting won't help.' Gwen's voice rippled through her,

and she felt the power of the water witch roll over her, examining her, in the distracted way someone might examine a puzzle. 'In fact, fighting makes it worse. Surrender to it. The truth will set you free. That's the secret of the mask. But you know that, don't you, Ariadne Walker? You're clever. You worked it out.'

'It's yours.' She didn't know where she managed to get the air to make those words. Her voice was thin and desperate, but she forced it out. She felt delirious with pain.

'It is far older than anything on this earth. But it was mine, for a time. Don't fight, Ariadne. Endure. Survive, if you can.'

Don't fight, she repeated to herself. *Endure it. Surrender to her.*

Gwen got to her feet and walked to stand in front of her, looking up at her... what, her sacrifice? Her offering?

The feeling of becoming untethered from the world returned. Ari was drifting. Mist closed around her.

Simon's hands took hers, their fingers tangling together as they used to, long ago.

'You left me,' she told him. 'You told me you didn't love me anymore.' The constriction round her throat eased just a little. She gasped for air. But all she inhaled was freezing mist. Without the pendant there, she felt like a vital part of her was missing, her last connection to him.

'*I know,*' Simon replied, taking pity on her. How desperate did your situation have to be for the Servant of Death itself to have pity for you? '*I'm sorry, but it was too late by then.*' He glanced at Gwen. '*I didn't realise what it would mean. When I died...*' His voice trailed off in a sigh.

Ari felt the throb of her heart, like an open wound. She could speak now. 'When you died, I fell to pieces. But I was broken before that. Simon, you shattered me. How could I trust again? How could I trust anyone?' How could she trust Rafael, she wanted to say. But she couldn't. What if he could still hear her? She wasn't even sure if she was speaking out loud or not. It didn't matter. Simon seemed to know anyway.

'*You need to let go, Ari,*' Simon whispered. '*You need to let me go. I never deserved you anyway.*'

'Yes.' The word came out as a sob, all that heartbreak she had kept locked away inside her. 'Yes you did.'

She closed her eyes and tried to remember the two of them together, the day she'd given him the pendant, sitting together on the cliffs, in bed, studying in the college library, laughing, his kiss...

But the arms that held her closest were Rafael's, the form her body remembered cradling her most clearly was Rafael's. The man she trusted, the one she was starting to believe in. The reason she was doing this.

'*Ari,*' Simon said softly, and pressed his icy lips to hers. No words, no pointless protestations, no lies. Not a single lie. Just his kiss. '*I should have loved you better. I should have gone with you. But I was selfish. I wanted too much. Let go now, my love. Embrace a future. Stop running.*'

She surrendered to it and felt the mask loosen. Just a little. And the words came out of her in a rush. 'I still love you, I always did. All I had left was that necklace. The last piece of us.'

The words hurt. God, they hurt. But there was not a word of a lie in them. She wanted to deny it, but she knew that would kill her. Now more than ever. Yes, she still loved Simon. Part of her would always love Simon.

She barely knew Rafael, but somehow he touched her more deeply than anyone had before. It was a different kind of love. Neither one detracted from the other.

'*Mon coeur,*' Simon murmured, his lips pulling back from hers. '*You have to let go. You have to release yourself.*'

Simon's hands on hers tightened for a moment, squeezing her fingers. She opened her eyes and he was there with her, floating like a dream in the nothingness surrounding her. She met his gaze again, and there were tears on his face. Simon Poullain, who had been everything to her, was just a ghost now. His cold touch, his pale face, his white hair... he was no longer the man she had known. He hadn't been for a very long time.

How could she heave those words into her mouth? How could she give voice to them? But she had to. She understood that now. She had to.

'I will. I love you, Simon, but I forgive you and I release you.'

But the mask still didn't come loose. It clung to her, little barbs of pain digging into her skin.

Golden lights raced through him. His hair turned fair instead of white, his skin sun-kissed instead of deathly pale. Slowly he changed back to Simon, her Simon.

Ari smiled. She couldn't help herself. She reached out a shaking hand to touch his cold face.

And felt the world dimming, her eyes failing her as the mask drained the last of her away.

'*Ari...*' She heard his voice, the last thing she heard. Not Simon. *Rafael.*

All around her, the icy mist crept higher and Simon reached out, picking the mask off her face. '*This is not for you,* chérie. *You have a life. You have a future. Go back.*'

It came away effortlessly and she stood there, facing him. Mist surrounded them, so cold, impenetrable. She knew if she stepped into it, she would be lost and her life would be over. She didn't know how she knew, but she did.

But there was one thing she still needed to know, one question that still had to be answered.

'Why did you write that letter, Simon?'

'*I had no choice. I wish I never had. But she swore she would kill you if you came. I sent you the pendant so you would know... to protect you, Morvarc'h... to carry you to safety. I wrote the coordinates of the place I hid the mask on the letter just in case. I barely knew why. Perhaps... perhaps it was just blind hope. Perhaps the mask wanted to be found and I knew I could trust you. All I could do was try to stop her. I knew you would figure it out.'*

He smiled, a brief and fleeting expression. The loss it conveyed made her heart lurch inside her, made it wrench itself up inside her ribcage, trying to tear its way free. It was awful, too cruel. She'd thought the worst of him when, really, he'd been trying to protect her. That's all he had ever done.

'I never expected to come back, but Dahut gave me another chance. She loved me. Isn't that the strangest thing? Beyond enchantments and magic. She loved me. She called me her champion. And when you came back, I told her you'd save Rafael.'

Simon kissed her one last time, his lips cold, his touch so gentle, like a winter breeze against her skin. And then he was gone.

Another mouth replaced his, not in a kiss, but something else. Air filled her lungs. And then hands on her chest, rhythmic compressions, then his mouth again...

Rafael, his mouth, his kiss, desperately trying to save her life.

Gasping for air, she half sat up, and crashed into him.

She was stretched out on the stone floor of the cave. The mask was gone, completely gone, and Rafael du Lac was holding her, breathing life back into her.

He whispered to her and she felt his breath on the side of her neck, warm with life, playing against her skin the way it had when she'd made love with him.

She shivered, still cold to the core. What had happened to her?

But Rafael held her, his fingers on her skin so hot in contrast. 'Breathe,' he said. 'Please, Ari. Breathe. I'll do anything, give anything...'

'Money can't help here, Rafael.' Her voice was a croak.

Rafael gave her a look of complete exasperation. 'I don't mean money. I meant... Why did you put it on, *mon coeur?*'

Mon coeur. It meant my heart. The way he said it... It meant so much more. She touched his face, her hand trembling.

'I couldn't let you do it. And you would have. We both know that. You like being a hero too much.'

From somewhere, he dredged up a smile. 'Rather than your princess, yes.'

'Damsel in distress,' she told him, suddenly giddy with elation.

'Lie still, I had to resuscitate you. Your brain is probably starved of oxygen. You aren't making sense.' But she caught the relieved smile lingering in the corner of his mouth.

But when another voice spoke, it faltered to alarm and he jerked himself up, as if he would protect her with his life if needs be.

'He always loved to be a hero,' Gwen said, her voice echoing across the chamber. The candles had burned down, puddles of wax on the stone, guttering flames. 'They all do. *Du Lacs.* What family renames itself after a made-up hero? But it is always a Poullain who saves you in the end, isn't it, *du Lac?*'

Ari shook her head. 'I'm not...'

Gwen smiled. 'You might as well be. He named you as such. Simon knew. In his heart, you were always his wife. Even when he loved me, he still loved you. Hearts are strange and fickle things. A different kind of love. He said you would save Rafael. This was our accord.'

'From what?' she whispered. 'The curse was broken.'

'From Laure, from fate...' Gwen glanced at him with all too knowing an expression. 'From himself.'

'Why me? I couldn't save Simon.'

'No one could do that, Ariadne. Not even me.'

Ari's eyes burned with tears again and that open wound

inside her was back. Her hand came up to grab the pendant, but it was gone. Somewhere, the pieces of it were lost on the floor of this chamber. Gone forever. Her last remembrance of Simon.

Rafael gathered her closer in his arms. 'I didn't hear the mask when I held it. Not the last time. Why didn't it work?'

Gwen smiled. 'You're lucky you kept Séraphine's charm on you. It kept you safe, just as she promised. Laure always refused them, you know. She couldn't even indulge an old woman who loved her. I wonder if she's really Théo's child at all. Yvette was the same. Cold to the core. Driven. Like I used to be. Before I learned of real love.'

'My mother,' Rafael growled. 'How am I going to—'

'Well, that's your problem,' Gwen said and rose to her feet, graceful as a dancer. 'I'm sure you'll work it out. You're very good at that sort of thing. I can take care of things here. You should leave.'

'But Laure...'

She glared at the sleeping body of his sister and all the humour drained out of her. 'She's mine now. She used my mask, my magic, for her own ends. She killed my Simon. There's a price. There is always a price, especially when you abuse the gifts of a water witch. And when you anger us. She joins me, cursed as I was cursed, my servant forever. But don't worry, I'll keep her in check. In the meantime, you need to go. Now. Once I release the spell, the cave is going to collapse. I should have done it long ago. Sentiment stopped me, I suppose. There isn't much time.'

The cave began to shake again. Dust and dirt rained down on them. A crack lanced through the rock overhead and the ground trembled wildly. They could hear the sound of the sea pounding against the rocks.

'Gwen, please!' Rafael shouted. 'Don't do this.'

'And what would you do with her, Rafael? How would you explain to the police what happened? Enough. Much as I love my retreat, this place must be destroyed. It is too dangerous to leave standing. I should have done it years ago. There is no curse of Ys anymore. Nothing to protect. Take Ariadne and go. Run.'

She turned her back on them both.

Scrambling to his feet, Rafael lifted Ari in his arms. The roof was coming down. They didn't have time to hesitate, plunging into the tunnels again. But she knew carrying her was slowing him down. Without words, she struggled free and they ran together, even if she had to lean on him more than she would have liked. There was almost no light, but they moved on instinct, fleeing, the sound deafening behind them. She could smell the dust and the sea, feel the world tearing itself apart just behind them. Somehow, they found their way back to the opening, a combination of the marks on the cave walls, unconscious memory and blind luck.

Rafael almost hurled her up through the gap and she grabbed the rope, pulling herself the rest of the way.

'Ari!' Jason screamed her name from outside and pounced on her, dragging her clear.

But Rafael didn't emerge after her. Ari turned like a feral animal, her hands reaching after him in the darkness, but he'd gone.

Back down the tunnel, trying to get to the cavern to save Laure, even if she only wanted him dead, even if she was a murderess and attempted murderess... she was still his sister.

'Get back from the edge,' Nico yelled hoarsely. 'The cliffs are unstable.'

She didn't care. Couldn't care. Rafael was down there somewhere, maybe trapped, maybe dead. Just when she had gathered her wits to jump back down, she saw him, his hands first, clutching the rope in the last ray of light to make it down into the hole.

'Help me,' she shouted to the other two and hauled their end of the rope, dragging him up.

He was covered in dirt and dust, his face streaked with it and tears. Blood ran from a gash on his head. He tumbled out of the darkness and lay on the track cutting through the bracken and gorse. His chest heaved.

'I couldn't reach them,' he said. 'I couldn't get back. The whole thing has come down. It's all gone.'

CHAPTER TWENTY-EIGHT

The lights were blinding and the Paris studio was peculiarly airless. Ari perched on a tall thin stool opposite a woman who looked like a sexy little doll newly brought to life. They'd taken one look at Ari's outfit, a rather neat if affordable black suit, and sighed, muttered and conferred until she was whisked off to a wardrobe department somewhere. She emerged wearing something far more stylish, her hair and make-up transformed.

The blue of the blouse did at least bring out her eyes, or so the make-up artist had informed her. That might have helped if she hadn't sounded like it was a miracle. It softened her appearance, made her more approachable. She hadn't been aware she was unapproachable before and instantly wished she was again.

Ari brought her hand up to her neck. She felt strangely exposed without the necklace and the little bone pendant. But that was long gone, the pieces buried under Castelmeur.

Emergency services had found nothing, no way into the cave system, no signs of life. They even sent in rescue divers through the sea cave at the end of the point, but the pathway to Ys was gone. Too much debris to continue, they'd said. No hope of finding survivors. No one should have been down there in the first place.

Ari agreed with every word. No one should ever have been down there.

They still had the coin and once they could dive again along with Nico and Simon, she had been able to locate the remains of the mosaic between Castelmeur and Îlot D'Or. But that meant the university and the department were swarming all over the place and the treasure hunt was over. It was a find of national importance. And international interest.

The media descended on them.

Jason seemed remarkably calm about it all. He'd proved his point, she supposed. The people who had dismissed him, ridiculed him, now had to admit that he had been right about the lost city of Ys and that seemed to be enough for him. There was talk of a television series, book deals and more. He was loving it. Besides, he had Nico. And that meant more to him than all the fame in the world.

While Jason charmed the world's media and sparkled, the roguish adventurer to the core, Ari was summoned more and more to be the voice of reason and academic responsibility. The documentary team had seemed the most reasonable and Rafael had arranged something. He had made some calls, found an agent for them, and had his own people go over the contracts. She suspected he was using them as a way to avoid doing it himself. Though his involvement was well known, more than a few people complained that he seemed to have vanished from the face of the earth the moment the story broke.

They'd barely spoken since their escape. Ari just kept remembering his face when she tried to talk to him afterwards, the hope dying in his eyes that Laure might be found, even then, after everything, after all her confessions and her plans for him.

But then Ari knew how she felt about Jason. Family was family, no matter what. She couldn't help but blame herself.

Rafael was trying to unravel the mess in his company. He sounded exhausted on the phone. She didn't have the heart to pester him. So she just let him slip away and waited until the next lull when she could do the same.

'So what could have caused the city to sink?' asked the willowy presenter, balanced on the ridiculous stool opposite Ari, in the studio, while a screen behind them showed the view from Castelmeur. Why they couldn't have just done the interview there, Ari didn't know. Their hair, maybe? Or the stools?

'We really don't know. That's one of the problems with archaeological finds. They need to be studied and that takes time. The university will issue findings.' She forced herself to ignore the camera, like Jason had told her, and direct her attention to the interviewer, just as if she was teaching a class. 'I think... that is, we think... there was a volcanic eruption in Iceland around 536. Cassiodorus wrote about it, so did Procopius.'

The presenter winced, off camera, of course. Maybe they'd cut that statement out. Keep it simple, they'd told her.

Ari ploughed on. 'The ash cloud blocked out the sun and the ensuing winter caused famine and was seen as heralding the end of the world. There are theories it might have been a comet or a meteorite. We'll never know. But whatever it was, if it hit the water, it could have caused a tsunami. Tsunamis build over distance and only stop when they hit land.'

Behind her, someone brought up a map of the north Atlantic, little dots marking the locations as arranged. Ari smiled. That had worked, at least. There had been a long debate and Jason had called someone or other an idiot. That might be another reason why she was here right now.

'If Ys, or the settlement at Castelmeur which became known as Ys, was in the direct path of a mega-tsunami coming right across the Atlantic, it wouldn't have stood a chance. In the story, the sea gates were left open. If the later maps are even vaguely accurate, a big enough wave would have swept right over the city whether the gates were open or not. And it would have been big. The damage a tsunami can do is catastrophic, as we know from the Indian Ocean tsunami in 2004 or the Tohoku earthquake and tsunami in 2011, which almost caused a meltdown at Fukushima nuclear reactor.'

Somewhere, a phone went off, *her* phone, she realised, and swore under her breath. She should have turned it off, or at least put it on silent.

'Cut,' someone yelled from somewhere unseen, another part of the studio.

'I'm sorry,' she said, embarrassed.

'Not at all,' the presenter – Wendy, she seemed to remember – said. 'Why don't we take a quick break and get back to it? I want to take a look at that map again. There's got to be a way to make this more viewer-friendly.'

Ari fished out her phone as everyone wandered away.

Rafael's name. No picture. She'd never taken a picture. Just his name in stark white letters on her screen with 'missed call' beside it. Several missed calls actually. She muted it and shoved it back into her pocket.

Ari chewed on the inside of her cheek and tried to push thoughts of him from her mind. He had no place here. She was pretty sure he didn't want to see her. Not after what had happened. And she wouldn't be here much longer. She wouldn't even be in France. She needed to focus and—

'We're going to need more location shots,' Wendy was saying as she came back. 'Preferably with you, Ari. I think this description might work better on site, don't you? Would tomorrow suit? I can arrange the cars now. It's a bit of a long haul down there, but I think it will be worth it. We'll put you up somewhere, of course.'

She didn't mention the gîte. She didn't want to imagine poor Wendy's face if she realised people lived like that.

'Are you sure you wouldn't prefer Jason? He's much more natural at this and he's already there.'

Wendy smiled, understanding. 'He's diving with another team tomorrow. I did check. Besides, you're as much the story here. Our very own Lara Croft.'

Ari glanced down at the peacock-blue blouse. That was not very *Tomb Raider*. 'Yeah, I'm not very comfortable with that.'

'Nonsense, you're a natural,' came another voice from the darkness by the doorway. One which sent every hair on her body upright and made the air leave her body in a rush.

Rafael.

What on earth was he doing here? Why was he ringing her phone if he was here?

He stepped out into the light and he had never looked better to her. Just for a moment, she wasn't sure she remembered how to breathe.

'Monsieur du Lac!' Wendy almost did a dance when she saw him. In an instant, she was transformed to her flirty, sexy TV persona. 'Oh, how wonderful. You got our invitation. I have been dying to interview you about this marvellous discovery, but your people never got back to me. I know you've been so busy, but I'd do *anything* to accommodate you.'

Rafael's jaw tightened and he got that deer in the headlights look that Ari was beginning to recognise as a logical reaction to Wendy and her team. He was, as many people had pointed out to her in the last couple of weeks, one of France's most eligible men, known for his beautiful girlfriends and his smouldering glare.

The glare was having completely the opposite effect on Wendy than the one he intended. And he looked even more annoyed by that. And uncomfortable.

For a moment, Ari just enjoyed it. She couldn't help herself. Then she stepped in to rescue him.

'Monsieur du Lac and I need to discuss a few matters, Wendy. Relating to the find. It is his property we're planning to invade, after all. I hope you don't mind.'

The relief on his face made her heart stutter inside her, but she tried to ignore it. The look she sent Wendy might have been pleading. She couldn't talk to him out here where anyone could be watching them. Or worse, recording them.

Wendy looked more than a bit chagrined, but she relented graciously. If she wanted Rafael in her show, she was clearly willing to be magnanimous. 'Oh, of course, of course, you can use my dressing room. It's quite private.'

She showed them the way and as she shut the door behind them, she gave Ari a wildly exaggerated wink.

Great. Just the kind of rumour she needed the TV people picking up on.

Rafael leaned against the back of a neat little velvet sofa, which made him look like a giant. 'Do you think she's listening outside? Should we check for bugs?'

Ari had to force herself to speak. The words, of course, all came out wrong. 'What are you doing here?'

Rafael smiled. 'I heard you were in Paris. I came to see you, of course.' The eternally irritating smile of his grew even more amused. His eyes had no right to twinkle like that.

Ari stopped, frowning at him, trying to work out if he was making fun of her or not. She was fairly certain he was, but he was too straight-faced to tell. Infuriating man. 'You... you just vanished, Rafael.'

A look of contrition finally replaced the smile. 'I know. I'm sorry. I tried to keep in touch, but...' He sighed and pinched the bridge of his nose as if he had a headache. 'There was so much to sort out, but it's done now. Please, Ari. I just want to talk to you. Make it up to you, if I can. If you'll let me.'

Ari shook her head, not in denial but disbelief. 'Fine,' she said at last. She could give him that much, couldn't she? 'But you can't solve this by throwing money around.'

'Really? I'm very good at that. Or so you're fond of telling me.'

She caught the glint of amusement returning to his eyes, and realised she'd missed this, missed him. Far more than she had the courage to admit right now.

'I brought you something,' he told her. 'As an apology. A peace offering.'

He held out a small octagonal jewellery box, tied with silken ribbons. It was beautiful in itself, the name of the shop printed discreetly in gold. Even looking at it, she knew it was from some exclusive designer in Paris – more money, more riches thrown around carelessly, because it didn't make a difference to him. He didn't understand. He probably never would. He was a hopeless case.

Ari glared at him, realised he wasn't going to give in and then took it, opening it expecting diamonds, platinum and any number of gemstones.

It was nothing of the sort.

Simon's pendant nestled in a satin hollow, fully repaired, slim traces of gold holding the pieces together, a magic horse, running on water, Morvarc'h. It hung on a delicate chain rather than the leather thong she'd always used. She touched it, barely able to believe what she was seeing, or how beautiful it was.

'I saved it from the cave, the pieces. I mean, before we escaped. I just... I couldn't leave it. I knew what it meant to you. You said it was all you had left of him. Of you and Simon.'

So he had heard her, every word she said to Simon back there in the cave, she realised. And that must have hurt him.

She ran her fingertips over the pendant, hardly able to believe it.

When she said nothing, Rafael went on. 'And there's an

artist I know, whose work is based on *kintsugi*, the Japanese ethos of making the broken whole again and embracing the damage to make something even more special. I thought... I thought you'd want it back.'

She looked up at him and unexpected tears rolled down her face. The make-up artist was going to kill her. But she didn't care. 'You did this for me?'

Rafael leaned forward and carefully wiped her cheeks. 'Of course, Ari. I'd do anything for you. Don't you know that yet?'

'But you left. Like he left. And I... I didn't.' She hadn't left. She'd hung on for once, waiting. She hadn't run away, and he hadn't come back.

Until now.

'I'm sorry. I don't know how to make it up to you, but I want to try. Here, let me...' He took the box and lifted the pendant out by the chain. He held it out to her, ready to put it on.

She turned around, and his breath brushed against her neck as he stepped closer. The pendant was heavier than it had been before, and hung lower against her chest. But it felt perfect. Broken and put back together, like her, like both of them.

She turned around faster than he expected and suddenly she was in his arms, right where she had dreamed of being once again. His eyes were endlessly dark, so warm with love and desire. 'You didn't have to come here. You could have sent it.'

'No,' he murmured, leaning in closer. 'I had to come. I missed you more than I could bear, Ari, but I had to confront my mother. The accountants found problems with the company finances and I had to sort that out. And then the police were involved. They were already suspicions about Laure's disappearance. I thought they were going to arrest me at one point. But my mother broke down and confessed everything. We kept most of it out of the media and I have to admit the work you and your brother are doing has served as a wonderful distraction. They can't prove murder, but fraud on that scale is almost as bad in the current climate. I wanted to keep you out of it. I had to. It wouldn't have been fair. The press were swarming all over us and I thought you'd be safe in Sainte Sirène. But when I found out you weren't there, I thought...'

He'd thought she'd gone. He thought she'd run away again. And she could hardly blame him. That was what she did. He'd told her so himself.

'I'm here, Rafael. I didn't leave.' Much as she had been tempted to. Much as she had feared she would need to.

He gave a brief laugh, as if ashamed of himself, or simply embarrassed. 'I forgot about this. And then the production company said you'd be here and I... I had to come. I'm going back to Sainte Sirène tonight. Come with me?'

She gripped his shoulders, needing something to hold on to. His mouth was so close to hers, she could feel the warmth of his skin.

'Is there any news of Gwen? Or...' She couldn't say Laure. She could see the hurt ghost through his eyes.

'No. She's gone. No one in the village knows where. Like the Itron Gwenn, the White Lady, the spirit who vanishes with the morning mist. It's better, I think.'

Probably. Better for all of them, including Gwen. *The White Lady*, she thought, the words slotting together in her head. She felt like a fool. Gwen, Blanche, White. She hadn't even disguised herself very well.

'I made sure Mémé was all right. Nolvene is looking after her and there's a nursing agency coming in to the Manoir now. But she's so much better these days. And then...' He stared at her, the words drying up.

'Then? I'm meant to be leaving, Rafael. I'm meant to be going back to Oxford.' She didn't say home. It had never felt like home.

He drew in a breath, more for courage than anything else, she suspected. He closed his eyes, then opened them again, looking down at her, great pools of warmth and darkness. 'If I let you go now, I'd never forgive myself. Simon came back from the dead for you. I could at least travel to Oxford. I'll open an office. I'll buy a house.'

'Where?' She half smiled. He wasn't throwing money at her, not exactly. He was just throwing it all around her. He'd given her something that money simply couldn't buy. He'd restored her one piece of Simon.

He waved one arm around vaguely, never breaking their gaze for a moment. 'I don't know yet. It doesn't matter. Somewhere nearby. Somewhere pretty. Somewhere to be with you.'

She shook her head, more in amusement than denial, but his hand on her face stopped her.

'I'm serious, Ari. Whatever you want, wherever you want. If you aren't happy there, we can go back to Sainte Sirène, to the Manoir.'

'I have a contract. A job.' It was silly. Yes, she might not love teaching, but it was a job. She might find the school utterly ridiculous, but she was comfortable there, safe. She just hadn't managed to get back there yet. Not with the current whirlwind her life had become. Mainly thanks to him.

Rafael arched a sardonic eyebrow at her. 'What kind of contract did you sign? Is it indentured servitude? Don't worry. I have excellent lawyers and loads of money, remember?'

She laughed suddenly. He was relentless. But her laughter seemed to give him hope and he pulled her even closer, his voice gentling.

'We can do anything. Anything you want. Just as long as we're together. I... I love you.'

He'd never said that before. She knew it just from the way he said it now, the way he looked into her eyes as he spoke those forbidden words, like he might still bolt any second. She knew because she knew Rafael, knew the depths of him. She wasn't sure how that had happened, but she couldn't deny it.

A thousand words of doubt assailed her all at once. He barely knew her, they'd spent so little time together, neither of them knew how to trust another person. Except she did. Now. She trusted him implicitly. And when push came to shove, he had never actually let her down. Even if she thought he had. He'd been protecting her. Because that was Rafael through and through.

Always the hero, Gwen had said. Or at least, he always wanted to be the hero.

Maybe, just this once, she should let him.

'Well then,' she said, and kissed him slowly, taking her time, exploring his mouth and body, holding him against her. His hands slid up her back, moulding her to his frame. 'Since you love me...'

'Ari?' He sounded worried, afraid she was mocking him or he'd done something wrong again, and she realised she'd have to be careful with him, as careful as he was trying to be with her. Rafael du Lac's heart was a fragile, precious thing, to be treasured and cared for.

'I love you,' he'd said. Just like that. He'd put himself out there for her, and even given all they had been through, she thought it might be the bravest thing she'd seen.

Could she be that brave? It was only the truth, after all, and as she had learned in the caves beneath the Pointe de Castelmeur, in the last remnants of Ys, no matter how hard, no matter how frightening, the truth set you free.

'I love you too,' she told him, 'and I'm not running away again. I promise.'

Rafael's sigh of relief was lost in their kiss.

A LETTER FROM JESSICA

Dear reader,

I want to say a huge thank you for choosing to read *The Water Witch*. If you did enjoy it, and want to keep up to date with all my latest releases, just sign up at the following link. Your email address will never be shared and you can unsubscribe at any time.

www.bookouture.com/jessica-thorne

Sadly, there is no manor house or village at the Pointe de Castelmeur. The point reaches out into the sea at the end of Cap Sizun, the Atlantic lashing against its western side. Ancient rocks, endless, weather-beaten and resolute – they hold a magic we know deep down in our bones, one we breathe like the salt-heavy air there, electric and wild. Brittany is a place of magic and always has been.

Ys may be a myth, impossible by modern standards, but there is something buried in those stories, a tale of greed and retribution, of grief and regret, of self-recrimination and redemption. Was Ys real? Probably not. Neither is my Sainte Sirène, or the du Lac Manoir – but Île Tristan is a real island, and the oppidum can still be found on the Pointe de Castelmeur. The Pointe du Raz, the Pointe du Van and the Baie des Trépassés are all real places at the very end of the world. Sound travels strangely over water and it is still possible to hear bells ringing or that strange and terrible crash as the gates of a lost city break under the waves.

I would like to thank Alley Valkyrie, Laura Amilar, Karina Coldrick and Kate Pearce for reading the manuscript and offering their wisdom. I am also indebted to Leah Koch-Michael for answering my bizarre underwater archaeology questions. Thanks as ever to my wonderful friends, including Alison May, Imogen Howson, Kate Johnson, Jeevani Charika, Sheila McClure, Janet Gover, Sarah Rees Brennan, Catie Murphy and Susan Connolly for all their encouragement and support. Thanks also to my agent Sallyanne and my editor Ellen. And, of course, to my kids, who have spent so many holidays with me in one of my favourite parts of the world. Even with all the visits to the rocks.

Finally, thanks as ever to my husband Pat, who had to come on the research trip, did all the driving, and forced himself to stay in the wonderful Hôtel le Goyen with me. Together we discovered the magic of Castelmeur.

I hope you loved *The Water Witch* and if you did I would be very grateful if you could write a review. I'd love to hear what you think, and it makes such a difference helping new readers to discover one of my books for the first time.

I love hearing from my readers – you can get in touch on my Facebook page, through Twitter, Goodreads or my website.

Thanks,

Jessica Thorne

www.rflong.com/jessicathorne

facebook.com/JessThorneBooks
twitter.com/JessThorneBooks

Printed in Great Britain
by Amazon